THE MEASURE
OF MALICE

THE MEASURE OF MALICE

Scientific Detection Stories

edited and introduced by

MARTIN EDWARDS

BRITISH LIBRARY

First published 2019 by
The British Library
96 Euston Road
London NW1 2DB

Cataloguing in Publication Data
A catalogue record for this publication is available from the British Library

ISBN 978 0 7123 5289 5
eISBN 978 0 7123 6491 1

Front cover image © Mary Evans Picture Library

Typeset by Tetragon, London
Printed and bound by TJ International, Padstow, Cornwall

MIX
Paper from
responsible sources
FSC
www.fsc.org   FSC® C013056

CONTENTS

INTRODUCTION

Long before the days of DNA testing and mobile phone tracking, science and technology played a crucial part in the detection of crime, real and fictional. *The Measure of Malice* gathers together classic mystery stories united by a common ingredient. The stories illustrate ways in which a host of writers, some still renowned, others long forgotten, made use of scientific and technical know-how (often fresh and exciting at the time the stories were written, even if now seemingly quaint or obvious) in weaving their puzzles.

The connection between science and the crime genre goes back to the early days of the genre. Ronald R. Thomas, an American professor of English, has pointed out in *Detective Fiction and the Rise of Forensic Science* (1999) that the nineteenth century saw authors "sometimes anticipating the actual technologies being developed by forensic science, sometimes appropriating or popularising them".

Thomas describes "the virtually occult power forensic science came to possess over the human image in modern mass society on both sides of the Atlantic, a phenomenon which helped to establish the fingerprint, the mug shot, and the lie detector as central elements in the sometimes dangerous arsenal of law enforcement devices", and argues that: "These features of the nineteenth-century detective story help to make the modern world of DNA fingerprinting, satellite surveillance and crime-scene computer simulation imaginable to us."

One of the earliest and most insightful historians of detective fiction was Dorothy L. Sayers, an author fascinated by the implications of scientific advance. In her introduction to *Great Short Stories of Detection, Mystery and Horror* (1928), she discussed the pioneering work of two notable Victorian novelists, J. Sheridan Le Fanu and Wilkie Collins, in the field of scientific detection. As she pointed out, the plot of Le Fanu's *Checkmate* (1871) "actually turns on the complete alteration of the criminal's appearance by a miracle of plastic surgery". Sayers expressed surprise that more use had not been made of this technique (writers soon made up for lost time in this respect), while highlighting a couple of obscure stories where "the alterations include the tattooing of the criminal's eyes from blue to brown". Sayers also admired Collins' use of the effects of opium as a plot device in *The Moonstone* (1868); this book and *Checkmate* were, in her opinion, "the distinguished forbears of a long succession of medical and scientific stories which stretches down to the present day".

L. T. Meade, who originally made her reputation writing stories for girls, developed the scientific detective story in conjunction with collaborators who supplied the necessary technical know-how. As Sayers said, their stories "dealt with such subjects as hypnotism, catalepsy..., somnambulism, lunacy, murder by the use of X-rays and hydrocyanic gas".

Crime writers have regularly consulted scientific experts over the years, and several have followed Meade's lead in not merely taking professional advice but collaborating in more formal fashion. Meade's most notable co-author was Robert Eustace, a doctor who would later work with Sayers on a highly ambitious and oddly underestimated epistolary novel, *The Documents in the Case* (1930), as well as combining with Edgar Jepson to produce a notable mystery puzzle in the "locked room" vein, "The Tea Leaf", which was included in the British Library anthology *Capital Crimes* (2015).

The New Zealander Ngaio Marsh, one of the so-called "Queens of Crime" from the Golden Age, collaborated on *The Nursing Home*

Murder (1935) with Henry Jellett, an Irish-born gynaecologist who also helped her to adapt the book into a stage play. Coming up to the present day, crime writer Margaret Murphy has collaborated with two experts in forensic pathology: after writing with Professor Dave Barclay as A. D. Garrett, she launched a new series under the name Ashley Dyer, co-authoring her books with Helen Pepper.

Scientific progress has fuelled the writing of stories about murder committed by unexpected means. As Sayers observed, "It is fortunate for the mystery-monger that, whereas, up to the present, there is only one known way of getting born, there are endless ways of getting killed. Here is a brief selection of handy short cuts to the grave: Poisoned tooth-stoppings; licking poisoned stamps; shaving-brushes inoculated with dread diseases; poisoned boiled eggs...; poison-gas; a cat with poisoned claws; poisoned mattresses;... electrocution by telephone...; air-bubbles injected into the arteries... hypodermic injections shot from air-guns... guns concealed in cameras; a thermometer which explodes a bomb when the temperature of the room reaches a certain height..."

Medical men such as Arthur Conan Doyle and Richard Austin Freeman naturally made use of their expertise in their detective fiction. Their influence in particular extended beyond crime writers who followed in their footsteps; at the dawn of the twenty-first century, Britain's premier forensic entomologist Dr Zakaria Erzinclioglu said in his intriguing memoir *Maggots, Murder and Men* (2000) that "the Sherlock Holmes stories, which emphasise the central importance of physical evidence in criminal investigation, were actually used as instruction manuals by the Chinese and Egyptian police forces for many years, and the French Sûreté named their great forensic laboratory at Lyon after him". Sherlock's surname is also referenced in HOLMES 2, the Home Office Large Major

Enquiry System, which at the time of writing remains the principal IT system used by UK police forces engaged in the investigation of major crimes such as murder and high-value fraud.

J. J. Connington, a major figure during "the Golden Age of Murder" between the two world wars, was not himself a doctor, but rather a professor of chemistry whose factual publications included *Recent Advances in Inorganic Chemistry*. His intricate "fair play" detective novels gain a good deal of their strength from his plausible descriptions of scientific and technological developments. Cunningly plotted books such as *The Case with Nine Solutions* (1928) demonstrate his command of scientific techniques, although it is fair to add that some of the ideas that seemed daring and up-to-the-minute during the 1920s and 1930s have not aged well.

Five of the authors featured in this book were doctors, two were engineers, and another was an academic chemist. The stories collected here display the wide variety of ways in which science came to the aid of (or, occasionally, helped to bamboozle) fiction's detectives, as well as the varied ways in which crime writers of the past made use of science in their stories. The anthology also highlights some of the difference between science of the past and of the present.

Today's readers can enjoy classic crime stories on more than one level, appreciating each tale on its own merits whilst also gaining an insight into vanished ways of life, and having the chance to see how scientific detection has in some respects over the years changed beyond all recognition—and how in certain essentials, it has not.

My thanks go to Nigel Moss, Jamie Sturgeon, and John Cooper, fellow enthusiasts for classic crime whose suggestions for stories to include in these anthologies are always invaluable. Mike Grost's internet page on scientific detection, which also covers many American stories, was also helpful. And, as ever, I'm grateful to the publications team at the British Library for their continuing support.

MARTIN EDWARDS

www.martinedwardsbooks.com

THE BOSCOMBE VALLEY MYSTERY

Arthur Conan Doyle

Arthur Conan Doyle (1859–1930) made admirable use of his scientific knowledge in his stories about Sherlock Holmes. The sage of 221b Baker Street was modelled in part upon the Scottish surgeon and lecturer Dr Joseph Bell. Doyle studied under Bell, and worked as his clerk; many years later, he said in a letter to Bell: *"It is most certainly to you that I owe Sherlock Holmes... round the centre of deduction and inference and observation which I have heard you inculcate I have tried to build up a man."* Holmes has been described, by no less an authority than the forensic entomologist Zakaria Erzinclioglu, as "a pioneer forensic scientist. It was he who introduced the idea of taking plaster casts of footprints... We owe him a great debt of gratitude."

"The Boscombe Valley Mystery", which first appeared in the *Strand Magazine* in October 1891 and was later gathered up in *The Adventures of Sherlock Holmes*, was the first short story in the canon to feature murder, and also the first to feature Inspector Lestrade. The Scotland Yard man had originally been introduced in the novel *A Study in Scarlet* (1887), and ultimately appeared in fourteen entries in the series. Summoned to Herefordshire by Lestrade, Holmes solves the puzzle thanks largely to his ability to analyse footprints. He also makes use of knowledge gained from compiling his monograph "on the ashes of 140 different varieties of pipe, cigar and cigarette tobacco".

WE WERE SEATED AT BREAKFAST ONE MORNING, MY WIFE and I, when the maid brought in a telegram. It was from Sherlock Holmes, and ran in this way:

> "Have you a couple of days to spare? Have just been wired for from the West of England in connection with Boscombe Valley tragedy. Shall be glad if you will come with me. Air and scenery perfect. Leave Paddington by the 11.15."

"What do you say, dear?" said my wife, looking across at me. "Will you go?"

"I really don't know what to say. I have a fairly long list at present."

"Oh, Anstruther would do your work for you. You have been looking a little pale lately. I think that the change would do you good, and you are always so interested in Mr. Sherlock Holmes' cases."

"I should be ungrateful if I were not, seeing what I gained through one of them," I answered. "But if I am to go I must pack at once, for I have only half an hour."

My experience of camp life in Afghanistan had at least had the effect of making me a prompt and ready traveller. My wants were few and simple, so that in less than the time stated I was in a cab with my valise, rattling away to Paddington Station. Sherlock Holmes was pacing up and down the platform, his tall, gaunt figure made even gaunter and taller by his long grey travelling cloak, and close-fitting cloth cap.

"It is really very good of you to come, Watson," said he. "It makes a considerable difference to me, having some one with me on whom I can thoroughly rely. Local aid is always either worthless or else biassed. If you will keep the two corner seats I shall get the tickets."

We had the carriage to ourselves save for an immense litter of papers which Holmes had brought with him. Among these he rummaged and read, with intervals of note-taking and of meditation, until we were past Reading. Then he suddenly rolled them all into a gigantic ball, and tossed them up on to the rack.

"Have you heard anything of the case?" he asked.

"Not a word. I have not seen a paper for some days."

"The London press has not had very full accounts. I have just been looking through all the recent papers in order to master the particulars. It seems, from what I gather, to be one of those simple cases which are so extremely difficult."

"That sounds a little paradoxical."

"But it is profoundly true. Singularity is almost invariably a clue. The more featureless and commonplace a crime is, the more difficult is it to bring it home. In this case, however, they have established a very serious case against the son of the murdered man."

"It is a murder, then?"

"Well, it is conjectured to be so. I shall take nothing for granted until I have the opportunity of looking personally into it. I will explain the state of things to you, as far as I have been able to understand it, in a very few words.

"Boscombe Valley is a country district not very far from Ross, in Herefordshire. The largest landed proprietor in that part is a Mr. John Turner, who made his money in Australia, and returned some years ago to the old country. One of the farms which he held, that of Hatherley, was let to Mr. Charles McCarthy, who was also an ex-Australian. The men had known each other in the Colonies, so that it was not unnatural that when they came to settle down they should do so as near each other as possible. Turner was apparently the richer man, so McCarthy became his tenant, but still remained, it seems, upon terms of perfect equality, as they were frequently together. McCarthy had one son, a lad of eighteen, and Turner had an only daughter of the same age, but neither of them had wives living. They appear to have avoided the society of the neighbouring English families, and to have led retired lives, though both the McCarthys were fond of sport, and were frequently seen at the race meetings of the neighbourhood. McCarthy kept two servants—a man and a girl. Turner had a considerable household, some half-dozen at the least. That is as much as I have been able to gather about the families. Now for the facts.

"On June 3, that is, on Monday last, McCarthy left his house at Hatherley about three in the afternoon, and walked down to the Boscombe Pool, which is a small lake formed by the spreading out of the stream which runs down the Boscombe Valley. He had been out with his serving-man in the morning at Ross, and he had told the man that he must hurry, as he had an appointment of importance to keep at three. From that appointment he never came back alive.

"From Hatherley Farmhouse to the Boscombe Pool is a quarter of a mile, and two people saw him as he passed over this ground. One was an old woman, whose name is not mentioned, and the other was William Crowder, a gamekeeper in the employ of Mr. Turner. Both these witnesses depose that Mr. McCarthy was walking alone. The gamekeeper adds that within a few minutes of his seeing Mr. McCarthy pass he had seen his son, Mr. James McCarthy, going the same way with a gun under his arm. To the best of his belief, the father was actually in sight at the time, and the son was following him. He thought no more of the matter until he heard in the evening of the tragedy that had occurred.

"The two McCarthys were seen after the time when William Crowder, the gamekeeper, lost sight of them. The Boscombe Pool is thickly wooded round, with just a fringe of grass and of reeds round the edge. A girl of fourteen, Patience Moran, who is the daughter of the lodge-keeper of the Boscombe Valley Estate, was in one of the woods picking flowers. She states that while she was there she saw, at the border of the wood and close by the lake, Mr. McCarthy and his son, and that they appeared to be having a violent quarrel. She heard Mr. McCarthy the elder using very strong language to his son, and she saw the latter raise up his hand as if to strike his father. She was so frightened by their violence that she ran away, and told her mother when she reached home that she had left the two McCarthys quarrelling near Boscombe Pool, and that she was afraid that they were going to fight. She had hardly said the words when young Mr. McCarthy came running up to the lodge to say that he had found his father dead in the wood, and to ask for the help of the lodge-keeper. He was much excited, without either his gun or his hat, and his right hand and sleeve were observed to be stained with fresh blood. On following him they found the dead body of his father stretched out upon the grass beside the Pool. The head had been beaten in by repeated blows of some heavy and blunt weapon. The injuries were such as might very well have been inflicted by the butt-end of his son's gun, which was found lying on the grass within a few paces of the body. Under these circumstances the young man was instantly arrested, and a verdict of 'Wilful Murder' having been returned at the inquest on Tuesday, he was on Wednesday brought before the magistrates at Ross, who have referred the case to the next assizes. Those are the main facts of the case as they came out before the coroner and at the police-court."

"I could hardly imagine a more damning case," I remarked. "If ever circumstantial evidence pointed to a criminal it does so here."

"Circumstantial evidence is a very tricky thing," answered Holmes, thoughtfully, "It may seem to point very straight to one thing, but if you shift your own point of view a little, you may find it pointing in an equally uncompromising manner to something entirely different. It must be confessed, however, that the case looks exceedingly grave against the young man, and it is very possible that he is indeed the culprit. There are several people in the neighbourhood, however, and among them Miss Turner, the daughter of the neighbouring landowner, who believe in his innocence, and who have retained Lestrade, whom you may remember in connection with the Study in Scarlet, to work out the case in his interest. Lestrade, being rather puzzled, has referred the case to me, and hence it is that two middle-aged gentlemen are flying westward at fifty miles an hour, instead of quietly digesting their breakfasts at home."

"I am afraid," said I, "that the facts are so obvious that you will find little credit to be gained out of this case."

"There is nothing more deceptive than an obvious fact," he answered, laughing. "Besides, we may chance to hit upon some other obvious facts which may have been by no means obvious to Mr. Lestrade. You know me too well to think that I am boasting when I say that I shall either confirm or destroy his theory by means which he is quite incapable of employing, or even of understanding. To take the first example to hand, I very clearly perceive that in your bedroom the window is upon the right-hand side, and yet I question whether Mr. Lestrade would have noted even so self-evident a thing as that."

"How on earth—!"

"My dear fellow, I know you well. I know the military neatness which characterises you. You shave every morning, and in this season you shave by the sunlight, but since your shaving is less and less complete as we get further back on the left side, until it becomes positively slovenly as we get round the angle of the jaw, it is surely very clear that that side is less well illuminated than the other. I could not imagine a man of your habits looking at himself in an equal light, and being satisfied with such a result. I only quote this as a trivial example of observation and inference. Therein lies my *métier*, and it is just possible that it may be of some service in the investigation which lies before us. There are one or two minor points which were brought out in the inquest, and which are worth considering."

"What are they?"

"It appears that his arrest did not take place at once, but after the return to Hatherley Farm. On the inspector of constabulary informing him that he was a prisoner, he remarked that he was not surprised to hear it, and that it was no more than his deserts. This observation of his had the natural effect of removing any traces of doubt which might have remained in the minds of the coroner's jury."

"It was a confession," I ejaculated.

"No, for it was followed by a protestation of innocence."

"Coming on the top of such a damning series of events, it was at least a most suspicious remark."

"On the contrary," said Holmes, "it is the brightest rift which I can at present see in the clouds. However innocent he might be, he could not be such an absolute imbecile as not to see that the circumstances were very black against him. Had he appeared surprised at his own arrest, or feigned indignation at it, I should have looked upon it as highly suspicious, because such surprise or anger would not be natural under the circumstances, and yet might appear to be the best policy to a scheming man. His frank acceptance of the situation marks him as either an innocent man, or else as a man of considerable self-restraint and firmness. As to his remark about his deserts, it was also not unnatural if you consider that he stood by the dead body of his father, and that there is no doubt that he had that very day so far forgotten his filial duty as to bandy words with him, and even, according to the little girl whose evidence is so important, to raise his hand as if to strike him. The self reproach and contrition which are displayed in his remark appear to me to be the signs of a healthy mind, rather than of a guilty one."

I shook my head. "Many men have been hanged on far slighter evidence," I remarked.

"So they have. And many men have been wrongfully hanged."

"What is the young man's own account of the matter?"

"It is, I am afraid, not very encouraging to his supporters, though there are one or two points in it which are suggestive. You will find it here, and may read it for yourself."

He picked out from his bundle a copy of the local Herefordshire paper, and having turned down the sheet, he pointed out the paragraph in which the unfortunate young man had given his own statement of what had occurred. I settled myself down in the corner of the carriage, and read it very carefully. It ran in this way:—

Mr. James McCarthy, the only son of the deceased, was then called, and gave evidence as follows:—"I had been away from home for three days at Bristol, and had only just returned upon the morning of last Monday, the 3rd. My father was absent from home at the time of my arrival, and I was informed by the maid that he had driven over to Ross with John Cobb, the groom. Shortly after my return I heard the wheels of his trap in the yard, and, looking out of my window, I saw him get out and walk rapidly out of the yard, though I was not aware in which direction he was going. I then took my gun, and strolled out in the direction of the Boscombe Pool, with the intention of visiting the rabbit warren which is upon the other side. On my way I saw William Crowder, the gamekeeper, as he has stated in his evidence; but he is mistaken in thinking that I was following my father. I had no idea that he was in front of me. When about a hundred yards from the Pool I heard a cry of 'Cooee!' which was a usual signal between my father and myself. I then hurried forward, and found him standing by the Pool. He appeared to be much surprised at seeing me, and asked me rather roughly what I was doing there. A conversation ensued, which led to high words, and almost to blows, for my father was a man of a very violent temper. Seeing that his passion was becoming ungovernable, I left him, and returned towards Hatherley Farm. I had not gone more than one hundred and fifty yards, however, when I heard a hideous outcry behind me, which caused me to run back again. I found my father expiring on the ground, with his head terribly injured. I dropped my gun, and held him in my arms, but he almost instantly expired. I knelt beside him for some minutes, and then made my way to Mr. Turner's lodge-keeper, his house being the nearest, to ask for assistance. I saw no one near my father when I returned, and I have no idea how he came by his injuries. He was not a popular man, being somewhat cold and forbidding in his manners; but he had, as far as I know, no active enemies. I know nothing further of the matter."

THE CORONER: "Did your father make any statement to you before he died?"

WITNESS: "He mumbled a few words, but I could only catch some allusion to a rat."

THE CORONER: "What did you understand by that?"

WITNESS: "It conveyed no meaning to me. I thought that he was delirious."

THE CORONER: "What was the point upon which you and your father had this final quarrel?"

WITNESS: "I should prefer not to answer."

THE CORONER: "I am afraid that I must press it."

WITNESS: "It is really impossible for me to tell you. I can assure you that it has nothing to do with the sad tragedy which followed."

THE CORONER: "That is for the Court to decide. I need not point out to you that your refusal to answer will prejudice your case considerably in any future proceedings which may arise."

WITNESS: "I must still refuse."

THE CORONER: "I understand that the cry of 'Cooee' was a common signal between you and your father?"

WITNESS: "It was."

THE CORONER: "How was it, then, that he uttered it before he saw you, and before he even knew that you had returned from Bristol?"

WITNESS (*with considerable confusion*): "I do not know."

A JURYMAN: "Did you see nothing which aroused your suspicions when you returned on hearing the cry, and found your father fatally injured?"

WITNESS: "Nothing definite."

THE CORONER: "What do you mean?"

WITNESS: "I was so disturbed and excited as I rushed out into the open, that I could think of nothing except of my father. Yet I have a vague impression that as I ran forward something lay upon the ground to the left of me. It seemed to me to be something grey in colour, a coat of some sort, or a plaid perhaps. When I rose from my father I looked round for it, but it was gone."

"Do you mean that it disappeared before you went for help?"

"Yes, it was gone."

"You cannot say what it was?"

"No, I had a feeling something was there."

"How far from the body?"

"A dozen yards or so."

"And how far from the edge of the wood?"

"About the same."

"Then if it was removed it was while you were within a dozen yards of it?"

"Yes, but with my back towards it."

This concluded the examination of the witness.

"I see," said I, as I glanced down the column, "that the coroner in his concluding remarks was rather severe upon young McCarthy. He calls attention, and with reason, to the discrepancy about his father having signalled to him before seeing him, also to his refusal to give details of his conversation with his father, and his singular account of his father's dying words. They are all, as he remarks, very much against the son.

Holmes laughed softly to himself, and stretched himself out upon the cushioned seat. "Both you and the coroner have been at some pains," said he, "to single out the very strongest points in the young man's favour. Don't you see that you alternately give him credit for having too much imagination and too little? Too little, if he could not invent a cause of quarrel which would give him the sympathy of the jury; too much, if he evolved from his own inner consciousness anything so *outré* as a dying reference to a rat, and the incident of the vanishing cloth. No, sir, I shall approach this case from the point of view that what this young man says is true, and we shall see whither that hypothesis will lead us. And now here is my pocket Petrarch, and not another word shall I say of this case until we are on the scene of action. We lunch at Swindon, and I see that we shall be there in twenty minutes."

It was nearly four o'clock when we at last, after passing through the beautiful Stroud Valley, and over the broad gleaming Severn, found ourselves at the pretty little country town of Ross. A lean, ferret-like man, furtive and sly-looking, was waiting for us upon the platform. In spite of the light brown dustcoat and leather leggings which he wore in deference to his rustic surroundings, I had no difficulty in recognising Lestrade, of Scotland Yard. With him we drove to the Hereford Arms, where a room had already been engaged for us.

"I have ordered a carriage," said Lestrade, as we sat over a cup of tea. "I knew your energetic nature, and that you would not be happy until you had been on the scene of the crime."

"It was very nice and complimentary of you," Holmes answered. "It is entirely a question of barometric pressure."

Lestrade looked startled. "I do not quite follow," he said.

"How is the glass? Twenty-nine, I see. No wind, and not a cloud in the sky. I have a caseful of cigarettes here which need smoking, and the sofa is very much superior to the usual country hotel abomination. I do not think that it is probable that I shall use the carriage tonight."

Lestrade laughed indulgently. "You have, no doubt, already formed your conclusions from the newspapers," he said. "The case is as plain as a pikestaff, and the more one goes into it the plainer it becomes. Still, of course, one can't refuse a lady, and such a very positive one, too. She had heard of you, and would have your opinion, though I repeatedly told her that there was nothing which you could do which I had not already done. Why, bless my soul! Here is her carriage at the door."

He had hardly spoken before there rushed into the room one of the most lovely young women that I have ever seen in my life. Her violet eyes shining, her lips parted, a pink flush upon her cheeks, all thought of her natural reserve lost in her overpowering excitement and concern.

"Oh, Mr. Sherlock Holmes!" she cried, glancing from one to the other of us, and finally, with a woman's quick intuition, fastening upon my companion, "I am so glad that you have come. I have driven down to tell you so. I know that James didn't do it. I know it, and I want you to start upon your work knowing it, too. Never let yourself doubt upon that point. We have known each other since we were little children, and I know his faults as no one else does; but he is too tender-hearted to hurt a fly. Such a charge is absurd to any one who really knows him."

"I hope we may clear him, Miss Turner," said Sherlock Holmes. "You may rely upon my doing all that I can."

"But you have read the evidence. You have formed some conclusion? Do you not see some loophole, some flaw? Do you not yourself think that he is innocent?"

"I think that it is very probable."

"There now!" she cried, throwing back her head, and looking defiantly at Lestrade. "You hear! He gives me hopes."

Lestrade shrugged his shoulders. "I am afraid that my colleague has been a little quick in forming his conclusions," he said.

"But he is right. Oh! I know that he is right. James never did it. And about his quarrel with his father, I am sure that the reason why he would not speak about it to the coroner was because I was concerned in it."

"In what way?" asked Holmes.

"It is no time for me to hide anything. James and his father had many disagreements about me. Mr. McCarthy was very anxious that there should be a marriage between us. James and I have always loved each other as brother and sister, but of course he is young, and has seen very little of life yet, and—and—well he naturally did not wish to do anything like that yet. So there were quarrels, and this, I am sure, was one of them."

"And your father?" asked Holmes. "Was he in favour of such a union?"

"No, he was averse to it also. No one but Mr. McCarthy was in favour of it." A quick blush passed over her fresh young face as Holmes shot one of his keen, questioning glances at her.

"Thank you for this information," said he. "May I see your father if I call tomorrow?"

"I am afraid the doctor won't allow it."

"The doctor?"

"Yes, have you not heard? Poor father has never been strong for years back, but this has broken him down completely. He has taken to his bed, and Dr. Willows says that he is a wreck, and that his nervous system is shattered. Mr. McCarthy was the only man alive who had known dad in the old days in Victoria."

"Ha! In Victoria! That is important."

"Yes, at the mines."

"Quite so; at the gold mines, where, as I understand, Mr. Turner made his money."

"Yes, certainly."

"Thank you, Miss Turner. You have been of material assistance to me."

"You will tell me if you have any news tomorrow. No doubt you will go to the prison to see James. Oh, if you do, Mr. Holmes, do tell him that I know him to be innocent."

"I will, Miss Turner."

"I must go home now, for dad is very ill, and he misses me so if I leave him. Good-bye, and God help you in your undertaking." She hurried from the room as impulsively as she had entered, and we heard the wheels of her carriage rattle off down the street.

"I am ashamed of you, Holmes," said Lestrade with dignity, after a few minutes' silence. "Why should you raise up hopes which you are bound to disappoint? I am not over-tender of heart, but I call it cruel."

"I think that I see my way to clearing James McCarthy," said Holmes. "Have you an order to see him in prison."

"Yes, but only for you and me."

"Then I shall reconsider my resolution about going out. We have still time to take a train to Hereford and see him tonight?"

"Ample."

"Then let us do so. Watson, I fear that you will find it very slow, but I shall only be away a couple of hours."

I walked down to the station with them, and then wandered through the streets of the little town, finally returning to the hotel, where I lay upon the sofa and tried to interest myself in a yellow-backed novel. The puny plot of the story was so thin, however, when compared to the deep mystery through which we were groping, and I found my attention wander so constantly from the fiction to the fact, that I at last flung it across the room, and gave myself up entirely to a consideration of the events of the day. Supposing that this unhappy young man's story was absolutely true, then what hellish thing, what absolutely unforeseen and extraordinary calamity could have occurred between the time when he parted from his father, and the moment when, drawn back by his screams, he rushed into the glade? It was something terrible and deadly. What could it be? Might not the nature of the injuries reveal something to my medical instincts? I rang the bell, and called for the weekly county paper, which contained a verbatim account of the inquest. In the surgeon's deposition it was stated that the posterior third of the left parietal bone and the left half of the occipital bone had been shattered by a heavy blow from a blunt weapon. I marked the spot upon my own head. Clearly such a blow must have been struck from behind. That was to some extent in favour of the accused, as when seen quarrelling he was face to face with his father. Still, it did not go for very much, for the older man might have turned his back before the blow fell. Still, it might be worth while to call Holmes' attention to it. Then there was the peculiar dying reference to a rat. What could that mean? It could not be delirium. A man dying from a sudden blow does not commonly become delirious. No, it was more likely to be an attempt to explain how he met his fate. But what could it indicate? I cudgelled my brains to find some possible explanation. And then the incident of the grey cloth, seen by young McCarthy. If that were true, the murderer must have dropped some part of his dress, presumably his overcoat, in his flight, and must have had the hardihood to return and carry it away at the instant when the son was kneeling with his back turned not a dozen paces off. What a tissue of mysteries and improbabilities the whole thing was! I did not wonder at Lestrade's opinion, and yet I had so much faith in Sherlock Holmes' insight that I could not lose hope as long as every fresh fact seemed to strengthen his conviction of young McCarthy's innocence.

It was late before Sherlock Holmes returned. He came back alone, for Lestrade was staying in lodgings in the town.

"The glass still keeps very high," he remarked, as he sat down. "It is of importance that it should not rain before we are able to go over the ground. On the other hand, a man should be at his very best and keenest for such nice work as that, and I did not wish to do it when fagged by a long journey. I have seen young McCarthy."

"And what did you learn from him?"

"Nothing."

"Could he throw no light?"

"None at all. I was inclined to think at one time that he knew who had done it, and was screening him or her, but I am convinced now that he is as puzzled as every one else. He is not a very quick-witted youth, though comely to look at, and, I should think, sound at heart."

"I cannot admire his taste," I remarked, "if it is indeed a fact that he was averse to a marriage with so charming a young lady as this Miss Turner."

"Ah, thereby hangs a rather painful tale. This fellow is madly, insanely in love with her, but some two years ago, when he was only a lad, and before he really knew her, for she had been away five years at a boarding-school, what does the idiot do but get into the clutches of a barmaid in Bristol, and marry her at a registry office? No one knows a word of the matter, but you can imagine how maddening it must be to him to be upbraided for not doing what he would give his very eyes to do, but what he knows to be absolutely impossible. It was sheer frenzy of this sort which made him throw his hands up into the air when his father, at their last interview, was goading him on to propose to Miss Turner. On the other hand, he had no means of supporting himself, and his father, who was by all accounts a very hard man, would have thrown him over utterly had he known the truth. It was with his barmaid wife that he had spent the last three days in Bristol, and his father did not know where he was. Mark that point. It is of importance. Good has come out of evil, however, for the barmaid, finding from the papers that he is in serious trouble, and likely to be hanged, has thrown him over utterly, and has written to him to say that she has a husband already in the Bermuda Dockyard, so that there is really no tie between them. I think that that bit of news has consoled young McCarthy for all that he has suffered."

"But if he is innocent, who has done it?"

"Ah! who? I would call your attention very particularly to two points. One is that the murdered man had an appointment with some one at the Pool, and that the some one could not have been his son, for his son was away, and he did not know when he would return. The second is that the murdered man was heard to cry, 'Cooee!' before he knew that his son had returned. Those are the crucial points upon which the case depends. And now let us talk about George Meredith, if you please, and we shall leave all minor matters until tomorrow."

There was no rain, as Holmes had foretold, and the morning broke bright and cloudless. At nine o'clock Lestrade called for us with the carriage, and we set off for Hatherley Farm and the Boscombe Pool.

"There is serious news this morning," Lestrade observed. "It is said that Mr. Turner, of the Hall, is so ill that his life is despaired of."

"An elderly man, I presume?" said Holmes.

"About sixty; but his constitution has been shattered by his life abroad, and he has been in failing health for some time. This business has had a very bad effect upon him. He was an old friend of McCarthy's, and, I may add, a great benefactor to him, for I have learned that he gave him Hatherley Farm rent free."

"Indeed! That is interesting," said Holmes.

"Oh, yes! In a hundred other ways he has helped him. Everybody about here speaks of his kindness to him."

"Really! Does it not strike you as a little singular that this McCarthy, who appeals to have had little of his own, and to have been under such obligations to Turner, should still talk of marrying his son to Turner's daughter, who is, presumably, heiress to the estate, and that in such a very cocksure manner, as if it was merely a case of a proposal and all else would follow? It is the more strange since we know that Turner himself was averse to the idea. The daughter told us as much. Do you not deduce something from that?"

"We have got to the deductions and the inferences," said Lestrade, winking at me. "I find it hard enough to tackle facts, Holmes, without flying away after theories and fancies."

"You are right," said Holmes, demurely; "you do find it very hard to tackle the facts."

"Anyhow, I have grasped one fact which you seem to find it difficult to get hold of," replied Lestrade, with some warmth.

"And that is?"

"That McCarthy, senior, met his death from McCarthy, junior, and that all theories to the contrary are the merest moonshine."

"Well, moonshine is a brighter thing than fog," said Holmes, laughing. "But I am very much mistaken if this is not Hatherley Farm upon the left."

"Yes, that is it." It was a widespread, comfortable-looking building, two-storied, slate-roofed, with great yellow blotches of lichen upon the grey walls. The drawn blinds and the smokeless chimneys, however, gave it a stricken look, as though the weight of this horror still lay heavy upon it. We called at the door, when the maid, at Holmes' request, showed us the boots which her master wore at the time of his death, and also a pair of the son's, though not the pair which he had then had. Having measured these very carefully from seven or eight different points, Holmes desired to be led to the courtyard, from which we all followed the winding track which led to Boscombe Pool.

Sherlock Holmes was transformed when he was hot upon such a scent as this. Men who had only known the quiet thinker and logician of Baker-street would have failed to recognise him. His face flushed and darkened. His brows were drawn into two hard, black lines, while his eyes shone out from beneath them with a steely glitter. His face was bent downwards, his shoulders bowed, his lips compressed, and the veins stood out like whipcord in his long, sinewy neck. His nostrils seemed to dilate with a purely animal lust for the chase, and his mind was so absolutely concentrated upon the matter before him, that a question or remark fell unheeded upon his ears, or at the most, only provoked a quick, impatient snarl in reply. Swiftly and silently he made his way along the track which ran through the meadows, and so by way of the woods to the Boscombe Pool. It was damp, marshy ground, as is all that district, and there were marks of many feet, both upon the path, and amid the short grass which bounded it on either side. Sometimes Holmes would hurry on, sometimes stop dead, and once he made quite a little *détour* into the meadow. Lestrade and I walked behind him, the detective indifferent and contemptuous, while I watched my friend with the interest which sprang from the conviction that every one of his actions were directed towards a definite end.

The Boscombe Pool, which is a little reed-girt sheet of water some fifty yards across, is situated at the boundary between the Hatherley Farm and the private park of the wealthy Mr. Turner. Above the woods which lined it upon the further side we could see the red jutting pinnacles which marked the site of the rich land-owner's dwelling. On the Hatherley side of the Pool the woods grew very thick, and there was a narrow belt of sodden grass twenty paces across between the edge of the trees and the reeds which lined the lake. Lestrade showed us the exact spot at which the body had been found, and, indeed, so moist was the ground, that I could plainly see the traces which had been left by the fall of the stricken man. To Holmes, as I could see by his eager face and peering eyes, very many other things were to be read upon the trampled grass. He ran round, like a dog who is picking up a scent, and then turned upon my companion.

"What did you go into the Pool for?" he asked.

"I fished about with a rake. I thought there might be some weapon or other trace. But how on earth—?"

"Oh, tut, tut! I have no time! That left foot of yours with its inward twist is all over the place. A mole could trace it, and there it vanishes among the reeds. Oh, how simple it would all have been had I been here before they came like a herd of buffalo, and wallowed all over it. Here is where the party with the lodge-keeper came, and they have covered all tracks for six or eight feet round the body. But here are three separate tracks of the same feet." He drew out a lens, and lay down upon his waterproof to have a better view, talking all the time rather to himself than to us. "These are young McCarthy's feet. Twice he was walking, and once he ran swiftly so that the soles are deeply marked, and the heels hardly visible. That bears out his story. He ran when he saw his father on the ground. Then here are the father's feet as he paced up and down. What is this, then? It is the butt end of the gun as the son stood listening. And this? Ha, ha! What have we here? Tip-toes! Tip-toes! Square, too, quite unusual boots! They come, they go, they come again—of course that was for the cloak. Now where did they come from?" He ran up and down, sometimes losing, sometimes finding the track until we were well within the edge of the wood, and under the shadow of a great beech, the largest tree in the neighbourhood. Holmes traced his way to the further side of this, and lay down once more upon his face with a little cry of satisfaction. For a long time he remained there, turning over the leaves and dried sticks, gathering up what seemed to me to be dust into an envelope, and examining with his lens not only the ground, but even the bark of the tree as far as he could reach. A jagged stone was lying among the moss, and this also he carefully examined and retained. Then he followed a pathway through the wood until he came to the high road, where all traces were lost.

"It has been a case of considerable interest," he remarked, returning to his natural manner. "I fancy that this grey house on the right must be the lodge. I think that I will go in and have a word with Moran, and perhaps write a little note. Having done that, we may drive back to our luncheon. You may walk to the cab, and I shall be with you presently."

It was about ten minutes before we regained our cab, and drove back into Ross, Holmes still carrying with him the stone which he had picked up in the wood.

"This may interest you, Lestrade," he remarked, holding it out. "The murder was done with it."

"I see no marks."

"There are none."

"How do you know, then?"

"The grass was growing under it. It had only lain there a few days. There was no sign of a place whence it had been taken. It corresponds with the injuries. There is no sign of any other weapon."

"And the murderer?"

"Is a tall man, left-handed, limps with the right leg, wears thick-soled shooting boots and a grey cloak, smokes Indian cigars, uses a cigar-holder, and carries a blunt penknife in his pocket. There are several other indications, but these may be enough to aid us in our search."

Lestrade laughed. "I am afraid that I am still a sceptic," he said. "Theories are all very well, but we have to deal with a hard-headed British jury."

"*Nous verrons*," answered Holmes, calmly. "You work your own method, and I shall work mine. I shall be busy this afternoon, and shall probably return to London by the evening train."

"And leave your case unfinished?"

"No, finished."

"But the mystery?"

"It is solved."

"Who was the criminal, then?"

"The gentleman I describe."

"But who is he?"

"Surely it would not be difficult to find out. This is not such a populous neighbourhood."

Lestrade shrugged his shoulders. "I am a practical man," he said, "and I really cannot undertake to go about the country looking for a left-handed gentleman with a game leg. I should become the laughing-stock of Scotland-yard."

"All right," said Holmes, quietly. "I have given you the chance. Here are your lodgings. Good-bye. I shall drop you a line before I leave."

Having left Lestrade at his rooms we drove to our hotel, where we found lunch upon the table. Holmes was silent and buried in thought with a pained expression upon his face, as one who finds himself in a perplexing position.

"Look here, Watson," he said, when the cloth was cleared; "just sit down in this chair and let me preach to you for a little. I don't quite know what to do, and I should value your advice. Light a cigar, and let me expound."

"Pray do so."

"Well, now, in considering this case there are two points about young McCarthy's narrative which struck us both instantly, although they impressed me in his favour and you against him. One was the fact that his father should, according to his account, cry 'Cooee!' before seeing him. The other was his singular dying reference to a rat. He mumbled several words, you understand, but that was all that caught the son's ear. Now from this double point our research must commence, and we will begin it by presuming that what the lad says is absolutely true."

"What of this 'Cooee!' then?"

"Well, obviously it could not have been meant for the son. The son, as far as he knew, was in Bristol. It was mere chance that he was within earshot. The 'Cooee!' was meant to attract the attention of whoever it was that he had the appointment with. But 'Cooee' is a distinctly Australian cry, and one which is used between Australians. There is a strong presumption that the person whom McCarthy expected to meet him at Boscombe Pool was some one who had been in Australia."

"What of the rat, then?"

Sherlock Holmes took a folded paper from his pocket and flattened it out on the table. "This is a map of the Colony of Victoria," he said. "I wired to Bristol for it last night." He put his hand over part of the map. "What do you read?" he asked.

"ARAT," I read.

"And now?" He raised his hand.

"BALLARAT."

"Quite so. That was the word the man uttered, and of which his son only caught the last two syllables. He was trying to utter the name of his murderer. So-and-so of Ballarat."

"It is wonderful!" I exclaimed.

"It is obvious. And now, you see, I had narrowed the field down considerably. The possession of a grey garment was a third point which, granting the son's statement to be correct, was a certainty. We have come now out of mere vagueness to the definite conception of an Australian from Ballarat with a grey cloak."

"Certainly."

"And one who was at home in the district, for the Pool can only be approached by the farm or by the estate, where strangers could hardly wander."

"Quite so."

"Then comes our expedition of today. By an examination of the ground I gained the trifling details which I gave to that imbecile Lestrade, as to the personality of the criminal."

"But how did you gain them?"

"You know my method. It is founded upon the observance of trifles."

"His height I know that you might roughly judge from the length of his stride. His boots, too, might be told from their traces."

"Yes, they were peculiar boots."

"But his lameness?"

"The impression of his right foot was always less distinct than his left. He put less weight upon it. Why? Because he limped—he was lame."

"But his left-handedness."

"You were yourself struck by the nature of the injury as recorded by the surgeon at the inquest. The blow was struck from immediately behind, and yet was upon the left side. Now, how can that be unless it were by a left-handed man? He had stood behind that tree during the interview between the father and son. He had even smoked there. I found the ash of a cigar, which my special knowledge of tobacco ashes enabled me to pronounce as an Indian cigar. I have, as you know, devoted some attention to this, and written a little monograph on the ashes of 140 different varieties of pipe, cigar, and cigarette tobacco. Having found the ash, I then looked round and discovered the stump among the moss where he had tossed it. It was an Indian cigar, of the variety which are rolled in Rotterdam."

"And the cigar-holder?"

"I could see that the end had not been in his mouth. Therefore he used a holder. The tip had been cut off, not bitten off, but the cut was not a clean one, so I deduced a blunt penknife."

"Holmes," I said, "you have drawn a net round this man from which he cannot escape, and you have saved an innocent human life as truly as if you had cut the cord which was hanging him. I see the direction in which all this points. The culprit is—"

"Mr. John Turner," cried the hotel waiter, opening the door of our sitting-room, and ushering in a visitor.

The man who entered was a strange and impressive figure. His slow, limping step and bowed shoulders gave the appearance of decrepitude, and yet his hard, deep-lined, craggy features, and his enormous limbs showed that he was possessed of unusual strength of body and of character. His tangled beard, grizzled hair, and outstanding, drooping eyebrows combined to give an air of dignity and power to his appearance, but his face was of an ashen white, while his lips and the corners of his nostrils were tinged with a shade of blue. It was clear to me at a glance that he was in the grip of some deadly and chronic disease.

"Pray sit down on the sofa," said Holmes, gently. "You had my note?"

"Yes, the lodge-keeper brought it up. You said that you wished to see me here to avoid scandal."

"I thought people would talk if I went to the Hall."

"And why did you wish to see me?" He looked across at my companion with despair in his weary eyes, as though his question were already answered.

"Yes," said Holmes, answering the look rather than the words. "It is so. I know all about McCarthy."

The old man sank his face in his hands. "God help me!" he cried. "But I would not have let the young man come to harm. I give you my word that I would have spoken out if it went against him at the Assizes."

"I am glad to hear you say so," said Holmes, gravely.

"I would have spoken now had it not been for my dear girl. It would break her heart—it will break her heart when she hears that I am arrested."

"It may not come to that," said Holmes.

"What!"

"I am no official agent. I understand that it was your daughter who required my presence here, and I am acting in her interests. Young McCarthy must be got off, however."

"I am a dying man," said old Turner. "I have had diabetes for years. My doctor says it is a question whether I shall live a month. Yet I would rather die under my own roof than in a gaol."

Holmes rose and sat down at the table with his pen in his hand and a bundle of paper before him. "Just tell us the truth," he said. "I shall jot down the facts. You will sign it, and Watson here can witness it. Then I could produce your confession at the last extremity to save young McCarthy. I promise you that I shall not use it unless it is absolutely needed."

"It's as well," said the old man; "it's a question whether I shall live to the Assizes, so it matters little to me, but I should wish to spare Alice the shock. And now I will make the thing clear to you; it has been a long time in the acting, but will not take me long to tell.

"You didn't know this dead man, McCarthy. He was a devil incarnate. I tell you that. God keep you out of the clutches of such a man as he. His grip has been upon me these twenty years, and he has blasted my life. I'll tell you first how I came to be in his power.

"It was in the early sixties at the diggings. I was a young chap then, hot-blooded and reckless, ready to turn my hand to anything; I got among bad companions, took to drink, had no luck with my claim, took to the bush, and, in a word, became what you would call over here a highway robber. There were six of us, and we had a wild, free life of it, sticking up a station from time to time, or stopping the waggons on the road to the diggings. Black Jack of Ballarat was the name I went under, and our party is still remembered in the colony as the Ballarat Gang.

"One day a gold convoy came down from Ballarat to Melbourne, and we lay in wait for it and attacked it. There were six troopers and six of us, so it was a close thing, but we emptied four of their saddles at the first volley. Three of our boys were killed, however, before we got the swag. I put my pistol to the head of the waggon-driver, who was this very man McCarthy. I wish to the Lord that I had shot him then, but I spared him, though I saw his wicked little eyes fixed on my face, as though to remember every feature. We got away with the gold, became wealthy men, and made our way over to England without being suspected. There I parted from my old pals, and determined to settle down to a quiet and respectable life. I bought this estate which chanced to be in the market, and I set myself to do a little good with my money, to make up for the way in which I had earned it. I married, too, and though my wife died young, she left me my dear little Alice. Even when she was just a baby her wee hand seemed to lead me down the right path as nothing else had ever done. In a word, I turned over a new leaf, and did my best to make up for the past. All was going well when McCarthy laid his grip upon me.

"I had gone up to town about an investment, and I met him in Regent Street with hardly a coat to his back or a boot to his foot.

"'Here we are, Jack,' says he, touching me on the arm; 'we'll be as good as a family to you. There's two of us, me and my son, and you can have the keeping of us. If you don't—it's a fine, law-abiding country is England, and there's always a policeman within hail.'

"Well, down they came to the West country, there was no shaking them off, and there they have lived rent free on my best land ever since. There was no rest for me, no peace, no forgetfulness; turn where I would, there was his cunning, grinning face at my elbow. It grew worse as Alice grew up, for he soon saw I was more afraid of her knowing my past than of the police. Whatever he wanted he must have, and whatever it was I gave him without question, land, money, houses, until at last he asked a thing which I could not give. He asked for Alice.

"His son, you see, had grown up, and so had my girl, and as I was known to be in weak health, it seemed a fine stroke to him that his lad should step into the whole property. But there I was firm. I would not have his cursed stock mixed with mine; not that I had any dislike to the lad, but his blood was in him, and that was enough. I stood firm. McCarthy threatened. I braved him to do his worst. We were to meet at the Pool midway between our houses to talk it over.

"When I went down there I found him talking with his son, so I smoked a cigar, and waited behind a tree until he should be alone. But as I listened to his talk all that was black and bitter in me seemed to come uppermost. He was urging his son to marry my daughter with as little regard for what she might think as if she were a slut from off the streets. It drove me mad to think that I and all that I held most dear should be in the power of such a man as this. Could I not snap the bond? I was already a dying and a desperate man. Though clear of mind and fairly strong of limb, I knew that my own fate was sealed. But my memory and my girl! Both could be saved, if I could but silence that foul tongue. I did it, Mr. Holmes. I would do it again. Deeply as I have sinned, I have led a life of martyrdom to atone for it. But that my girl should be entangled in the same meshes which held me was more than I could suffer. I struck him down with no more compunction than if he had been some foul and venomous beast. His cry brought back his son; but I had gained the cover of the wood, though I was forced to go back to fetch the cloak which I had dropped in my flight. That is the true story, gentlemen, of all that occurred."

"Well, it is not for me to judge you," said Holmes, as the old man signed the statement which had been drawn out. "I pray that we may never be exposed to such a temptation."

"I pray not, sir. And what do you intend to do?"

"In view of your health, nothing. You are yourself aware that you will soon have to answer for your deed at a higher Court than the Assizes. I will keep your confession, and, if McCarthy is condemned, I shall be forced to use it. If not, it shall never be seen by mortal eye; and your secret, whether you be alive or dead, shall be safe with us."

"Farewell! then," said the old man, solemnly. "Your own death-beds, when they come, will be the easier for the thought of the peace which you have given to mine." Tottering and shaking in all his giant frame, he stumbled slowly from the room.

"God help us!" said Holmes, after a long silence. "Why does fate play such tricks with poor helpless worms? I never hear of such a case as this that I do not think of Baxter's words, and say, 'There, but for the grace of God, goes Sherlock Holmes.'"

James McCarthy was acquitted at the Assizes, on the strength of a number of objections which had been drawn out by Holmes, and submitted to the defending counsel. Old Turner lived for seven months after our interview, but he is now dead; and there is every prospect that the son and daughter may come to live happily together, in ignorance of the black cloud which rests upon their past.

THE HORROR OF STUDLEY GRANGE

L. T. Meade and Clifford Halifax

L. T. Meade was the pseudonym adopted by Elizabeth Thomasina Meade Smith (1844–1914) after she took up writing at the age of seventeen. The daughter of an Irish clergyman, and a fluent story-teller, Meade became an extraordinarily prolific writer of stories for girls as well as mysteries and tales of adventure. In addition, she founded and edited *Atalanta*, a magazine aimed primarily at young women and which featured such authors as R. L. Stevenson, H. Rider Haggard, and Frances Hodgson Burnett. A feminist, Meade was a member of the progressive and egalitarian Pioneer Club for women.

She co-wrote a number of books with male collaborators. Dr Clifford Halifax, was also a pen-name, concealing the identity of a Yorkshire-born medical man, Edgar Beaumont (1860–1921). Their first joint effort was *This Troublesome World* (1893), featuring a doctor who uses psychotropic drugs for his own purposes. The following year saw the publication of *Stories for the Diary of a Doctor*, narrated by Halifax, from which this tale is taken; it dates from 1894, and originally appeared in the *Strand Magazine*. "The Horror of Studley Grange" is a pleasingly atmospheric mystery which culminates in an experiment with a laryngoscope.

I WAS IN MY CONSULTING-ROOM ONE MORNING, AND HAD JUST said good-bye to the last of my patients, when my servant came in and told me that a lady had called who pressed very earnestly for an interview with me.

"I told her that you were just going out, sir," said the man, "and she saw the carriage at the door; but she begged to see you, if only for two minutes. This is her card."

I read the words, "Lady Studley".

"Show her in," I said, hastily, and the next moment a tall, slightly made, fair-haired girl entered the room.

She looked very young, scarcely more than twenty, and I could hardly believe that she was, what her card indicated, a married woman.

The colour rushed into her cheeks as she held out her hand to me. I motioned her to a chair, and then asked her what I could do for her.

"Oh, you can help me," she said, clasping her hands and speaking in a slightly theatrical manner. "My husband, Sir Henry Studley, is very unwell, and I want you to come to see him—can you?—will you?"

"With pleasure," I replied. "Where do you live?"

"At Studley Grange, in Wiltshire. Don't you know our place?"

"I daresay I ought to know it," I replied, "although at the present moment I can't recall the name. You want me to come to see your husband. I presume you wish me to have a consultation with his medical attendant?"

"No, no, not at all. The fact is, Sir Henry has not got a medical attendant. He dislikes doctors, and won't see one. I want you to come and stay with us for a week or so. I have heard of you through mutual friends—the Onslows. I know you can effect remarkable cures, and you have a great deal of tact. But you can't possibly do anything for my husband unless you are willing to stay in the house and to notice his symptoms."

Lady Studley spoke with great emphasis and earnestness. Her long, slender hands were clasped tightly together. She had drawn off her gloves and was bending forward in her chair. Her big, childish, and somewhat restless blue eyes were fixed imploringly on my face.

"I love my husband," she said, tears suddenly filling them—"and it is dreadful, dreadful, to see him suffer as he does. He will die unless someone comes to his aid. Oh, I know I am asking an immense thing, when I beg of you to leave all your patients and come to the country. But we can pay. Money is no object whatever to us. We can, we will, gladly pay you for your services."

"I must think the matter over," I said. "You flatter me by wishing for me, and by believing that I can render you assistance, but I cannot take a step of this kind in a hurry. I will write to you by tonight's post if you will give me your address. In the meantime, kindly tell me some of the symptoms of Sir Henry's malady."

"I fear it is a malady of the mind," she answered immediately, "but it is of so vivid and so startling a character, that unless relief is soon obtained, the body must give way under the strain. You see that I am very young, Dr. Halifax. Perhaps I look younger than I am—my age is twenty-two. My husband is twenty years my senior. He would, however, be considered by most people still a young man. He is a great scholar, and has always had more or less the habits of a recluse. He is fond of living in his library, and likes nothing better than to be surrounded by books of all sorts. Every modern book worth reading is forwarded to him by its publisher. He is a very interesting man and a brilliant conversationalist. Perhaps I ought to put all this in the past tense, for now he scarcely ever speaks—he reads next to nothing—it is difficult to persuade him to eat—he will not leave the house—he used to have a rather ruddy complexion— he is now deadly pale and terribly emaciated. He sighs in the most heartrending manner, and seems to be in a state of extreme nervous tension. In short, he is very ill, and yet he seems to have no bodily disease. His eyes have a terribly startled expression in them—his hand trembles so that he can scarcely raise a cup of tea to his lips. In short, he looks like a man who has seen a ghost."

"When did these symptoms begin to appear?" I asked.

"It is mid-winter now," said Lady Studley. "The queer symptoms began to show themselves in my husband in October. They have been growing worse and worse. In short, I can stand them no longer," she continued, giving way to a short, hysterical sob. "I felt I must come to someone—I have heard of you. Do, do come and save us. Do come and find out what is the matter with my wretched husband."

"I will write to you tonight," I said, in as kind a voice as I could muster, for the pretty, anxious wife interested me already. "It may not be possible for me to stay at Studley Grange for a week, but in any case I can promise to come and see the patient. One visit will probably be sufficient—what your husband wants is, no doubt, complete change."

"Oh, yes, yes," she replied, standing up now. "I have said so scores of times, but Sir Henry won't stir from Studley—nothing will induce him to go away. He won't even leave his own special bedroom, although I expect he has dreadful nights." Two hectic spots burnt in her cheeks as she spoke. I looked at her attentively.

"You will forgive me for speaking," I said, "but you do not look at all well yourself. I should like to prescribe for you as well as your husband."

"Thank you," she answered, "I am not very strong. I never have been, but that is nothing—I mean that my health is not a thing of consequence at present. Well, I must not take up any more of your time. I shall expect to get a letter from you tomorrow morning. Please address it to Lady Studley, Grosvenor Hotel, Victoria."

She touched my hand with fingers that burnt like a living coal and left the room.

I thought her very ill, and was sure that if I could see my way to spending a week at Studley Grange, I should have two patients instead of one. It is always difficult for a busy doctor to leave home, but after carefully thinking matters over, I resolved to comply with Lady Studley's request.

Accordingly, two days later saw me on my way to Wiltshire, and to Studley Grange. A brougham with two smart horses was waiting at the station. To my surprise I saw that Lady Studley had come herself to fetch me.

"I don't know how to thank you," she said, giving me a feverish clasp of her hand. "Your visit fills me with hope—I believe that you will discover what is really wrong. Home!" she said, giving a quick, imperious direction to the footman who appeared at the window of the carriage.

We bowled forward at a rapid pace, and she continued:—

"I came to meet you today to tell you that I have used a little guile with regard to your visit. I have not told Sir Henry that you are coming here in the capacity of a doctor."

Here she paused and gave me one of her restless glances.

"Do you mind?" she asked.

"What have you said about me to Sir Henry?" I inquired.

"That you are a great friend of the Onslows, and that I have asked you here for a week's change," she answered immediately. "As a guest, my husband will be polite and delightful to you—as a doctor, he would treat you with scant civility, and would probably give you little or none of his confidence."

I was quite silent for a moment after Lady Studley had told me this. Then I said:—

"Had I known that I was not to come to your house in the capacity of a medical man, I might have reconsidered my earnest desire to help you."

She turned very pale when I said this, and tears filled her eyes.

"Never mind," I said now, for I could not but be touched by her extremely pathetic and suffering face, by the look of great illness which was manifested in every glance. "Never mind now; I am glad you have told me exactly the terms on which you wish me to approach your husband; but I think that I can so put matters to Sir Henry that he will be glad to consult me in my medical capacity."

"Oh, but he does not even know that I suspect his illness. It would never do for him to know. I suspect! I see! I fear! but I say nothing. Sir Henry would be much more miserable than he is now, if he thought that I guessed that there is anything wrong with him."

"It is impossible for me to come to the Grange except as a medical man," I answered, firmly. "I will tell Sir Henry that you have seen some changes in him, and have asked me to visit him as a doctor. Please trust me. Nothing will be said to your husband that can make matters at all uncomfortable for you."

Lady Studley did not venture any further remonstrance, and we now approached the old Grange. It was an irregular pile, built evidently according to the wants of the different families who had lived in it. The building was long and rambling, with rows of windows filled up with panes of latticed glass. In front of the house was a sweeping lawn, which, even at this time of the year, presented a velvety and well-kept appearance. We drove rapidly round to the entrance door, and a moment later I found myself in the presence of my host and patient. Sir Henry Studley was a tall man with a very slight stoop, and an aquiline and rather noble face. His eyes were dark, and his forehead inclined to be bald. There was a courtly, old-world sort of look about him. He greeted me with extreme friendliness, and we went into the hall, a very large and lofty apartment, to tea.

Lady Studley was vivacious and lively in the extreme. While she talked, the hectic spots came out again on her cheeks. My uneasiness about her increased as I noticed these symptoms. I felt certain that she was not only consumptive, but in all probability she was even now the victim of an advanced stage of phthisis. I felt far more anxious about her than about her husband, who appeared to me at that moment to be nothing more than a somewhat nervous and hypochondriacal person. This state of things seemed easy to account for in a scholar and a man of sedentary habits.

I remarked about the age of the house, and my host became interested, and told me one or two stories of the old inhabitants of the Grange. He said that tomorrow he would have much pleasure in taking me over the building.

"Have you a ghost here?" I asked, with a laugh.

I don't know what prompted me to ask the question. The moment I did so, Sir Henry turned white to his lips, and Lady

Studley held up a warning finger to me to intimate that I was on dangerous ground. I felt that I was, and hastened to divert the conversation into safer channels. Inadvertently I had touched on a sore spot. I scarcely regretted having done so, as the flash in the baronet's troubled eyes, and the extreme agitation of his face, showed me plainly that Lady Studley was right when she spoke of his nerves being in a very irritable condition. Of course, I did not believe in ghosts, and wondered that a man of Sir Henry's calibre could be at all under the influence of this old-world fear.

"I am sorry that we have no one to meet you," he said, after a few remarks of a commonplace character had divided us from the ghost question. "But tomorrow several friends are coming, and we hope you will have a pleasant time. Are you fond of hunting?"

I answered that I used to be in the old days, before medicine and patients occupied all my thoughts.

"If this open weather continues, I can probably give you some of your favourite pastime," rejoined Sir Henry; "and now perhaps you would like to be shown to your room."

My bedroom was in a modern wing of the house, and looked as cheerful and as un-ghostlike as it was possible for a room to be. I did not rejoin my host and hostess until dinner-time. We had a sociable little meal, at which nothing of any importance occurred, and shortly after the servants withdrew, Lady Studley left Sir Henry and me to ourselves. She gave me another warning glance as she left the room. I had already quite made up my mind, however, to tell Sir Henry the motive of my visit.

The moment the door closed behind his wife, he started up and asked me if I would mind coming with him into his library.

"The fact is," he said, "I am particularly glad you have come down. I want to have a talk with you about my wife. She is extremely unwell."

I signified my willingness to listen to anything Sir Henry might say, and in a few minutes we found ourselves comfortably established in a splendid old room, completely clothed with books from ceiling to floor.

"These are my treasures," said the baronet, waving his hand in the direction of an old bookcase, which contained, I saw at a glance, some very rare and precious first editions.

"These are my friends, the companions of my hours of solitude. Now sit down, Dr. Halifax; make yourself at home. You have come here as a guest, but I have heard of you before, and am inclined to confide in you. I must frankly say that I hate your profession as a rule. I don't believe in the omniscience of medical men, but moments come in the lives of all men when it is necessary to unburden the mind to another. May I give you my confidence?"

"One moment first," I said. "I can't deceive you, Sir Henry. I have come here, not in the capacity of a guest, but as your wife's medical man. She has been anxious about you, and she begged of me to come and stay here for a few days in order to render you any medical assistance within my power. I only knew, on my way here today, that she had not acquainted you with the nature of my visit."

While I was speaking, Sir Henry's face became extremely watchful, eager, and tense.

"This is remarkable," he said. "So Lucilla is anxious about me? I was not aware that I ever gave her the least clue to the fact that I am not—in perfect health. This is very strange—it troubles me."

He looked agitated. He placed one long, thin hand on the little table which stood near, and pouring out a glass of wine, drank it off.

I noticed as he did so the nervous trembling of his hand. I glanced at his face, and saw that it was thin to emaciation.

"Well," he said, "I am obliged to you for being perfectly frank with me. My wife scarcely did well to conceal the object of your visit. But now that you have come, I shall make use of you both for myself and for her."

"Then you are not well?" I asked.

"Well!" he answered, with almost a shout. "Good God, no! I think that I am going mad. I know—I know that unless relief soon comes I shall die or become a raving maniac."

"No, nothing of the kind," I answered, soothingly; "you probably want change. This is a fine old house, but dull, no doubt, in winter. Why don't you go away?—to the Riviera, or some other place where there is plenty of sunshine? Why do you stay here? The air of this place is too damp to be good for either you or your wife."

Sir Henry sat silent for a moment, then he said, in a terse voice:—

"Perhaps you will advise me what to do after you know the nature of the malady which afflicts me. First of all, however, I wish to speak of my wife."

"I am ready to listen," I replied.

"You see," he continued, "that she is very delicate?"

"Yes," I replied; "to be frank with you, I should say that Lady Studley was consumptive."

He started when I said this, and pressed his lips firmly together. After a moment he spoke.

"You are right," he replied. "I had her examined by a medical man—Sir Joseph Dunbar—when I was last in London; he said her lungs were considerably affected, and that, in short, she was far from well."

"Did he not order you to winter abroad?"

"He did, but Lady Studley opposed the idea so strenuously that I was obliged to yield to her entreaties. Consumption does not seem to take quite the ordinary form with her. She is restless, she longs for cool air, she goes out on quite cold days, in a closed carriage, it is true. Still, except at night, she does not regard herself in any sense as an invalid. She has immense spirit—I think she will keep up until she dies."

"You speak of her being an invalid at night," I replied. "What are her symptoms?"

Sir Henry shuddered quite visibly.

"Oh, those awful nights!" he answered. "How happy would many poor mortals be but for the terrible time of darkness. Lady Studley has had dreadful nights for some time: perspirations, cough, restlessness, bad dreams, and all the rest of it. But I must hasten to tell you my story quite briefly. In the beginning of October we saw Sir Joseph Dunbar. I should then, by his advice, have taken Lady Studley to the Riviera, but she opposed the idea with such passion and distress, that I abandoned it."

Sir Henry paused here, and I looked at him attentively. I remembered at that moment what Lady Studley had said about her husband refusing to leave the Grange under any circumstances. What a strange game of cross-purposes these two were playing. How was it possible for me to get at the truth?

"At my wife's earnest request," continued Sir Henry, "we returned to the Grange. She declared her firm intention of remaining here until she died.

"Soon after our return she suggested that we should occupy separate rooms at night, reminding me, when she made the request, of the infectious nature of consumption. I complied with her wish on condition that I slept in the room next hers, and that on the smallest emergency I should be summoned to her aid. This arrangement was made, and her room opens into mine. I have sometimes heard her moving about at night—I have often heard her cough, and I have often heard her sigh. But she has never once sent for me, or given me to understand that she required my aid. She does not think herself very ill, and nothing worries her more than to have her malady spoken about. That is the part of the story which relates to my wife."

"She is very ill," I said. "But I will speak of that presently. Now will you favour me with an account of your own symptoms, Sir Henry?"

He started again when I said this, and going across the room, locked the door and put the key in his pocket.

"Perhaps you will laugh at me," he said, "but it is no laughing matter, I assure you. The most terrible, the most awful affliction has come to me. In short, I am visited nightly by an appalling apparition. You don't believe in ghosts, I judge that by your face. Few scientific men do."

"Frankly, I do not," I replied. "So-called ghosts can generally be accounted for. At the most they are only the figments of an over-excited or diseased brain."

"Be that as it may," said Sir Henry, "the diseased brain can give such torture to its victim that death is preferable. All my life I have been what I consider a healthy minded man. I have plenty of money, and have never been troubled with the cares which torture men of commerce, or of small means. When I married, three years ago, I considered myself the most lucky and the happiest of mortals."

"Forgive a personal question," I interrupted. "Has your marriage disappointed you?"

"No, no; far from it," he replied with fervour. "I love my dear wife better and more deeply even than the day when I took her as a bride to my arms. It is true that I am weighed down with sorrow about her, but that is entirely owing to the state of her health."

"It is strange," I said, "that she should he weighed down with sorrow about you for the same cause. Have you told her of the thing which terrifies you?"

"Never, never. I have never spoken of it to mortal. It is remarkable that my wife should have told you that I looked like a man who has seen a ghost. Alas! alas! But let me tell you the cause of my shattered nerves, my agony, and failing health."

"Pray do, I shall listen attentively," I replied.

"Oh, doctor, that I could make you feel the horror of it!" said Sir Henry, bending forward and looking into my eyes. "Three months ago I no more believed in visitations, in apparitions, in so-called ghosts, than you do. Were you tried as I am, your scepticism would receive a severe shock. Now let me tell you what occurs. Night after night Lady Studley and I retire to rest at the same hour. We say good-night, and lay our heads on our separate pillows. The door of communication between us is shut. She has a night-light in her room—I prefer darkness. I close my eyes and prepare for slumber. As a rule I fall asleep. My sleep is of short duration. I awake with beads of perspiration standing on my forehead, with my heart thumping heavily and with every nerve wide awake, and waiting for the horror which will come. Sometimes I wait half an hour—sometimes longer. Then I know by a faint, ticking sound in the darkness that the Thing, for I can clothe it with no name, is about to visit me. In a certain spot of the room, always in the same spot, a bright light suddenly flashes; out of its midst there gleams a preternaturally large eye, which looks fixedly at me with a diabolical expression. As time goes, it does not remain long; but as agony counts, it seems to take years of my life away with it. It fades as suddenly into grey mist and nothingness as it comes, and, wet with perspiration, and struggling to keep back screams of mad terror, I bury my head in the bed-clothes."

"But have you never tried to investigate this thing?" I said.

"I did at first. The first night I saw it, I rushed out of bed and made for the spot. It disappeared at once. I struck a light—there was nothing whatever in the room."

"Why do you sleep in that room?"

"I must not go away from Lady Studley. My terror is that she should know anything of this—my greater terror is that the apparition, failing me, may visit her. I daresay you think I'm a fool, Halifax; but the fact is, this thing is killing me, brave man as I consider myself."

"Do you see it every night?" I asked.

"Not quite every night, but sometimes on the same night it comes twice. Sometimes it will not come at all for two nights, or even three. It is the most ghastly, the most horrible form of torture that could hurry a sane man into his grave or into a madhouse."

"I have not the least shadow of doubt," I said, after a pause, "that the thing can be accounted for."

Sir Henry shook his head. "No, no," he replied, "it is either as you suggest, a figment of my own diseased brain, and therefore just as horrible as a real apparition; or it is a supernatural visitation. Whether it exists or not, it is reality to me and in no way a dream. The full horror of it is present with me in my waking moments."

"Do you think anyone is playing an awful practical joke?" I suggested.

"Certainly not. What object can anyone have in scaring me to death? Besides, there is no one in the room, that I can swear. My outer door is locked, Lady Studley's outer door is locked. It is impossible that there can be any trickery in the matter."

I said nothing for a moment. I no more believed in ghosts than I ever did, but I felt certain that there was grave mischief at work. Sir Henry must be the victim of a hallucination. This might only be caused by functional disturbance of the brain, but it was quite serious enough to call for immediate attention. The first thing to do was to find out whether the apparition could be accounted for in any material way, or if it were due to the state of Sir Henry's nerves. I began to ask him certain questions, going fully into the case in all its bearings. I then examined his eyes with the ophthalmoscope. The result of all this was to assure me beyond doubt that Sir Henry Studley was in a highly nervous condition, although I could detect no trace of brain disease.

"Do you mind taking me to your room?" I said.

"Not tonight," he answered. "It is late, and Lady Studley might express surprise. The object of my life is to conceal this horror from her. When she is out tomorrow you shall come to the room and judge for yourself."

"Well," I said, "I shall have an interview with your wife tomorrow, and urge her most strongly to consent to leave the Grange and go away with you."

Shortly afterwards we retired to rest, or what went by the name of rest in that sad house, with its troubled inmates. I must confess that, comfortable as my room was, I slept very little. Sir Henry's story stayed with me all through the hours of darkness. I am neither nervous nor imaginative, but I could not help seeing that terrible eye, even in my dreams.

I met my host and hostess at an early breakfast. Sir Henry proposed that as the day was warm and fine, I should ride to a neighbouring meet. I was not in the humour for this, however, and said frankly that I should prefer remaining at the Grange. One glance into the faces of my host and hostess told me only too plainly that I had two very serious patients on my hands. Lady Studley looked terribly weak and excited—the hectic spots on her cheeks, the gleaming glitter of her eyes, the parched lips, the long, white, emaciated hands, all showed only too plainly the strides the malady under which she was suffering was making.

"After all, I cannot urge that poor girl to go abroad," I said to myself. "She is hastening rapidly to her grave, and no power on earth can save her. She looks as if there were extensive disease of the lungs. How restless her eyes are, too! I would much rather testify to Sir Henry's sanity than to hers."

Sir Henry Studley also bore traces of a sleepless night—his face was bloodless; he averted his eyes from mine; he ate next to nothing.

Immediately after breakfast, I followed Lady Studley into her morning-room. I had already made up my mind how to act. Her husband should have my full confidence—she only my partial view of the situation.

"Well," I said, "I have seen your husband and talked to him. I hope he will soon be better. I don't think you need be seriously alarmed about him. Now for yourself, Lady Studley. I am anxious to examine your lungs. Will you allow me to do so?"

"I suppose Henry has told you I am consumptive?"

"He says you are not well," I answered. "I don't need his word to assure me of that fact—I can see it with my own eyes. Please let me examine your chest with my stethoscope."

She hesitated for a moment, looking something like a wild creature brought to bay. Then she sank into a chair, and with trembling fingers unfastened her dress. Poor soul, she was almost a walking skeleton—her beautiful face was all that was beautiful about her.

A brief examination told me that she was in the last stage of phthisis—in short, that her days were numbered.

"What do you think of me?" she asked, when the brief examination was over.

"You are ill," I replied.

"How soon shall I die?"

"God only knows that, my dear lady," I answered.

"Oh, you needn't hide your thoughts," she said. "I know that my days are very few. Oh, if only, if only my husband could come with me! I am so afraid to go alone, and I am fond of him, very fond of him."

I soothed her as well as I could.

"You ought to have someone to sleep in your room at night," I said. "You ought not to be left by yourself."

"Henry is near me—in the next room," she replied. "I would not have a nurse for the world—I hate and detest nurses."

Soon afterwards she left me. She was very erratic, and before she left the room she had quite got over her depression. The sun shone out, and with the gleam of brightness her volatile spirits rose.

"I am going for a drive," she said. "Will you come with me?"

"Not this morning," I replied. "If you ask me tomorrow, I shall be pleased to accompany you."

"Well, go to Henry," she answered. "Talk to him—find out what ails him, order tonics for him. Cheer him in every way in your power. You say he is not ill—not seriously ill—I know better. My impression is that if my days are numbered, so are his."

She went away, and I sought her husband. As soon as the wheels of her brougham were heard bowling away over the gravel sweep, we went up together to his room.

"That eye came twice last night," he said in an awestruck whisper to me. "I am a doomed man—a doomed man. I cannot bear this any longer."

We were standing in the room as he said the words. Even in broad daylight, I could see that he glanced round him with apprehension. He was shaking quite visibly. The room was decidedly old-fashioned, but the greater part of the furniture was modern. The bed was an Albert one with a spring mattress, and light, cheerful dimity hangings. The windows were French—they were wide open, and let in the soft, pleasant air, for the day was truly a spring one in winter. The paper on the walls was light.

"This is a quaint old wardrobe," I said. "It looks out of place with the rest of the furniture. Why don't you have it removed?"

"Hush," he said, with a gasp. "Don't go near it—I dread it, I have locked it. It is always in that direction that the apparition appears. The apparition seems to grow out of the glass of the wardrobe. It always appears in that one spot."

"I see," I answered. "The wardrobe is built into the wall. That is the reason it cannot be removed. Have you got the key about you?"

He fumbled in his pocket, and presently produced a bunch of keys.

"I wish you wouldn't open the wardrobe," he said. "I frankly admit that I dislike having it touched."

"All right," I replied. "I will not examine it while you are in the room. You will perhaps allow me to keep the key?"

"Certainly! You can take it from the bunch, if you wish. This is it. I shall be only too glad to have it well out of my own keeping."

"We will go downstairs," I said.

We returned to Sir Henry's library. It was my turn now to lock the door.

"Why do you do that?" he asked.

"Because I wish to be quite certain that no one overhears our conversation."

"What have you got to say?"

"I have a plan to propose to you."

"What is it?"

"I want you to change bedrooms with me tonight."

"What can you mean?—what will Lady Studley say?"

"Lady Studley must know nothing whatever about the arrangement. I think it very likely that the apparition which troubles you will be discovered to have a material foundation. In short, I am determined to get to the bottom of this horror. You have seen it often, and your nerves are much shattered. I have never seen it, and my nerves are, I think, in tolerable order. If I sleep in your room tonight—"

"It may not visit you."

"It may not, but on the other hand it may. I have a curiosity to lie on that bed and to face that wardrobe in the wall. You must yield to my wishes, Sir Henry."

"But how can the knowledge of this arrangement be kept from my wife?"

"Easily enough. You will both go to your rooms as usual. You will bid her good night as usual, and after the doors of communication are closed I will enter the room and you will go to mine, or to any other that you like to occupy. You say your wife never comes into your room during the hours of the night?"

"She has never yet done so."

"She will not tonight. Should she by any chance call for assistance, I will immediately summon you."

It was very evident that Sir Henry did not like this arrangement. He yielded, however, to my very strong persuasions, which almost took the form of commands, for I saw that I could do nothing unless I got complete mastery over the man.

Lady Studley returned from her drive just as our arrangements were fully made. I had not a moment during all the day to examine the interior of the wardrobe. The sick woman's restlessness grew greater as the hours advanced. She did not care to leave her husband's side. She sat with him as he examined his books. She followed him from room to room. In the afternoon, to the relief of everyone, some fresh guests arrived. In consequence we had a cheerful evening. Lady Studley came down to dinner in white from top to toe. Her dress was ethereal in texture and largely composed of lace. I cannot describe woman's dress, but with her shadowy figure and worn, but still lovely face, she looked spiritual. The gleam in her large blue eyes was pathetic. Her love for her husband was touching to behold. How soon, how very soon, they must part from each other! Only I as a doctor knew how impossible it was to keep the lamp of life much longer burning in the poor girl's frame.

We retired as usual to rest. Sir Henry bade me a cheerful goodnight. Lady Studley nodded to me as she left the room.

"Sleep well," she said, in a gay voice.

It was late the next morning when we all met round the breakfast table. Sir Henry looked better, but Lady Studley many degrees worse, than the night before. I wondered at her courage in retaining her post at the head of her table. The visitors, who came in at intervals and took their seats at the table, looked at her with wonder and compassion.

"Surely my hostess is very ill?" said a guest who sat next my side.

"Yes, but take no notice of it," I answered.

Soon after breakfast I sought Sir Henry.

"Well—well?" he said, as he grasped my hand. "Halifax, you have seen it. I know you have by the expression of your face."

"Yes," I replied, "I have."

"How quietly you speak. Has not the horror of the thing seized you?"

"No," I said, with a brief laugh. "I told you yesterday that my nerves were in tolerable order. I think my surmise was correct, and that the apparition has tangible form and can be traced to its foundation."

An unbelieving look swept over Sir Henry's face.

"Ah," he said, "doctors are very hard to convince. Everything must be brought down to a cold material level to satisfy them; but several nights in that room would shatter even your nerves, my friend."

"You are quite right," I answered, "I should be very sorry to spend several nights in that room. Now I will tell you briefly what occurred."

We were standing in the library. Sir Henry went to the door, locked it, and put the key in his pocket.

"Can I come in?" said a voice outside.

The voice was Lady Studley's.

"In a minute, my darling," answered her husband. "I am engaged with Halifax just at present."

"Medically, I suppose?" she answered.

"Yes, medically," he responded.

She went away at once, and Sir Henry returned to my side.

"Now speak," he said. "Be quick. She is sure to return, and I don't like her to fancy that we are talking secrets."

"This is my story," I said. "I went into your room, put out all the lights, and sat on the edge of the bed."

"You did not get into bed, then?"

"No I preferred to be up and to be ready for immediate action should the apparition, the horror, or whatever you call it, appear."

"Good God, it is a horror, Halifax!"

"It is, Sir Henry. A more diabolical contrivance for frightening a man into his grave could scarcely have been contrived. I can comfort you on one point, however. The terrible thing you saw is not a figment of your brain. There is no likelihood of a lunatic asylum in your case. Someone is playing you a trick."

"I cannot agree with you—but proceed," said the baronet, impatiently.

"I sat for about an hour on the edge of the bed," I continued. "When I entered the room it was twelve o'clock—one had sounded before there was the least stir or appearance of anything, then the ticking noise you have described was distinctly audible. This was followed by a sudden bright light, which seemed to proceed out of the recesses of the wardrobe."

"What did you feel when you saw that light?"

"Too excited to be nervous," I answered, briefly. "Out of the circle of light the horrible eye looked at me."

"What did you do then? Did you faint?"

"No, I went noiselessly across the carpet up to the door of the wardrobe and looked in."

"Heavens! you are daring. I wonder you are alive to tell this tale."

"I saw a shadowy form," I replied—"dark and tall—the one brilliant eye kept on looking past me, straight into the room. I made a very slight noise; it immediately disappeared. I waited for some time—nothing more happened. I got into your bed, Sir Henry, and slept. I can't say that I had a comfortable night, but I slept, and was not disturbed by anything extraordinary for the remaining hours of the night."

"Now what do you mean to do? You say you can trace this thing to its foundation. It seems to me that all you have seen only supports my firm belief that a horrible apparition visits that room."

"A material one," I responded. "The shadowy form had substance, of that I am convinced. Sir Henry, I intend to sleep in that room again tonight."

"Lady Studley will find out."

"She will not. I sleep in the haunted room again tonight, and during the day you must so contrive matters that I have plenty of time to examine the wardrobe. I did not do so yesterday because I had not an opportunity. You must contrive to get Lady Studley out of the way, either this morning or afternoon, and so manage matters for me that I can be some little time alone in your room."

"Henry, Henry, how awestruck you look!" said a gay voice at the window. Lady Studley had come out, had come round to the library window, and, holding up her long, dark-blue velvet dress, was looking at us with a peculiar smile.

"Well, my love," replied the baronet. He went to the window and flung it open. "Lucilla," he exclaimed, "you are mad to stand on the damp grass."

"Oh, no, not mad," she answered. "I have come to that stage when nothing matters. Is not that so, Dr. Halifax?"

"You are very imprudent," I replied.

She shook her finger at me playfully, and turned to her husband.

"Henry," she said, "have you taken my keys? I cannot find them anywhere."

"I will go up and look for them," said Sir Henry. He left the room, and Lady Studley entered the library through one of the French windows.

"What do you think of my husband this morning?" she asked.

"He is a little better," I replied. "I am confident that he will soon be quite well again."

She gave a deep sigh when I said this, her lips trembled, and she turned away. I thought my news would make her happy, and her depression surprised me.

At this moment Sir Henry came into the room.

"Here are your keys," he said to his wife.

He gave her the same bunch he had given me the night before. I hoped she would not notice that the key of the wardrobe was missing.

"And now I want you to come for a drive with me," said Sir Henry.

He did not often accompany her, and the pleasure of this unlooked-for indulgence evidently tempted her.

"Very well," she answered. "Is Dr. Halifax coming?"

"No, he wants to have a ride."

"If he rides, can he not follow the carriage?"

"Will you do that, Halifax?" asked my host.

"No, thank you," I answered; "I must write some letters before I go anywhere. I will ride to the nearest town and post them presently, if I may." I left the room as I spoke.

Shortly afterwards I saw from a window Sir Henry and his wife drive away. They drove in a large open landau, and two girls who were staying in the house accompanied them. My hour had come, and I went up at once to Sir Henry's bedroom. Lady Studley's room opened directly into that of her husband, but both rooms had separate entrances.

I locked the two outer doors now, and then began my investigations. I had the key of the wardrobe in my pocket.

It was troublesome to unlock, because the key was a little rusty, and it was more than evident that the heavy doors had not been opened for some time. Both these doors were made of glass. When shut they resembled in shape and appearance an ordinary old-fashioned window. The glass was set in deep mullions. It was thick, was of a peculiar shade of light blue, and was evidently of great antiquity. I opened the doors and went inside. The wardrobe was so roomy that I could stand upright with perfect comfort. It was empty, and was lined through and through with solid oak. I struck a light and began to examine the interior with care. After a great deal of patient investigation I came across a notch in the wood. I pressed my finger on this, and immediately a little panel slid back, which revealed underneath a small button. I turned the button and a door at the back of the wardrobe flew open. A flood of sunlight poured in, and stepping out, I found myself in another room. I looked around me in astonishment. This was a lady's chamber. Good heavens! What had happened? I was in Lady Studley's room. Shutting the mysterious door of the wardrobe very carefully, I found that all trace of its existence immediately vanished.

There was no furniture against this part of the wall. It looked absolutely bare and smooth. No picture ornamented it. The light paper which covered it gave the appearance of a perfectly unbroken pattern. Of course, there must be a concealed spring somewhere, and I lost no time in feeling for it. I pressed my hand and the tips of my fingers in every direction along the wall. Try as I would, however, I could not find the spring, and I had at last to leave Lady Studley's room and go back to the one occupied by her husband, by the ordinary door.

Once more I re-entered the wardrobe and deliberately broke off the button which opened the secret door from within. Anyone who now entered the wardrobe by this door, and shut it behind him, would find it impossible to retreat. The apparition, if it had material foundation, would thus find itself trapped in its own net.

What could this thing portend?

I had already convinced myself that if Sir Henry were the subject of a hallucination, I also shared it. As this was impossible, I felt certain that the apparition had a material foundation. Who was the person who glided night after night into Lady Studley's room, who knew the trick of the secret spring in the wall, who entered the old wardrobe, and performed this ghastly, this appalling trick on Sir Henry Studley? I resolved that I would say nothing to Sir Henry of my fresh discovery until after I had spent another night in the haunted room.

Accordingly, I slipped the key of the wardrobe once more into my pocket and went downstairs.

I had my way again that night. Once more I found myself the sole occupant of the haunted room. I put out the light, sat on the edge of the bed, and waited the issue of events. At first there was silence and complete darkness, but soon after one o'clock I heard the very slight but unmistakable tick-tick, which told me that the apparition was about to appear. The ticking noise resembled the quaint sound made by the death spider. There was no other noise of any sort, but a quickening of my pulses, a sensation which I could not call fear, but which was exciting to the point of pain, braced me up for an unusual and horrible sight. The light appeared in the dim recess of the wardrobe. It grew clear and steady, and quickly resolved itself into one intensely bright circle. Out of this circle the eye looked at me. The eye was unnaturally large—it was clear, almost transparent, its expression was full of menace and warning. Into the circle of light presently a shadowy and ethereal hand intruded itself. The fingers beckoned me to approach, while the eye looked fixedly at me. I sat motionless on the side of the bed. I am stoical by nature and my nerves are well seasoned, but I am not ashamed to say that I should be very sorry to be often subjected to that menace and that invitation. The look in that eye, the beckoning power in those long, shadowy fingers would soon work havoc even in the stoutest nerves. My heart beat uncomfortably fast, and I had to say over and over to myself, "This is nothing more than a ghastly trick." I had also to remind myself that I in my turn had prepared a trap for the apparition. The time while the eye looked and the hand beckoned might in reality have been counted by seconds; to me it seemed like eternity. I felt the cold dew on my forehead before the rapidly waning light assured me that the apparition was about to vanish. Making an effort I now left the bed and approached the wardrobe. I listened intently. For a moment there was perfect silence. Then a fumbling noise was distinctly audible. It was followed by a muffled cry, a crash, and a heavy fall. I struck a light instantly, and taking the key of the wardrobe from my pocket, opened it. Never shall I forget the sight that met my gaze.

There, huddled up on the floor, lay the prostrate and unconscious form of Lady Studley. A black cloak in which she had wrapped herself partly covered her face, but I knew her by her long, fair hair. I pulled back the cloak, and saw that the unhappy girl had broken a blood-vessel, and even as I lifted her up I knew that she was in a dying condition.

I carried her at once into her own room and laid her on the bed. I then returned and shut the wardrobe door, and slipped the key into my pocket. My next deed was to summon Sir Henry.

"What is it?" he asked, springing upright in bed.

"Come at once," I said, "your wife is very ill."

"Dying?" he asked, in an agonised whisper.

I nodded my head. I could not speak.

My one effort now was to keep the knowledge of the ghastly discovery I had made from the unhappy husband.

He followed me to his wife's room. He forgot even to question me about the apparition, so horrified was he at the sight which met his view.

I administered restoratives to the dying woman, and did what I could to check the haemorrhage. After a time Lady Studley opened her dim eyes.

"Oh, Henry!" she said, stretching out a feeble hand to him, "come with me, come with me. I am afraid to go alone."

"My poor Lucilla," he said. He smoothed her cold forehead, and tried to comfort her by every means in his power.

After a time he left the room. When he did so she beckoned me to approach.

"I have failed," she said, in the most thrilling voice of horror I have ever listened to. "I must go alone. He will not come with me."

"What do you mean?" I asked.

She could scarcely speak, but at intervals the following words dropped slowly from her lips:—

"I was the apparition. I did not want my husband to live after me. Perhaps I was a little insane. I cannot quite say. When I was told by Sir Joseph Dunbar that there was no hope of my life, a most appalling and frightful jealousy took possession of me. I pictured my husband with another wife. Stoop down."

Her voice was very faint. I could scarcely hear her muttered words. Her eyes were glazing fast, death was claiming her, and yet hatred against some unknown person thrilled in her feeble voice.

"Before my husband married me, he loved another woman," she continued. "That woman is now a widow. I felt certain that immediately after my death he would seek her out and marry her. I could not bear the thought—it possessed me day and night. That, and the terror of dying alone, worked such a havoc within me that I believe I was scarcely responsible for my own actions. A mad desire took possession of me to take my husband with me, and so to keep him from her, and also to have his company when I passed the barriers of life. I told you that my brother was a doctor. In his medical-student days the sort of trick I have been playing on Sir Henry was enacted by some of his fellow students for his benefit, and almost scared him into fever. One day my brother described the trick to me, and I asked him to show me how it was done. I used a small electric lamp and a very strong reflector."

"How did you find out the secret door of the wardrobe?" I asked.

"Quite by chance. I was putting some dresses into the wardrobe one day and accidentally touched the secret panel. I saw at once that here was my opportunity."

"You must have been alarmed at your success," I said, after a pause. "And now I have one more question to ask: Why did you summon me to the Grange?"

She made a faint, impatient movement.

"I wanted to be certain that my husband was really very ill," she said. "I wanted you to talk to him—I guessed he would confide in you; I thought it most probable that you would tell him that he was a victim of brain hallucinations. This would frighten him and would suit my purpose exactly. I also sent for you as a blind. I felt sure that under these circumstances neither you nor my husband could possibly suspect me."

She was silent again, panting from exhaustion.

"I have failed," she said, after a long pause. "You have discovered the truth. It never occurred to me for a moment that *you* would go into the room. He will recover now."

She paused; a fresh attack of haemorrhage came on. Her breath came quickly. Her end was very near. Her dim eyes could scarcely see.

Groping feebly with her hand she took mine.

"Dr. Halifax—promise."

"What?" I asked.

"I have failed, but let me keep his love, what little love he has for me, before he marries that other woman. Promise that you will never tell him."

"Rest easy," I answered, "I will never tell him."

Sir Henry entered the room.

I made way for him to kneel by his wife's side.

As the grey morning broke Lady Studley died.

Before my departure from the Grange I avoided Sir Henry as much as possible. Once he spoke of the apparition and asked if I had seen it. "Yes," I replied.

Before I could say anything further, he continued:—

"I know now why it came; it was to warn me of my unhappy wife's death." He said no more. I could not enlighten him, and he is unlikely now ever to learn the truth.

The following day I left Studley Grange. I took with me, without asking leave of anyone, a certain long black cloak, a small electric lamp, and a magnifying glass of considerable power.

It may be of interest to explain how Lady Studley in her unhealthy condition of mind and body performed the extraordinary trick by which she hoped to undermine her husband's health, and ultimately cause his death.

I experimented with the materials which I carried away with me, and succeeded, so my friends told me, in producing a most ghastly effect.

I did it in this way. I attached the mirror of a laryngoscope to my forehead in such a manner as to enable it to throw a strong reflection into one of my eyes. In the centre of the bright side of the laryngoscope a small electric lamp was fitted. This was connected with a battery which I carried in my hand. The battery was similar to those used by the ballet girls in Drury Lane Theatre, and could be brought into force by a touch and extinguished by the removal of the pressure. The eye which was thus brilliantly illumined looked through a lens of some power. All the rest of the face and figure was completely covered by the black cloak. Thus the brightest possible light was thrown on the magnified eye, while there was corresponding increased gloom around.

When last I heard of Studley Grange it was let for a term of years and Sir Henry had gone abroad. I have not heard that he has married again, but he probably will, sooner or later.

THE TRAGEDY OF A THIRD SMOKER

C. J. Cutcliffe Hyne

Charles John Cutcliffe Wright Hyne (1866–1944) is not widely remembered in the twenty-first century, certainly as far as readers of crime fiction are concerned. In his day he was a well-known author, more of a rival to H. G. Wells than to Doyle, given that his most successful novel was *The Lost Continent: The Story of Atlantis* (1900). He was also the creator of Captain Owen Kettle, who appeared in a long series of short stories for the magazines as well as in novels. Kettle, a much-travelled seaman, spent time as a riverboat pilot in the Congo, and it has even been suggested that Joseph Conrad was influenced by Hyne's work in writing his classic novel *Heart of Darkness* (1899).

Hyne was born in Gloucestershire but raised in Yorkshire and educated at Cambridge University. A prolific writer under his own name, he also wrote as Weatherby Chesney. "The Tragedy of a Third Smoker" first appeared in the *Harmsworth Monthly Pictorial Magazine* in 1898, at a time when Hyne was dabbling in crime stories with an ingredient of elementary forensic science. He did not make a sustained contribution to the genre, but this is an enjoyable railway mystery with a pleasingly provocative opening line. Interestingly, the storyline anticipates that of a very early Dr Thorndyke story, "The Blue Sequin", written by R. Austin Freeman a decade later.

"I ABOMINATE DETECTIVE STORIES," SAID THE Q.C., LAYING down his cue along the corner of the billiard-table and going across to the shelf where the cigar-boxes stood. "You see, when a man makes a detective story to write down on paper, he begins at the butt-end and works backwards. He notes his points and manufactures his clues to suit 'em, so it's all bound to work out right. In real life it's very different,"—he chose a Partaga, looking at it through his glasses thoughtfully—"and I ought to know; I've been studying the criminal mind for half my working life."

"But," said O'Malley, "a defending counsel is a different class of animal from the common detective."

"Oh, is he?" said the Q.C.; "that's all you know about it." He dragged one of the big chairs up into the deep chimney corner and settled himself in it, after many luxurious shruggings; then he spoke on, between whiffs at the Partaga.

"Now I'll just state you a case, and you'll see for yourself how we sometimes have to ravel out things. The solicitor who put the brief in my hands was, as solicitors go, a smart chap. He had built up a big business out of nothing, but criminal work was slightly out of his line. He had only taken up this case to oblige an old client, and I must say he made an uncommonly poor show of it. I never had such a thin brief given me in my life.

"The prisoner was to be tried on the capital charge; and if murder really had been committed, it was one of a most cold-blooded nature. Hanging would follow conviction as surely as night comes on the heels of day; and a client who gets the noose given him always damages his counsel's reputation, whether that counsel deserves it or not.

"As my brief put it, the case fined down to this:

"Two men got into an empty third-class smoking compartment at Addison Road. One of them, Guide, was a drain contractor; the other, Walker, was a foreman in Guide's employ. The train took them past the Shepherd's Bush and Grove Road Hammersmith stations without anything being reported; but at Shaftesbury Road Walker was found on the floor, stone dead, with a wound in the skull, and on the seat of the carriage was a small miner's pickaxe with one of its points smeared with blood.

"It was proved that Guide had been seen to leave the Shaftesbury Road station. He was dishevelled and agitated at the time, and this made the ticket collector notice him specially amongst the crowd of out-going passengers. After it was found out who he was, inquiries were made at his home. His wife stated that she had not seen him since Monday—the morning of Walker's death. She also let out that Walker had been causing him some annoyance of late, but she did not know about what. Subsequently—on the Friday, four days later—Guide was arrested at the West India Dock. He was trying to obtain employ as coal trimmer on an Australian steamer, obviously to escape from the country. On being charged he surrendered quietly, remarking that he supposed it was all up with him.

"That was the gist of my case, and the solicitor suggested that I should enter a plea of insanity.

"Now, when I'd conned the evidence over—additional evidence to what I've told you, but all tending to the same end—I came to the conclusion that Guide was as sane as any of us are, and that, as a defence, insanity wouldn't have a leg to stand upon. 'The fellow,' I said, 'had much better enter a plea of guilty and let me pile up a long list of extenuating circumstances. A jury will always listen to those, and feeling grateful for being excused a long and wearisome trial, recommend to mercy out of sheer gratitude.' I wrote a note to this effect. On its receipt the solicitor came to see me—by the way, he was Barnes, a man of my own year at Cambridge.

"'My dear Grayson,' said he, 'I'm not altogether a fool. I know as well as you do that Guide would have the best chance if he pleaded guilty; but the difficult part of it is that he flatly refuses to do any such thing. He says he no more killed this fellow Walker than you or I did. I pointed out to him that the man couldn't very conveniently have slain himself, as the wound was well over at the top of his head, and had obviously been the result of a most terrific blow. At the P.M. it was shown that Walker's skull was of abnormal thickness, and the force required to drive through it even a heavy, sharp-pointed instrument like the pickaxe must have been something tremendous.

"'I tell you, Grayson, I impressed upon the fellow that the case was as black as ink against him, and that he'd only irritate the jury by holding out; but I couldn't move him. He held doggedly to his tale—he had not killed Andrew Walker.'

"'He's not the first man who's stuck to an unlikely lie like that,' I remarked.

"'The curious part of it is,' said Barnes, 'I'm convinced that the man believes himself to be telling the absolute truth.'

"'Then what explanation has he to offer?'

"'None worth listening to. He owns that he and Walker had a fierce quarrel over money matters, which culminated in a personal struggle. He knows that he had one blow on the head which dazed him, and fancies that he must have had a second which reduced him to unconsciousness. When next he knew what was happening, he saw Walker lying on the floor, stone dead, though he was still warm and supple. On the floor was the pickaxe, with one of its points slimy with blood. How it came to be so he couldn't tell. He picked it up and laid it on a seat. Then in an instant the thought flashed across him how terribly black things looked against himself. He saw absolutely no chance of disproving them, and with the usual impulse of crude minds resolved at once to quit the country. With that idea he got out at the Shaftesbury Road Station, and being an ignorant man and without money, made his way down to the Ratcliff Highway—beg its pardon, St. George's High Street. Using that as a centre, he smelt about the docks at Limehouse and Millwall trying for a job in the stokehold; but as that neighbourhood is one of the best watched spots on earth, it is not a matter for surprise that he was very soon captured. That's about all I can tell you.'

"'I'm afraid it doesn't lighten matters up very much.'

"'I never said it would. The gist of this is down in your brief, Grayson. I only came round to chambers because of your letter.'

"'Still,' I persisted, 'you threw out a hint that Guide had offered some explanation.'

"'Oh, yes; but such a flimsy, improbable theory that no sane man could entertain it for a minute. In fact, he knew it to be absurd himself. After pressing him again and again to suggest how Walker could have been killed (with the view of extorting a confession), he said, in his slow, heavy way, "Why, I suppose, Mr. Barnes, someone else must ha' done it. Don't you think as a man could ha' got into the carriage whilst I was lying there stupid, and hit Walker with the pick and got out again afore I come to? Would that do, sir?"

"'I didn't think,' added Barnes, drily, 'that it was worth following that theory any deeper. What do you say?'

"I thought for a minute and then spoke up. 'Look here, Barnes; if in the face of this cock-and-bull story Guide persists in his innocence, there may be something in it after all; and if by any thousand-to-one chance we could bring him clear, it would be a red feather in the caps of both of us. Do you object to my seeing the man personally?'

"'It's a bit irregular,' said Barnes, doubtfully.

"'I know it is bang in the teeth of etiquette. But suppose we compromise, and you come with me?'

"'No, I won't do that. My time's busy just now; and besides, I don't want to run up the costs of this case higher than necessary. But if you choose to shove your other work aside and waste a couple of hours, just go and interview him by yourself, and we'll waive ceremony. I'll get the necessary prison order, and send it round to you tomorrow.'

"Next afternoon I went down to see Guide in the waiting-room at the Old Bailey. He was a middle-aged man, heavy-faced, and evidently knocked half stupid by the situation in which he found himself. He was perhaps as great a fool to his own interests as one might often meet with. There was no getting the simplest tale out of him except by regular question-and-answer cross-examination. What little he did tell seemed rather to confirm his guilt than otherwise; though, strange to say, I was beginning to believe him when he kept on assuring me between every other sentence that he did not commit the murder. Perhaps it was the stolid earnestness of the fellow in denying the crime which convinced me. One gets to read a good deal from facial expression when a man has watched what goes on in the criminal dock as long as I have done; and one can usually spot guilt under any mask.

"'But tell me,' I said, 'what did you quarrel about in the first instance?'

"'Money,' said Guide, moodily.

"'That's vague. Tell me more. Did he owe you money?'

"'No, sir, it was t'other way on.'

"'Wages in arrear?'

"'No, it was money he had advanced me for the working of my business. You see Walker had always been a hard man, and he'd saved. He said he wanted his money back, he knowing that I was pinched a bit just then and couldn't pay. Then he tried to thrust himself into partnership with me in the business, which was a thing I didn't want. I'd good contracts on hand which I expected would bring me in a matter of nine thousand pounds, and I didn't want to share it with any man, least of all him. I told him so, and that's how the trouble began. But it was him that hit me first.'

"'Still, you returned the blow?'

"Guide passed a hand wearily over his forehead. 'I may have struck him back, sir—I was dazed, and I don't rightly remember. But before God I'll swear that I never lifted that pick to Andrew Walker—it was his pick.'

"'But,' I persisted, 'Walker couldn't very conveniently have murdered himself.'

"'No, sir, no—no, he couldn't. I thought of that myself since I been in here, and I said to Mr. Barnes that perhaps somebody come into the carriage when I was knocked silly, and killed him; but Mr. Barnes he said that was absurd. Besides, who could have done it?'

"'Don't you know anybody, then, who would have wished for Walker's death?'

"'There was them that didn't like him,' said Guide, drearily.

"That was all I could get out of him, and I went away from the prison feeling very dissatisfied. I was stronger than ever in the belief that Guide was in no degree guilty, and yet for the life of me I did not see how to prove his innocence. He had not been a man of any strong character to begin with, and the shock of what he had gone through had utterly dazed him. It was hopeless to expect any reasonable explanation from him; he had resigned himself to puzzlement. If he had gone melancholy mad before he came up to trial, I should not have been one whit surprised.

"I brooded over the matter for a couple of days, putting all the rest of my practice out of thought, but I didn't get any forwarder with it. I hate to give anything up as a bad job, and in this case I felt that there was on my shoulders a huge load of responsibility. Guide, I had thoroughly persuaded myself, had not murdered Andrew Walker; as sure as the case went into court, on its present grounding, the man would be hanged out of hand; and I persuaded myself that then I, and I alone, should be responsible for an innocent man's death.

"At the end of those two days only one course seemed open to me. It was foreign to the brief I held, but the only method left to bring in my client's innocence.

"I must find out who did really murder the man. I must try to implicate some third actor in the tragedy.

"To begin with, there was the railway carriage; but a little thought showed me that nothing was to be done there. The compartment would have been inspected by the police, and then swept and cleaned and garnished, and coupled on to its train once more, and used by unconscious passengers for weeks since the uproar occurred in it.

"All that I had got to go upon were the notes and relics held at Scotland Yard.

"The police authorities were very good. Of course, they were keen enough to bring off the prosecution with professional *éclat*; but they were not exactly anxious to hand over a poor wretch to the hangman if he was not thoroughly deserving of a dance on nothing. They placed at my disposal every scrap of their evidence, and said that they thought the reading of it all was plain beyond dispute. I thought so, too, at first. They sent an inspector to my chambers as their envoy.

"On one point, though, after a lot of thought, I did not quite agree with them. I held a grisly relic in my hand, gazing at it fixedly. It was a portion of Walker's skull—a disc of dry bone with a splintered aperture in the middle.

"'And so you think the pickaxe made that hole,' I said to the inspector.

"'I don't think there can be any doubt about it, Mr. Grayson. Nothing else could have done it, and the point of the pick was smeared with blood.'

"'But would there be room to swing such a weapon in a third-class Metropolitan railway carriage?'

"'We thought of that, and at first it seemed a poser. The roof is low, and both Guide and Walker are tall men; but if Guide had gripped the shaft by the end, so, with his right hand pretty near against the head, so, he'd have had heaps of room to drive it with a sideways swing. I tried the thing for myself; it acted perfectly. Here's the pickaxe: you can see for yourself.'

"I did see, and I wasn't satisfied; but I didn't tell the inspector what I thought. It was clearer to me than ever that Guide had not committed the murder. What I asked the inspector was this: 'Had either of the men got any luggage in the carriage?'

"The inspector answered, with a laugh, 'Not quite, Mr. Grayson, or you would see it here.'

"Then I took on paper a rough outline of that fragment of bone, and an accurate sketch of exact size of the gash in it, and the inspector went away. One thing his visit had shown me. Andrew Walker was not slain by a blow from behind by the pickaxe.

"I met Barnes whilst I was nibbling lunch, and told him this. He heard me doubtfully. 'You may be right,' said he, 'but I'm bothered if I see what you have to go upon.'

"'You know what a pickaxe is like?' I said.

"'Certainly.'

"'A cross-section of one of the blades would be what?'

"'Square—or perhaps oblong.'

"'Quite so. Rectangular. What I want to get at is this: it wouldn't even be diamond shape, with the angles obtuse and acute alternately.'

"'Certainly not. The angles would be clean right-angles.'

"'Very good. Now look at this sketch of the hole in the skull, and tell me what you see.'

"Barnes put on his glasses, and gazed attentively for a minute or so, and then looked up. 'The pick point has crashed through without leaving any marks of its edges whatever.'

"'That is to say, there are none of your right-angles showing.'

"'None. But that does not go to prove anything.'

"'No. It's only about a tenth of my proof. It gives the vague initial idea. It made me look more carefully, and I saw this'—I pointed with my pencil to a corner of the sketch.

"Barnes whistled. 'A clean arc of a circle,' said he, 'cut in the bone as though a knife had done it. You saw that pickaxe. Was it much worn? Were the angles much rounded near the point?'

"'They were not. On the contrary, the pick, though an old one, had just been through the blacksmith's shop to be re-sharpened, and had not been used since. There was not a trace of wear upon it: of that I am certain.'

"Barnes whistled again in much perplexity. At length said he, 'It's an absolutely certain thing that Walker was not killed in the way they imagine. But I don't think this will get Guide off scot-free.

There's too much other circumstantial evidence against him. Of course you'll do your best, but—'

"'It would be more than a toss-up if I could avoid a conviction. Quite so. We must find out more. The question is, how was this wound made? Was there a third man in it?'

"'Guide may have jobbed him from behind with some other instrument, and afterwards thrown it out of window.'

"'Yes,' said I, 'but that is going on the assumption that Guide did the trick, which I don't for a moment think is the case. Besides, if he did throw anything out of window, it would most assuredly have been found. They keep the permanent way very thoroughly inspected upon the Metropolitan. No, Barnes. There is some other agent in this case, animate or inanimate, which so far we have overlooked completely; and an innocent man's life depends upon our ravelling it out.'

"Barnes lifted his shoulders helplessly, and took another sandwich. 'I don't see what we can do.'

"'Nor I, very clearly. But we must start from the commencement, and go over the ground inch by inch.'

"So wrapped up was I in the case by this time, that I could not fix my mind to anything else. Then and there I went out and set about my inquiries.

"With some trouble I found the compartment in which the tragedy had taken place, but learnt nothing new from it. The station and the railway people at Addison Road, Kensington, were similarly drawn blank. The ticket inspector at Shaftesbury Road, who distinctly remembered Guide's passage, at first seemed inclined to tell me nothing new, till I dragged it out of him by a regular emetic of questioning.

"Then he did remember that Guide had been carrying in his hand a carpenter's straw bass as he passed through the wicket. He did not recollect whether he had mentioned this to the police: didn't see that it mattered.

"I thought differently, and with a new vague hope in my heart, posted back to the prison. I had heard no word of this hand-baggage from Guide. It remained to be seen what he had done with it.

"They remembered me from my previous visit, and let me in to the prisoner without much demur. Guide owned up to the basket at once. 'Yes,' he said, 'I had some few odd tools to carry from home, and as I couldn't find anything else handy to put them in I used the old carpenter's bass. I had an iron eye to splice on to the end of a windlass rope, a job that I like to do myself, to make sure it's done safe. I never thought about telling you of that bass before, sir. I didn't see as how it mattered.'

"'Where is the bass now?'

"'In the Left Luggage Office at Shaftesbury Road Station. Name of Hopkins. I've lost the ticket.'

"'Where did you put your basket on entering the carriage at Addison Road?'

"'On the seat, sir, in the corner by the window.'

"And with that I left him.

"'Now,' thought I, 'I believe I can find out whether you murdered Walker or not,' and drove back to Hammersmith.

"I inquired at the cloak-room. Yes, the carpenter's bass was there, beneath a dusty heap of other unclaimed luggage. There was demurrage to pay on it, which I offered promptly to hand over, but as I could produce no counterfoil bearing the name of Hopkins, the clerk, with a smile, said that he could not let me have it. However, when he heard what I wanted, he made no objection to my having an overhaul.

"The two lugs of the bass were threaded together with a hammer. I took this away, and opened the sides. Within was a ball of marline, another of spun-yarn, a grease-pot, and several large iron eyes. Also a large marline-spike. It was this last that fixed my attention. It was brand new, with a bone handle and a bright brass ferrule. Most of the iron also was bright, but three inches of the point were stained with a faint dark brown. From a casual inspection I should have put this down to the marline-spike having been last used to make a splice on tarred rope: but now my suspicions made me think of something else.

"I raised the stained point to my nose. There was no smell of tar whatever. On the bright part there was the indefinable odour of iron; at the tip, that thin coat of dark brown varnish had blotted this scent completely away.

"I think my fingers trembled when I turned to the bass again.

"Yes, there, opposite to where the point of the marline-spike had been lying—it was tilted up over the ball of spun-yarn—was a closed-up gash in the side of the bass. The spike had passed through there, and then been withdrawn. Round the gash was a dim discoloration which I knew to be dried human blood.

"In my mind's eye I saw the whole ghastly accident clearly enough now. The two men had been standing up, struggling. Guide had gone down under a blow, knocked senseless, and Walker had stumbled over him. Pitching forward, face downwards, on to the seat before he could recover, his head had dashed violently against the carpenter's bass. The sharp marline-spike inside, with its heel resting against the solid wall of the carriage, had entered the top of his skull like a bayonet. No human hand had been raised against him, and yet he had been killed.

"I kept my own particular ramblings in this case remarkably quiet, and in court led up to my facts through ordinary cross-examination.

"At the proper psychological moment I called attention to the shape of the puncture in Walker's skull, and then dramatically sprang the bass and the marline-spike upon them unawares. After that, as the papers put it, 'there was applause in court, which was instantly suppressed'."

"Oh, the conceit of the man," said O'Malley, laughing.

Grayson laughed too. "Well," he said, "I was younger then, and I suppose I was a trifle conceited. The Crown didn't throw up. But the jury chucked us a 'Not guilty' without leaving the box, and then leading counsel for the other side came across and congratulated me on having saved Guide from the gallows. 'Now I'd have bet anything on hanging that man,' said he."

THE MAN WHO DISAPPEARED

L. T. Meade and Robert Eustace

L. T. Meade's collaboration with Robert Eustace enjoyed even more success than her work with Clifford Halifax. For many years, there was speculation about Eustace's identity, but it has now been established that in real life he was a doctor called Eustace Robert Barton (1871–1943). Meade and Eustace created several notable characters, including the sleuth Florence Cusack (so young, so beautiful, and so wealthy that "it was almost impossible to believe that she was a power in the police courts, and highly respected by every detective in Scotland Yard"), whose cases are narrated by a male physician, Dr Lonsdale. The duo's female villains, such as Madame Sara, were also distinctive and ahead of their time.

This story which first appeared in the *Strand Magazine* in December 1901, demonstrates the authors' enthusiasm for the impossible crime puzzle; their *A Master of Mysteries* (1898) has been described by Douglas Greene and Jack Adrian in *Death Locked In* (1987) as "the first collection of stories entirely dedicated to impossible crimes"; Greene and Adrian consider "The Man Who Disappeared" to be one of Meade and Eustace's finest forays into the "miracle problem".

C HARLES PLEYDELL, A VERY CLEVER LAWYER BY PROFESSION, was with me to the end of the allotted month before he told me his story. It was a few days before he left me to join his young wife that I extracted from him the following most remarkable tale:—

I am a lawyer by profession, and have a snug set of offices in Chancery Lane. My name is Charles Pleydell. I have many clients, and can already pronounce myself a rich man.

On a certain morning towards the end of September in the year 1897 I received the following letter—

"SIR,—

"I have been asked to call on you by a mutual friend, General Cornwallis, who accompanied my step-daughter and myself on board the *Osprey* to England. Availing myself of the General's introduction, I hope to call to see you or to send a representative about eleven o'clock today.

"The General says that he thinks you can give me advice on a matter of some importance.

"I am a Spanish lady. My home is in Brazil, and I know nothing of England or of English ways. I wish, however, to take a house near London and to settle down. This house must be situated in the neighbourhood of a large moor or common. It must have grounds surrounding it, and must have extensive cellars or basements, as my wish is to furnish a laboratory in order to carry on scientific research. I am willing to pay any sum in reason for a desirable habitation, but one thing is essential: the house must be as near London as is possible under the above conditions.

"Yours obediently,
"STELLA SCAIFE."

This letter was dated from the Carlton Hotel.

Now, it so happened that a client of mine had asked me a few months before to try and let his house—an old-fashioned and somewhat gruesome mansion, situated in a lonely part of Hampstead Heath. It occurred to me that this house would exactly suit the lady whose letter I had just read.

At eleven o'clock one of my clerks brought me in a card. On it were written the words, "Miss Muriel Scaiffe". I desired the man to show the lady in, and a moment later a slight fair-haired English girl entered the room.

"Mrs. Scaiffe is not quite well and has sent me in her stead. You have received a letter from my step-mother, have you not, Mr. Pleydell?"

"I have," I replied. "Will you sit down, Miss Scaife?"

She did so. I looked at her attentively. She was young and pretty. She also looked good, and although there was a certain anxiety about her face which she could not quite repress, her smile was very sweet.

"Your step-mother," I said, "requires a house with somewhat peculiar conditions?"

"Oh, yes," the girl answered. "She is very anxious on the subject. We want to be settled within a week."

"That is a very short time in which to take and furnish a house," I could not help remarking.

"Yes," she said, again. "But, all the same, in our case it is essential. My stepmother says that anything can be done if there is enough money."

"That is true in a sense," I replied, smilingly. "If I can help you I shall be pleased. You want a house on a common?"

"On a common or moor."

"It so happens, Miss Scaiffe, that there is a place called The Rosary at Hampstead which may suit you. Here are the particulars. Read them over for yourself and tell me if there is any use in my giving you an order to view."

She read the description eagerly, then she said—

"I am sure Mrs. Scaiffe would like to see this house. When can we go?"

"Today, if you like, and if you particularly wish it I can meet you at The Rosary at three o'clock."

"That will do nicely," she answered.

Soon afterwards she left me.

The rest of the morning passed as usual, and at the appointed hour I presented myself at the gates of the Rosary. A carriage was already drawn up there, and as I approached a tall lady with very dark eyes stepped out of it.

A glance showed me that the young lady had not accompanied her.

"You are Mr. Pleydell?" she said, holding out her hand to me, and speaking in excellent English.

"Yes," I answered.

"You saw my step-daughter this morning?"

"Yes," I said again.

"I have called to see the house," she continued. "Muriel tells me that it is likely to suit my requirements. Will you show it to me?"

I opened the gates, and we entered a wide carriage-drive. The Rosary had been unlet for some months, and weeds partly covered the avenue. The grounds had a desolate and gloomy appearance, leaves were falling thickly from the trees, and altogether the entire place looked undesirable and neglected.

The Spanish lady, however, seemed delighted with everything. She looked around her with sparkling glances. Flashing her dark eyes into my face, she praised the trees and avenue, the house, and all that the house contained.

She remarked that the rooms were spacious, the lobbies wide; above all things, the cellars numerous.

"I am particular about the cellars, Mr. Pleydell," she said.

"Indeed!" I answered. "At all events, there are plenty of them."

"Oh, yes! And this one is so large. It will quite suit our purpose. We will turn it into a laboratory.

"My brother and I— Oh, I have not told you about my brother. He is a Spaniard—Señor Merello—he joins us here next week. He and I are scientists, and I hope scientists of no mean order. We have come to England for the purpose of experimenting. In this land of the free we can do what we please. We feel, Mr. Pleydell—you look so sympathising that I cannot help confiding in you—we feel that we are on the verge of a very great—a very astounding discovery, at which the world, yes, the whole world will wonder. This house is the one of all others for our purpose. When can we take possession, Mr. Pleydell?"

I asked several questions, which were all answered to my satisfaction, and finally returned to town, prepared to draw up a lease by which the house and grounds known as The Rosary, Hampstead Heath, were to be handed over at a very high rent to Mrs. Scaiffe.

I felt pleased at the good stroke of business which I had done for a client, and had no apprehensions of any sort. Little did I guess what that afternoon's work would mean to me, and still more to one whom I had ever been proud to call my greatest friend.

Everything went off without a hitch. The Rosary passed into the hands of Mrs. Scaiffe, and also into the hands of her brother, Señor Merello, a tall, dark, very handsome man, bearing all over him the well-known characteristics of a Spanish don.

A week or two went by and the affair had well-nigh passed my memory, when one afternoon I heard eager, excited words in my clerks' room, and the next moment my head clerk entered, followed by the fair-haired English-looking girl who had called herself Muriel Scaiffe.

"I want to speak to you, Mr. Pleydell," she said, in great agitation. "Can I see you alone, and at once?"

"Certainly," I answered. I motioned to the clerk to leave us and helped the young lady to a chair.

"I cannot stay a moment," she began. "Even now I am followed. Mr. Pleydell, he has told me that he knows you; it was on that account I persuaded my step-mother to come to you about a house. You are his greatest friend, for he has said it."

"Of whom are you talking?" I asked, in a bewildered tone.

"Of Oscar Digby!" she replied. "The great traveller, the great discoverer, the greatest, most single-minded, the grandest man of his age. You know him? Yes—yes."

She paused for breath. Her eyes were full of tears.

"Indeed, I do know him," I answered. "He is my very oldest friend. Where is he? What is he doing? Tell me all about him."

"He is on his way to England," she answered. "Even now he may have landed. He brings great news, and the moment he sets foot in London he is in danger."

"What do you mean?"

"I cannot tell you what I mean. I dare not. He is your friend, and it is your province to save him."

"But from what, Miss Scaiffe? You have no right to come here and make ambiguous statements. If you come to me at all you ought to be more explicit."

She trembled, and now, as though she could not stand any longer, dropped into a chair.

"I am not brave enough to explain things more fully," she said. "I can only repeat my words, 'Your friend is in danger.' Tell him—if you can, if you will—to have nothing to do with *us*. Keep him, at all risks, away from *us*. If he mentions us pretend that you do not know anything about us. I would not speak like this if I had not cause—the gravest. When we took The Rosary I did not believe that matters were so awful; indeed, then I was unaware that Mr. Digby was returning to London. But last night I overheard… Oh! Mr. Pleydell, I can tell you no more. Pity me and do not question me. Keep Oscar Digby away from The Rosary and, if possible, do not betray me; but if in no other way you can insure his leaving us alone, tell him that I—yes, I, Muriel Scaiffe—wish it. There, I cannot do more."

She was trembling more terribly than ever. She took out her handkerchief to wipe the moisture from her brow.

"I must fly," she said. "If this visit is discovered my life is worth very little."

After she had gone I sat in absolute amazement. My first sensation was that the girl must be mad. Her pallor, her trembling, her vague innuendoes pointed surely to a condition of nerves the reverse of sane. But although the madness of Muriel Scaiffe seemed the most possible solution of her strange visit, I could not cast the thing from my memory. I felt almost needlessly disturbed by it. All day her extraordinary words haunted me, and when, on the next day, Digby, whom I had not seen for years, unexpectedly called, I remembered Miss Scaiffe's visit with a queer and ever-increasing sense of apprehension.

Digby had been away from London for several years. Before he went he and I had shared the same rooms, had gone about together, and had been chums in the fullest sense of the word. It was delightful to see him once again. His hearty, loud laugh fell refreshingly on my ears, and one or two glances into his face removed my fears. After all, it was impossible to associate danger with one so big, so burly, with such immense physical strength. His broad forehead, his keen, frank blue eyes, his smiling mouth, his strong and muscular hands, all denoted strength of mind and body. He looked as if he were muscle all over.

"Well," he said, "here I am, and I have a good deal to tell you. I want your help also, old man. It is your business to introduce me to the most promising and most enterprising financier of the day. I have it in my power, Pleydell, to make his fortune, and yours, and my own, and half a dozen other people's as well."

"Tell me all about it," I said. I sat back in my chair, prepared to enjoy myself.

Oscar was a very noted traveller and thought much of by the Geographical Society.

He came nearer to me and dropped his voice a trifle.

"I have made an amazing discovery," he said, "and that is one reason why I have hurried back to London. I do not know whether you are sufficiently conversant with extraordinary and out-of-the-way places on our globe. But anyhow, I may as well tell you that there is a wonderful region, as yet very little known, which lies on the watershed of the Essequibo and Amazon rivers. In that region are situated the old Montes de Cristæs or Crystal Mountains, the disputed boundary between British Guiana and Brazil. There also, according to the legend, was supposed to be the wonderful lost city of Manos. Many expeditions were sent out to discover it in the seventeenth century, and it was the Eldorado of Sir Walter Raleigh's famous expedition in 1615, the failure of which cost him his head."

I could not help laughing.

"This sounds like an old geography lesson. What have you to do with this *terra incognita?*"

He leant forward and dropped his voice.

"Do not think me mad," he said, "for I speak in all sanity. I have found the lost Eldorado!"

"Nonsense!" I cried.

"It is true. I do not mean to say that I have found the mythical city of gold; that, of course, does not exist. But what I have discovered is a spot close to Lake Amacu that is simply laden with gold. The estimates computed on my specimens and reports make it out to be the richest place in the world. The whole thing is, as yet, a close secret, and I have come to London now to put it into the hands of a big financier. A company must be formed with a capital of something like ten millions to work it."

"By Jove!" I cried. "You astonish me."

"The thing will create an enormous sensation," he went on, "and I shall be a millionaire; that is, if the secret does not leak out."

"The secret," I cried.

"Yes, the secret of its exact locality."

"Have you charts?"

"Yes, but those I would rather not disclose, even to you, old man, just yet."

I was silent for a moment, then I said—

"Horace Lancaster is the biggest financier in the whole of London. He is undoubtedly your man. If you can satisfy him with your reports, charts, and specimens he can float the company. You must see him, Digby."

"Yes, that is what I want," he cried.

"I will telephone to his office at once."

I rang the bell for my clerk and gave him directions.

He left the room. In a few moments he returned with the information that Lancaster was in Paris.

"He won't be back for a week, sir," said the clerk.

He left the room, and I looked at Digby.

"Are you prepared to wait?" I asked.

He shrugged his great shoulders.

"I must, I suppose," he said. "But it is provoking. At any moment another may forestall me. Not that it is likely; but there is always the possibility. Shall we talk over matters tonight, Pleydell? Will you dine with me at my club?"

"With all my heart," I answered.

"By the way," continued Digby, "some friends of mine— Brazilians—ought to be in London now: a lady of the name of Scaiffe, with her pretty little step-daughter, an English girl. I should like to introduce you to them. They are remarkably nice people. I had a letter from Mrs. Scaiffe just as I was leaving Brazil telling me that they were *en route* for England and asking me to look her up in town. I wonder where they are? Her brother, too, Señor Merello, is a most charming man. Why, Pleydell, what is the matter?"

I was silent for a moment; then I said: "If I were you I would have nothing to do with these people. I happen to know their whereabouts, and—"

"Well?" he said, opening his eyes in amazement.

"The little girl does not want you to call on them, Digby. Take her advice. She looked true and good." To my astonishment I saw that the big fellow seemed quite upset at my remarks.

"True!" he said, beginning to pace the room. "Of course the little thing is true. I tell you, Pleydell, I am fond of her. Not engaged, or anything of that sort, but I like her. I was looking forward to meeting them. The mother—the step-mother, I mean—is a magnificent woman. I am great friends with her. I was staying at their Quinta last winter. I also know the brother, Señor Merello. Has little Muriel lost her head?"

"She is anxious and frightened. The whole thing seems absurd, of course, but she certainly did beg of me to keep you away from her step-mother, and I half promised to respect her secret and not to tell you the name of the locality where Mrs. Scaiffe and Señor Merello are at present living."

He tried not to look annoyed, but he evidently was so. A few moments later he left me.

That evening Digby and I dined together. We afterwards went exhaustively into the great subject of his discovery. He showed me his specimens and reports, and, in short, so completely fired my enthusiasm that I was all impatience for Lancaster's return. The thing was a big thing, one worth fighting for. We said no more about Mrs. Scaiffe, and I hoped that my friend would not fall into the hands of a woman who, I began to fear, was little better than an adventuress.

Three or four days passed. Lancaster was still detained in Paris, and Digby was evidently eating his heart out with impatience at the unavoidable delay in getting his great scheme floated.

One afternoon he burst noisily into my presence.

"Well," he cried. "The little girl has discovered herself. Talk of women and their pranks! She came to see me at my hotel. She declared that she could not keep away. I just took the little thing in my arms and hugged her. We are going to have a honeymoon when the company is floated, and this evening, Pleydell, I dine at The Rosary. Ha! ha! my friend. I know all about the secret retreat of the Scaiffes by this time. Little Muriel told me herself. I dine there tonight, and they want you to come, too."

I was about to refuse when, as if in a vision, the strange, entreating, suffering face of Muriel Scaiffe, as I had seen it the day she implored me to save my friend, rose up before my eyes. Whatever her present inexplicable conduct might mean, I would go with Digby tonight.

We arrived at The Rosary between seven and eight o'clock. Mrs. Scaiffe received us in Oriental splendour. Her dress was a wonder of magnificence. Diamonds flashed in her raven black hair and glittered round her shapely neck. She was certainly one of the most splendid-looking women I had ever seen, and Digby was not many moments in her company before he was completely subjugated by her charms.

The pale little Muriel looked washed-out and insignificant beside this gorgeous creature. Señor Merello was a masculine edition of his handsome sister: his presence and his wonderful courtly grace of manner seemed but to enhance and accentuate her charms.

At dinner we were served by Spanish servants, and a repulsive-looking negro of the name of Samson stood behind Mrs. Scaiffe's chair.

She was in high spirits, drank freely of champagne, and openly alluded to the great discovery.

"You must show us the chart, my friend," she said.

"No!" he answered, in an emphatic voice. He smiled as he spoke and showed his strong, white teeth.

She bent towards him and whispered something. He glanced at Muriel, whose face was deadly white. Then he rose abruptly.

"As regards anything else, command me," he said; "but not the chart."

Mrs. Scaiffe did not press him further. The ladies went into the drawing-room, and by and by Digby and I found ourselves returning to London.

During the journey I mentioned to him that Lancaster had wired to say that he would be at his office and prepared for a meeting on Friday. This was Monday night.

"I am glad to hear that the thing will not be delayed much longer," he answered. "I may as well confess that I am devoured by impatience."

"Your mind will soon be at rest," I replied. "And now, one thing more, old man. I must talk frankly. I do not like Mrs. Scaiffe—I do not like Señor Merello. As you value all your future, keep that chart out of the hands of those people."

"Am I mad?" he questioned. "The chart is seen by no living soul until I place it in Lancaster's hands. But all the same, Pleydell," he added, "you are prejudiced. Mrs. Scaiffe is one of the best of women."

"Think her so, if you will," I replied; "but, whatever you do, keep your knowledge of your Eldorado to yourself. Remember that on Friday the whole thing will be safe in Lancaster's keeping."

He promised, and I left him.

On Tuesday I saw nothing of Digby.

On Wednesday evening, when I returned home late, I received the following letter:—

"I am not mad. I have heavily bribed the kitchen-maid, the only English woman in the whole house, to post this for me. I was forced to call on Mr. Digby and to engage myself to him at any cost. I am now strictly confined to my room under pretence of illness. In reality I am quite well, but a close prisoner. Mr. Digby dined here again last night, and, under the influence of a certain drug introduced into his wine, has given away the whole of his discovery *except* the exact locality.

"He is to take supper here late tomorrow night (Thursday) and to bring the chart. If he does, he will never leave The Rosary alive. All is prepared. *I speak who know.* Don't betray me, but save him."

The letter fell from my hands. What did it mean? Was Digby's life in danger, or had the girl who wrote to me really gone mad? The letter was without date, without any heading, and without signature. Nevertheless, as I picked it up and read it carefully over again, I was absolutely convinced beyond a shadow of doubt of its truth. Muriel Scaiffe was not mad. She was a victim, to how great an extent I did not dare to think. Another victim, one in even greater danger, was Oscar Digby. I must save him. I must do what the unhappy girl who was a prisoner in that awful house implored of me.

It was late, nearly midnight, but I knew that I had not a moment to lose. I had a friend, a certain Dr. Garland, who had been police surgeon for the Westminster Division for several years. I went immediately to his house in Eaton Square. As I had expected, he was up, and without any preamble I told him the whole long story of the last few weeks.

Finally, I showed him the letter. He heard me without once interrupting. He read the letter without comment. When he folded it up and returned it to me I saw that his keen, clean-shaven face was full of interest. He was silent for several minutes, then he said—

"I am glad you came to me. This story of yours may mean a very big thing. We have four prima facie points. *One:* Your friend has this enormously valuable secret about the place in Guiana or on its boundary; a secret which may be worth anything. *Two:* He is very intimate with Mrs. Scaiffe, her step-daughter, and her brother. The intimacy started in Brazil. *Three:* He is engaged to the step-daughter, who evidently is being used as a sort of tool, and is herself in a state of absolute terror, and, so far as one can make out, is not specially in love with Digby nor Digby with her. *Four:* Mrs. Scaiffe and her brother are determined, at any risk, to secure the chart which Digby is to hand to them tomorrow evening. The girl thinks this so important that she has practically risked her life to give you due warning. By the way, when did you say Lancaster would return? Has he made an appointment to see Digby and yourself?"

"Yes; at eleven o'clock on Friday morning."

"Doubtless Mrs. Scaiffe and her brother know of this."

"Probably," I answered. "As far as I can make out they have such power over Digby that he confides everything to them."

"Just so. They have power over him, and they are not scrupulous as to the means they use to force his confidence. If Digby goes to The Rosary tomorrow evening the interview with Lancaster will, in all probability, never take place."

"What do you mean?" I cried, in horror.

"Why, this. Mrs. Scaiffe and Señor Merello are determined to learn Digby's secret. It is necessary for their purpose that they should know the secret, and also that they should be the *sole possessors* of it. You see why they want Digby to call on them? They must get his secret from him *before* he sees Lancaster. The chances are that if he gives it up he will never leave the house alive."

"Then, what are we to do?" I asked, for Garland's words confirmed the suspicions which had impelled me to seek counsel with him over the letter.

"Leave this matter in my hands. I am going immediately to see Inspector Frost. I will communicate with you directly anything serious occurs."

The next morning I called upon Digby and found him breakfasting at his club. He looked worried, and, when I came in, his greeting was scarcely cordial.

"What a solemn face, Pleydell!" he said. "Is anything wrong?" He motioned me to a seat near, I sank into it.

"I want you to come out of town with me," I said. "I can take a day off. Shall we both run down to Brighton? We can return in time for our interview with Lancaster tomorrow."

"It is impossible," he answered. "I should like to come with you, but I have an engagement for tonight."

"Are you going to The Rosary?" I asked.

"I am," he replied, after a moment's pause. "Why, what is the matter?" he added. "I suppose I may consider myself a free agent." There was marked irritation in his tone.

"I wish you would not go," I said.

"Why not?"

"I do not trust the people."

"Folly, Pleydell. In the old days you used not to be so prejudiced."

"I had not the same cause. Digby, if ever people are trying to get you into their hands, they are those people. Have you not already imparted your secret to them?"

"How do you know?" he exclaimed, springing up and turning crimson.

"Well, can you deny it?"

His face paled.

"I don't know that I want to," he said. "Mrs. Scaiffe and Merello will join me in this matter. There is no reason why things should be kept dark from them."

"But is this fair or honourable to Lancaster? Remember, I have already written fully to him. Do, I beg of you, be careful."

"Lancaster cannot object to possible wealthy shareholders," was Digby's answer. "Anyhow," he added, laughing uneasily, "I object to being interfered with. Pray understand that, old man, if we are to continue friends; and now bye-bye for the present. We meet at eleven o'clock tomorrow at Lancaster's."

His manner gave me no pretext for remaining longer with him, and I returned to my own work. About five o'clock on that same day a telegram was handed to me which ran as follows:—

"Come here at once.—GARLAND."

I left the house, hailed a hansom, and in a quarter of an hour was shown into Garland's study. He was not alone. A rather tall, grey-haired, grey-moustached, middle-aged man was with him. This man was introduced to me as Inspector Frost.

"Now, Pleydell," said Garland, in his quick, incisive way, "listen to me carefully. The time is short. Inspector Frost and I have not ceased our inquiries since you called on me last night. I must tell you that we believe the affair to be of the most serious kind. Time is too pressing now to enter into all details, but the thing amounts to this. There is the gravest suspicion that Mrs. Scaiffe and her brother, Señor Merello, are employed by a notorious gang in Brazil to force Digby to disclose the exact position of the gold mine. We also know for certain that Mrs. Scaiffe is in constant and close communication with some very suspicious people both in London and in Brazil.

"Now listen. The crisis is to be tonight. Digby is to take supper at The Rosary, and there to give himself absolutely away. He will take his chart with him; that is the scheme. Digby must not go—that is, if we can possibly prevent him. We expect you to do what you can under the circumstances, but as the case is so serious, and as it is more than probable that Digby will not be persuaded, Inspector Frost and myself and a number of men of his division will surround the house as soon as it becomes dark, and if Digby should insist on going in every protection in case of difficulty will be given him. The presence of the police will also insure the capture of Mrs. Scaiffe and her brother."

"You mean," I said, "that you will, if necessary, search the house?"

"Yes."

"But how can you do so without a warrant?"

"We have thought of that," said Garland, with a smile. "A magistrate living at Hampstead has been already communicated with. If necessary, one of our men will ride over to his house, and procure the requisite instrument to enforce our entrance."

"Very well," I answered; "then I will go at once to Digby's, but I may as well tell you plainly that I have very little hope of dissuading him."

I drove as fast as I could to my friend's rooms, but was greeted with the information that he had already left, and was not expected back until late that evening. This was an unlooked-for blow.

I went to his club—he was not there. I then returned to Dr. Garland.

"I failed to find him," I said. "What can be done? Is it possible that he has already gone to his fate?"

"That is scarcely likely," replied Garland, after a pause. "He was invited to supper at The Rosary, and according to your poor young friend's letter the time named was late. There is nothing for it but to waylay him on the grounds before he goes in. You will come with us tonight, will you not, Pleydell?"

"Certainly," I answered.

Garland and I dined together. At little after nine we left Eaton Square, and, punctually at ten o'clock, the hansom we had taken put us down at one of the roads on the north side of the Heath. The large house which I knew so well loomed black in the moonlight.

The night was cold and fresh. The moon was in its second quarter and was shining brightly. Garland and I passed down the dimly lit lane beside the wall. A tall, dark figure loomed from the darkness, and, as it came forward, I saw that it was Inspector Frost.

"Mr. Digby has not arrived yet," he said. "Perhaps, sir," he added, looking at me, "you can even now dissuade him, for it is a bad business. All my men are ready," he continued, "and at a signal the house will be surrounded; but we must have one last try to prevent his entering it. Come this way, please, sir," he added, beckoning to me to follow him.

We passed out into the road.

"I am absolutely bewildered, inspector," I said to him. "Do you mean to say there is really great danger?"

"The worst I ever knew," was his answer. "You cannot stop a man entering a house if he wishes to; but I can tell you, Mr. Pleydell, I do not believe his life is worth that if he goes in." And the inspector snapped his fingers.

He had scarcely ceased speaking when the jingling of the bells of a hansom sounded behind us. The cab drew up at the gates and Oscar Digby alighted close to us.

Inspector Frost touched him on the shoulder.

He swung round and recognised me.

"Halloa! Pleydell," he said, in no very cordial accents. "What in the name of Heaven are you doing here? What does this mean? Who is this man?"

"I am a police officer, Mr. Digby, and I want to speak to you. Mr. Pleydell has asked you not to go into that house. You are, of course, free to do as you like, but I must tell you that you are running into great danger. Be advised by me and go away."

For answer Digby thrust his hand into his breast-pocket. He pulled out a note which he gave me.

"Read that, Pleydell," he said; "and receive my answer." I tore the letter from its envelope and read in the moonlight—

"Come to me. I am in danger and suffering. Do not fail me.—MURIEL."

"A hoax! A forgery!" I could not help crying. "For God's sake, Digby, don't be mad."

"Mad or sane, I go into that house," he said. His bright blue eyes flashed with passion and his breath came quickly.

"Hands off, sir. Don't keep me."

He swung himself away from me.

"One word," called the inspector after him. "How long do you expect to remain?"

"Perhaps an hour. I shall be home by midnight."

"And now, sir, please listen. You can be assured, in case of any trouble, that we are here, and I may further tell you that if you are not out of the house by one o'clock we shall enter with a search warrant."

Digby stood still for a moment, then he turned to me.

"I cannot but resent your interference, but I believe you mean well. Good-bye!" He wrung my hand and walked quickly up the drive.

We watched him ring the bell. The door was opened at once by the negro servant. Digby entered. The door closed silently. Inspector Frost gave a low whistle.

"I would not be that man for a good deal," he said.

Garland came up to us both.

"Is the house entirely surrounded, Frost?" I heard him whisper. Frost smiled, and I saw his white teeth gleam in the darkness. He waved his hand.

"There is not a space of six feet between man and man," I heard him say; "and now we have nothing to do but to wait and hope for at least an hour and a half. If in an hour's time Mr. Digby does not reappear I shall send a man for the warrant. At one o'clock we enter the house."

Garland and I stood beneath a large fir tree in a dense shade and within the enclosed garden. The minutes seemed to crawl. Our conversation was limited to low whispers at long intervals.

Eleven o'clock chimed on the church clock near by; then half-past sounded on the night air. My ears were strained to catch the expected click of the front door-latch, but it did not come. The house remained wrapt in silence. Once Garland whispered—

"Hark!" We listened closely. It certainly seemed to me that a dull, muffled sound, as of pounding or hammering, was just audible; but whether it came from the house or not it was impossible to tell.

At a quarter to twelve the one remaining lighted window on the first floor became suddenly dark. Still there was no sign of Digby. Midnight chimed.

Frost said a word to Garland and disappeared, treading softly. He was absent for more than half an hour. When he returned I heard him say—

"I have got it," and he touched his pocket with his hand as he spoke.

The remaining moments went by in intense anxiety, and, just as the deep boom of one o'clock was heard the inspector laid his hand on my shoulder.

"Come along quietly," he whispered.

Some sign, conveyed by a low whistle, passed from him to his men, and I heard the bushes rustle around us.

The next moment we had ascended the steps, and we could hear the deep whirr of the front door bell as Frost pressed the button.

In less time than we had expected we heard the bolts shot back. The door was opened on a chain and a black face appeared at the slit.

"Who are you and what do you want?" said a voice.

"I have called for Mr. Digby," said Frost. "Go and tell him that his friend, Mr. Pleydell, and also Doctor Garland want to see him immediately."

A look of blank surprise came over the negro's face.

"But no one of the name of Digby lives here," he said.

"Mrs. Scaiffe lives here," replied the inspector, "and also a Spanish gentleman of the name of Señor Merello. Tell them that I wish to see them immediately, and that I am a police officer."

A short conversation was evidently taking place within. The next moment the door was flung open, electric lights sprang into being, and my eyes fell upon Mrs. Scaiffe.

She was dressed with her usual magnificence. She came forward with a stately calm and stood silently before us. Her large black eyes were gleaming.

"Well, Mr. Pleydell," she said, speaking in an easy voice, "what is the reason of this midnight disturbance? I am always glad to welcome you to my house, but is not the hour a little late?"

Her words were interrupted by Inspector Frost, who held up his hand.

"Your attitude, madam," he said, "is hopeless. We have all come here with a definite object. Mr. Oscar Digby entered this house at a quarter past ten tonight. From that moment the house has been closely surrounded. He is therefore still here."

"Where is your authority for this unwarrantable intrusion?" she said. Her manner changed, her face grew hard as iron. Her whole attitude was one of insolence and defiance.

The inspector immediately produced his warrant.

She glanced over it and uttered a shrill laugh.

"Mr. Digby is not in the house," she said.

She had scarcely spoken before an adjoining door was opened, and Señor Merello, looking gaunt and very white about the face approached. She looked up at him and smiled, then she said, carelessly:—

"Gentlemen, this is my brother, Señor Merello."

The Señor bowed slightly, but did not speak.

"Once more," said Frost, "where is Mr. Digby?"

"I repeat once more," said Mrs. Scaiffe, "that Mr. Digby is not in this house."

"But we saw him enter at a quarter past ten."

She shrugged her shoulders.

"He is not here now."

"He could not have gone, for the house has been surrounded."

Again she gave her shoulders a shrug. "You have your warrant, gentlemen," she said; "you can look for yourselves."

Frost came up to her.

"I regret to say, madam, that you, this gentlemen, and all your servants must consider yourselves under arrest until we find Mr. Oscar Digby."

"That will be for ever, then," she replied; "but please yourselves."

My heart beat with an unwonted sense of terror. What could the woman mean? Digby, either dead or alive, must be in the house.

The operations which followed were conducted rapidly. The establishment, consisting of Mrs. Scaiffe, her brother, two Spanish men-servants, two maids, one of Spanish extraction, and the negro who had opened the door to us, were summoned and placed in the charge of a police-sergeant.

Muriel Scaiffe was nowhere to be seen.

Then our search of the house began. The rooms on the ground-floor, consisting of the drawing-room, dining-room, and two other big rooms, were fitted up in quite an everyday manner. We did not take much time going through them.

In the basement, the large cellar which had attracted Mrs. Scaiffe's pleased surprise on the day when I took her to see The Rosary had now been fitted up as a laboratory. I gazed at it in astonishment. It was evidently intended for the manufacture of chemicals on an almost commercial scale. All the latest chemical and electrical apparatus were to be found there, as well as several large machines, the purposes of which were not evident. One in particular I specially noticed. It was a big tank with a complicated equipment for the manufacture of liquid air in large quantities.

We had no time to give many thoughts to the laboratory just then. A foreboding sense of ever-increasing fear was upon each and all of us. It was sufficient to see that Digby was not there.

Our search in the upper regions was equally unsuccessful. We were just going down stairs again when Frost drew my attention to a door which we had not yet opened. We went to it and found it locked. Putting our strength to work, Garland and I between us burst it open. Within, we found a girl crouching by the bed. She was only partly dressed, and her head was buried in her hands. We went up to her. She turned, saw my face, and suddenly clung to me.

"Have you found him? Is he safe?"

"I do not know, my dear," I answered, trying to soothe her. "We are looking for him. God grant us success."

"Did he come to the house? I have been locked in here all day and heavily drugged. I have only just recovered consciousness and scarcely know what I am doing. Is he in the house?"

"He came in. We are searching for him; we hope to find him."

"That you will never do!" She gave a piercing cry and fell unconscious on the floor.

We placed the unhappy girl on the bed. Garland produced brandy and gave her a few drops; she came to in a couple of minutes and began to moan feebly. We left her, promising to return. We had no time to attend to her just then.

When we reached the hall Frost stood still.

"The man is not here," he muttered.

But he is here, was Garland's incisive answer. "Inspector, you have got to tear the place to pieces."

The latter nodded.

The inspector's orders were given rapidly, and dawn was just breaking when ten policemen, ordered in from outside, began their systematic search of the entire house from roof to basement.

Pick and crowbar were ruthlessly applied, and never have I seen a house in such a mess. Floorings were torn up and rafters cut through.

Broken plaster littered the rooms and lay about on the sumptuous furniture. Walls were pierced and bored through. Closets and cupboards were ransacked. The backs of the fireplaces were torn out and the chimneys explored.

Very little was said as our investigation proceeded, and room after room was checked off.

Finally, an exhaustive examination of the basement and cellars completed our search.

"Well, Dr. Garland, are you satisfied?" asked the inspector.

We had gone back to the garden, and Garland was leaning against a tree, his hands thrust in his pockets and his eyes fixed on the ground. Frost pulled his long moustache and breathed quickly.

"Are you satisfied?" he repeated.

"We must talk sense or we shall all go mad," was Garland's answer. "The thing is absurd, you know. Men don't disappear. Let us work this thing out logically. There are only three planes in space and we know matter is indestructible. If Digby left this house he went up, down, or horizontally. *Up is out of the question.* If he disappeared in a balloon or was shot off the roof he must have been seen by us, for the house was surrounded. He certainly did not pass through the cordon of men. *He did not go down*, for every cubic foot of basement and cellar has been accounted for, as well as *every* cubic foot of space in the house.

"So we come to the chemical change of matter, dissipation into gas by heat. There are no furnaces, no ashes, no gas cylinders, nor dynamos, nor carbon points. The time when we lost sight of him to the time of entrance was exactly two hours and three-quarters. There is no way out of it. He is still there."

"He is not there," was the quiet retort of the inspector. "I have sent for the Assistant Commissioner to Scotland Yard, and will ask him to take over the case. It is too much for me."

The tension in all our minds had now reached such a state of strain that we began to fear our own shadows.

Oscar Digby, standing, as it were, on the threshold of a very great future, the hero of a legend worthy of old romance, had suddenly and inexplicably vanished. I could not get my reason to believe that he was not still in the house, for there was not the least doubt that he had not come out. What would happen in the next few hours?

"Is there no secret chamber or secret passage that we have overlooked?" I said, turning to the inspector.

"The walls have been tapped," he replied. "There is not the slightest indication of a hollow. There are no underground passages. The man is not within these walls."

He now spoke with a certain degree of irritation in his voice which the mystery of the case had evidently awakened in his mind. A few moments later the sound of approaching wheels caused us to turn our heads. A cab drew up at the gates, out of which alighted the well-known form of Sir George Freer.

Garland had already entered the house, and on Sir George appearing on the scene he and I followed him.

We had just advanced across the hall to the room where the members of the household, with the exception of poor Muriel Scaiffe, were still detained, when, to our utter amazement, a long strange peal of laughter sounded from below. This was followed by another, and again by another. The laughter came from the lips of Garland. We glanced at each other. What on earth did it mean? Together we darted down the stone steps, but before we reached the laboratory another laugh rang out. All hope in me was suddenly changed to a chilling fear, for the laugh was not natural. It had a clanging, metallic sound, without any mirth.

In the centre of the room stood Garland. His mouth was twitching and his breath jerked in and out convulsively.

"What is it? What is the matter?" I cried.

He made no reply, but, pointing to a machine with steel blocks, once more broke into a choking, gurgling laugh which made my flesh creep.

Had he gone mad? Sir George moved swiftly across to him and laid his hand on his shoulder.

"Come, what is all this, Garland?" he said, sternly, though his own face was full of fear.

I knew Garland to be a man of extraordinary self-control, and I could see that he was now holding himself in with all the force at his command.

"It is no use—I cannot tell you," he burst out.

"What—you know what has become of him?"

"Yes."

"You can prove it?"

"Yes."

"Speak out, man."

"He is not here," said Garland.

"Then where is he?"

He flung his hand out towards the Heath, and I saw that the fit was taking him again, but once more he controlled himself. Then he said in a clear, level voice:—

"He is dead, Sir George, and you can never see his body. You cannot hold an inquest for there is nothing to hold it on. The winds have taken him and scattered him in dust on the Heath. Don't look at me like that, Pleydell. I am sane, although it is a wonder we are not all mad over this business, Look and listen."

He pointed to the great metal tank.

"I arrived at my present conclusion by a process of elimination," he began. "Into that tank which contained liquid air Digby, gagged and bound, must have been placed violently, probably after he had given away the chart. Death would have been instantaneous, and he would have been frozen into complete solidity in something like forty minutes. The ordinary laboratory experiment is to freeze a rabbit, which can then be powdered into mortar like any other friable stone. The operation here has been the same. It is only a question of size. Remember we are dealing with 312 deg. below Fahrenheit, and then—well, look at this and these."

He pointed to a large machine with steel blocks and to a bench littered with saws, chisels, pestles, and mortars.

"That machine is a stone-breaker," he said. "On the dust adhering to these blocks I found this."

He held up a test tube containing a blue liquid.

"The Guiacum test," he said. "In other words, blood. This fact taken with the facts we already know, that Digby never left the house; that the only other agent of destruction of a body, fire, is out of the question; that this tank is the receptacle of that enormous machine for making liquid air in very large quantities; and, above all, the practical possibility of the operation being conducted by the men who are at present in the house, afford me absolutely conclusive proof beyond a possibility of doubt as to what has happened. The body of that unfortunate man is as if it had never been, without a fragment of pin-point size for identification or evidence. It is beyond the annals of all the crimes that I have ever heard of. What law can help us? Can you hold an inquest on nothing? Can you charge a person with murder where no victim or trace of a victim can be produced?"

A sickly feeling came over me. Garland's words carried their own conviction, and we knew that we stood in the presence of a horror without a name. Nevertheless, to the police mind horror *per se* does not exist. To them there is always a mystery, a crime, and a solution. That is all. The men beside me were police once more. Sentiment might come later.

"Are there any reporters here?" asked Sir George.

"None," answered Frost.

"Good. Mr. Oscar Digby has disappeared. There is no doubt how. There can, of course, be no arrest, as Dr. Garland has just said. Our official position is this. We suspect that Mr. Digby has been murdered, but the search for the discovery of the body has failed. That is our position."

Before I left that awful house I made arrangements to have Muriel Scaiffe conveyed to a London hospital. I did not consult Mrs. Scaiffe on the subject. I could not get myself to say another word to the woman. In the hospital a private ward was secured for the unhappy girl, and there for many weeks she hovered between life and death.

Meanwhile, Mrs. Scaiffe and her brother were detained at The Rosary. They were closely watched by the police, and although they made many efforts to escape they found it impossible. Our hope was that when Muriel recovered strength she would be able to substantiate a case against them. But, alas! this hope was unfounded, for, as the girl recovered, there remained a blank in her memory which no efforts on our part could fill. She had absolutely and completely forgotten Oscar Digby, and the house on Hampstead Heath was to her as though it had never existed. In all other respects she was well. Under these circumstances the Spaniard and his sister were tried for the murder of Oscar Digby. They escaped conviction on technical grounds and returned to their own country, our one most earnest hope being that we might never see or hear of them again.

Meanwhile, Muriel grew better. I was interested in her from the first. When she was well enough I placed her with some friends of my own. A year ago she became my wife. I think she is happy. A past which is forgotten cannot trouble her. I have long ago come to regard her as the best and truest woman living.

THE CYPRIAN BEES

Anthony Wynne

Anthony Wynne's reputation as a detective novelist languished in obscurity for decades following the appearance of his final novel in 1950. Interest in his work has revived as a result of the republication in the British Library Crime Classics series of *Murder of a Lady* (aka *The Silver Scale Mystery*, 1931), set in the author's native Scotland. That novel is a clever example of the impossible crime mystery, a subgenre in which Wynne developed a specialism. In real life, Wynne was Robert McNair Wilson, a former house surgeon at Glasgow Western Infirmary who became a long-serving medical correspondent for *The Times*. Keenly interested in politics and economics, he stood twice for Parliament as a Liberal Party candidate in the 1920s, but without success.

Wynne's long-serving series detective was the snuff-taking Dr Eustace Hailey, and many of Hailey's cases, including this one, make effective use of his creator's scientific and medical know-how. "The Cyprian Bees" is, by a distance, Wynne's most famous short story, first appearing in *Hutchinson's Mystery-Story Magazine* in 1924. It was collected in *Sinners Go Secretly* (1927), and the following year in Dorothy L. Sayers' ground-breaking omnibus *Great Short Stories of Detection, Mystery and Horror*.

I NSPECTOR BILES, OF SCOTLAND YARD, PLACED A SMALL WOODEN box on the table in front of Doctor Hailey.

"There," he remarked in cheerful tones, "is a mystery which even you, my dear doctor, will scarcely be able to solve."

Doctor Hailey bent his great head and examined the box with minute care. It was merely a hollowed-out block of wood to which a lid, also of wood, was attached at one point by a nail. The lid rotated on this nail. He put out his hand to open it; but Biles checked that intention immediately.

"Take care," he exclaimed, "there are three live bees in that box." He added: "There were four originally but one of them stung a colleague of mine who was incautious enough to pull the lid open without first finding out what it covered."

He leaned back in his chair and drew a long whiff of the excellent cigar with which Doctor Hailey had supplied him. He remained silent while a heavy vehicle went lumbering down Harley Street. Then he said:

"Last night one of my men found the box lying in the gutter in Piccadilly Circus, just opposite the Criterion Theatre. He thought it looked peculiar and brought it down to the Yard. We have a bee-keeper of some distinction on the staff and he declares that these insects are all workers and that only a lunatic would carry them about in this fashion. Queens, it appears, are often transported in boxes."

Doctor Hailey raised his eyeglass and set it in his eye.

"So I have heard." He opened his snuff-box and took a large pinch. "You know, of course, my dear Biles," he added, "what this particular box contained before the bees were put into it?"

"No, I don't."

"Serum; either anti-diphtheria serum or one of the other varieties. Practically every manufacturer of these products uses this type of receptacle for them."

"H'm!" Biles leaned forward in his chair. "So that means that, in all probability, the owner of the bees is a doctor. How very interesting."

Doctor Hailey shook his head.

"It doesn't follow," he remarked. "The box was perhaps left in a patient's house after its contents had been used. The patient may have employed it for its present purpose."

Biles nodded. He appeared to hesitate a moment, then he said:

"The reason why I troubled you was that, last night, a woman was found dead at the wheel of a motorcar—a closed coupé—in Leicester Square. She had been stung by a bee just before her death."

He spoke in quiet tones, but his voice nevertheless revealed the fact that the disclosure he was making had assumed a great importance in his mind. He added:

"The body was examined by a doctor almost immediately. He observed the sting which was in her forehead. The dead bee was recovered, later, from the floor of the car."

As he spoke he took another box from his pocket, and opened it. He held it out to the doctor.

"You will notice that there are rather unusual markings on the bee's body; those yellow rings. Our expert says, that they indicate a special breed, the Cyprian, and that these insects are notoriously very ill-natured. The peculiar thing is that the bees in the wooden box are also Cyprian bees."

Doctor Hailey picked up a large magnifying glass which lay on the table beside him and focused it on the body of the insect. His knowledge of bees was not extensive but he recognised that this was not the ordinary brown English type. He set the glass down again and leaned back in his chair.

"It is certainly very extraordinary," he declared. "Have you any theory?"

Biles shook his head. "None. Beyond the supposition that the shock caused by the sting was probably the occasion for the woman's sudden collapse. She was seen to pull quickly into the side of the road to stop the car, so she must have had a presentiment of what was coming. I suppose heart failure might be induced by a sting?"

"It is just possible." Doctor Hailey took more snuff. "Once, long ago," he said, "I had personal experience of a rather similar case; that of a bee-keeper who was stung some years after he had given up his own apiary. He died in about five minutes. But that was a clear case of anaphylaxis."

"I don't understand."

Doctor Hailey thought a moment. "Anaphylaxis," he explained, "is the name given to one of the most amazing phenomena in the whole of medical science. If a human being receives an injection of serum or blood or any extract or fluid from the animal body, a tremendous sensitiveness is apt to develop, afterwards, towards that particular substance. For example, an injection of the white of a duck's egg will, after the lapse of a week or so, render a man so intensely sensitive to this particular egg white, that, if a further injection is given, instant death may result. Even if a duck's egg is eaten there may be violent sickness and collapse, though hens' eggs will cause no ill effect. Queerly enough, however, if the injection is repeated within, say a day of its first administration, no trouble occurs. For the sensitiveness to develop it is essential that time should elapse between the first injection and the second one. Once the sensitiveness has developed it remains active for years. The bee-keeper, whose death I happened to witness, had often been stung before: but he had not been stung for a very long time."

"Good God!" Biles' face wore an expression of keen interest. "So it's possible that this may actually be a case of *murder*."

He pronounced the word in tones of awe. Doctor Hailey saw that already his instincts as a man hunter were quickening.

"It is just possible. But do not forget, my dear Biles, that the murderer using this method would require to give his victim a preliminary dose—by inoculation—of bee-poison, because a single sting would scarcely be enough to produce the necessary degree of sensitiveness. That is to say he would require to exercise an amount of force which would inevitably defeat his purpose, *unless he happened to be a doctor*."

"Ah! the wooden serum box!"

The detective's voice thrilled.

"Possibly! A doctor undoubtedly could inject bee-poison, supposing he possessed it, instead of ordinary serum or an ordinary vaccine. It would hurt a good deal—but patients expect inoculations to hurt them."

Biles rose. "There is no test—is there," he asked, "by which it would be possible to detect the presence of this sensitiveness you speak of, in a dead body?"

"None."

"So we can only proceed by means of circumstantial evidence." He drew a sharp breath. "The woman has been identified as the widow of an artist, named Bardwell. She had a flat, a luxurious one, in Park Mansions, and seems to have been well off. But we have not been able to find any of her relatives so far." He glanced at his watch. "I am going there now. I suppose I couldn't persuade you to accompany me?"

Doctor Hailey's rather listless eyes brightened. For answer he rose, towering above the detective in that act.

"My dear Biles, you know that you can always persuade me."

The flat in Park Mansions was rather more, and yet rather less, than luxurious. It bespoke prodigality, but it bespoke also restlessness of mind, as though its owner had felt insecure in her enjoyment of its comforts. The rooms were too full, and their contents were saved from vulgarity only by the sheer carelessness of their bestowal. This woman seemed to have bought anything and to have cared for nothing. Thus, in her dining-room, an exquisite Queen Anne sideboard was set, cheek by jowl, with a most horrible Victorian armchair made of imitation walnut. In the drawing-room there were flower glasses of the noblest period of Venetian craftsmanship, in which Beauty was held captive in wonderful strands of gold, and, beside these, shocking and obscene examples of "golden glass" ware from some third-rate Bohemian factory. Doctor Hailey began to form a mental picture of the dead woman. He saw her changeable, greedy, gaudy, yet with a certain instinctive charm; the kind of woman who, if she is young and beautiful, gobbles a man up. Women of that sort, his experience had shown him, were apt to drive their lovers to despair with their extravagance or their infidelities. Had the owner of the bees embarked on his terrible course in order to secure himself against the mortification of being supplanted by some more attractive rival? Or was he merely removing from his path a woman of whom he had grown tired? In any case, if the murder theory was correct, he must have stood in the relationship to the dead girl of doctor to patient and he must have possessed an apiary of his own.

A young detective, whom Biles introduced as Todcaster, had already made a careful examination of the flat. He had found nothing, not even a photograph. Nor had the owners of neighbouring flats been able to supply any useful information. Mrs. Bardwell, it appeared, had men friends who had usually come to see her after dark. They had not, apparently, been in the habit of writing to her, or if they had—she had destroyed all their letters. During the last few weeks she seemed to have been without a servant.

"So you have found nothing?" Biles' tones were full of disappointment.

"Nothing, sir. Unless, indeed, this is of any importance."

Todcaster held out a crumpled piece of paper. It was a shop receipt, bearing the name of the Times Book Club, for a copy of *The Love Songs of Robert Browning*. There was no name on it. Biles handed it to Doctor Hailey, who regarded it for a few moments in silence and then asked:

"Where did you find this?"

"In the fireplace of the bedroom."

The doctor's eyes narrowed.

"It does not strike me," he said, "that such a collection of poems would be likely to interest the owner of this flat."

He folded the slip and put it carefully into his pocket-book. He added:

"On the other hand, Browning's Love Songs do appeal very strongly to some women." He fixed his eyeglass and regarded the young detective. "You have not found the book itself, have you?"

"No, sir. There are a few novels in the bedroom but no poetry of any kind."

Doctor Hailey nodded. He asked to be shown the collection and made a detailed examination of it. The novels were all of the lurid, sex type. It was as he had anticipated. He opened each of the books and glanced at the fly leaves. They were all blank. He turned to Biles:

"I am ready to bet that Mrs. Bardwell did not pay that bill at the Book Club," he declared. "And I am ready to bet also that this book was not bought for her."

The detective shrugged his shoulders.

"Probably not," he said unconcernedly.

"Then, why should the receipt for it be lying in this room?'

"My dear doctor, how should I know? I suppose because the man who possessed it chose to throw it away here."

The doctor shook his head.

"Men do not buy collections of Love Songs for themselves, nor, for that matter, do women. They buy them almost invariably, to give to people they are interested in. Everybody, I think, recognises that."

He broke off. A look of impatience came into Biles' face.

"Well?"

"Therefore a man does not, as a rule, reveal to one woman the fact that he has made such a purchase on behalf of another. I mean, it is difficult to believe that any man on intimate terms with Mrs. Bardwell would have invited her jealousy by leaving such plain evidence of his interest in another woman lying about in her room. I assume, you see, that no man would give that poor lady this particular book."

Biles shrugged his shoulders. The point seemed to him immaterial. He glanced round the bedroom with troubled eyes.

"I wish," he declared, "that we had something to go on—something definite leading towards some individual."

His words were addressed impartially to his subordinate and to Doctor Hailey. The former looked blank. But the doctor's expression was almost eager. He raised his eyeglass and put it into his eye.

"My dear Biles," he said, "we have something definite to go on. I was about to suggest to you, when you interrupted me, that the receipt for the books probably fell from the pocket of the purchaser through a hole in that pocket, just as the little box containing the additional bees which he had not found it necessary to release was destined to fall later, when the man, having assured himself that an insect of unimpaired vigour was loose and on the wing, descended in Piccadilly Circus from Mrs. Bardwell's car."

He paused. The detective had turned to him, interested once more. The thought crossed Doctor Hailey's mind that it was a pity Biles had not been gifted by Providence with an appreciation of human nature as keen as his grasp of material circumstances. He allowed his eyeglass to drop in a manner which proclaimed that he had shot his bolt. He asked:

"You have not perhaps taken occasion to watch a man receiving a shop receipt for goods he has just bought and paid for? Believe me, a spectacle full of instruction in human nature. The receipt is handed, as a rule, by a girl, and the man, as a rule, pushes it into his nearest pocket, because he does not desire to be so rude or so untidy as to drop it on the floor. Shyness, politeness and tidiness, my dear Biles, are all prominent elements in our racial character."

Again he broke off, this time to take a pinch of snuff. The two detectives watched that process with some impatience.

"A man with a hole in his coat pocket—a hole not very large, yet large enough to allow a piece of crumpled paper to work its way out as the wearer of the coat strode up and down the floor of the room—is not that a clue? A doctor perhaps with, deep in his soul, the desire for such women as Mrs. Bardwell, cheap, yet attractive women."

"I thought you expressed the opinion that he bought the love songs for some other woman," Biles snapped.

"Exactly. Some other woman sufficiently like Mrs. Bardwell to attract him, though evidently possessed of a veneer of education to which Mrs. Bardwell could lay no claim." Doctor Hailey's large and kindly face grew thoughtful. "Has it not struck you," he asked, "that though a man may not be faithful to any one woman, he is almost always faithful to a type? Again and again I have seen in first and second wives the same qualities of mind and appearance, both good and bad. Indeed, I would go so far as to say that our first loves and our last are kindred spirits, recognised and chosen by needs and desires which do not change, or change but little, throughout the course of life."

"Even so, my dear Hailey."

Biles' look of perplexity had deepened. The doctor, however, was too eager to be discouraged.

"If Mrs. Bardwell was in fact murdered," he continued, "the figure of her murderer is not, I think, very difficult to visualise: a doctor in early middle life—because the dead woman is about thirty—with a practice in the country, but the tastes of a towns-man, a trifle careless of his clothes, since he tolerates holes in his pockets, a sentimental egoist, since he buys Browning's Love Songs while plans of murder are turning over in his mind." He broke off and thought a moment. "It is probable that Mrs. Bardwell was an expensive luxury. Some women, too, fight like tigers for the pos-session of the men they rely on. Yet, though she had undoubtedly obtained a great, perhaps a terrible, hold on him, she had failed to make him marry her."

He turned to Biles and readjusted his eyeglass.

"Why, do you suppose," he asked, "Mrs. Bardwell failed to make this doctor marry her?"

"I have no idea." The detective's tones were crisp almost to the point of abruptness.

Doctor Hailey moved across the room to a writing table which stood near the window. He took a sheet of paper and marked a small circle on it. Around this he drew a much larger circle. He returned to the detective who had been watching him.

"Here is London," he said, pointing to the small circle. "And here is the country round it up to a distance of forty miles—that is to say, up to a two-hour journey by motor-car. As our doctor seems to make frequent visits to town that is not, I think, too narrow a radius. Beyond about forty miles, London is no longer within easy reach."

He struck his pencil at two places through the circumference of the larger circle, marking off a segment.

"Here," he went on, "are the Surrey Highlands, the area within our district, where heather grows and where, in consequence, almost everyone keeps bees."

He raised his head and faced the two men, whose interest he seemed to have recaptured:

"It should not," he suggested, "be impossible to discover whether or not, within this area, there is a doctor in practice who keeps Cyprian bees, is constantly running up to London, wears an overcoat with a hole in one of the pockets, and lives apart from his wife."

"Good heavens!" Biles drew his breath sharply. His instincts as a man-hunter had reasserted themselves. He glanced at the doctor with an enthusiasm which lacked nothing of generosity. The younger detective, however, retained his somewhat critical expression.

"Why should the doctor be living apart from his wife?" he asked.

"Because, had she not left him as soon as he tired of her, he would probably have killed her long ago. And in that case he would almost certainly have married Mrs. Bardwell during the first flush of his devotion to her. I know these sensualists who are also puffed up with literary vanity. Marriage possesses for them an almost incredible attractiveness."

He glanced at his watch as he spoke. The recollection of a professional appointment had come suddenly to his memory.

"If you care to follow up the luce, my dear Biles," he remarked as he left the flat, "I hope you will let me know the result. *The Medical Directory* should serve as a useful starting point."

Doctor Hailey was kept fully occupied during the next day and was unable, in consequence, to pursue the mystery of the Cyprian bees any further. In the late afternoon, however, he rang up Inspector Biles at Scotland Yard. A voice, the tones of which were sufficiently dispirited, informed him that the whole of the Home Counties did not contain a doctor answering the description with which he had furnished the police.

"Mrs. Bardwell," Biles added, "kept a maid, who has been on holiday. She returned last night and has now told us that her mistress received very few men at her flat and that a doctor was not among the number. Of course it is possible that a doctor may have called during the last fortnight, in the girl's absence. But in the circumstances, I'm afraid, we must look on the murder theory as rather far-fetched. After all, the dead woman possessed a car and may have been in the country herself on the morning on which she was stung. Bees often get trapped in cars."

Doctor Hailey hung up the receiver and took a pinch of snuff. His face wore a puzzled expression. He sat down in his big armchair and closed his eyes that he might pass in fresh review the various scraps of evidence he had collected. If the dead woman had not received the doctor at her house then the idea that they were on intimate terms could scarcely be maintained. In that case the whole of his deductions must be invalidated. He got up and walked down Harley Street to the Times Book Club. He showed the receipt which he had retained and asked if he might see the assistant who had conducted the sale. This girl remembered the incident quite clearly. It had occurred about a week earlier. The man who had bought the volume of poems was accompanied by a young woman.

"Did you happen to notice," Doctor Hailey asked, "what his companion looked like?"

"I think she was very much 'made up.' She had fair hair. But I can't say that I noticed her carefully."

"And the man?"

The girl shrugged her shoulders. "I'm afraid I don't remember him clearly. A business man, perhaps." She thought a moment. "He was a good deal older than she was, I should say."

Doctor Hailey left the shop and walked back towards Harley Street. On one point at least he had not been mistaken. The purchaser of the Love Songs was a man and he had bought them for a woman who was not Mrs. Bardwell—Biles had mentioned that this lady had auburn hair. Why should the man have visited Mrs. Bardwell so soon after making this purchase? He sighed. After all, though, why not? Biles was quite right in thinking that no jury in the world would listen to evidence the only basis of which was character-reading at second hand. He reached his door and was about to let himself into the house, when a cab drew up beside him. The young detective, Todcaster, to whom Biles had introduced him at Park Mansions, got out.

"Can I see you a moment, doctor?" he asked.

They entered the house together. Todcaster produced a letter from his pocket and handed it to Doctor Hailey. It was a prescription, written on Mrs. Bardwell's note paper and signed only with initials, which were nearly indecipherable.

"I found it after you had gone," the young man explained. "It was dispensed as you can see by a local chemist. Today I have seen him and he says he has had other similar prescriptions to dispense. But he has no idea who the writer is. Mrs. Bardwell had the medicine a few days ago."

Doctor Hailey read the prescription, which was a simple iron tonic. The signature was illegible. He shook his head.

"This does not carry us much further, I'm afraid," he declared.

"You can't tell from the initials who the doctor is?"

"No."

"In that case, I think we shall have to throw our hands in." Todcaster's voice expressed considerable disappointment. It was obvious that he had hoped to make his reputation out of the solution of the mystery. "Your reasoning, yesterday," he added, "impressed me very much, sir, if I may say so."

Doctor Hailey inclined his head. But his eyes were vacant. So a doctor *had* called on the dead woman recently, and also, apparently, made earlier visits; a doctor, too, whose prescriptions were unfamiliar to the local chemist. He turned to the young detective:

"I have just heard from Biles," he said, "that the maid has come back. Do you happen to know if she has any recollection of these professional visits?"

"I asked her that myself. She says that she knows nothing about them."

Again the far-away look came to the doctor's eyes. The fact that the prescriptions were written on Mrs. Bardwell's note paper showed that they had been given during an attendance at the flat. For what reason had the dead woman been at pains to hide the doctor's visits from her maid?

"Should I be troubling you very much," he said, "if I asked you to take me back to Park Mansions? I confess that I would like to ask that girl a few questions. A doctor can obtain information which is not likely to be imparted to any layman."

As they drove through the crowded streets, Doctor Hailey asked himself again the question which had caused him to embark on this fresh investigation. What reason had Mrs. Bardwell for hiding her need of medical attendance from her maid? Even supposing that her doctor was also her lover, there seemed to be no sense in such a concealment. He opened his eyes and saw the stream of London's home-going population surging around the cab. Sweet-faced girls and splendid youths, mingled with women whose eyes told their story of disappointment and men who wore pressing responsibility as habitual expression. No wonder the police despaired of finding any nameless human being in this vast tide of humanity, of hopes and fears, of desires and purposes!

The cab stopped. They entered the lift and came to the door of the flat. Todcaster rang the bell. A moment later the door was opened by a young girl who invited them to enter in tones which scarcely disguised the anxiety she apparently felt at the return of the police. She closed the door and then led the way along the dim entrance corridor. She opened the door of the drawing-room.

As the light from the windows fell on her face Doctor Hailey repressed an exclamation of amazement. He started as though a new idea had sprung to his mind. A slight flush mounted to his cheek. He raised his eyeglass and inserted it quickly in his eye.

"I have troubled you," he said to the girl, "because there are a few points about Mrs. Bardwell's health, before her fatal seizure, which I think you can help us to understand. I may say that I am a doctor assisting the police."

"Oh, yes!"

The girl's voice was low. Her pretty, heavily powdered face seemed drawn with anxiety and her eyes moved restlessly from one man to the other. She raised her hand in a gesture of uneasiness and clasped her brow, seeming to press her golden curls into the white flesh.

"Perhaps it might be better if I spoke to you alone?"

Doctor Hailey's tones were very gentle. He looked at Todcaster as he spoke and the detective immediately got up and left the room. Then he turned to the girl.

"Your mistress," he asked, "discharged you from her employment a fortnight ago?"

The girl started violently and all the blood seemed to ebb from her cheeks. Wild fear stared at him from her big, lustrous eyes.

"No!"

"My dear girl, if I may say so, you have everything to gain, nothing to lose, by telling the truth."

He spoke coldly. Yet there was a reassuring note in his voice. He saw fear give place a little to that quality of weakness which he had expected to find in her character—the quality which had attracted Mrs. Bardwell's lover which explained, in some subtle fashion, the gift of the Love Songs. He repeated his question. The girl hung her head. She consented. He let his eyeglass fall.

"Because of your intimacy with a man she had been accustomed to look on as her own particular friend?"

"Oh, no! No! It is not true!"

Again her eyes challenged him; she had thrown back her head, revealing the full roundness of her throat. The light gleamed among her curls. No wonder that this beauty had been able to dispossess her mistress!

"Listen to me!" Doctor Hailey's face had grown stern. "You have denied that any doctor came to this flat—at least so far as you know. As it happens, however, a number of prescriptions were dispensed for Mrs. Bardwell by the local chemist. So that either she took great pains to hide from you the fact that she was calling in a doctor, or you have not been speaking the truth."

"She did not tell me."

He raised his hand. "It will be easy," he said, "to get an answer to that question. If your mistress was really hiding her doctor's visits from you, she must have taken her prescriptions herself to the chemist. I shall find out from him later on whether or not that is so."

Again the girl's mood changed. She began to whimper, pressing a tiny lace handkerchief to her eyes in coquettish fashion. Doctor Hailey drew a deep breath. He waited a moment before framing his next remark. Then he said:

"You realise, I suppose, that if a girl helps a man to commit a crime, she is as guilty as he is in the eyes of the law."

"What do you mean?"

All her defences now were abandoned. She stood before him, abject in her terror, with staring eyes and trembling lips.

"That your presence here today proves you have had a share in this business. Why did you return to the flat?"

"Because—because—"

"Because he—the man you are shielding—wanted to find out what the police were doing in the place?"

She tottered towards him. She laid her hands on his arm.

"Oh, God, I am so frightened," she whimpered.

"You have reason to be frightened."

He led her to a chair. But suddenly, she seemed to gather her strength anew. Her grasp on his arm tightened.

"I didn't want him to do it," she cried in tones of anguish. "I swear that I didn't. And I swear that I have no idea, even yet, what he did do. We were going to be married—immediately."

"Married!" His voice seemed to underline the word.

"I swear that. It was honest and above-board, only he had her on his hands and she had wasted so much of his money." For the first time her voice rang true. She added: "His wife cost a lot too, though she was not living with him. She died a month ago."

They stood facing one another. In the silence of the room, the ticking of an ornate little clock on the mantelshelf was distinctly audible.

Doctor Hailey leaned forward.

"His name?" he asked.

"No. I shall not tell you."

She had recaptured her feeble courage. It gleamed from her eyes for an instant, transforming even her weakness. The vague knowledge that she loved this man in her paltry, unmoral way, came to him. He was about to repeat his demand when the door of the room opened. Todcaster came in with a small, leather-bound volume in his hand.

The girl uttered a shrill cry and sprang towards him. But Doctor Hailey anticipated that move. He held her firmly.

"It is the collection of Browning's Love Songs," the detective said, "I found it lying open in the next room. There is an inscription signed Michael Cornwall."

He held the book out for the doctor's inspection. But Doctor Hailey's face was as pale, almost, as that of the girl by his side.

He repeated the name "Michael Cornwall" almost like a man in a dream.

The place was hidden among its trees. Doctor Hailey walked up the avenue with slow steps. The thought of the mission which had brought him to this lovely Hampstead house lay, as it had lain through all the hours of the night—like death on his spirit. Michael Cornwall, the well-known Wimpole Street bacteriologist, and he had been boys together at Uppingham. They were still acquaintances. He came to the front door and was about to ring the bell when the man he was looking for appeared round the side of the house, accompanied by an old man and a girl.

"Hailey! Well I'm dashed!"

Doctor Cornwall advanced with outstretched hand. His deep, rather sinister eyes welcomed his colleague with an enthusiasm which was entirely unaffected. He introduced: "My uncle, Colonel Cornwall, and my cousin, Miss Patsy Cornwall, whom you must congratulate on having just become engaged," in his quick staccato manner.

"We're just going round the garden," he explained, "and you must accompany us. And, after that, to luncheon. Whereupon, my dear Hailey, if you have—as I feel sure you have—great business to discuss with me, we shall discuss it."

His bantering tones accorded well with his appearance, which had changed but little in the years. He was the same astute, moody, inordinately vain fellow who had earned for himself, once upon a time, the nickname of "The Lynx". They strolled across the lawn and came to a brick wall of that rich, russet hue which only time and the seasons can provide. Doctor Cornwall opened a door in the wall and stood back for his companions to enter. A sight of entrancing beauty greeted them; lines of fruit trees in full blossom, as though the snows of some Alpine sunset had been spread, in all their glowing tints, on the English garden. Doctor Hailey, however, had no eye for this loveliness. His gaze was fixed on a row of white-painted bee-hives which gleamed in the sunlight under the distant wall. Patsy Cornwall exclaimed in sheer wonder. Then a new cry of delight escaped her as she detected in a large greenhouse which flanked the wall, a magnificent display of scarlet tulips. She took Doctor Hailey, in whose eyes the melancholy expression seemed to have deepened, to inspect them while her father and cousin strolled on up the garden path. She stood with him in the narrow gangway of the greenhouse and feasted ecstatic eyes on the wonderful blossoms.

"Don't they make you wish to gather them all and take them away somewhere where there are no flowers?"

She turned to him. But he had sprung away from her side.

A cry, shrill and terrible, pierced the lazy silence of the morning. She saw her father and cousin fleeing back, pursued by an immense swarm of winged insects, towards the garden gate.

Blindly, frantically, they sought to ward off the dreadful onslaught. The old man stumbled and must have fallen had not his nephew caught him in his arms. She had a momentary glimpse of his face; it was as though she had looked on the face of death.

"The bees!"

The words broke from Doctor Hailey's lips as a moan of despair. He had come to the closed door of the greenhouse and seemed to be about to open it. But at the same moment one of the infuriated insects, in delirious flight, struck the glass frame beside him. Then another... another... and another. He came back towards the girl.

"Lie down on the gangway," he shouted at the pitch of his voice. "There may be a broken pane somewhere."

She turned her horror-stricken eyes to him:

"My father, oh God!"

"Lie down for your life!"

He stood beside her, watching, ready to strike if one of the bees succeeded in entering the greenhouse. Only once did he remove his straining eyes from this task. The sight which then greeted them wrung a fresh cry from his lips.

The terrible swarm hung like a dust-cloud in the air above the garden gate, rising and falling in swift undulations, which caused the light to flash and scintillate on a myriad gilded bodies and shining wings. A faint, shrill piping came to his ears across the silence. The door in the wall was open; and the garden now quite empty.

Biles leaned forward.

"Mrs. Bardwell's maid has confessed that she rung up Doctor Cornwall immediately before luncheon this morning," he said. "She tried to communicate with him before, but he had gone to the country, to a case, overnight. He got her warning that the police suspected him of being responsible for her mistress' death just after had carried his second victim, his uncle, in a dying condition, from the garden."

The detective stuck a match and relit his cigar. Doctor Hailey sat watching him with sorrowful eyes.

"Ten minutes later, as you know," he went on, "Cornwall blew his brains out. He had the wit to see that the game was up. He had been badly stung, of course, but his long experience of the bees made this a less serious matter than it would have been in the case of an ordinary outsider. In any case, moreover, he had to accept that risk if his plan was to succeed."

Silence fell in the big consulting room; then the doctor remarked:

"Miss Cornwall has recently become engaged to be married?"

"Yes." Biles drew a long whiff. "That was the circumstance which made speed essential to her cousin's murderous plan. He was hopelessly in debt, as a result of Mrs. Bardwell's extravagance, and only his uncle's money, which is considerable, could have saved him. If Miss Cornwall had married he must have lost all hope of obtaining it, and so of marrying the girl on whom he had set his fickle heart. I have ascertained that he insisted on inoculating both father and daughter against spring catarrh a month ago and that the injections he gave them hurt them terribly. No doubt Mrs. Bardwell received a similar injection about the same time. Thus for each of these three individuals a single bee sting, on your showing, meant instant death."

Doctor Hailey inclined his head.

"The moment I saw the swarm the truth flashed across my mind," he declared. "These Cyprian bees, as I have been at pains to find out and as your bee-keeping friend told you, are exceedingly ill-natured. But no bees, unless they have been previously roused to fury, ever attack at sight people who have not even approached their hives. It was all too clear, even in that first terrible moment, that the swarm was part of a carefully prepared plan."

The detective rose and held out his hand

"But for you, my dear friend," he said, "Miss Cornwall must inevitably have shared her father's fate; and the most devilish murder of which I have ever so much as heard would, almost certainly, have gone unsuspected and unpunished."

THE ENGLISH FILTER

C. E. Bechhofer Roberts

Carl Erich Bechhofer Roberts (1894–1949) was of German descent but born and raised in London. As a young man, he travelled the world, and some of his early work was published in leading literary magazines such as *The New Age* in Britain and H. L. Mencken's *The Smart Set* in the US. During the First World War he was a trooper of the 9th Lancers, and met Rasputin in St Petersburg. Prevailing anti-German sentiment caused him to publish some of his writings under the Anglicised pen-name Charles Brookfarmer, and also as "Ephesian", a tribute to the distinguished lawyer and politician F. E. Smith. A man of many parts, Bechhofer Roberts was himself a barrister and a student of true crime. When he turned his attention to detective fiction in the 1920s, he created A. B. C. Hawkes, a brilliant scientist firmly in the tradition of the Great Detective, whose cases are narrated by his admiring friend, an archæologist called Johnstone. Today the Hawkes books are sought-after collectors' items, while the handful of crime novels Bechhofer Roberts co-wrote with the prolific George Goodchild are not much easier to find.

"The English Filter" first appeared in the *Strand Magazine* in 1926. It's a locked room mystery—complete with a plan of the scene of the crime—written with so much gusto that one can forgive the dubious science. Optography, the concept at the heart of the plot, fascinated the Victorians, but had been widely questioned by the time the story was written. Belief in it persisted nevertheless, and in 1927, the shooting in Essex of P.C. George Gutteridge through each eye was thought to reflect a fear that a picture of the murderer would be implanted on the retina of the luckless constable.

I AM UNLIKELY EVER TO FORGET THE VISIT THAT MY FRIEND, A. B. C. Hawkes, the scientist, and I paid to Rome. "A. B. C.", as I always call him, had let only one man know we were coming—his old acquaintance, Professor Castagni, the bacteriologist. We were astonished, therefore, to find at least a hundred people awaiting us at the station.

Castagni introduced many of them, a lengthy business, and I was amused to discover that his instinctive Italian love of pageantry had apparently caused him to marshal representatives of every branch of learning in the city. I found myself, for example, walking to the hotel with an elderly historian on one side, who knew a little French and less English, and delivered himself of an uninterrupted flow of words in both languages, while at the other ear was a still older professor of philosophy who spoke only Italian—of which tongue I am ignorant, although this did not seem to prevent his addressing me in it.

Hawkes, in the inevitable grey frock-coat and sponge-bag trousers, with a rose in his buttonhole, was submerged in an excited crowd, from whom there arose a Babel of welcome and congratulation. Our arrival was a comic triumph.

The moment we reached our hotel, however, they all bowed, shook our hands, and withdrew.

"What a nerve-racking experience, A. B. C.," I commented, as my friend and I reached our rooms.

"And, of course, the one man I do want to meet wasn't there," Hawkes replied.

I asked who this was.

"Ribotta, the physicist," A. B. C. said. "He must be an old man now, and, I confess, I had never rated him very highly. But just lately he's published some really very remarkable papers on atomic magnetism. How he's managed to make up fifty years leeway in his work, I don't pretend to know. But that is what I've come to Rome to find out."

There was a tap at the door, and a young Italian entered.

"My name is Dorsi, Professor Castagni's assistant," he said in perfect English. "The professor wishes me to act as your guide here in Rome."

"That is most kind of you both," said Hawkes with assumed gratification. "But really, I mustn't trouble you."

"It is truly a pleasure. I appreciate the honour of coming into contact with so famous a man of science. Of course, if you wish to rest now after your journey, I will wait for you downstairs."

A. B. C. smiled resignedly.

"What my friend Johnstone and I really want," he said, "is an early lunch. I see it's just twelve—perhaps we may indulge our appetites. You will lunch with us, Mr. Dorsi, I trust?"

Our guest proved a sympathetic and intelligent young man. Educated partly in England, he had a sound knowledge of our language and tastes. I could see that Hawkes liked him as well as I did.

"Now, Mr. Dorsi," said A. B. C., as the waiter served the coffee and we lit our cigars. "You tell me that I may expect to be able to pay my formal call on Professor Castagni at three o'clock. Right! The only other visit I am anxious to make is to Professor Ribotta. His latest work interests me profoundly."

"That will be very simple," said Dorsi. "If you like, we can go there now—he is sure to be in his laboratory. And while you are there, gentlemen, I should advise you to talk to his assistant as well."

"You are trying to tell me something," remarked A. B. C., with a shrewd glance.

The Italian smiled.

"The facts are these, professor," he commenced.

"Holy Darwin! Don't call me 'professor'!" cried A. B. C. "Anything but that! The word suggests all the academic foibles I most detest—vanity, pedantry, untidiness, petty jealousies, and tyranny!"

"You must excuse this outburst, Mr. Dorsi," I laughed. "It is a form of address that always rouses his tempestuous nature."

Dorsi stole a humorous glance at the scientist's flaming red hair and smiled more broadly.

"Well, then, Mr. Hawkes," he began again—"That's better!" murmured A. B. C.—"I am perhaps being indiscreet, but your time is too valuable to be wasted. Professor Ribotta—I emphasise the title in this case—is not responsible for the theories you speak of. He takes the credit for them, but it is due to his assistant, Mr. Lavorello. You know the stupid system we have in our Continental universities—promotion goes by seniority, and a position may be held for life, or at least to a very advanced age, by any old man who does not wish to retire on a pension. That is the case of Professor Ribotta. He holds a chair for which, however well he may have filled it thirty years ago, he is today quite unqualified. You will see this for yourselves. But Lavorello—ah, there is a young man of the first quality, an experimenter without rival in all Italy, a scientific genius."

"I have heard of such cases before," said A. B. C. "I shall make a point of getting into touch with him. Thank you for your friendly advice. Shall we be going?"

The three of us set out for Ribotta's laboratory, which we found in an old part of the city, near the Pantheon. The entrance was remote from the main portion of the institute, and Dorsi told us that it led to Ribotta's and his assistant's rooms only.

The porter inside took off his cap to us and led us into a small room which, Dorsi told me, was the preserve of the laboratory attendant. It was dark and confined; the remains of a meal lay on the table and a couple of dirty overalls hung on a hook on the wall.

We stopped before another door, on which the porter knocked.

It was opened to us by Ribotta himself, to whom Dorsi swiftly explained who we were. The professor, an old man with a flowing beard and piercing eyes, then invited us to enter. He greeted A. B. C. effusively, led us to his desk, and motioned to us to sit down. He leaned forward in his chair, holding a hand to his ear.

"You speak not Italian, I think, Professor Hawkes?" he said in a broken English that I shall not attempt to reproduce exactly. "You do? Well, no matter; I prefer to speak English. Oh, I am very fond of England. Forty years ago I was at Cambridge under your great professors." He mentioned some famous names. "They taught me much—but I see you are too young to know them. I have not been in England since then, but I still have my great love for English things. I have many beautiful English things in my laboratory. I will call my assistant; he shall show them to you. Lavorello! Lavorello! Ah, he does not hear me. No matter, I will send the attendant to him. Carlo!" he called.

"That wretched attendant," the garrulous old man went on, "I cannot make him obey me. He attends only to Mr. Lavorello's work; he leaves my laboratory dirty. When he comes, he will hear from me. And now I will call my assistant myself."

He pounded on a door at the other side of the room. We heard a chair pushed back and the slamming of a door. Through an unglazed, barred window that gave on to a corridor—apparently the only ventilation of the room, for all the other windows were tightly closed—we saw a man pass.

Ribotta tittered. "You think it odd, perhaps," he said. "My assistant is in the next room, but he cannot come in through the connecting door. Ah, this is done on purpose. I do not want anybody to come into the room. So I locked that door twenty years ago, and it has remained locked ever since. He must come in the way you came, the only entrance. And that has a Yale lock, so that nobody can come in except myself and the attendant, unless I let them in myself. Only he and I have keys. Even the porter I never allow to enter. I want quiet, and in this way I get it. Ah, there must be Lavorello!"

He motioned to Dorsi, and our guide slipped across to unfasten the door. A young man entered, keen and dark, but very fleshy for his age—a point, we afterwards discovered, on which he was rather sensitive. I looked at him with interest, for he was the brilliant youth whose work had brought Hawkes to Rome.

"Sit down, Lavorello, sit down," cried Ribotta. "But no, I want you to show my English guests the great things that have come here from their country. First give them a glass of water from my filter."

Without a word the young man went over to a large glass tank, uncovered at the top and with some kind of filter and tap attached. It was one of the most noticeable objects in the peculiarly bare room. He filled a glass from it and brought this to us. Ribotta held it under Hawkes' nose.

"Taste!" he said. "What beautiful clear water! Rome water is not good to drink, but out of my English filter—ah, then one may drink with pleasure and safety. Lavorello, empty this ashtray and give me some matches!"

Expressionlessly Lavorello obeyed. Then Ribotta told him to get the cigars out of a drawer, and the old man offered them to A. B. C.,

Dorsi, and me—we refused them—and lit one of the rank things himself. He did not trouble to offer one to Lavorello, I noticed.

"Now you have seen the filter," he rattled on. "Next you must see the English microscope. Lavorello, bring the microscope and show it to Professor Hawkes."

It was, even as I could see, a very ordinary piece of laboratory apparatus, but the old man gloated over it as if it were a marvel.

"Very interesting indeed," murmured A. B. C.; "but have you any new results in your work on magnetism, sir?"

"No, I have not them here at the moment. I do not make the experiments myself these days; I leave them to the young men. Lavorello shall show you them in his laboratory. It is good work—I showed him how it should be done. The brains are mine; the hand is his. That is how it should be, is it not?"

For politeness' sake, we agreed.

"Do have another glass of water. Professor Hawkes. No? Ah, but it is good, thanks to my English filter. Your friend, then? Oh, you must! Lavorello, bring another glass of water! Quickly! If you drank more of this water, Lavorello, you would not be so fat! There is no water like this in Rome."

It tasted to me like any other water, but I thought it incumbent on me to express loud admiration.

"We must not take up any more of your time, sir," said Hawkes, rising from his chair. "With your permission, we shall just glance at Mr. Lavorello's work, and then we must be going away."

"Delighted to have seen you, professor," said Ribotta, shaking our hands. "I am always glad to welcome foreign scientists to my laboratory, especially from England. Lavorello, you are to show these gentlemen your work—*our* work—so that they may see that we old men can still keep pace with the young. Ah, but first give me some more matches."

As we left the laboratory through the little ante-room, the attendant hurried in. He was, I noticed, a sinister-looking fellow, the sort of man one would instinctively avoid on a dark night. He went past us into the professor's room, the door of which he opened with his pass-key, and we heard the old man greet him with a storm of angry words.

The corridor led us round towards Lavorello's room. Dorsi in a whisper called my attention to the cupboards and bookcases that were placed against the doors leading to the rest of the building—another example of Ribotta's insistence upon isolation. As we passed the barred window, we saw the attendant standing by the desk, gazing at the professor with a malicious glance. The old man was shouting and gesticulating, but, as he heard us go by, he turned and waved.

We reached Lavorello's laboratory, the whole atmosphere of which was very different from the old professor's, and A. B. C. and he were soon bent in eager interest over note-books and curves, with an occasional reference to some proof-sheets that lay on the table.

They forgot all about Dorsi and myself. The subject was far beyond either of us and we passed the time chatting.

"It's pretty clear," Dorsi said, after a long and bitter attack upon the old man in the next room, "with whom Mr. Hawkes finds himself more at home."

I sympathised with his denunciation of Ribotta's selfishness, his ridiculous pride in the very ordinary filter and microscope, and his bullying treatment of Lavorello, but, as a stranger, I thought it best not to be drawn into the expression of an opinion, and I looked round for an opportunity to change the subject.

"Hallo," I said, thankfully, "here is something I do understand a little about."

I walked over to a cabinet in the corner of the room, in which were ranged objects that I recognised as Italian and Greek-Italian antiques. There were coins and little statuettes and rings and toys and other trifles.

Lavorello happened to see us gazing at his collection. He smiled and unlocked the door of the cabinet.

"A hobby of mine," he said to me. "My country—I am a Sicilian, you know—is especially rich in such things."

"What are these?" asked Dorsi, pointing to some small white objects, which were familiar enough to me.

"Knucklebones," answered Lavorello, "with which I suppose our ancestors used to play. The queer glasses behind them are for another game, *cottabos*; and those square things on the same shelf are *tesserae*, the counterparts of modern dice."

A. B. C. called him back to the papers and Dorsi and I discussed the customs of the ancients and their survivals in modern times.

It was a long time before Hawkes was ready to leave. Then the three of us took leave of Lavorello and tip-toed along the corridor so as not to attract Ribotta's attention, for we had no desire to be called in to hear another harangue. We glanced in through the barred opening, and saw him at his desk, with his beloved filter beyond him underneath the clock. Fortunately he was absorbed in a newspaper and did not notice us pass.

"Shades of Cavendish!" whispered A. B. C. "It's three o'clock already!"

We hurried past the porter's lodge, to whose occupant the laboratory attendant was declaiming fiercely.

"The attendant's opinion of Ribotta," A. B. C. said to me when we got outside, "is not much higher than our own, I'm afraid. If my knowledge of Italian, or at least of the Roman dialect, is not in error, he was expressing a wish that the old professor might be devoured by hungry wolves. He added that, if they or some similar agents of destiny did not perform this necessary action, he himself would have to attend to it. I must confess, after comparing Ribotta's and Lavorello's capacity, I have some sympathy with the attendant's desire."

"Lavorello is a good man, is he?" I said.

"First-rate," said my friend. "A brilliant, ingenious brain with a magnificent grasp of scientific possibilities! If he has a fault, it's a tendency to rush at conclusions, to go the short way to a result when a longer and more patient method would be more suitable. But he'll go far! It's a crying shame that he should be held back by that old charlatan. And for the latter to steal the credit of Lavorello's researches is an insult to science."

For a moment Hawkes' round, good-natured face looked quite angry, but his usual smile soon reappeared.

We made a short call on Castagni, and spent the rest of the afternoon in the Forum. Not only did we visit the usual sights there, but, as honoured guests, we were invited to view various collections and excavations not open to the general public.

For once I was able to display more knowledge than Hawkes, and, to his mock awe, I traced resemblances between some of the exhibits and various specimens I had unearthed on the more successful of my archæological expeditions in England. A. B. C. was in his element, however, with some ancient scientific instruments, and his identification of their uses has now, I understand, been officially adopted. I learned from the director of the excavations that Lavorello had performed a similar service at the time of some earlier discoveries.

We were to meet Dorsi for dinner at the "Ulpia", which he recommended as the most picturesque restaurant in the city. We found it in an ancient basilica, whose curved brick walls, arching to the roof, made a curious and sombre background for the bright napery and electric lights. The blend of old and new—so typical of Rome—was carried down to the smallest details; the lamps, for example, were fixed in amphoræ of antique form, and the menu was rolled like an old parchment scroll. The place amused us, and we settled down patiently to await our guest.

An hour after the agreed time we despaired of his arrival and decided to begin. At ten o'clock, just as we were about to leave, he came in.

"Forgive my absence," he said, "but a terrible thing has happened. Professor Ribotta has been murdered!"

"Murdered!" I exclaimed.

"He was found poisoned in his laboratory this afternoon," Dorsi went on. A pallid smile flickered on his lips as he added, "The poison was apparently administered in the filter of which he was so proud."

"Who did it?" A. B. C. asked.

"The attendant has disappeared, and the police are in search of him. The chief of police is in the laboratory now, and, as you were among the last people to see the professor alive, he wishes to interrogate you. He was going to send to your hotel, but I volunteered to come here and fetch you."

We called for the bill and left the restaurant in silence. We walked through the warm night to the laboratory, and found it ablaze with lights. A group of men were standing in the dead man's room, among them Lavorello and the porter, both much moved.

The body had been removed to a neighbouring mortuary for examination. They told us that the professor had been found sitting upright at his desk, just as we had seen him as we tip-toed out that same afternoon. Tightly grasped in his hand was a glass of water, of which he had drunk perhaps a half; and his eyes were fixed in a rigid stare.

The chief of police asked Hawkes a string of questions, writing the replies in a note-book.

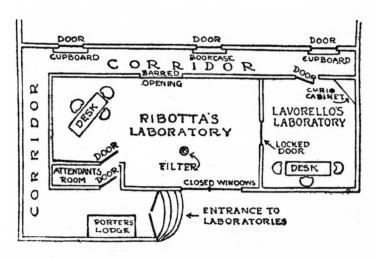

PLAN OF PROFESSOR RIBOTTA'S LABORATORY

"There seems no doubt," Dorsi said to me, "that the attendant is the villain. We all heard the quarrel and the threats he uttered against the old man. He, the attendant, was seen to leave the building a few minutes after three o'clock; in fact, he did not go back into the laboratory after we left. Lavorello says that at a quarter past five, on his way out to the baths that he visits every afternoon to try to reduce his weight, he spoke to Ribotta through the barred window from the corridor. The porter confirms that Lavorello went out at that time. Now comes the important evidence: at half-past five the attendant came in—not too sober, the porter thinks, and still muttering threats against the old man—and entered his little room, through which alone, as you know, it is possible to enter this laboratory.

"He came out ten minutes later and has not been seen since. At six o'clock, twenty minutes after the attendant went away, the porter knocked on the inner door to give the professor a message. Alarmed at receiving no reply, he went round to the barred window and called to him. When he saw that the old gentleman did not move, he called some students who were passing by. They had, of course, to smash down the door to enter, and they discovered old Ribotta dead with the glass in his hand."

I was considering these facts when a stir outside was followed by the appearance of a couple of policeman with the attendant.

The villain was even more unprepossessing than before; he was both drunk and frightened.

The chief of police told him that he was suspected of causing the professor's death, and the man, moistening his parched lips, vehemently denied the charge. Ordered to account for his movements that afternoon, he said the professor had driven him past endurance and he had gone away in a temper. He thought this must have been about three o'clock.

He went to a wine-shop and had some drinks and then made up his mind to go home to his village, a few miles out of the city, but on his way he remembered that he had left some personal belongings in his room and came back to fetch them. After making a parcel of them, he said, he went away again, without entering the laboratory at all. Then he took the tram to his home, where the police had just arrested him.

He repeatedly denied that he had gone into the professor's laboratory during his short return. He had, he insisted, stayed in his own little room and made his parcel.

Asked whether he had not uttered threats against the professor's life earlier in the afternoon, he at first said he had not. But, confronted with the evidence of the porter and ourselves, he had to admit that in the heat of his anger he might have done so.

His account in other respects certainly tallied with the previous statements. But the damning facts remained that only he and the dead man had keys to the laboratory and that he had admittedly been in the ante-room between the time Ribotta was last seen alive—by Lavorello, at a quarter past five—and the time of his being found dead at six o'clock.

Suddenly the chief turned to the porter. "And you?" he said. "Did you enter the laboratory during that period?" A. B. C. interpreted all this to me.

"The professor never permitted me inside," answered the porter. "And I had no key. No one had a key, not even Signor Lavorello, except the professor and the attendant."

"Perhaps the professor opened the door to somebody else, or the murderer had provided himself with a third key?"

"Even so," was the reply, "my lodge is opposite the door of the ante-room, and I should have seen anyone enter it. Nobody did. There is no other entrance to the laboratory."

The chief went round the room examining it. As he showed us, there was indeed no other entrance than by the door from the attendant's room. The door to Lavorello's room was still bolted, and it was clear that it had not been opened. The dust on the skylight and on the windows proved that they, too, had not been tampered with. As for the window to the corridor, the bars were firmly fixed in the mortar; a baby could not have climbed between them.

We were asked to accompany the party to the mortuary. A sheet was reverently pulled back and the dead man's face revealed. I watched the attendant. He shuddered and crossed himself surreptitiously. One might have said that his very emotion testified to his guilt.

The unnatural rigidity of the dead man's features seemed to interest Hawkes. He took a glass from his pocket and intently examined the staring eyes for some minutes. Then he entered upon a conversation with the doctors in a corner of the room, where they were working.

When the rest of us went out, glad to leave the presence of death, A. B. C. did not immediately follow. Dorsi and I waited outside, after seeing the prisoner removed, protesting violently, by the police. My friend came out at last.

"Gentlemen," he said, "you must excuse me. Johnstone, take Mr. Dorsi back to the hotel and entertain him—and Mr. Lavorello too, if he will accompany you. I am going to help with the medical examination."

"What a gruesome idea!" I said.

"My erudite friend," he replied, "you ought to know my interest in the border-line between physics and physiology. Good night." And he hurried back inside the mortuary.

We walked to the hotel, discussing the terrible event.

"I suppose," I said, "it is certain the poor man was poisoned?"

"Of that there is no doubt," said Dorsi. "The doctors suspected it from the first, and Mr. Hawkes, who seems to know everything, agrees with them. They all think it is a poison of the strychnine class, although probably not strychnine itself."

"It ought to be easy to find where the attendant procured it," I suggested.

"In England it might be," smiled Lavorello, "but not, I fear, in Rome. However, as no one but the attendant could possibly have entered and dropped it in the filter, the question where he obtained it hardly seems to matter."

"Can it possibly have been introduced through the walls or the roof or the windows?" I asked.

"Impossible," said Dorsi. "Stupid and deaf as the old man was, he was very keen-sighted, and, sitting at his desk with the filter right in front of him, he would have noticed any attempt to tamper with it. Besides, how on earth could anyone have done so, when it was in the very middle of the room?"

I had to admit that they were right.

They would not come in with me, and we parted at the entrance to my hotel. I sat in my room for some time, but I saw nothing to shake my conviction that the attendant was guilty. This seemed established beyond the possibility of doubt.

Hawkes did not return all that night, nor was he in the hotel when I left it the next morning to visit St. Peter's and one of the Vatican galleries. I lunched in a little restaurant near the Cathedral and returned to the hotel in the middle of the afternoon.

I found A. B. C. waiting for me. From his look I guessed that he had spent the whole night on his researches.

"Well, what news?" he asked.

"I look to you for that, A. B. C.," I replied. "Has the attendant confessed?"

"Not yet; but things are very black against him."

"You look tired," I said. "Why don't you lie down for a while?"

"I am little fatigued," he admitted. "Between you and me, Ribotta dead presents more scientific interest than he did alive, but he is equally wearying in both states. I fear you will think that remark in bad taste. I don't think I'll lie down, however. What would you say to taking a Turkish bath—a Roman bath, I suppose I ought to call it here? Our full-bodied friend Lavorello patronises the baths every afternoon, it seems, like the lover of antique Roman customs that he is, and I have arranged to visit one of them with him today. I hope you will accompany us."

I readily agreed, and we drove off to the laboratory and picked up Lavorello. We took the opportunity to glance in at the dead man's room, and I confirmed my impressions of the case. Nobody could possibly have entered it except through the attendant's room.

The three of us were soon in the baths enjoying the delights that Lavorello, lying on a slab near us, assured us were the daily pleasures of the ancient Romans. His admiration for my friend was so evident, and he addressed his conversation so exclusively to him, that A. B. C. seemed to fear that I was being unduly relegated to the background.

"Cease to emulate the modest violet, friend Johnstone," he smiled. "Discourse to us upon topics suitable to the occasion. An archæologist like you ought to welcome the society of a fellow-enthusiast like Mr. Lavorello—Professor Lavorello, I suppose his friends will call him now. Expound to us, my able adjutant, the pastimes of antique Roman society in the baths they frequented."

"Surely, A. B. C.," I said, "Mr. Lavorello is better qualified than I? His collection shows him to be a specialist."

"I doubt it," said Hawkes. "He has been too busy, I am sure, adequately to interest himself in the subject; is that not so, Lavorello?"

"Oh, I don't know," replied Lavorello; "I have found time in my leisure moments to study it with a certain thoroughness."

"Theory, theory, all is theory!" A. B. C. scoffed. "I'll wager for example, that you, Lavorello, couldn't even tell me the right way to hold those old knucklebones that are in your cabinet."

"Surely knucklebones are played today pretty much as they ever were?" said the Italian. "The simplest and yet the most difficult game is to toss them one after the other in the air and to endeavour to catch the whole set—three or five—on the back of your hand. It is difficult, but after long practice I found I could do it."

"So you have joined practice to theory after all," said A. B. C. "I apologise for my unworthy doubts. Now, Johnstone, I give you one more chance to retrieve your reputation as an archæologist. Tell me some other game that the ancients played on such occasions as these—and in such prodigious heat as this."

"That's easy," I said. "I was reminded of it yesterday. Mr. Lavorello has the instruments in his cabinet. It is the old game of *cottabos*."

"Oh, how do you play that, friend Lavorello?"

"I am afraid," replied he, laughing, "my knowledge stops short at knucklebones. As you hinted, I am not a universal genius."

"Now, splendid Johnstone, cover yourself with glory! Tell us how the royal and ancient game of *cottabos* was played."

"As far as I remember," I said, "the players amused themselves with it at drinking parties. The aim of the game was to throw wine from a specially shaped glass in such a way that the liquid travelled through the air without scattering. This was done, according to German scholars, who know everything about everything, by a particular twirling movement imparted to the glass. The object was to sink a little metal saucer floating in a sunken tank by casting the wine into it. Isn't that right, Mr. Lavorello?"

Just at that moment Dorsi entered, smiling at the sight of us three in our scanty attire.

"What stifling heat!" he said. "You sent for me, Mr. Hawkes?"

"Yes," said A. B. C. "I wanted you to know that I have discovered the murderer of Professor Ribotta."

"You have?" we exclaimed, in one breath.

"I thought, sir, the police arrested him yesterday," said Dorsi.

"No, dear Dorsi, no. The attendant had no hand in the crime."

"But it was proved—" I began.

"It was proved, my intelligent compatriot, that the attendant entered the building at half-past five for a few minutes. The corpse was not discovered till six, and so it was taken for granted that the man had entered the professor's room and dropped the poison in the filter."

"Exactly," I said.

"But when I saw the corpse," A. B. C. went on, "I was struck at once by the peculiar red discoloration of the eyes. There is a certain obscure poison of the strychnine class which produces this effect. It also produces almost instantaneous death. As you know the eye is like a camera, with the retina at the back like a sensitive plate, on which the different pictures are continually formed. Now, this poison makes the lens lose its transparency, with the result that no light enters, and the eyeball becomes like a camera with the shutter closed.

"It occurred to me, therefore, that the picture that was cast on the retina at the moment of death might have persisted. Of course, we should not perceive this picture direct. I thought, however, that it might be possible, as it were, to develop the image. The doctors agreed to allow me to try. I will not give you details of the method, for they are not particularly pleasant to hear. We were not successful with the first eye; the work was more difficult than I had suspected. But from the second I got a blurred picture—not a studio photograph, perhaps, but sufficient for our purpose. That picture told me all I wanted to know."

"What did it show?" I asked.

"Just the clock on the wall, on which, as I took the trouble to observe this afternoon, the rays of the afternoon sun fall. Now that photograph on the dead man's retina, which was the last thing he saw in this life, showed with clearness that, at the moment of his death, the hands of the clock stood at exactly five o'clock!"

"Five o'clock," cried Dorsi. "Then the attendant had not yet returned!"

"Before he came back on that unfortunate visit to his room," said A. B. C. solemnly, "the professor was already dead."

"But nobody else had entered the laboratory," I objected.

"And nobody had!" said A. B. C. "That's what made me so curious about the game of *cottabos*. You see, a really skilled player, standing in the corridor with the proper kind of glass, might well throw the poison through the barred window into the filter. It would be difficult, I admit, but a practised hand could achieve it. The professor at his desk would not notice the liquid passing across the room."

A choking sound came from the slab where Lavorello lay. He was gasping as if unable to draw his breath. A. B. C. strode across to him and spoke softly but distinctly in his ear, while Dorsi and I watched with a terrible suspicion in our minds.

"Lavorello," said Hawkes, sternly, "*you* understand!"

The young scientist groaned and fought for air. Then a sudden agitation of his body threw him off the slab on to the floor. Dorsi and I rushed to raise him, but A. B. C. waved us back.

"It's too late," he said. "I knew his heart was weak—he was foolish to use these hot rooms. The heat of the bath, the strain of his recent crime, and the knowledge that it had been detected have killed him. I must confess that this was my reason for staging this little scene here. We may now be able to avert a very nasty scandal; whereas, if it had come to a public trial—" He shook his head. "Yes, he was a great experimenter, was young Lavorello, but his ambition was too great for him. A true scientist should await results, not force them, even when a stupid, vain old man stands in the way."

THE CONTENTS OF A MARE'S NEST

R. Austin Freeman

Richard Austin Freeman (1862–1943) qualified as a doctor and worked in Africa as Assistant Colonial Surgeon until poor health caused him to return to England. He started writing to supplement a modest income from his day job, and after a couple of false starts made his name as the creator of Dr John Evelyn Thorndyke, who (like Holmes) had a real-life inspiration. His professional expertise was modelled on that of Dr Alfred Swaine Taylor, whom Freeman described as "the father of medical jurisprudence". Freeman also endowed Thorndyke with good looks and an amiable if slightly austere character; he is entirely lacking in the personality quirks that make Sherlock Holmes so memorable.

"The Contents of a Mare's Nest" was included in *The Magic Casket*, published in 1927, when Freeman's fame was at its peak; this was a period when no less an authority than T. S. Eliot, an enthusiast of detective fiction and occasional critic of the genre, ranked Austin Freeman alongside Freeman Wills Crofts as the two leading British detective writers—ahead, in other words, of Agatha Christie and Dorothy L. Sayers. This clever story demonstrates Freeman's authoritative handling of forensic investigation.

"IT IS VERY UNSATISFACTORY," SAID MR. STALKER, OF THE 'Griffin' Life Assurance Company, at the close of a consultation on a doubtful claim. "I suppose we shall have to pay up."

"I am sure you will," said Thorndyke. "The death was properly certified, the deceased is buried, and you have not a single fact with which to support an application for further inquiry."

"No," Stalker agreed. "But I am not satisfied. I don't believe that doctor really knew what she died from. I wish cremation were more usual."

"So, I have no doubt, has many a poisoner," Thorndyke remarked dryly.

Stalker laughed, but stuck to his point. "I know you don't agree," said he, "but from our point of view it is much more satisfactory to know that the extra precautions have been taken. In a cremation case, you have not to depend on the mere death certificate; you have the cause of death verified by an independent authority, and it is difficult to see how any miscarriage can occur."

Thorndyke shook his head. "It is a delusion, Stalker. You can't provide in advance for unknown contingencies. In practice, your special precautions degenerate into mere formalities. If the circumstances of a death appear normal, the independent authority will certify; if they appear abnormal, you won't get a certificate at all. And if suspicion arises only after the cremation has taken place, it can neither be confirmed nor rebutted."

"My point is," said Stalker, "that the searching examination would lead to discovery of a crime before cremation."

"That is the intention," Thorndyke admitted. "But no examination, short of an exhaustive post-mortem, would make it safe to destroy a body so that no reconsideration of the cause of death would be possible.'

Stalker smiled as he picked up his hat. "Well," he said, "to a cobbler there is nothing like leather, and I suppose that to a toxicologist there is nothing like an exhumation," and with this parting shot he took his leave.

We had not seen the last of him, however. In the course of the same week he looked in to consult us on a fresh matter.

"A rather queer case has turned up," said he. "I don't know that we are deeply concerned in it, but we should like to have your opinion as to how we stand. The position is this: Eighteen months ago, a man named Ingle insured with us for fifteen hundred pounds, and he was then accepted as a first-class life. He has recently died—apparently from heart failure, the heart being described as fatty and dilated—and his wife, Sibyl, who is the sole legatee and executrix, has claimed payment. But just as we were making arrangements to pay, a caveat has been entered by a certain Margaret Ingle, who declares that she is the wife of the deceased and claims the estate as next of kin. She states that the alleged wife, Sibyl, is a widow named Huggard who contracted a bigamous marriage with the deceased, knowing that he had a wife living."

"An interesting situation," commented Thorndyke, "but, as you say, it doesn't particularly concern you. It is a matter for the Probate Court."

"Yes," agreed Stalker. "But that is not all. Margaret Ingle not only charges the other woman with bigamy; she accuses her of having made away with the deceased."

"On what grounds?"

"Well, the reasons she gives are rather shadowy. She states that Sibyl's husband, James Huggard, died under suspicious circumstances—there seems to have been some suspicion that he had been poisoned—and she asserts that Ingle was a healthy, sound man and could not have died from the causes alleged."

"There is some reason in that," said Thorndyke, "if he was really a first-class life only eighteen months ago. As to the first husband, Huggard, we should want some particulars: as to whether there was an inquest, what was the alleged cause of death, and what grounds there were for suspecting that he had been poisoned. If there really were any suspicious circumstances, it would be advisable to apply to the Home Office for an order to exhume the body of Ingle and verify the cause of death."

Stalker smiled somewhat sheepishly. "Unfortunately," said he, "that is not possible. Ingle was cremated."

"Ah!" said Thorndyke, "that is, as you say, unfortunate. It clearly increases the suspicion of poisoning, but destroys the means of verifying that suspicion."

"I should tell you," said Stalker, "that the cremation was in accordance with the provisions of the will."

"That is not very material," replied Thorndyke. "In fact, it rather accentuates the suspicious aspect of the case; for the knowledge that the death of the deceased would be followed by cremation might act as a further inducement to get rid of him by poison. There were two death certificates, of course?"

"Yes. The confirmatory certificate was given by Dr. Halbury, of Wimpole Street. The medical attendant was a Dr. Barber, of

Howland Street. The deceased lived in Stock-Orchard Crescent, Holloway."

"A good distance from Howland Street," Thorndyke remarked. "Do you know if Halbury made a post-mortem? I don't suppose he did."

"No, he didn't," replied Stalker.

"Then," said Thorndyke, "his certificate is worthless. You can't tell whether a man has died from heart failure by looking at his dead body. He must have just accepted the opinion of the medical attendant. Do I understand that you want me to look into this case?"

"If you will. It is not really our concern whether or not the man was poisoned, though I suppose we should have a claim on the estate of the murderer. But we should like you to investigate the case; though how the deuce you are going to do it I don't quite see."

"Neither do I," said Thorndyke. "However, we must get into touch with the doctors who signed the certificates, and possibly they may be able to clear the whole matter up."

"Of course," said I, "there is the other body—that of Huggard—which might be exhumed—unless he was cremated, too."

"Yes," agreed Thorndyke; "and for the purposes of the criminal law, evidence of poisoning in that case would be sufficient. But it would hardly help the Griffin Company, which is concerned exclusively with Ingle deceased. Can you let us have a précis of the facts relating to this case, Stalker?"

"I have brought one with me," was the reply; "a short statement, giving names, addresses, dates, and other particulars. Here it is"; and he handed Thorndyke a sheet of paper bearing a tabulated statement.

When Stalker had gone Thorndyke glanced rapidly through the précis and then looked at his watch. "If we make our way to

Wimpole Street at once," said he, "we ought to catch Halbury. That is obviously the first thing to do. He signed the 'C' certificate, and we shall be able to judge from what he tells us whether there is any possibility of foul play. Shall we start now?"

As I assented, he slipped the précis in his pocket and we set forth. At the top of Middle Temple Lane we chartered a taxi by which we were shortly deposited at Dr. Halbury's door and a few minutes later were ushered into his consulting room, and found him shovelling a pile of letters into the waste-paper basket.

"How d'ye do?" he said briskly, holding out his hand. "I'm up to my eyes in arrears, you see. Just back from my holiday. What can I do for you?"

"We have called," said Thorndyke, "about a man named Ingle."

"Ingle—Ingle," repeated Halbury. "Now, let me see—"

"Stock-Orchard Crescent, Holloway," Thorndyke explained.

"Oh, yes. I remember him. Well, how is he?"

"He's dead," replied Thorndyke.

"Is he really?" exclaimed Halbury. "Now that shows how careful one should be in one's judgments. I half suspected that fellow of malingering. He was supposed to have a dilated heart, but I couldn't make out any appreciable dilatation. There was excited, irregular action. That was all. I had a suspicion that he had been dosing himself with trinitrine. Reminded me of the cases of cordite chewing that I used to meet with in South Africa. So he's dead, after all. Well, it's queer. Do you know what the exact cause of death was?"

"Failure of a dilated heart is the cause stated on the certificates—the body was cremated; and the 'C' Certificate was signed by you."

"By me!" exclaimed the physician. "Nonsense! It's a mistake. I signed a certificate for a Friendly Society—Mrs. Ingle brought it here for me to sign—but I didn't even know he was dead. Besides, I went away for my holiday a few days after I saw the man and only came back yesterday. What makes you think I signed the death certificate?"

Thorndyke produced Stalker's précis and handed it to Halbury, who read out his own name and address with a puzzled frown. "This is an extraordinary affair," said he. "It will have to be looked into."

"It will, indeed," assented Thorndyke; "especially as a suspicion of poisoning has been raised."

"Ha!" exclaimed Halbury. "Then it was trinitrine, you may depend. But I suspected him unjustly. It was somebody else who was dosing him; perhaps that sly-looking baggage of a wife of his. Is anyone in particular suspected?"

"Yes. The accusation, such as it is, is against the wife."

"H'm. Probably a true bill. But she's done us. Artful devil. You can't get much evidence out of an urnful of ashes. Still, somebody has forged my signature. I suppose that is what the hussy wanted that certificate for—to get a specimen of my handwriting. I see the 'B' certificate was signed by a man named Meeking. Who's he? It was Barber who called me in for an opinion."

"I must find out who he is," replied Thorndyke. "Possibly Dr. Barber will know. I shall go and call on him now."

"Yes," said Dr. Halbury, shaking hands as we rose to depart, "you ought to see Barber. He knows the history of the case, at any rate."

From Wimpole Street we steered a course for Howland Street, and here we had the good fortune to arrive just as Dr. Barber's car drew up at the door. Thorndyke introduced himself and me, and then introduced the subject of his visit, but said nothing, at first, about our call on Dr. Halbury.

"Ingle," repeated Dr. Barber. "Oh, yes, I remember him. And you say he is dead. Well, I'm rather surprised. I didn't regard his condition as serious."

"Was his heart dilated?" Thorndyke asked.

"Not appreciably. I found nothing organic; no valvular disease. It was more like a tobacco heart. But it's odd that Meeking didn't mention the matter to me—he was my locum, you know. I handed the case over to him when I went on my holiday. And you say he signed the death certificate?"

"Yes; and the 'B' certificate for cremation, too."

"Very odd," said Dr. Barber. "Just come in and let us have a look at the day book."

We followed him into the consulting room, and there, while he was turning over the leaves of the day book, I ran my eye along the shelf over the writing-table from which he had taken it; on which I observed the usual collection of case books and books of certificates and notification forms, including the book of death certificates.

"Yes," said Dr. Barber, "here we are; 'Ingle, Mr., Stock-Orchard Crescent'. The last visit was on the 4th of September, and Meeking seems to have given some sort of certificate. Wonder if he used a printed form." He took down two of the books and turned over the counterfoils.

"Here we are," he said presently; "'Ingle, Jonathan, 4th September. Now recovered and able to resume duties.' That doesn't look like dying, does it? Still, we may as well make sure."

He reached down the book of death certificates and began to glance through the most recent entries.

"No," he said, turning over the leaves, "there doesn't seem to be—Hullo! What's this? Two blank counterfoils; and about the date, too; between the 2nd and 13th of September. Extraordinary! Meeking is such a careful, reliable man."

He turned back to the day book and read through the fortnight's entries. Then he looked up with an anxious frown.

"I can't make this out," he said. "There is no record of any patient having died in that period."

"Where is Dr. Meeking at present?" I asked.

"Somewhere in the South Atlantic," replied Barber. "He left here three weeks ago to take up a post on a Royal Mail Boat. So he couldn't have signed the certificate in any case."

That was all that Dr. Barber had to tell us, and a few minutes later we took our departure.

"This case looks pretty fishy," I remarked, as we turned down Tottenham Court Road.

"Yes," Thorndyke agreed. "There is evidently something radically wrong. And what strikes me especially is the cleverness of the fraud; the knowledge and judgment and foresight that are displayed."

"She took pretty considerable risks," I observed.

"Yes, but only the risks that were unavoidable. Everything that could be foreseen has been provided for. All the formalities have been complied with—in appearance. And you must notice, Jervis, that the scheme did actually succeed. The cremation has taken place. Nothing but the incalculable accident of the appearance of the real Mrs. Ingle, and her vague and apparently groundless suspicions, prevented the success from being final. If she had not come on the scene, no questions would ever have been asked."

"No," I agreed. "The discovery of the plot is a matter of sheer bad luck. But what do you suppose has really happened?"

Thorndyke shook his head.

"It is very difficult to say. The mechanism of the affair is obvious enough, but the motives and purpose are rather incomprehensible. The illness was apparently a sham, the symptoms being produced by nitro-glycerine or some similar heart poison. The doctors were called in, partly for the sake of appearances and partly to get specimens of their handwriting. The fact that both the doctors happened to be away from home and one of them at sea at the time when verbal questions might have been asked—by the undertaker, for instance—suggests that this had been ascertained in advance. The death certificate forms were pretty certainly stolen by the woman when she was left alone in Barber's consulting-room, and, of course, the cremation certificates could be obtained on application to the crematorium authorities. That is all plain sailing. The mystery is, what is it all about? Barber or Meeking would almost certainly have given a death certificate, although the death was unexpected, and I don't suppose Halbury would have refused to confirm it. They would have assumed that their diagnosis had been at fault."

"Do you think it could have been suicide, or an inadvertent overdose of trinitrine?"

"Hardly. If it was suicide, it was deliberate, for the purpose of getting the insurance money for the woman, unless there was some further motive behind. And the cremation, with all its fuss and formalities, is against suicide; while the careful preparation seems to exclude inadvertent poisoning. Then, what was the motive for the sham illness except as a preparation for an abnormal death?"

"That is true," said I. "But if you reject suicide, isn't it rather remarkable that the victim should have provided for his own cremation?"

"We don't know that he did," replied Thorndyke. "There is a suggestion of a capable forger in this business. It is quite possible that the will itself is a forgery."

"So it is!" I exclaimed. "I hadn't thought of that."

"You see," continued Thorndyke, "the appearances suggest that cremation was a necessary part of the programme; otherwise these extraordinary risks would not have been taken. The woman was sole executrix and could have ignored the cremation clause. But if the cremation was necessary, why was it necessary? The suggestion is that there was something suspicious in the appearance of the body; something that the doctors would certainly have observed or that would have been discovered if an exhumation had taken place."

"You mean some injury or visible signs of poisoning?"

"I mean something discoverable by examination even after burial."

"But what about the undertaker? Wouldn't he have noticed anything palpably abnormal?"

"An excellent suggestion, Jervis. We must see the undertaker. We have his address: Kentish Town Road—a long way from the deceased's house, by the way. We had better get on a bus and go there now."

A yellow omnibus was approaching as he spoke. We hailed it and sprang on, continuing our discussion as we were borne northward.

Mr. Burrell, the undertaker, was a pensive-looking, profoundly civil man who was evidently occupied in a small way, for he combined with his funeral functions general carpentry and cabinet making. He was perfectly willing to give any required information, but he seemed to have very little to give.

"I never really saw the deceased gentleman," he said in reply to Thorndyke's cautious inquiries. "When I took the measurements, the corpse was covered with a sheet; and as Mrs. Ingle was in the room, I made the business as short as possible."

"You didn't put the body in the coffin, then?"

"No. I left the coffin at the house, but Mrs. Ingle said that she and the deceased gentleman's brother would lay the body in it."

"But didn't you see the corpse when you screwed the coffin-lid down?"

"I didn't screw it down. When I got there it was screwed down already. Mrs. Ingle said they had to close up the coffin, and I dare say it was necessary. The weather was rather warm; and I noticed a strong smell of formalin."

"Well," I said, as we walked back down the Kentish Town Road, "we haven't got much more forward."

"I wouldn't say that," replied Thorndyke. "We have a further instance of the extraordinary adroitness with which this scheme was carried out; and we have confirmation of our suspicion that there was something unusual in the appearance of the body. It is evident that this woman did not dare to let even the undertaker see it. But one can hardly help admiring the combination of daring and caution, the boldness with which these risks were taken, and the care and judgment with which they were provided against. And again I point out that the risks were justified by the result. The secret of that man's death appears to have been made secure for all time."

It certainly looked as if the mystery with which we were concerned were beyond the reach of investigation. Of course, the woman could be prosecuted for having forged the death certificates, to say nothing of the charge of bigamy. But that was no concern of ours or Stalker's. Jonathan Ingle was dead, and no one could say how he died.

On our arrival at our chambers we found a telegram that had just arrived, announcing that Stalker would call on us in the evening; and as this seemed to suggest that he had some fresh information we looked forward to his visit with considerable interest. Punctually at six o'clock he made his appearance and at once opened the subject.

"There are some new developments in this Ingle case," said he. "In the first place, the woman, Huggard, has bolted. I went to the house to make a few inquiries and found the police in possession.

They had come to arrest her on the bigamy charge, but she had got wind of their intentions and cleared out. They made a search of the premises, but I don't think they found anything of interest except a number of rifle cartridges; and I don't know that they are of much interest either, for she could hardly have shot him with a rifle."

"What kind of cartridges were they?" Thorndyke asked.

Stalker put his hand in his pocket.

"The inspector let me have one to show you," said he; and he laid on the table a military cartridge of the pattern of some twenty years ago. Thorndyke picked it up, and taking from a drawer a pair of pliers drew the bullet out of the case and inserted into the latter a pair of dissecting forceps. When he withdrew the forceps, their points grasped one or two short strings of what looked like cat-gut.

"Cordite!" said I. "So Halbury was probably right, and this is how she got her supply." Then, as Stalker looked at me inquiringly, I gave him a short account of the results of our investigations.

"Ha!" he exclaimed, "the plot thickens. This juggling with the death certificates seems to connect itself with another kind of juggling that I came to tell you about. You know that Ingle was Secretary and Treasurer to a company that bought and sold land for building estates. Well, I called at their office after I left you and had a little talk with the chairman. From him I learned that Ingle had practically complete control of the financial affairs of the company, that he received and paid all moneys and kept the books. Of late, however, some of the directors have had a suspicion that all was not well with the finances, and at last it was decided to have the affairs of the company thoroughly overhauled by a firm of, chartered accountants. This decision was communicated to Ingle, and a couple of days later a letter arrived from his wife saying that he had had a severe heart attack and asking that the audit of the books might be postponed until he recovered and was able to attend at the office."

"And was it postponed?" I asked.

"No," replied Stalker. "The accountants were asked to get to work at once, which they did; with the result that they discovered a number of discrepancies in the books and a sum of about three thousand pounds unaccounted for. It isn't quite obvious how the frauds were carried out, but it is suspected that some of the returned cheques are fakes with forged endorsements."

"Did the company communicate with Ingle on the subject?" asked Thorndyke.

"No. They had a further letter from Mrs. Ingle—that is, Huggard—saying that Ingle's condition was very serious; so they decided to wait until he had recovered. Then, of course, came the announcement of his death, on which the matter was postponed pending the probate of the will. I suppose a claim will be made on the estate, but as the executrix has absconded, the affair has become rather complicated."

"You were saying," said Thorndyke, "that the fraudulent death certificates seem to be connected with these frauds on the company. What kind of connection do you assume?"

"I assume—or, at least, suggest," replied Stalker, "that this was a case of suicide. The man, Ingle, saw that his frauds were discovered, or were going to be, and that he was in for a long term of penal servitude, so he just made away with himself. And I think that if the murder charge could be dropped, Mrs. Huggard might be induced to come forward and give evidence as to the suicide."

Thorndyke shook his head.

"The murder charge couldn't be dropped," said he. "If it was suicide, Huggard was certainly an accessory; and in law, an accessory to suicide is an accessory to murder. But, in fact, no official charge of murder has been made, and at present there are no means of sustaining such a charge. The identity of the ashes might be assumed to be that stated in the cremation order, but the difficulty is the cause of death. Ingle was admittedly ill. He was attended for heart disease by three doctors. There is no evidence that he did not die from that illness."

"But the illness was due to cordite poisoning," said I.

"That is what we believe. But no one could swear to it. And we certainly could not swear that he died from cordite poisoning."

"Then," said Stalker, "apparently there is no means of finding out whether his death was due to natural causes, suicide, or murder?"

"There is only one chance," replied Thorndyke. "It is just barely possible that the cause of death might be ascertainable by an examination of the ashes."

"That doesn't seem very hopeful," said I. "Cordite poisoning would certainly leave no trace."

"We mustn't assume that he died from cordite poisoning," said Thorndyke. "Probably he did not. That may have masked the action of a less obvious poison, or death might have been produced by some new agent."

"But," I objected, "how many poisons are there that could be detected in the ashes? No organic poison would leave any traces, nor would metallic poisons such as mercury, antimony, or arsenic."

"No," Thorndyke agreed. "But there are other metallic poisons which could be easily recovered from the ashes; lead, tin, gold, and silver, for instance. But it is useless to discuss speculative probabilities. The only chance that we have of obtaining any new facts is by an examination of the ashes. It seems infinitely improbable that we shall learn anything from it, but there is the bare possibility and we ought not to leave it untried."

Neither Stalker nor I made any further remark, but I could see that the same thought was in both our minds. It was not often that Thorndyke was "gravelled"; but apparently the resourceful Mrs. Huggard had set him a problem that was beyond even his powers. When an investigator of crime is reduced to the necessity of examining a potful of ashes in the wild hope of ascertaining from them how the deceased met his death, one may assume that he is at the very end of his tether. It is a forlorn hope indeed.

Nevertheless, Thorndyke seemed to view the matter quite cheerfully, his only anxiety being lest the Home Secretary should refuse to make the order authorising the examination. And this anxiety was dispelled a day or two later by the arrival of a letter giving the necessary authority, and informing him that a Dr. Hemming—known to us both as an expert pathologist—had been deputed to be present at the examination and to confer with him as to the necessity for a chemical analysis.

On the appointed day Dr. Hemming called at our chambers and we set forth together for Liverpool Street; and as we drove thither it became evident to me that his view of our mission was very similar to my own. For, though he talked freely enough, and on professional topics, he maintained a most discreet silence on the subject of the forthcoming inspection; indeed, the first reference to the subject was made by Thorndyke himself just as the train was approaching Corfield, where the crematorium was situated.

"I presume," said he, "you have made all necessary arrangements, Hemming?"

"Yes," was the reply. "The superintendent will meet us and will conduct us to the catacombs, and there, in our presence, will take

the casket from its niche in the columbarium and have it conveyed
to the office, where the examination will be made. I thought it best
to use these formalities, though, as the casket is sealed and bears the
name of the deceased, there is not much point in them."

"No," said Thorndyke, "but I think you were right. It would be
easy to challenge the identity of a mass of ashes if all precautions
were not taken, seeing that the ashes themselves are unidentifiable."

"That was what I felt," said Hemming; and then, as the train
slowed down, he added: "This is our station, and that gentleman
on the platform, I suspect, is the superintendent."

The surmise turned out to be correct; but the cemetery official
was not the only one present bearing that title; for as we were mutu-
ally introducing ourselves, a familiar tall figure approached up the
platform from the rear of the train—our old friend Superintendent
Miller of the Criminal Investigation Department.

"I don't wish to intrude," said he, as he joined the group and
was presented by Thorndyke to the strangers, "but we were notified by the Home Office that an investigation was to be made, so I
thought I would be on the spot to pick up any crumbs of information that you may drop. Of course, I am not asking to be present
at the examination."

"You may as well be present as an additional witness to the
removal of the urn," said Thorndyke; and Miller accordingly joined
the party, which now made its way from the station to the cemetery.

The catacombs were in a long, low arcaded building at the end
of the pleasantly wooded grounds, and on our way thither we
passed the crematorium, a smallish, church-like edifice with a per-
forated chimney-shaft partly concealed by the low spire. Entering
the catacombs, we were conducted to the "columbarium", the walls
of which were occupied by a multitude of niches or pigeon-holes,

each niche accommodating a terra-cotta urn or casket. The super-intendent proceeded to near the end of the gallery, where he halted, and opening the register, which he had brought with him, read out a number and the name "Jonathan Ingle", and then led us to a niche bearing that number and name, in which reposed a square casket, on which was inscribed the name and date of death. When we had verified these particulars, the casket was tenderly lifted from its place by two attendants, who carried it to a well-lighted room at the end of the building, where a large table by a window had been covered with white paper. Having placed the casket on the table, the attendants retired, and the superintendent then broke the seals and removed the cover.

For a while we all stood looking in at the contents of the casket without speaking; and I found myself contrasting them with what would have been revealed by the lifting of a coffin-lid. Truly corrup-tion had put on incorruption. The mass of snow-white, coral-like fragments, delicate, fragile, and lace-like in texture, so far from being repulsive in aspect, were almost attractive. I ran my eye, with an anatomist's curiosity, over these dazzling remnants of what had lately been a man, half-unconsciously seeking to identify and give a name to particular fragments, and a little surprised at the difficulty of determining that this or that irregularly shaped white object was a part of any one of the bones with which I had thought myself so familiar.

Presently Hemming looked up at Thorndyke and asked: "Do you observe anything abnormal in the appearance of these ashes? I don't."

"Perhaps," replied Thorndyke, "we had better turn them out on to the table, so that we can see the whole of them."

This was done very gently, and then Thorndyke proceeded to spread out the heap, touching the fragments with the utmost delicacy—for they were extremely fragile and brittle—until the whole collection was visible.

"Well," said Hemming, when we had once more looked them over critically, "what do you say? I can see no trace of any foreign substance. Can you?"

"No," replied Thorndyke. "And there are some other things that I can't see. For instance, the medical referee reported that the proposer had a good set of sound teeth. Where are they? I have not seen a single fragment of a tooth. Yet teeth are far more resistant to fire than bones, especially the enamel caps."

Hemming ran a searching glance over the mass of fragments and looked up with a perplexed frown.

"I certainly can't see any sign of teeth," he admitted; "and it is rather curious, as you say. Does the fact suggest any particular significance to you?"

By way of reply, Thorndyke delicately picked up a flat fragment and silently held it out towards us. I looked at it and said nothing; for a very strange suspicion was beginning to creep into my mind.

"A piece of a rib," said Hemming. "Very odd that it should have broken across so cleanly. It might have been cut with a saw."

Thorndyke laid it down and picked up another, larger fragment, which I had already noticed.

"Here is another example," said he, handing it to our colleague.

"Yes," agreed Hemming. "It is really rather extraordinary. It looks exactly as if it had been sawn across."

"It does," agreed Thorndyke. "What bone should you say it is?"

"That is what I was just asking myself," replied Hemming, looking at the fragment with a sort of half-vexed smile. "It seems ridiculous that a competent anatomist should be in any doubt with as large a portion as this, but really I can't confidently give it a name.

The shape seems to me to suggest a tibia, but of course it is much too small. Is it the upper end of the ulna?"

"I should say no," answered Thorndyke. Then he picked out another of the larger fragments, and handing it to Hemming, asked him to name it.

Our friend began to look somewhat worried.

"It is an extraordinary thing, you know," said he, "but I can't tell you what bone it is part of. It is clearly the shaft of a long bone, but I'm hanged if I can say which. It is too big for a metatarsal and too small for any of the main limb bones. It reminds one of a diminutive thigh bone."

"It does," agreed Thorndyke; "very strongly." While Hemming had been speaking he had picked out four more large fragments, and these he now laid in a row with the one that had seemed to resemble a tibia in shape. Placed thus together, the five fragments bore an obvious resemblance.

"Now," said he, "look at these. There are five of them. They are parts of limb bones, and the bones of which they are parts were evidently exactly alike, excepting that three were apparently from the left side and two from the right. Now, you know, Hemming, a man has only four limbs and of those only two contain similar bones. Then two of them show distinct traces of what looks like a saw-cut."

Hemming gazed at the row of fragments with a frown of deep cogitation.

"It is very mysterious," he said. "And looking at them in a row they strike me as curiously like tibiæ—in shape; not in size."

"The size," said Thorndyke, "is about that of a sheep's tibia."

"A sheep's!" exclaimed Hemming, staring in amazement, first at the calcined bones and then at my colleague.

"Yes; the upper half, sawn across in the middle of the shank."

Hemming was thunderstruck.

"It is an astounding affair!" he exclaimed. "You mean to suggest—"

"I suggest," said Thorndyke, "that there is not a sign of a human bone in the whole collection. But there are very evident traces of at least five legs of mutton."

For a few moments there was a profound silence, broken only by a murmur of astonishment from the cemetery official and a low chuckle from Superintendent Miller, who had been listening with absorbed interest. At length Hemming spoke.

"Then, apparently, there was no corpse in the coffin at all?"

"No," answered Thorndyke. "The weight was made up, and the ashes furnished, by joints of butcher's meat. I dare say, if we go over the ashes carefully, we shall be able to judge what they were. But it is hardly necessary. The presence of five legs of mutton and the absence of a single recognisable fragment of a human skeleton, together with the forged certificates, gives us a pretty conclusive case. The rest, I think we can leave to Superintendent Miller."

"I take it, Thorndyke," said I, as the train moved out of the station, "that you came here expecting to find what you did find?"

"Yes," he replied. "It seemed to me the only possibility, having regard to all the known facts."

"When did it first occur to you?"

"It occurred to me as a possibility as soon as we discovered that the cremation certificates had been forged; but it was the under-taker's statement that seemed to clench the matter."

"But he distinctly stated that he measured the body."

"True. But there was nothing to show that it was a dead body. What was perfectly clear was that there was something that must on no account be seen; and when Stalker told us of the embezzlement we had a body of evidence that could point to only one conclusion. Just consider that evidence.

"Here we had a death, preceded by an obviously sham illness and followed by cremation with forged certificates. Now, what was it that had happened? There were four possible hypotheses. Normal death, suicide, murder, and fictitious death. Which of these hypotheses fitted the facts?

"Normal death was apparently excluded by the forged certificates.

"The theory of suicide did not account for the facts. It did not agree with the careful, elaborate preparation. And why the forged certificates? If Ingle had really died, Meeking would have certified the death. And why the cremation? There was no purpose in taking those enormous risks.

"The theory of murder was unthinkable. These certificates were almost certainly forged by Ingle himself, who we know was a practised forger. But the idea of the victim arranging for his own cremation is an absurdity.

"There remained only the theory of fictitious death; and that theory fitted all the facts perfectly. First, as to the motive. Ingle had committed a felony. He had to disappear. But what kind of disappearance could be so effectual as death and cremation? Both the prosecutors and the police would forthwith write him off and forget him. Then there was the bigamy—a criminal offence in itself. But death would not only wipe that off; after 'death' he could marry Huggard regularly under another name, and he would have shaken off his deserted wife for ever. And he stood to gain fifteen hundred pounds from the Insurance Company. Then see how this theory explained the other facts. A fictitious death made necessary a fictitious illness. It necessitated the forged certificates, since there was no corpse. It made cremation highly desirable; for suspicion might easily have arisen, and then the exhumation of a coffin containing a dummy would have exploded the fraud. But successful cremation would cover up the fraud for ever. It explained the concealment of the corpse from the undertaker, and it even explained the smell of formalin which he noticed."

"How did it?" I asked.

"Consider, Jervis," he replied. "The dummy in this coffin had to be a dummy of flesh and bone which would yield the correct kind of ash. Joints of butcher's meat would fulfil the conditions. But the quantity required would be from a hundred and fifty to two hundred pounds. Now Ingle could not go to the butcher and order a whole sheep to be sent the day before the funeral. The joints would have to be bought gradually and stored. But the storage of meat in warm weather calls for some kind of preservative; and formalin is highly effective, as it leaves no trace after burning.

"So you see that the theory of fictitious death agreed with all the known circumstances, whereas the alternative theories presented inexplicable discrepancies and contradictions. Logically, it was the only possible theory, and, as you have seen, experiment proved it to be the true one."

As Thorndyke concluded, Dr. Hemming took his pipe from his mouth and laughed softly.

"When I came down today," said he, "I had all the facts which you had communicated to the Home Office, and I was absolutely convinced that we were coming to examine a mare's nest. And yet, now I have heard your exposition, the whole thing looks perfectly obvious."

"That is usually the case with Thorndyke's conclusions," said I. "They are perfectly obvious—when you have heard the explanation."

Within a week of our expedition, Ingle was in the hands of the police. The apparent success of the cremation adventure had misled him to a sense of such complete security that he had neglected to cover his tracks, and he had accordingly fallen an easy prey to our friend Superintendent Miller. The police were highly gratified, and so were the directors of the Griffin Life Assurance Company.

AFTER DEATH THE DOCTOR

J. J. Connington

J. J. Connington was the literary alias of Alfred Walter Stewart (1880–1947), a Scottish professor of chemistry who turned to dystopian fiction with *Nordenholt's Millions* (1923), a novel of ecocatastrophe, but soon decided to concentrate on detective stories. His principal sleuth was Sir Clinton Driffield, a tough-minded Chief Constable, and his plots frequently turn on questions of science or technology. Like Austin Freeman, whose work he admired, he was a founder member of the Detection Club.

In his memoir *Alias J. J. Connington*, published in the year of his death, the author mused on the contrast between scientific investigation and detective story writing, concluding that: "There is not the slightest parallelism between these two lines, except that in both a logical mind is required." Warming to his theme, he said that: "In scientific research, the inquirer plays the part of the detective in real life… working from details towards a solution." In contrast, he thought that the detective writer typically began with a preconceived solution to a puzzle, and worked backwards to the details of his plot; this led him to express the view that "the closest likeness to the writing of a detective story is to be found in the composition of a chess-problem". Primarily a novelist rather than a writer of short stories, he contributed "After Death the Doctor" to the *News Chronicle*, and it was subsequently included in *The First Class Omnibus* (1934). The part played in the plot by a contemporary scientific gadget is typical Connington.

"BETTER GO IN, NOW, DOCTOR?" SERGEANT LONGRIDGE SUG-gested. "You'll be here later on?" he added to Jack Sparkford. "I'll have to ask you a few questions then."

It was the sergeant's first murder case, and though outwardly confident, he felt a shade diffident in the presence of the more experienced police surgeon.

Hastily summoned, Longridge had tramped up to the house, breakfastless, planning his procedure as he came. The first thing to do, obviously, was to examine the room and the body, with no outsiders to worry him while he made his notes. It was with some relief that he saw Dr. Shefford's car drive up to the front door as he reached it himself.

Here was the room, with that comfortless and untidy look which rooms have in the morning, before the disorder of the night has been repaired; the chairs set at odd angles, the ashtrays unemptied, the cushions crumpled and awry, a newspaper thrown carelessly on the floor.

It seemed a cross between a sitting-room and an office, with a wireless set, bookcases, filing cabinets, a couple of occasional tables, and a pedestal desk against the wall in one corner. The furniture was good, but shabby like the clothes of a man who has come down in the world.

"Regular old bachelor's den," the doctor observed. "Not a flower anywhere, though they've plenty in the garden."

He put down his bag and went over to the corner of the room. The sergeant was not sensitive, and it cost him no qualms to examine the body of Barnaby Leadburn as it lay back in the office chair before the pedestal desk. A bit weird, he reflected, to see an old gent one knew by sight, lying there with his throat cut.

Dr. Shefford's interest was more professional.

"Not so much blood as I'd have expected," he commented.

His examination of the body became more technical; and Longridge, understanding little of what the doctor was doing, bethought himself that he had a task of his own. He opened his note-book and began to jot down things which seemed important.

The French window was open, but only one of the curtains was drawn back from it. The electric light had been switched off. In the empty grate were some ashes of burnt paper, with printing showing black on the grey background: a piece of newspaper, the sergeant guessed. And when he picked up the newspaper from the floor, he found about a quarter of one of the sheets torn away.

The desk bore a neat array of account-books, and on the open pages of the one nearest the body lay a sheet of note-paper. Longridge, craning over the doctor, read on it the words: *"I, Barnaby Leadburn…"* Then came the regular trail of blotches caused by a pen rolling along the paper; and the pen itself lay on the desk surface to the right of the book.

For some moments Sergeant Longridge puzzled over this sinister hiatus in the manuscript, trying to imagine how the incomplete sentence had been meant to run. At last an idea occurred to him.

"Do you think, sir, that he could have been making his will? I never made a will myself—not worth while, seeing I've nothing to leave—but don't they run: 'I, So-and-so, hereby give and bequeath…' That's how I've heard say."

Dr. Shefford seemed to think that he had enough to do in his own sphere, without entrenching on the sergeant's.

"They usually start by appointing executors," he said dryly. "This looks a very clean cut, sergeant. It might almost have been done with a razor, from the look of it."

"How long do you think he's been dead, sir?" Longridge inquired, glancing at his watch.

Dr. Shefford shrugged his shoulders rather impatiently.

"He probably died round about midnight, I should guess; but it's no use pretending that you can tell to a minute from medical evidence alone. Things vary far too much for that. Hadn't you better hunt about and see if you can find the weapon it was done with, if it happens to be in the room?"

The sergeant's feelings were ruffled by this reflection on his zeal and efficiency.

"Well, sir, if you'll stand aside for a moment, I'll have a look with my flashlamp in the well of the desk. I don't see any weapon lying about anywhere else."

Dr. Shefford stood aside; and the sergeant, cautiously grovelling with his flash-lamp, explored the cavity under the desk. An exclamation of triumph told the doctor that something had been found.

"Here's what it was done with, sir. Look! That's a rummy sort of knife. I'll fetch it out."

Gingerly he picked up the weapon and placed it on the desk: a stout blade four or five inches long embedded in a straight wooden handle, with a steel lever at the side.

"It's the sort of knife artists use for cutting mill-board or for trimming prints," the doctor explained. "You can alter the amount of blade that sticks out of the handle by setting that steel catch on the side. I rather wondered how that wound was made, but this evidently did it, to judge by the blood on the blade. By the way, sergeant, you'd better inquire if the old man was left-handed. This gash has been made from right to left, by the look of it. If old Leadburn was right-handed, then it isn't suicide. And you might ask if the light was on or off this morning. Suicides aren't usually so economical as to switch off before they put their own light out. Though, from what I've heard, old Leadburn was mean enough to have taken the precaution."

"Very good, sir," the sergeant agreed. "And now, sir, I think I'll leave you and make some inquiries from the house people."

"Just pull the curtains before you go, and switch on the lights. It's hardly decent to carry on further in full view of anyone who happens to cross the lawn."

Jack Sparkford and his younger brother, Sydney, were in the hall as the sergeant emerged from the room. Between Jack, at twenty-five, and the fifteen-year-old schoolboy, the family likeness was unmistakable even down to the weakly obstinate chins.

"They look bothered, but not just tearful," Longridge reflected. "Not much wonder, either, if old Leadburn was the tartar he got the name of being. They hadn't the lives of dogs, if all tales were true."

"Have you found anything?" Jack demanded anxiously.

The sergeant put up his hand defensively.

"One thing at a time, sir. We've got no facts yet. I'd like to see the maid who discovered the…"

"Ring for Hart, Sydney," Jack ordered. "We'd better go in here. No use interviewing her in the hall."

In a few moments a young, rather good-looking housemaid appeared, evidently in a very shaken state of nerves.

"Your name's Jenny Hart, isn't it?" demanded the sergeant. "Tell me just how you came to discover Mr. Leadburn this morning."

The girl seemed taken aback by this official tone from a person with whom she already had a nodding acquaintance.

"It was this way," she explained nervously. "I went into that room about seven o'clock to clear it up and set things to rights."

"Was the electric light on?"

"No. So the first thing I did was to go and draw the curtains back from the window, and when I'd drawn the first one, I saw Mr. Leadburn lying there in his blood on the chair, and I screamed and ran out of the room."

"Was the French window open when you drew the curtain?"

"Yes, it was. It must have stood open all night. Mr. Leadburn always liked to have it open, but he used to shut it when he went up to bed, last thing."

The sergeant could think of no further questions to ask the maid just then, so he dismissed her and turned to the two nephews of Barnaby Leadburn.

"Did anything out of the common—sounds or what not—attract your attention in the night?" he asked Jack Sparkford.

Jack shook his head.

"I went up to my room about eleven o'clock," he explained. "My uncle was busy with his accounts and so forth. I heard nothing suspicious."

"And you, sir?" Longridge inquired, turning to Sydney.

"I heard nothing inside the house," the boy answered at once. "But I heard Cæsar—that's our big retriever, you know—I heard him give a long howl, a funny sort of noise, about twenty past twelve. I never heard him make a noise like that before—a kind of howl, very long-drawn-out."

"How do you know it was twenty past twelve then?" demanded the sergeant sceptically.

"Because the down express passed almost immediately afterwards. It goes through at 12.25. I was kept awake part of the night with toothache, you see. And, by the way," he added, "I haven't seen Cæsar this morning."

"You'd better get hold of him," Jack said at once, "he might do damage to somebody if he's left on the loose."

"Savage, is he?" inquired the sergeant, who had heard some rumours about the dog.

"A bit nasty with everybody barring ourselves, I'm afraid," Jack admitted. "My brother Timothy's the only outsider he takes to. Even the gardener at the lodge is in terror of him. Cæsar hates him for some reason or other. My uncle had him let loose in the grounds at night. Nobody would dare to come a-burgling here with Cæsar off the chain. It would be as much as his life was worth."

"What the girl said about open windows is right?" inquired Longridge.

"Oh, yes. We've all got a tendency to consumption in our family. My brother Timothy's in a bad way with it. Naturally we believe in fresh air, and my uncle was all for open windows."

"H'm!" said Longridge. "Now about this dog, sir. Had your uncle any enemies, that he kept a savage dog about the place at night?"

"Not that I know of," Jack replied frankly enough.

Something in Sydney's expression caught the sergeant's eye, and he put the same question to the boy.

"I don't know about enemies," Sydney answered doubtfully. "He had a bit of a row with Corfe—that's our gardener—last night. Something to do with our housemaid, Hart. I heard the two of them slanging each other and Corfe seemed a bit above himself with rage. He's engaged to Hart, you know. Something about my uncle accusing her of stealing. I couldn't help hearing some of it, but I didn't listen on purpose. It was in the garden."

Sergeant Longridge veiled his interest in this new piece of evidence by changing the subject. He described the knife and asked if it belonged to anyone in the house.

"Oh, yes, it's mine," Sydney admitted promptly. "It always lies on the desk, in there. I use it for trimming the white edges off my Kodak prints."

"Oh, it's your knife and it always lies on the desk," Sergeant Longridge repeated mechanically, as he noted the facts in his book. "Thanks. Now another question, Mr. Sparkford. Did any visitors call on your uncle last night?"

"Visitors? Not that I know of," Jack answered. "Unless you call my brother Timothy a visitor. He came in after dinner and left again about ten o'clock. I saw him down to the road then. His eyesight's bad, and I went with him down the short cut to save him stumbling about in the dark."

"He left at ten p.m.," noted the sergeant. "Have you notified him about the death, sir?"

"Yes, I rang him up. But he was sick, last night; he had to call a doctor in the small hours, he told me. Probably he's a bit shaky this morning and hasn't felt up to coming over here yet."

"He lives across the railway, I think?"

Longridge's question was merely formal. He knew Timothy Sparkford by sight and reputation; but he believed in getting "the evidence of a witness" to put down in his notes.

"Yes, he lives in Moss Cottage," Jack replied.

"I remember, sir. He moved over there after he had a bit of luck in the Sweep, didn't he? By the way, your uncle didn't seem nervous about anything when you saw him last night?"

Jack shook his head decidedly.

"Nothing of that sort, not a sign of it."

"Nothing missing, that you've noticed, sir? No valuables gone, or a safe opened?"

"Nothing whatever in that line, so far as I know. There's no safe in the house. He kept everything in the bank."

"I see, sir. Now I think I'd like to have your maid back again just to ask her a question or two more."

But when Hart was summoned, they learned that she had left the house, apparently to talk to the gardener; and it was a few minutes before she came back. When she reappeared the sergeant interviewed her alone.

"Now, my girl," he began in his most paternal tone, "you don't want to be keeping anything back in a bad case like this. It wouldn't do. People would begin to think there was something wrong, you see, if you did that. So just tell me what this bit of trouble was that you had with old Mr. Leadburn."

At the question, the prim maidservant vanished and in her stead a virago appeared, furious, bitter, and yet uneasy.

"If anybody says I stole anything, they're taking away my character, and I'll have the law on them," she burst out breathlessly.

"The truth of it is, I was dusting his desk and I happened to pull open a drawer, and a note dropped out, and I picked it up, and I was standing there with it in my hand when he came in. He'd been out there in the garden, sneaking behind the bushes, watching me through the window.

"Spying on me! That's a nice occupation for a man with thousands a year, I don't think! I wouldn't demean myself so. And then he swore I'd stolen the note, and he'd been missing money for some time, for he kept a good check on it, which was like his mean, miserly ways. And I said I'd never touched a penny of any money in the house, and *he* said he was going to send for the police and see I was jailed for it, for he knew to a penny how much I'd taken—fancy!

"And I went and told Simmy—my boy, he is, and we're going to be married in three months. And Simmy was real angry, as who wouldn't be, and he went and told Mr. Leadburn straight just what he thought about it, and then Mr. Leadburn said he'd have no thieves on his premises and if Simmy married me he could look out for another job, for he wouldn't be kept on at the lodge.

"And Simmy was angry, of course, for with things as they are nowadays it's not likely he'd get another job, and so we wouldn't be able to get married after all. And they got to words about it, and you can't wonder at Simmy, and that's the plain truth. You can ask Simmy and see if it isn't."

"I see," said Longridge non-committally, when the torrent ceased. "Quite so."

He had a shrewd idea that most likely there had been faults on both sides in that affair; but he had no desire to start inquiring into petty larceny in the midst of a murder case. He noted that there had been bad feeling between the gardener and his employer.

"Now, tell me," he went on, "did you see anything that might throw light on this business?"

The girl seemed to realise that she might have done more harm than good by her outbreak, and when she spoke again, it was in a cooler tone.

"I happened to be going through the hall last night; about half-past nine or so, it was: and I heard them at it, hammer and tongs, in that room. It was about Mr. Jack's engagement and an extra allowance for him to get married on. Mr. Timothy was there, and the old man was as mad as a hornet at the idea and wouldn't hear of it. And he seemed to be threatening Mr. Timothy, too, for I heard something about 'discreditable doings', and you know what Mr. Timothy is.

"They were fair shouting at each other. That old man seemed to have a fair down on people getting married: Simmy and me, first of all, and then Mr. Jack and his girl. And he didn't seem to like the other thing any better, neither, if you go by the way he was storming at Mr. Timothy. One would think he expected everyone to live like monks and nuns."

"A bad quarrel, it sounded like?"

"Oh, of course they were always quarrelling, if it comes to that," Jenny answered. "What else would you expect, with that old skinflint holding on to the cash and doling it out to grown men as if they were kids? It wasn't a happy household, as you might say."

"No, I suppose not," Longridge agreed. "Now, just another question. Was Mr. Leadburn left-handed?"

"Not he," Jenny replied. Then, after a pause, she added, "It's Mr. Timothy that's left-handed. Was that what you meant? What do you want to know for?"

The sergeant was saved from answering by the hasty entrance of Sydney Sparkford, evidently in a state of excitement.

"We've found Cæsar!" he exclaimed breathlessly. "He's dead, poor old dog! Poisoned, by the look of him. You'd better come and see him for yourself. He's in the shrubbery close to my bedroom window. That's why his howl waked me up, I expect, coming from so near at hand."

Longridge followed the boy to the shrubbery, where they found Jack Sparkford before them, staring thoughtfully at the dead dog. The sergeant got the impression that its end gave him more regret than the loss of his uncle seemed to do.

"What do you make of this?" he demanded, as they approached.

Longridge went down on his knees and examined the dog which, even in death, looked a formidable brute. As he bent close, the merest whiff of a familiar odour came to his keen nostrils: the scent of bitter almonds.

"This'll be a job for the vet, sir," he said, tacitly admitting his own lack of expert knowledge. "I'll just have a look round, though."

He ferreted about for some minutes without success, but at last he discovered the thing for which he had been searching: a piece of raw liver. By holding it close to his nose he managed to detect the faint smell of bitter almonds from it also.

"That's how it was done, sir," he explained in triumph, holding out the meat to Jack. "Just you smell it, sir: same smell as the dog's mouth has."

Jack evidently disdained a personal verification; but Sydney eagerly sniffed first at the dog and then at the liver.

"I know what it is!" he declared jubilantly. "Cyanide, that's what it smells of. Just the same as the stuff in my butterfly killing-bottle."

The sight of the dead retriever had led Longridge to revise some of his ideas abruptly. "An outside job" was his new verdict. The dog had been friendly with the house people, and with Timothy Sparkford.

Any one of them could have got at old Leadburn without this huge brute interfering. But an outsider would need to dispose of it before he could penetrate to its master. Cyanide? Well, that should be an easy enough poison to trace. You had to sign for that at the druggist's before you got it.

He was stirred from his musing by the approach of a fresh figure: Timothy Sparkford, whom the sergeant knew by sight. He came forward with the hesitating walk of a man suffering from very defective vision, and as he reached the group he peered closely at each face before he greeted his brothers.

With his shambling gait, low stature, powerful physique, and deep-set eyes, he had something about him which contrasted sharply with the appearance of his younger brothers; and when he spoke, it was with a certain truculence.

"Who's this?" he demanded, after he had scrutinised the sergeant at close quarters.

"It's Sergeant Longridge, Tim," Jack explained. "I rang up the police before I got on to you on the phone."

Timothy acknowledged the introduction with a casual nod.

"Has the old geezer kicked the bucket?" he asked brutally. "Best news I've had in a month of Sundays. No use being mealy-mouthed about these things, is there? No flowers, by request. That's the right spirit in this case."

The ribald tone made Longridge prick up his ears, and it occurred to him suddenly that not one of the people he had questioned had shown the slightest regret for Barnaby Leadburn's death. They had not vented their spite like Timothy, but their restraint had been almost equally significant. They had not thought it worth while to pay even a tribute of hypocrisy to his memory.

"Sorry I couldn't get over sooner," Timothy went on. "When I got home last night I started some electro-plating, and in the middle of it I got the most frightful attack of gripes and sickness. Must have been the remains of some shrimp paste I had for supper. Been left open too long, I suspect. Ptomaine poisoning, likely. Anyhow, after the bout I had, I could barely crawl to the phone and ring up Dr. Ackworth. He came along, not over-pleased at being dragged out at half-past twelve, I gathered. All he did, when he arrived, was to stand around and let nature take its course. Anyhow, it's over now, and I feel a bit better. Still a bit shaky though."

Then, completely ignoring the sergeant, he took his brother's arm.

"Come along and tell me all about it."

Longridge was going to call him back and question him when on the drive he saw the police surgeon beckoning to him. He hurried off, leaving Sydney to join his brothers.

"Oh, sergeant," Dr. Shefford said when they met. "You can rub one notion off your slate. This affair wasn't suicide. He was strangled first of all, and then his throat was cut to hide the marks of the cord. At least, so one may suppose. That's why he made no noise when he died. And, naturally, with the heart stopped, he didn't bleed as much as one might have expected from the wound. There'll be an inquest, of course. There'll have to be some arrangements made for a p.m., I expect."

"Very good, sir."

Sergeant Longridge's investigations lasted longer than he had expected, but a couple of days later he was summoned—not for the first time—to give an account of his stewardship to Inspector Dronfield. The inspector was deep in a study of various documents, and he rubbed his eyes wearily as Longridge presented himself. He was a tall man who concealed a natural alertness behind an air of lassitude.

"Not clear yet?" he grumbled. "Suppose we take it step by step. Systematically, I mean. Must have been either an inside or an outside job. That's obvious. Insiders first. Not the cook?"

Sergeant Longridge shook his head. That suggestion was absurd.

"No. She's got a first-class character and she's only been in that place a couple of months. She hasn't had time to raise a grievance big enough to account for the job."

"The maid, Hart, then?"

"I don't somehow see her strangling the old man and then cutting his throat," the sergeant declared. "She might, but it's not my idea of her."

The inspector made a non-committal noise.

"Hardly sounds like the schoolboy, either," he confessed, "though one never knows what some kids may get up to in these days. That leaves Jack Sparkford as a possible."

He picked up a document from the table.

"Your stuff about the family's all gossip. Still, it seems pretty sound. I've had it checked up. Old Leadburn did get round his widowed sister before she died, and he drafted her will for her. She trusted him, it seems.

"Here's a copy of the will. Got it from Somerset House. Leadburn was to draw the income from the estate—about four thousand pounds a year—until the youngest son reached twenty-one. Then the four of them were to divide the capital in equal shares. Meanwhile, Leadburn was to allow each of them annually a sum equal to his own personal expenditure for the year. I suppose she thought that meant a very comfortable income for each of them.

"What happened was that he turned out to be a miserly old skinflint who lived on about a pound a week himself, and he paid his nephews at the same rate. Shows how the best intentions may go wrong. And he wouldn't let them take up any trade or profession.

"Coming into a thousand pounds a year apiece, later on, they didn't need it, he said. Then there's a clause about any of them forfeiting all rights if he contests the will. Another clause allowing Leadburn to disqualify any of them for 'discreditable conduct'. No definition given."

"Fairly had 'em by the short hairs," the sergeant admitted. "No wonder they disliked him."

"Must have been feathering his nest to the tune of over three thousand pounds a year," the inspector pointed out. "He pocketed the surplus each year. Nice little nest-egg for his old age. And this arrangement had still five or six years to run. The youngster's only fifteen."

He thought for a moment or two, then put a question.

"That girl of Jack Sparkford's; has she any money?"

"Not a stiver," the sergeant declared emphatically. "She's as poor as a church mouse. I fished that out quite definitely."

"So Jack Sparkford would have to wait six years before he could get into double harness. H'm! And now he can get spliced tomorrow, if he wants to. Possible motive there," the inspector concluded thoughtfully "He was in the house, handy, that night. And there was that quarrel the maid overheard, on this very point of an extra allowance. H'm! Put a query against his name, I think. That finishes the insiders."

"The outsiders are Timothy Sparkford, Corfe, and some person or persons unknown," Sergeant Longridge suggested, entering into the spirit of systematic inquiry.

"What about Timothy Sparkford then? Why doesn't he live with the rest of them?"

"He won two or three hundred last year on a share in a Sweep ticket," Longridge explained. "As soon as he got that money he cleared out and went to live by himself in a cottage in Moor End Road, across the railway from Leadburn's place, with the sidings in between. I don't blame him; I'd have cleared out myself if I'd been in his shoes. It was no life for a man of thirty, under the thumb of old Leadburn."

He paused momentarily and then added: "A bad lad, Timothy. Wine and women; a short life and a gay one: that's his motto. He's got consumption, poor beggar! and Leadburn wouldn't pay for sanatorium treatment in the early stages; said he didn't believe in it.

Just a fad, by his way of it. So he saved money. Timothy didn't love his uncle much; I could see that with half an eye."

The inspector looked up sharply.

"'Wine and women', eh? That fits in with the talk about discreditable doings that the maid heard. And 'discreditable conduct' are the words in the will. Old Leadburn must have been threatening to disqualify Timothy. That meant one less to share in the capital in the final divvy-up. Something in that, perhaps."

"He's got an alibi though," the sergeant pointed out. "He called in Dr. Ackworth, just as he told me. I've checked that. Still," he added ruminatively, "alibis aren't always sound. And he bought liver that morning. He fetches his own stuff from the butcher, living alone as he does.

"The butcher remembered him buying liver that day; and the dog was poisoned with liver. But Corfe bought liver, too, that day—so I fished out from his butcher. I wonder the dog would touch stuff with that smell on it; but it seems they fed it only in the morning—it being a watchdog—so probably it was ready to bolt anything by the time it came to midnight."

"Most likely," the inspector concurred. "But why should Timothy want to poison his own family dog which wouldn't interfere with him?"

"Corfe's more likely for that," the sergeant admitted. "And I've fished out that Corfe bought some cyanide that evening. I've seen the entry he signed in the poison-book of the druggist who sold it to him. And Corfe's coat was torn a bit when I saw him on the morning of the murder. The dog hated him, so they say. But he swore then that he'd gone to bed at ten and never waked up till the morning."

"He lied then," said the inspector. "Somebody saw a light in the lodge-room about midnight. Got a note of it here. You told him to call in just now, didn't you? See if he's turned up and we'll put him through it."

In a minute or two the sergeant returned with Corfe. The gardener had the coarse looks and powerful physique of a fine animal, but not altogether a good-natured one. Something in the eyes suggested a dangerous temper which might break out suddenly and furiously, though at this moment he seemed sullen and uneasy rather than angry.

"We want more information than you gave the sergeant, Corfe," the inspector began abruptly. "First of all, how did you get that tear in your jacket?"

"Caught it on a nail and tore it," Corfe declared sullenly.

"A nail doesn't make that shape of tear in cloth," retorted the inspector. "What had you for supper on the night of the murder?"

Corfe pondered for some seconds before answering, as though he were weighing alternatives.

"Sausages," he said at last.

"So you had the raw liver in the house? You bought liver at the butcher's that day."

Corfe had the wit to see the trend of this. Cæsar had been poisoned with raw liver. He corrected himself clumsily.

"My mistake. It was liver I had for supper, now I think of it. I ate the lot."

"What did you buy cyanide for?" the inspector continued.

This time the answer came promptly enough.

"To kill rats with. They're in my chicken run."

"Dangerous stuff to have lying about," commented Dronfield. "Could the dog have got at it?"

"No, it was inside my fence. I put it at the rats' holes, not in the run, of course. I'm not a fool."

"You are, in some ways," Dronfield said acidly. "Look here, my man, I advise you to tell the truth. It'll do you less harm than the lies you've given us. That's a plain warning. We know a bit more than you think. You'd better come across."

Corfe shifted uneasily from one foot to the other as he digested this advice. He was so long in making up his mind that the inspector grew suspicious.

"You needn't start making up a yarn," he said sharply. "If you're going to tell the truth, it won't need any thinking over. Come along now."

Corfe pondered for a few moments longer. Then he seemed to have his story ready.

"This was the way of it," he began hesitatingly, like a man not too sure of his ground. "After the row I had with that old blackguard Leadburn, I had to have a talk with Jenny, naturally. But when I went for to see her, she was busy with their dinner and we couldn't get more than a word.

"I do a bit of jobbing work in the evenings to make some extra money, and I had to go to Mr. Rigg's in Broomhill Drive, and I didn't expect to be back till after ten. Old Leadburn wouldn't have a maid outside his door after ten o'clock. So I slipped a word to Jenny to be at the window in the hall upstairs at midnight and I'd come up, so as to have a talk with her about things. I thought I'd be able to get up on a bit of wall there, and keep clear of the damned dog. I was about beyond caring about dogs, then, in the state of mind I was in.

"So when I got back from Broomhill Drive I hung about a bit, waiting till it was time, and then I went up for to see her. But the dog beat me. I took a stick with me; but stick or no stick, it near had me down. It tore my coat for me and I had to give up. If I'd managed to get past it, it'd have raised Cain anyhow, barking, and had the house all awake. Lucky it fought quiet, so there was no row, barring the growling, and that roused nobody. But I had to turn back and go home to the lodge. And that's the plain truth, believe it or not."

"Did you see a light in the room with the French window?" the inspector asked, without commenting on Corfe's statement.

"The curtains were drawn, but the light was burning."

"When was that?"

"I went up just before twelve o'clock, as I told you," Corfe declared. "Just as I was going to bed, after I got home, I heard the express pass. That's twelve twenty-five."

"Very well," said Dronfield. "That'll do for the present."

He dismissed Corfe, and in a few minutes the sergeant ushered Jenny Hart into the room.

"You're quite sure about those things you told the sergeant?" was the inspector's opening. "About the quarrel amongst the three men on the night of the murder?"

"I heard them at it."

"You heard something about an allowance? And Mr. Leadburn said something about 'discreditable doings'? Sure of that?"

"That's what I heard."

"The murder took place at midnight. Where were you then?"

"Sitting in the upstairs hall, waiting for Simmy. He said he'd come if he could get past the dog."

"Hear anything while you were there?"

"Yes. Cæsar gave a funny howl—sort of like a squeaking balloon it was, only louder, of course. Long-drawn-out sort of noise. And I was afraid, a bit, about Simmy. I waited for a while in case he turned up. When he didn't, and I heard the express go past, I took it that Simmy wouldn't be up that night, so I went to bed."

"Any bedrooms on that floor, opening off the hall?"

"Master Sydney's room opens off it on one side and Mr. Jack's on the other."

"Moonlight night, wasn't it? Notice if the bedroom doors were shut?"

"Master Sydney's was. Mr. Jack's was open. I thought he hadn't gone to bed. When I passed his door I saw his bed hadn't been slept in."

"So Jack Sparkford was out of his room until past midnight," the inspector mused, after Jenny had been dismissed. "That's a bit of fresh news. And that little piece seemed to be speaking the truth then, which is more than Corfe did. Let's think it over again. Start with what we've got."

The sergeant checked over the facts on his fingers.

"There's the dog poisoned with cyanide; and the raw liver; and the knife; and the unfinished writing; and the burned newspaper; and the left-handed cut in his throat; and the tear in Corfe's coat; and Jack Sparkford up until the small hours; and the quarrels, of course," he ended rather vaguely.

"That seems the lot," Dronfield agreed. "Well, it wasn't either of the maids. The cook has no motive; and Jenny Hart could get Corfe to do the job sooner than do it herself—unless they were both in it together."

"The boy had cyanide in his butterfly bottle, and he knew about the knife being on the table," the sergeant suggested.

"He'd no motive and no raw liver," the inspector objected impatiently.

"There's Corfe. He's been telling a pack of lies and he did get his coat torn by the dog that night. And he'd both liver and cyanide in hand. And *he* had a motive, right enough."

"Leave him aside for a moment. See how the rest of them stand."

"There's Timothy Sparkford," Longridge suggested rather doubt-fully. "I'd have put my shirt on him as the one that did it. He's got the temper for it, or I'm a Dutchman. If old Leadburn meant to use that clause about discreditable conduct against him, Timothy was going to be cut out altogether after waiting so long for his share. There's motive enough. And the bit of writing might be something about the cutting-out that Timothy just stopped in time. And the left-handed cut fits him, with his left-handedness. And the burnt newspaper may have been a bit that he used to wrap round the handle of the knife to keep his finger-prints off it; and he had to burn the paper afterwards on the same account."

"Anybody might have done the same," the inspector objected. "That doesn't fit Timothy specially."

"Then he bought some liver that day," Longridge continued, disregarding the interruption. "In fact, as I say, I'd have put my shirt on him. Only, it won't wash," he added regretfully.

"Are you so sure as all that?" the inspector demanded.

"It won't work," Longridge insisted. "You know the lie of the land about the house. To get from it to Timothy's cottage you've got to cross the railway. There's two bridges: one a quarter of a mile north of the house, and t'other one half a mile to the south. That makes it either half a mile or a mile by road from door to door.

"The dog was poisoned at 12.20 a.m. Besides, what would he poison the dog for, seeing he could walk past it without bother, seeing it was friendly? Well, it was poisoned at twelve-twenty. Then there was some time spent in doing the murder itself—ten minutes, at least, and likely longer. That makes it 12.30 a.m. before Timothy could start off home again.

"But it was just about half-past twelve when he rang up Dr. Ackworth from his cottage; and the doctor got there very soon afterwards to find him ghastly sick. I've seen Dr. Ackworth and them's the facts. Besides, he couldn't have got across either bridge without being seen, as it happens. The road was up at the north bridge, and there was a watchman on all night who swears that between eleven and two o'clock nobody passed him, barring a tall, slim young fellow in plus-fours, bare-headed, and wearing a white scarf.

"'That won't fit Timothy. He's short, with a figure like a gorilla. On t'other bridge there was a motorist in trouble, kept there for over an hour between eleven-thirty and twelve-thirty o'clock, fixing something under a street lamp. He and his passenger are certain nobody passed, bar one man: the same cove in the white scarf. He stopped to ask if he could lend a hand. That was about a quarter-past twelve, they say. Timothy's easy remembered, and he wasn't seen at either bridge."

"Well, what was to hinder him going straight across the railway line, making a bee-line from house to cottage?"

"It won't work," Longridge protested in an aggrieved tone. "Timothy suffers from something they call comical cornea. He's as blind as a bat, even on a bright moonlight night like that one.

"Now look how the land lies. There's a rock cutting from the one bridge to the station. He couldn't have climbed down that rock face and up t'other side, not with his sight. It's impossible; let alone there isn't the time. He couldn't get into the station. It's locked up at that time of night, and it's a solid block of building on the lip of the cutting. You can't get at the stair down to the platform without breaking in the door of the ticket-office. He didn't go that way.

"Beyond the station, just opposite the house, there's a barbed-wire fence on level ground, and a mass of sidings filled with odd trucks standing, and beyond the sidings there's another stiff fence on the Moss Cottage side of the line.

"I might be able to get across by that route in ten minutes myself, though it would be quick work: but a man with Timothy's comical cornea simply couldn't come near that time. He'd be absolutely lost among the trucks, let alone that he couldn't shin over the fences like a normal man who could see what he was doing.

"I've been over the ground myself. He simply couldn't have managed it. And farther north, beyond the sidings, there's another rock-cutting, sheer in the sides, that would take a man with all his sight to get down. No half-blind man did that job, you can take it from me."

"H'm!" said the inspector, convinced by this evidence, "then that leaves Jack Sparkford. But he doesn't fit in anyhow. It's his own dog, so he needn't be afraid of it interfering with him. Besides, he's in the house already and doesn't need to pass the dog."

"He had a motive," the sergeant insisted. "If old Leadburn was out of the way he could marry the girl. Maybe he was putting the screw on the old man and went a bit too far—killed him without actually planning to do it.

"Making him write out, 'I hereby agree to give Jack Sparkford an allowance fit to marry on,' or something of that sort. That would fit the facts. And he *was* up and about, late that night, by the girl's evidence. He kept his thumb on *that* bit when he was giving his own account of things."

"We'll go over and see him now," the inspector decided, after a glance at his watch. "Don't like his keeping back information this way. Not good enough."

They found Jack Sparkford at home, and after the sergeant had introduced his superior, the inspector opened the matter with his usual bluntness.

"You told Sergeant Longridge that you went up to bed at 11 p.m.

on the night of Mr. Leadburn's death, sir. Was that a slip, by any chance? Would you like to correct it?"

Jack seemed taken aback by this suggestion.

"What do you mean?" he demanded, rather uncertainly.

"You went up to bed about eleven," the inspector conceded. "But did you get into bed?"

Jack seemed to be all on the alert.

"What I said was perfectly accurate," he insisted. "I went upstairs at eleven o'clock."

"Yes, yes," said the inspector testily. "But what did you do after that? You didn't go to bed immediately. What were you doing?"

Jack paused for a moment or two, then he seemed to come to a decision.

"You seem to know something. I've nothing to conceal, so I'll be quite frank with you. I'd had a row with my uncle, a private matter, nothing to do with his death. He wouldn't come round to my view. It was an important matter to me. I saw my brother part of the way home when he left at ten o'clock. Then I came back again and tried to persuade my uncle again.

"It was no use; he was quite set in his view. So I went upstairs at eleven o'clock. I was worried, very worried, when I got up to my room. I knew it was no good going to bed, I'd never have slept. I sat about in my room for a while, about an hour, I should guess, thinking. Then I came downstairs and went out of the house. I wanted to walk off my troubles."

"What time was that?" the inspector demanded.

"I didn't look at my watch."

"How were you dressed?"

"Plus-fours—the same as I have on now. And I put on a white scarf because I'd had a touch of sore throat that day."

Jack unconsciously clinched the matter with his next words.

"I remember one thing that may help you," he added with something like a sneer. "On the bridge beyond the station I came across a fellow under a street lamp with a twelve-six Austin car. He'd been caught with a puncture with his spare wheel out of action. He'd patched up the puncture with a portable vulcaniser, put his wheel on again, and just as I got up he found the nail had gone through both sides of his inner tube, and he had missed the second hole when he had it down. He was just starting to take it off the wheel a second time when I passed him and offered to give him a hand. If you can get hold of him, he'll identify me, I expect. It must have been round about midnight when I had my talk with him."

"Which way did you come home again?" the inspector asked.

"By the other bridge. I don't know when I got in, certainly long after midnight."

"Did you see any light in the room with the French window as you came back?"

"No, not that I remember. I didn't look particularly. I'd left my uncle making up his accounts."

"You didn't see the dog Cæsar?"

"I saw him on my way out. He went part of the way down to the gate with me, and then I ordered him home. I didn't see him on my way back, but I thought nothing of that. By the way, I remember that the fellow with the Austin car glanced at his watch once while I was with him. He may remember what time it was, then, if you're really interested."

"Can you suggest any explanation of the uncompleted document your uncle was writing that night?" inquired Dronfield.

Jack shook his head.

"I haven't the faintest idea."

The inspector, quite satisfied, withdrew along with his subordinate. As they walked together down the drive, the sergeant broke silence.

"That's the lot of them cleared, if you take the evidence as sound."

"Corfe's story's unsupported except by that girl of his; and her evidence doesn't tell us what he really did," objected Dronfield. "It's on the cards that the two of them were in it, and just cooked up a yarn between them."

"Might be that," the sergeant agreed, thoughtfully.

"I've got to hurry off now," Dronfield said, with a glance at his watch. "I'll just save that appointment and no more."

"Merely a slight attack of conjunctivitis," the specialist assured Inspector Dronfield. "Nothing to worry about, though it's been a nuisance to you, I expect. I'll write you a prescription for some eye-drops."

He went over to his writing-table and jotted down something on a sheet of paper.

Meanwhile the inspector, left to himself, let his eyes wander over the various appliances of the oculist's armoury: the box of lenses, the ophthalmoscope, the perimeter, the astigmometer, and the case of test types with its concealed lamp. Finally his glance fell upon something which puzzled him by its very simplicity: a little disc, concentrically ringed like a target, with a hole where the bull's-eye should have been, and furnished with a handle like a lorgnette.

The inspector was the last patient on that day's list; and the oculist was a man who liked to relax after his work was done. As he came back with his completed prescription, he noticed Dronfield's interest in the little instrument.

"Looking at the Placido's disc?" he inquired with a smile. "I'll give you three guesses and see if you can spot what we use it for."

"I was just wondering, but I didn't get to the length of guessing," the inspector confessed. "It's beyond me. What *is* its use?"

"It's for diagnosing conical cornea," the specialist explained, picking it up as he spoke.

The inspector became alert. Conical cornea! Of course, that was what the sergeant had misheard and turned into "comical cornea". The trouble with Timothy Sparkford's eyesight. The inspector decided that there would be no harm in hearing more about that subject.

"Could you explain it, sir?" he asked, with obvious interest. "What *is* conical cornea?"

"It's a malformation of the eye. You know what the cornea is? The transparent covering at the front of the eyeball. In the normal eye, it's roughly spherical, and it acts as part of the mechanism of sight. If it's misshapen—conical in form instead of spherical—it distorts vision. Unfortunately you can't correct the distortion with spectacles."

"Not even with special spectacles? I see. And where does the little target-thing come in, sir?"

"It shows up the defect at once. I bring it up to the patient's eye, target side towards him. The rings are reflected in his cornea, as if it were a convex mirror; and by looking through his hole where the bull's-eye should be, I can examine the reflection. If he's got conical cornea, the reflection's distorted in a peculiar way that's recognisable at a glance. Very neat, isn't it?"

"Very neat indeed," the inspector acquiesced. "And you can't cure it with spectacles?"

"No, spectacles are of no use. In fact, until lately, it's been hopeless."

"Until lately?" demanded the inspector sharply. "You mean it can be cured now?"

The oculist leaned over and opened a box which lay on his table.

"Curiously enough, I had a patient here today to be tested for these things. They're what are called 'contact glasses'."

He showed Dronfield a series of tiny objects, almost hemispherical in form and made from glass so thin that they seemed the most fragile things Dronfield had seen.

"The idea is this," the oculist went on. "The essence of the trouble is that the outer surface of the patient's cornea is conical instead of spherical. Fill one of these little glass cups with saline solution and slip it under the eyelids, above and below. It sticks to the eyeball by surface tension, and the salt water fills up the gap between eye and glass.

"The net result is that you've now got a glass outer surface to your eyeball, and that new surface is shaped just like a normal cornea. You've merged the defective conical surface into a system with the same refractive index... but perhaps that's getting a bit too technical for you."

"And a man wearing one of these gadgets sees as well as a normal person?"

"So far as his conical cornea goes, yes. And what's more, no one would ever imagine that the patient was wearing anything. It's not like spectacles. These contact glasses, once they're in place, are almost unnoticeable, unless you've been told to look for them."

"I suppose they take some getting in, though?"

The oculist shook his head.

"Not a bit of it! The patient can do that for himself; insert them in the morning and take them out again when he goes to bed, if he wishes. They hardly cause the wearer any discomfort."

"I see, sir. That's wonderful. Very interesting indeed, sir. I'd no notion things of that sort were possible. And now I mustn't detain you any longer. This the prescription? Thank you, sir."

And with as much haste as courtesy allowed, the inspector bowed himself out of the consulting-room. His first call was at a druggist's, where he asked one or two questions. Then he returned to his headquarters and summoned Sergeant Longridge.

"We've got the Leadburn murderer at last," he said, as his subordinate entered the room.

"Can you prove it?" the sergeant asked sceptically. "Who is it?"

"I think so, if we've any luck in a search of the premises after we arrest him. It's Timothy Sparkford."

"But the thing's flat impossible," Longridge protested. "I've checked all the evidence to the last dot, in his case, because at the start I was dead sure he was the man we wanted. Even if you leave out his sight—and that makes the affair impossible in itself—the times won't fit. Nohow. See here. The dog was poisoned at 12.20 a.m.

"After that, he had to do the murder, get away, climb a fence, cross the siding, climb the other fence, and get to his cottage, all by 12.30 a.m., for he telephoned to Dr. Ackworth about that time. I've timed myself over that course, going as hard as I could, and it took me nine minutes from door to door. Where's the time required for murdering old Leadburn?

"Besides, Timothy had eaten some bad tinned stuff that evening and was deathly sick. We've Ackworth's evidence for that. A man as sick as all that simply couldn't commit a murder neatly and then do all the gymnastics required to get home in double-quick time, let alone he's as blind as a bat."

"You can wash out the 'blind as a bat' part," Dronfield declared. "He's only blind when he chooses to be."

And he explained the matter of the contact glasses to his subordinate, who opened his eyes at the information.

"Amazing what they can do," he admitted. "Still, you can't get over the rest of the facts."

"Let's take it step by step," suggested Dronfield, who prided himself on having a systematic mind.

"Here's how I figure it out. Timothy's been thinking of this for a good while. He goes up to London and gets himself fitted with contact glasses. That leaves no clue among the eye-specialists hereabouts. Of course he says nothing about the glasses to anyone. That equips him with fair normal sight, unknown to anyone in these parts. Now come to the day of the murder. He buys some liver. We know that. He's got cyanide to hand…"

"How?" demanded Longridge.

"From his electro-plating hobby. Cyanide's used in silver-plating. That fits him out for the dog-poisoning. He goes up to the house that evening to give his brother Jack a helping hand, and to make sure that all's favourable to his plans up to the last possible minute. Then he clears out at 10 p.m."

"That seems straight enough," Longridge admitted. "It's the next stage that's sticky."

"Well, he clears out at ten o'clock, and Jack has to see the poor blind bat half-way home. That's bound to come out in evidence, and it impresses his bad sight on simple fellows like you and me.

"Later on, he puts on his contact glasses and comes back. I don't know when, exactly. Just before midnight, probably, so as to catch old Leadburn before he finishes up his accounts. He passes the dog without its barking. One of the family. He tries to force old Leadburn into signing some document, probably something that would put an end to the avuncular tyranny.

"Method of persuasion: a cord round the neck. No chance of Leadburn yelling for help in these circs. Unfortunately, the cord gets drawn a bit too tight. Leadburn chokes. Timothy tries to cover up the cord marks by cutting the old man's throat. He holds the knife in a bit of newspaper and burns the paper afterwards. No finger-prints, in that way. But in the flurry he forgets all about left-handedness and leaves that clue for us. Then he goes off, calls up the dog, poisons it with cyanided liver..."

"Why?" demanded Longridge. "I don't see the point, there."

"I see two," retorted the inspector. "First, the dog-poisoning makes it look like an outsider's job. Second, beasts poisoned with cyanide give a loud cry; and Timothy takes care to lead the beast under his brother's window to kill it. The youngster's got toothache and isn't sleeping sound. The howl wakes him. That dates the poisoning at twelve-twenty all right, for Timothy would bear the express in mind. And we dropped into his trap and assumed the dog had been poisoned by an intruder on his way *in* to the house. Makes all the difference in the supposed timing of the affair. Gained Timothy all the time he took in the actual murder, see?"

"I see," said Longridge. "Go on."

"With his contact glasses on, he'd get to the cottage as quick as you could. Nine minutes, you said. He'd be home by 12.30 a.m. Then at once he rings up Ackworth and says he's been sick. He's no more sick than you are. But as soon as he's done phoning, he swallows an emetic."

"Ipecacuanha?" queried the sergeant, conquering the polysyllable by careful enunciation.

"No, it's too slow in acting. Copper sulphate would do the trick. It acts immediately. And he'd have it for his electro-plating stunt. By the time Ackworth arrives, Timothy's sick enough; and he tells that lie about some tinned stuff having given him the gripes. Naturally Ackworth suspects nothing. So there's a sound alibi established. See?"

"It sounds neat," Longridge admitted. "And it clears Corfe of the dog-poisoning, which was the sticker from my point of view. You're going to get a warrant?"

"Yes. You'll execute it. Take a man or two with you and comb his cottage thoroughly after he's in custody. What we want is cyanide, copper or zinc sulphate—they're both emetics—his contact glasses, any bills or papers you can find that bear on his purchase of the glasses. If you get these things, we have him by the short hairs, I think."

"You'll have to suggest some motive that'll pass with a jury," objected the sergeant.

"No difficulty about that," declared the inspector. "We know our Timothy. Great lad for wine and women. What about the discreditable conduct clause in the will? Besides, his lungs are gone, aren't they? He's thirty, now. I don't know how far gone he is, but most likely he thought he wouldn't be in any condition to enjoy his fortune if he had to wait six years more for it. 'A short life and a gay one' was his idea. But you can't be gay on £100 a year—not in that line of gaiety, anyhow. So it was a race between his consumption and the date of his inheritance. All he wanted was to shift that date a bit forward, so that he could enjoy his money while he was still fit for it. That's how I see it, anyhow."

"Lucky you had to see that eye-doctor," was Sergeant Longridge's reflection, which he kept to himself.

THE BROKEN TOAD

H. C. Bailey

When asked to list the leading lights of Golden Age fiction, few modern readers are likely to mention the name of H. C. Bailey, although some connoisseurs of the genre hold him in high esteem. His star may have faded, but between the wars, Henry Christopher Bailey (1878–1961) was one of the most renowned exponents of the form. In her essay "Detective Writers of England", Agatha Christie heaped praise on Bailey's principal detective, the surgeon and Home Office consultant Reggie Fortune: "Mr. Fortune is, undeniably, a great man. Now to label a man a great man and then write about him and *show* him to be a great man is a supreme literary feat!… Some of the best of the Fortune stories show the deduction of a whole malignant growth from one small isolated incident… underneath Fortune's smiling exterior there is cold steel. Reggie Fortune is for Justice—merciless and inexorable justice. His pity and indignation are aroused by the victims—in execution he is as ruthless as his own knife."

Bailey's mannered literary style is deeply out of fashion, but it is a pity that his merits are nowadays often overlooked. "The Broken Toad" first appeared in the October 1934 issue of *The Windsor Magazine*, and was collected in *Mr. Fortune Objects* the following year. Vivid and distinctive, this story about a "chain of murder" showcases Reggie's diagnostic flair and Bailey's storytelling at its best.

M R. FORTUNE'S EYES, DROWSY AND BENIGN, CONTEMPLATED
Mrs. Fortune. The shape of her face, the poise of her head,
and her amber hair were shown him against a background of
sunlit, misty blue, the August sky of his garden in the Cotswolds.
The shape of the rest of her, which was covered in amber silk,
had behind it the dark, shining green and the creamy flowers of
a fence of Mermaid roses. She was receiving the admiration of
the Chief of the Criminal Investigation Department and was gra-
ciously amused.

A maid arrived with tea. Mr. Fortune's eyes turned to consideration of the cake-stand. He sighed content. He wriggled in his long
chair to a position more adapted for eating. He gazed at his wife,
and said plaintively, "Joan!"

Mrs. Fortune and Lomas turned towards him. "The hungry sheep
look up and are not fed," said Lomas.

"He has so few pleasures," Mrs. Fortune apologised. "The per-
petual small boy."

"Oh, no. No. Very mature mind. Speakin' roughly, the only
mature mind I ever knew," Reggie murmured. "In a man." He took
a yellow cake of a bun formation. "Try this pleasure, Lomas. My
design, executed by Elise. Sort o' saffron cake, with interior clotted
cream and wild strawberry jam."

"Good Gad!" Lomas exclaimed. "Saffron!"

"Why not?" Reggie opened round eyes at him. "Oh, that!"

"Yes, exactly," said Lomas, with a grimace. "No accounting for taste," he shrugged. "You're a wonderful animal, Reginald." He turned to Mrs. Fortune and apologised. "I beg your pardon."

She smiled. "I do like to think he's rational—as often as I can." With affection she surveyed Reggie's delicate management of gushing jam and cream.

"Instincts very highly developed," Lomas admitted. "But we are making the man self-conscious." He steered the conversation away from the question of saffron in cake to life at large.

Reggie finished a second *gâteau* Elise, and returned to society to hear them talking morals... Lomas was talking... Lomas was being clever... something about goodness consisting of good taste.

"Just existing beautifully," said Mrs. Fortune. "Then you must be very good, Mr. Lomas."

"No. No. Certain activity required," Reggie protested.

"Hush." Lomas waved him out of it. "What's Mrs. Fortune's definition of goodness?"

"Being kind," she said.

"Yes. Both have glimpses of the truth," Reggie murmured. "Bein' kind isn't adequate. You've got to be kind within reason. Lots of nasty sin comes out of the other kind of kindness. That's where sound taste is useful. Love's done about as much harm in the world as hate. Devotion—self-sacrifice—dangerous, delusive virtues. Made some of the worst horrors."

"You do sometimes believe in something, don't you?" said Mrs. Fortune gently.

"Oh, yes. Yes. All the time, Joan. I believe in justice."

"And mercy," she said.

"Not by itself, no. Bein' always merciful produces fools and devils."

She looked at him severely. "Do you make my flesh creep? No, not when you're trying."

"He's doing worse," said Lomas. "He's talking shop," and turned the conversation to the new painter's picture of Mrs. Fortune…

The emotions of Lomas over saffron in cake and Mr. Fortune's criticism of unselfish love were alike inspired by the case of the broken toad. It is to be admitted that this has become a favourite subject with Mr. Fortune. He considers it—and has been thought too fond of saying so—the supreme example of crimes of affection; he maintains that study of it is necessary to a liberal education.

Police-constable Mills was the unhappy cause of bringing it before him. Early on a summer morning—that is to say, about eight o'clock—Mr. Fortune was waked to dislike the world by a telephone message asking him to go and see a policeman in the Langdon Hospital.

Sitting up in bed, he moaned into the receiver. "Who is speaking? Underwood? Have you a heart? No. You used to have some intelligence. What's the matter with the man?"

"The hospital won't give us anything definite. They say it might be some sort of stroke, or it might be concussion—blow on the head, you know. We'd got that far by ourselves. And, you see, we want to know good and quick which it was. If the poor chap was attacked, we've got to get busy."

"Horrible necessity. Well, well. What are the facts, if any?"

"Constable went out on his beat last night quite fit. Nothing known of him after that, till a milk van nearly ran over him this morning. He was lying in the road, helmet off, sort of groaning, the milkman says, but practically unconscious, and he's been like that ever since."

Langdon is one of the outlying suburbs of London, but most of it was built last century. Then it attracted men who were making comfortable, third-class fortunes. The result is that it consists chiefly of genteel villas, each in its own piece of ground, which have tried hard to be unlike one another with contortions of inconvenience. Some of these are still inhabited by the survivors or descendants of those who put them up. Others have been converted by the forces of progress into modern ugliness as blocks of flats offering modern comfort to those who do without babies.

Breakfastless and pallid, Reggie came to the hospital built in the lowest, dampest situation which the hills of Langdon provide.

Police-constable Mills had been put in a private room. He lay unconscious. The bulk of his body raised the bed-clothes to a long mound through which no tremor of movement came, so faintly life struggled in him with a gurgle of labouring breath.

"He had some spasms when he first came in," the doctor explained. "Only slight. He's been much like this for two hours—continuous and deepening coma."

"Yes. Collapse of central nervous system," Reggie murmured. He felt a feeble, irregular pulse, he bent over the patient…

In vigour Constable Mills must have been the popular ideal of a long-service policeman. But the cheeks, which ought to have been dark red, were livid behind the network of tiny purple veins; his unseeing eyes had sunk back into their puckered wrinkles; from the unknown into which his mind had passed the face reported pain and dread…

"That's a big bruise on the back of his head," the doctor pointed out.

"Yes, I did notice it. Yes," Reggie murmured. He was looking close into the moustache.

"He's a heavy fellow," the doctor continued to instruct. "It might have been made by a fall, if you assume he had a stroke, and he's the age and the habit of body to make that possible. Or he may have been slogged from behind. Anyhow I'm taking it as a case of concussion."

"Been sick, hasn't he?" Reggie murmured.

"Not since he came in. I should say he had been. There was some muck on his clothes. You often find sickness after concussion, don't you?"

"Yes, that is so. However. Try an apomorphine injection. Want to clean out the stomach if you can. And then give him dialysed iron."

"My Lord," the doctor exclaimed. "I never thought—"

"No. Don't blame you. Very bafflin', these cases of collapse. Get on with it now."

The doctor got on...

Over the hospital telephone Reggie spoke to Inspector Underwood. "He's gone, poor chap. As near as no matter. Not a chance left. No. He hasn't said anything. Never conscious. What? Yes, bad luck. Very bad luck."

"You think somebody did him in, sir?" Underwood said eagerly.

"Oh, yes. Yes. That is indicated. Not a natural death."

"Knocked on the head, was he?"

"Only by himself. As he fell. Bruise on the head irrelevant. Cause of death, irritant poisoning. Some analysis required, but no doubt the usual arsenic."

"Good Lord!" Underwood ejaculated.

"Yes. As you say. But human action is also indicated. Come on."

When Underwood reached the hospital, he found Reggie in the matron's room, eating buttered toast and drinking tea.

"Well, well." Reggie looked up at him and sighed. "A sad world. A horrible breakfast. And he's dead."

Underwood nodded gloomily. "Ah, it's a bad business, sir. Did he suffer much?"

"In the last hours—no. Quite a lot before. Not a nice game, the arsenic game." Reggie pushed back his chair, gazed at his toast with dislike, and lit his pipe.

"I never heard of a case like it," said Underwood.

"No. You wouldn't. In the nature of things. Dose of arsenic, followed by collapse, passes for a stroke or concussion, and the operator gets a nice, quiet burial of the victim. Same like this operator would have got, if you hadn't dragged me in to interfere with him. Bold operator. Takin' a risk, but a good risk. A big dose may go to the nervous system quick and omit the desirable, betrayin' symptoms. Boldness, and again boldness, is the motto for the murder industry. Quite a lot of arsenic poisonin' the police never hear of. Comfortin' thought. And every case you don't hear of leads to others. Your poisoner goes marchin' on—from victory to victory. However. We have heard of this case. We might catch the poisoner before there's another victim." He gazed at Underwood with dreamy, closing eyes. "Quite a novelty for the police force to avert a murder or two, very improbable novelty. We shall have to be very clever," he drawled. "Are you feelin' clever, Underwood. I am not. Oh, my hat, I am not." He looked with loathing at the congealed remains of his toast. "Question for you is the history of Constable Mills—with full and particular details of his last afternoon and evening here upon earth. Get on to it. You're the lucky man. I have to examine his remains."

That evening Mr. Fortune attended a conference at Scotland Yard. He came to it late. He found it already in session—Underwood and Superintendent Bell presided over by the Hon. Sidney Lomas, the Chief of the Criminal Investigation Department.

"Well, what are you going to tell us?" Lomas asked.

"Tell you I told you so." Reggie sank into a chair. "That's all.

Arsenic. Large dose. The customary arsenic trioxide. As from rat-killer, weed-killer, or what not."

"That's all very well," Lomas frowned. "But I never had a case like this—a constable poisoned out on his beat."

"No. Circumstances of case rare and bafflin'."

"I suppose it might have been suicide?"

"Possible theory. Not an attractive theory. Not likely a man arrangin' to poison himself should choose the hours he was walkin' his regular night beat to do the job. However. Try every hypothesis. Any reason to suspect suicide?"

"No, there isn't," said Bell, with some vehemence. "Underwood was just saying Mills's record is first class. Not brainy, but an honest ox of a man. They know him inside out at Langdon. He'd been there most of his time. Almost due for pension. Widower these ten years. No children. Lodged with an old woman who keeps house for her son, a jobbing gardener. The three of 'em all had the same meal yesterday evening before Mills went out on night duty—meat pie and tea, and the old girl and her son are fit and well. Besides, they're well known and respectable, and all they get by his death is losing their lodger. After he went out, I haven't found anybody who saw him. When do you reckon he had the poison, Mr. Fortune?"

"No certainty. Probably before midnight. Probably not many hours before. I should say he had it after goin' on duty. That's the medical evidence. Apply the higher intelligence, Lomas. What are you going to do about it?"

"What the devil can we do?" Lomas snapped. "There's nothing to work from. If he'd been knocked on the head, we could put it down to a burglar he'd come up against. But you don't ask me to believe in criminals who go round carrying arsenic and persuade the innocent constable to eat it out of their hands."

"I don't know so much," said Bell. "You're making it sound ridiculous, sir. It needn't be, though. Say there was a job planned and Mills had to be got out of the way, so one of the gang stood him a drink with a dose in it. That's all right."

"Haven't heard of any job, have we?" Lomas shrugged. "And it's a big job that's worth a preliminary murder."

"It might be coming," said Bell stubbornly. "Suppose Mills had got on to something that would give it away?"

"Judging by his record, he never got on to anything. And if he did he'd have run to his sergeant. This is mare's nesting, Bell. You can't make the case rational however you take it. The most probable explanation is, the poor devil was sick of life. You get that when men are just due to retire."

"Yes. It could be," Reggie murmured. "But not probable. As aforesaid. Other possibilities worth considering. Private possibilities. The deceased was the old-style constable. Kind of constable who is popular with the female servant, what? At home in many hospitable kitchens. Not a grave offence, Bell, what?"

Bell shook his disciplined head. "I wouldn't say. It all depends. He didn't ought to have gone into a kitchen, if that's what you mean. But, of course, constables do."

"I don't know whether he went indoors," Reggie sighed. "I have my limitations. But I think somebody gave him a little homely meal. Say cake and cocoa. Includin' arsenic trioxide."

Bell and Underwood stared at him. "Ah. That's getting us somewhere," said Bell.

"Is it?" Lomas exclaimed. "Damme, what does it come to? A wicked cook poisoned the man—because he was carrying on with the cook next door, I suppose. And what then? Are we to make a house-to-house visitation of Mills's beat to find out what cooks loved him?"

"No. Not necessary. No. We can narrow it down," Reggie murmured. "Underwood—is the widow lady Mills lodges with a Londoner?"

"Yes, sir. Thoroughbred Cockney."

"Good. That simplifies things. If you can find a house on Mills's beat where they're west-country people, I think we might get on."

"The devil you do!" said Lomas. "What's this theory, Reginald?"

"Not a theory. Rational inference. The late Constable Mills had been eating saffron cake. The last thing he did eat. The arsenic was in that. Saffron cake isn't a common confection. But much cherished in the western counties. This had cream and currants in it. What they call revel cake, or revel buns, in Devonshire. Because it's the stuff to give the company at a wake, funeral feast, or revel. Constable Mills had some revel cake for his own funeral. However. That may be an unintended irony. The inference stands—he was fed on poison from a house that knew something about west-country cooking."

"My oath!" Bell muttered, and looked reverently at his Mr. Fortune. "That's clever, sir." He turned to Underwood. "Now it's up to you, young fellow."

"Yes, that's given me a line all right," Underwood chuckled.

"Has it!" said Lomas. "If you make anything of it, I shall be surprised. Damme, Fortune, what do you think it means? A cook set herself to poison this middle-aged widower of a policeman—why?"

"I haven't the slightest idea," Reggie mumbled.

"It's fantastic." Lomas made contemptuous noises.

"Oh, yes. Yes. As it stands. It don't stand on anything. Bit of the top of a crime visible, and a bit of the bottom, without anything in between. Fantastic, impossible structure. Like a crag supported on mist, with a lake poking out underneath. Crag is nevertheless real. And Constable Mills is dead by poison. So there is a poisoner somewhere about, Lomas. Whether the poisonin' of Mills was intended or not."

There was a moment of silence. "Good Gad!" said Lomas. "Confound your variations. Why can't you talk straight? Mills got what was meant for someone else. That's your real opinion, is it?"

"Oh, no. No. Haven't any opinion. Not enough facts. Death of Mills may not have been according to plan. It could be. I wonder." He gazed at Lomas with dreamy eyes. "You're so irrelevant. Evadin' the true point. Which is that a bold poisoner is now operatin' in Langdon. Poisoners seldom stop at one victim. Thus demonstratin' the efficiency of the police force. Good night."

In his frequent comments on the case Mr. Fortune is apt to insist that its chequered course was determined by the unreliability of people's taste in eating. If everyone could be trusted to like what they ought to like, he will point out, its results might have been even more unjust. In this he finds sad proof of the mystery of evil…

The inquest on Constable Mills was opened and warily adjourned without any evidence to warn the world that the police knew he had been poisoned.

Some days afterwards, Underwood talked to Mr. Fortune over the telephone. "About that clue of yours, the saffron cake, sir. Well, I've pretty well combed out Mills's beat for west-country people, and I can only find one set. There's an old lady living in Belair Avenue— Miss Pearse by name. She's a Devonshire woman, and makes a bit of fuss about it. Pair of old Devonshire servants too. But I've had a talk with them, and they won't own to knowing Mills at all. I should say they're telling the truth. Keep themselves to themselves sort of women. So it looks like petering out."

"You think so?" Reggie murmured.

"I do. Pity. It seemed a real good line. But there you are."

"Oh, no. Not anywhere," Reggie murmured. "Miss Pearse, an old lady of Devon. Well, well." He became musical:

Tom Pearse, Tom Pearse, lend me your, grey mare,
All along, out along, down along lee—

"What's that, sir?" said Underwood.

Wi' Bill Brewer, Jan Stewer, Peter Gurney, Peter Davy,
Dan'l Whiddon, Harry Hawk, Old Uncle Tom Cobleigh and all.

Reggie concluded the Devonian ballad. "Where are you speakin' from? Langdon? The police station? All right I'll come out. We'll call on Miss Pearse of Belair Avenue."

"If you say so—" Underwood conveyed doubt and disapproval.

"Oh, my dear chap! Quite in order. I'm the medical man investigatin' Mills's death, introduced by Inspector Underwood, in charge of the case. Did she happen to know the poor man, his habits and what not and so forth? And we'll see what we can get."

You may now behold Inspector Underwood and Mr. Fortune walking from the police station of Langdon to the home of Miss Pearse, The Nest, Belair Avenue. Langdon is a suburb of hills, and the determination of Mr. Fortune to walk surprised Underwood. The reason given was a desire to get the atmosphere.

No part of the world is more peaceful than the umbrageous streets of Langdon in the afternoon. The superlative of their somnolence may be found in Belair Avenue. It climbs along the shoulder of one of the highest hills. The houses in it, some fifty years old, exhibit the opulent fancy of that period. The Nest is built in stone, and dowdily resembles a castle in a German fairy-tale. Next door to it, Bellagio is a tall conglomeration of purple brick, with oriel windows and a pagoda top. And so on.

A grey-haired maid, who sniffed at Underwood, let them into The Nest, left them on the mat, and, reappearing in time, conducted them up a narrow staircase which twisted mediævally to a room smelling of pot-pourri and lavender, and decorated with chintz, silhouettes, and miniatures. Two small lancet windows admitted some light, but no air. They seemed not made to open.

Reggie looked out on a garden descending in steps of lawn, so steeply the ground fell away behind the house, with flower-beds containing nothing but geraniums, calceolarias, and lobelia. He moaned at it. He looked beyond to the garden of Bellagio.

That at least was different. There the ground dropped still more steeply. From a little terrace behind the house a tall flight of steps led down to a rectangle paved with tiles, in which was a pool where dark water gleamed between lily leaves. All was uncared for, dirty, moss-grown, weed-grown. But it had been elaborate. Funereal shrubs grew out of the tiles. There were awful objects of art upon them: china dwarfs of German manufacture; at the foot of the steps leered, greenish-yellow, a china toad.

"Oh, my hat!" Reggie groaned, and directed his suffering eyes to look beyond.

The rest of the Bellagio garden sloped away into an artificial wilderness of shrubbery through which, on either side the path vanishing down the hill, loomed more images in crockery or plaster. Along the path a woman moved. She seemed to be tidying the unkempt shrubs, and weeding the path in spasms, without steady purpose. She was not beautiful. She wore a drab woollen coat and a cotton skirt faded into a dingy confusion of colour, and she seemed to have no more definite shape than these old clothes. She was lank and ungainly. In her tangle of hay-coloured hair no grey appeared, but her long face looked aged—it shone sallow, it was worried, fretful, dreamily earnest. She fussed out of sight.

Reggie's eyes came back to contemplate, with new horror, the terrace and the toad.

"You wished to see me?" said a small prim voice. And he turned, and seemed to be a child again meeting his grandmother. So imposing was the presence of Miss Pearse. She was a small woman; she was all black to her white hair and parchment face—a face little and meek and pretty, but with the perfect assurance of authority in this world and the next.

"It is about the poor policeman?" she went on. "Pray sit down. I shall be happy to give you any help which is possible." Her composure, her condescension, let them infer that she expected to be asked for help and was prepared. She surveyed them with pale blue eyes which were without expression.

After a moment the quiet voice spoke again. She had known Mills for many years; she discoursed on the proper relations of the police to ladies of importance, lamented his demise, and passed on to indicate her unique position in Langdon... It appeared that she was of its oldest and bluest blood, by divine right the leader of its society...

Underwood became restive, and interrupted with a brusque question: did she happen to see Mills the night he died?

Miss Pearse was affronted. She made an odd movement of neck and head, like a duck swallowing, and informed him that it was not her habit to go walking after nightfall.

Underwood told her that she didn't take the point. What they wanted was some information about Mills' condition—state of health and so on—as he went round his beat the night he died. For instance, there was the chance he might have come to her house.

Miss Pearse, biting the words, remarked that it was an improper suggestion. The inspector should be aware that she would not tolerate her servants entertaining a man.

"Sorry to distress you," Reggie murmured. "It's a very distressin' case. But we have to do the poor fellow justice, and I did hope you might help us. West-country man, wasn't he? Devon man?"

"Indeed?" For the first time Miss Pearse betrayed surprise. "I had no idea of that. I shouldn't have thought it."

"Really?" Reggie put up his eyebrows. "But you ought to be a judge. You're Devonshire."

Miss Pearse flushed. "I am of a Devonshire family."

"Oh, yes. Yes. That would be another reason for him coming to your house if he wanted help."

"If he was a Devon man." She spoke slowly; she stared. "But I tell you I have no reason to think so."

"Well, well," Reggie murmured. "Bafflin' case. Speakin' medically, you see, it's important to find somebody who met him the night he died." Under his grave eyes Miss Pearse admitted that she could understand that. "Two possible lines of enquiry," Reggie mumbled. "Do you know any other Devon people living hereabouts?"

"I cannot imagine why you insist on Devonshire people," she said.

"No? Other line of enquiry. Do you know any house where a constable would be welcome in the kitchen?"

Miss Pearse gave him a look of reproof. "That is an unpleasant question," she said acidly. "I should not be likely to observe such conduct." But it appeared to Reggie that she was considering whether she should say she had observed some. He proceeded to tempt her.

"Domestic conduct not what it was," he mourned. "People don't look after their homes." Miss Pearse was quick to agree. "Yes. You find that even in Langdon, what? I was wondering"—he gazed at her solemnly—"garden next door looked rather wild—I was wondering—is that a go-as-you-please place where a policeman might be in and out of the kitchen?"

Miss Pearse drew herself up. She really could not say. And she went on saying. Mrs. Colson had been at Bellagio for many years. It was built by her father-in-law. He had designed the garden; it was the delight of his life—such a sweet fanciful place it used to be. But now—!

"Rather neglected, what?" Reggie murmured.

Miss Pearse would not say that Mrs. Colson neglected things. But after the children grew up she had had nothing but trouble. Her father-in-law died; her husband died. She had been such a sweet happy creature before. But afterwards—No wonder. They were fine men. She was a devoted mother, absolutely devoted. She had only lived for her children. And they—! Really Miss Pearse could not endure the modern notion that parents must give up everything to their children—it made for nothing but misery.

"Nobody should give up everything to anybody, no," Reggie purred. "Quite immoral. Has Mrs. Colson many children?"

With a certain vehemence, as if she felt the number offensive, Miss Pearse told him there were two. Alfred Colson was a harmless creature enough, but absolutely dependent on his mother. It was a wonder he ever married. He and his wife were always at his mother's knee.

"Still lives in the maternal house?" Reggie murmured.

"Oh, they have a home of their own," said Miss Pearse. "One of the flats in that disgusting block where the Old Hall was; they can hardly know what it's like."

"United family," Reggie smiled. "Charming. And the daughter. Equally devoted?"

"I suppose Minnie has never been away from her mother a day," said Miss Pearse, with disdain. "The most affectionate creature. But Minnie is at anybody's service. She bustles in all the good works we have. Really, it is as if she hadn't time to have a self of her own."

"I see. Yes. Very interesting." Reggie encouraged more opinions of the Colson family.

But Miss Pearse decided that she had said all she wanted, or more. She smoothed down her dress, and met his look of enquiry with mild, innocent eyes in which there was something hard and assured. She was the grandmother who knew everything and had told the small boy all that was good for him.

"Thanks very much," he smiled. "And if anything should occur to you, you'll tell the police station, won't you?"

"I cannot conceive that anything else will occur to me," said Miss Pearse. "Good day."

When they were outside. "She's a hard case, sir," Underwood grinned. Reggie did not answer. He gazed pensively at the purple bulk of Bellagio and its dingy lace curtains, and his pace was slow. "Well, I don't know what you make of her, sir," Underwood went on. "I can't make up my mind whether we've drawn blank or got on to something."

"Not blank, no," Reggie mumbled.

"You shook her up all right," Underwood admitted. "She didn't like being told there was something Devonshire about Mills' death, did she? That bothered her quite a lot. Might mean you were right, sir, and he got his arsenic in her house."

"Yes. It could be."

"And then, that didn't look too good her telling the tale about the people next door. Very keen to run them down, wasn't she? Fishy, that was, there's no denying."

"You think so? Yes. Reaction to suggestion of the house next door very marked. Vivid description of the Colson family. I should say she's had them on her mind some time. Thoughtful person, our Miss Pearse."

"She's deep," Underwood nodded. "She knows something. She gave me the creeps now and then. I kept getting the idea she wasn't human—didn't feel things the natural way."

"Rather superhuman, yes. Old ladies are—when clever and lonely."

"I can imagine her doing anything," said Underwood. "But then, what's the sense of supposing she or her old servants poisoned a policeman?"

"Not likely. No. However. The provisional hypothesis is that the saffron cake wasn't meant for the policeman."

"You mean she might have sent a cake in next door?" Underwood cried. "She meant to poison some of the Colsons, and Mills got it? That's all right."

"Yes. It could be. I wonder. Some way to go yet. And the sooner it's over the sooner to sleep. Next step in the investigation quite obvious. Find out all about the Colson family and servants, if any. Miss Pearse's history of the Colsons has interest. A heart-to-heart talk with a Colson cook would be illuminatin'. Don't be official, Underwood. Use your charms. You should fascinate any cook."

"Thank you, sir," said Underwood bitterly.

"And, in the intervals of fascination, look up the deaths of the Colson father and grandfather. Miss Pearse was rather affectionate about them. Did you notice that?"

"Good Lord!" Underwood exclaimed. "You mean to say, maybe this wasn't the first time a saffron cake went from her house to the Colsons?"

"I wonder," Reggie murmured. "Some animosity towards the Colson family very marked. Yes. We'd better know what we can about the deaths of the past. Before the future brings more deaths. Well, well. Here's the police station. Futile institution, so far. Justify your existence, Underwood. If possible. Good-bye."

Some days afterwards he was called away from the composition of a monograph on influenza in rabbits to Scotland Yard.

Again he found Underwood with Bell and Lomas. He gazed at them with plaintive dislike. "Oh, my hat!" he moaned. "What's the matter now?"

"The reference is your infernal saffron cake, Reginald," Lomas said. "You don't mean to say you've forgotten it?"

"Oh, yes. Yes. I had. Absolutely. I'd done my job. The rest is simple police work. I was on something important."

"Simple!" said Lomas. "Good Gad! You've brought us up against a blank wall. Go on, Underwood. Tell him."

Underwood went off with a rush. "Well, sir, I got on to the Colsons' cook all right. I reckon I've pretty well turned her inside out—"

"My dear fellow!" Reggie purred admiration. "Your fatal charm."

"Nothing like that, sir," said Underwood severely. "She's old enough to be my mother. I took her round for a cup o' tea with the Langdon inspector—"

"Very proper, I'm sure," Bell grunted.

Underwood glowered at him. "Talking over poor Mills' death, that was the idea. She's desperate cut up about him. He did go into the Colsons' house that night, Mr. Fortune. She gave him a bun and a cup of cocoa, and he went off as right as rain."

"Oh, yes. Who made the bun?" Reggie murmured.

"That's where the catch comes. It was a saffron bun, like you said. That day the Colsons had the married son and his wife coming to tea, and Miss Minnie Colson made some special stuff herself—buns made with cream and currants and saffron—"

"Yes. I told you so. Revel buns, as in Devonshire."

"I dare say. The cook says Minnie Colson had the recipe from Miss Pearse next door. The Colsons have 'em now and again, and Miss Minnie always makes 'em. The son's wife is supposed to like 'em."

"Sound taste. They're very good," Reggie murmured. "Not quite right though. I've been thinkin' about that. Want a better fruit flavour. I—"

"Damme, let the man get on," Lomas cried.

"Oh, yes. Yes. Duty first. You were sayin'—they were made for the son's wife. By daughter Minnie."

"That's right. Cook wasn't in the kitchen when she made 'em. The buns went up to tea, and came down again untouched."

"The son's wife wouldn't have any. Well, well. Taste not reliable. Appetite not reliable. Very disconcertin' in a guest. Makes a lot of trouble. Look at this case."

"Made some trouble for poor Mills," Underwood said severely. "The buns came back to the kitchen. The cook don't like saffron herself. So she didn't eat any. She fed Mills on 'em when he looked in for his bit of supper. When she went to the cake tin next day, to send things up for tea again, the rest of the buns were gone. That's all she knows—so she says, and I believe her. So there's a nice old snag. We'll never be able to prove there was anything in the dam' buns at all."

"No. As you say. We shan't," Reggie murmured. "Nothing more from that line of investigation. We weren't quick enough."

"I don't know what more I could have done, sir," Underwood protested.

"Nothing. No. Not blamin' you. We don't have much luck. If Mills had been found sooner, I might have saved him. If we could have learnt his habits quicker, we might have got some effective evidence. However. Other means of usin' pressure. By the way, what about the deaths of Colson father and grandfather?"

"Colson grandfather died, aged seventy-five, in 1914, of a stroke. Colson father died, aged sixty-two, in 1925, of gastric influenza."

"Well, well." Reggie sank deep in his chair, and gazed at Lomas with closing eyes. "That's very interestin'."

"You're suspicious?" Lomas frowned.

"Yes. Both stated causes of death possibly veilin' arsenic. Complex case, this case, Lomas."

"Damme, it always was," said Lomas bitterly. "Now you want to make it into one of the devilish chains of murder. And we haven't one clear piece of evidence. I couldn't get an order to exhume these two men on your suspicions. And, if I did, if you found arsenic in the bodies, we should be no nearer proof."

"Oh, no. That's hopeless. At the best, we should only have association of arsenic with the Colson household, since the Colson children grew up. As Miss Pearse put it. No use."

"Thank you. I see that," Lomas snapped. "It's very gratifying, isn't it? A succession of murders, and we can do nothing."

"Not the first time," Bell growled. "These clever poisoners are the devil."

"Yes. One of the devil's best efforts," Reggie nodded. "But not invincible, when observed. Are we down-hearted? No. Action has been taken, Lomas. Pressure is bein' applied. The poisoner of Belair Avenue is now aware that the police are sittin' up and takin' notice. I made that clear to Miss Pearse. Underwood's been makin' it clear to servants. I should say there'll be consequences. Swift and fruitful consequences. Good-bye."

It is held by Superintendent Bell that the handling of this case was one of his most uncanny pieces of work. But this judgment may be biased by the speed with which results developed: a speed which, Mr. Fortune points out, was the natural consequence of the menace of frustration on the poisoner.

He had just got into his car, when a detective ran out and asked him to come back and speak to Mr. Lomas. Lomas and Underwood and Bell were still together when he returned.

"Here's your fruitful consequences, Reginald," Lomas said. "Young Colson's wife has been found dead. Drowned in a pool in old Mrs. Colson's garden."

"Well, well," Reggie murmured. "Who found her?"

"The daughter, Minnie Colson. Found her this morning. Body's been removed to the mortuary."

"Oh, Peter!" Reggie moaned. "Why?"

"Sorry. Minnie Colson pulled her out of the pool before she sent for a doctor. So we're told. You'll go and have a look at her, what?"

"Go and have a look at the pool," Reggie murmured. "Come on, Underwood."

A policeman admitted them to the murky hall of Bellagio. In a shabby morning-room the local detective-inspector received them.

He considered it a very queer business. They all told the same tale. "Miss Minnie Colson—she said she was going out to the girls' club at the church last night—"

"Cook's night out, wasn't it?" said Reggie, with a glance at Underwood.

"That's right, sir. That seems to be one of the points," the inspector agreed. "They only keep a cook and a daily girl. So the house was going to be left, except for old Mrs. Colson. That's why Miss Minnie telephoned to young Mrs. Colson to come and sit with the old lady. So she says. And young Mrs. Colson came, and Miss Minnie went out. That would be about seven to half past—as she says. Then there's old Mrs. Colson. She says the young woman didn't stay long, but went off about dusk. She can't put a time to it. The old lady was up in her own room—that's overhead in the front—and the young woman's short way home was to go through the garden at the back and out by the gate at the end. Then there's her husband's statement. He says he was dining at his club last night: says he often does. When he came home, about midnight, his wife wasn't there. They live in a flat. After a bit he got their servant out o' bed, but she couldn't tell him anything, except that there'd been a phone message and her mistress had gone out after. He says he sat up all night. I don't know. If you ask me, he don't think too much of his wife. And then this morning, about ten o'clock, so she says, Miss Minnie goes out to do a bit o' gardening, and sees young Mrs. Colson lying in a pool they have out in the garden, pulled her out, found her dead, and sent for the doctor. The doctor says the woman was drowned some time last night. He rang us up. I didn't get here till eleven fifteen—and by that time, you see, the body had been moved and mucked about, and the whole place was walked over."

"Yes. I see. Yes," Reggie murmured. "Tiresome. However. You've done very well. Nice, clear story. Now we'll look at what's left."

They went out on to the terrace above the garden, and the inspector demonstrated: big drop from the terrace to the lily pool in the rectangle of tiles and shrubs; the flight of steps which led down was steep; quite possible anybody in the dusk or dark might take a bad toss; the pool had a concrete bottom; it was two or three feet deep;

the young woman might have tumbled into it head first, and, if she did, she might have been stunned and lay till she drowned.

"Yes. It could be," Reggie nodded. "Quite good. All possibilities of the place considered and allowed for."

"I wouldn't call it likely myself," said Underwood. "Too much 'might have been'."

"I'm not saying it's likely," the inspector agreed. "It means a lot of chances came off. But you can't be sure the thing didn't happen that way."

"That's the devil of it," Underwood grunted. "It's so ruddy plausible."

"You think so?" Reggie murmured. "One difficulty. How was the toad broken?" He pointed a little finger at it. It lay on the tiles in jagged fragments of crockery.

"That—well, I don't know where it stood," the inspector answered. "I asked Minnie Colson; she didn't seem to know—very vague about it. If it was on the terrace here, or on the steps, the young woman might have tripped over it—and there you are."

"You think so?" Reggie murmured. He went slowly down the steps. "The other day, the toad was on the tiles about where it is now. I saw it from the next-door window." He picked up one of the larger fragments. "Yes. This is its regular place. You see, there's no moss on the tiles underneath. They're dry and clean. Yes. So the provisional hypothesis is, it was broken by the fall of young Mrs. Colson last night. And, if she fell on the toad, she didn't fall into the pool. She was put there by hand." He gazed solemnly at Underwood. "Broken toad indicates crime of determination." He bent over the toad's wreck. "Yes. Several signs of human contact with the broken toad. What was young Mrs. Colson wearing?"

"She had a long coat on, sir—rough, yellow stuff."

"Here you are. Strands of yellow woollen fabric. Thus confirmin' our hypothesis. Young Mrs. Colson fell down the steps on to the toad, and was stunned by the fall. Then dragged into the pool to drown while unconscious. Other indications confirm that. See the streaks in the moss on the tiles? Something was pulled across lately. Also the toad made further contacts. Somebody scraped a shoe on this fragment. You see? Black leather—fine leather. Probably kid. However. Not providin' any explanation of the first act—how she fell."

"Taking it altogether, I should say she was pushed," said Underwood.

"Yes. Quite possible. Perhaps probable. But further investigation required." Slowly he climbed the steps, again looking closely at each and the iron railings on either side. Just below the top he stood still. He pointed a little finger at the railings. "What about that, inspector?"

To the base of one rail a piece of string was tied—thin, green string. The loose end of it had been blown into the shrubs below. The inspector gathered it up. "Don't seem to have been broken. But there's a bit of dirt at the end. Tied to the other railing, and jerked off, I should say—the knot pulled loose—when the strain came. That's it, a trip line to bring the young woman down."

"Yes. That is indicated," Reggie drawled. "Tied with a granny-knot. Well, well." He gazed at the inspector and Underwood, and his round face was without expression. "Proceedin' on these facts, you'd better occupy the attention of the ladies Colson—telling 'em nothing—while Underwood goes through the house lookin' for green string and a black kid-shoe with a scratch on it. Is the man Colson here? No? Gone back to his widower's home? You might ask him to come and have another heart-to-heart talk. I should be ready for him this afternoon. I must go and have a look at the dead woman now. Oh—Underwood—drop in next door and ask our Miss Pearse where the first Colson had his stroke, will you? Sort of question to keep her interested—which might be useful. I was wonderin' if he had it on the tiles. And another little question—ask Cook if Minnie Colson eats saffron herself. Good-bye."

In the squalid mortuary of Langdon he examined the body of young Mrs. Colson. She was not beautiful in death. Her face stared at him, swollen and pale, the pencilling about her blood-shot eyes smeared on the pouches below, the grease-paint on her lips lurid and grotesque across the bloated pallor...

It was some hours before he came back to the Colson house, and, in that dingy room off the hall, told Underwood his results. "Cause of death, drowning. Several bruises on head and body before death. Tear in the coat. Provisional hypothesis thus confirmed. Also, she'd had some drink shortly before death. Probably cocktails. She drank a good deal. Didn't live a very nice life. That's the medical evidence. What have you got? Identified our criminal of determination?"

"I rather think I've got a case, sir. I've found a ball of green string. In a cupboard in the room Minnie Colson uses for a sort of study. You never saw such a muck of a place. It's a tumbled muddle of odds and ends—needlework, woolwork, church papers, girls' club stuff, letters, and accounts all over the place. In the cupboard she keeps gardening things—gloves and basket and clippers, and what not—and there was this ball of green string. And what else do you think I found?"

"Oh, weed-killer. Arsenical weed-killer."

"That's right," Underwood nodded. "It does look like a case now, don't it?"

"Yes. If we could prove Mills got his arsenic here. Which we can't. However. What about the shoes?"

"Minnie Colson's shoes, put out to clean last night, are black kid, and they're both scratched. Look here."

"Yes. As you say," Reggie murmured. "And what does the cook say? Does Minnie like saffron?"

"Never eats any cake, sir. Being bilious, I'm told. Only makes cakes and pastry for other people. So there you are."

"Yes. These defects of eatin' power are a factor. Dominatin' factor. If Mrs. Colson junior had only eaten normally, quite a different case. However. What about our Miss Pearse? Could she tell you where grandfather Colson had his stroke?"

"She could, sir. She said he was found out there on the tiles, below the terrace." Underwood looked at Reggie, rather like a dog, admiration and a certain awe in his brown eyes. "That was a facer to me. I don't know how you got to it."

"Workin' on a series," Reggie mumbled. "Repetitions probable. Grandfather found unconscious—like Mills—possibly after knock-out dose of arsenic—down there under the terrace—like young Mrs. Colson—possibly tripped on the steps. That was in 1914. Eighteen years ago. After the children grew up. As Miss Pearse was careful to indicate. By the way, has our Miss Pearse been in to condole with the bereaved?"

"Yes, sir. When I saw her, she said she must come in and see old Mrs. Colson, and she came and stayed some time."

"Very proper. She is proper," Reggie purred. "Well, well. At the time of grandfather's death, I should say Minnie was twenty-five or so. And her brother was—what?"

"Oh, about the same. He's over forty, I'll swear. I phoned for him, like you said, and he's come. He's with his mother." Reggie nodded, and sat silent in meditation which seemed gratifying. "Well—I suppose the next thing is to put Miss Minnie through it?" Underwood suggested.

Reggie gazed at him solemnly. "Is she with her mother, too?"

"No. Miss Pearse sent her away to lie down. She's in her own room."

"That's all right. Minnie can wait. I'll talk to mamma. Go and tell the son to clear out, and stand by."

Old Mrs. Colson's bedroom was large and furnished with mid-Victorian state. Through its close-curtained windows only dim light could enter, but that did not conceal the faded age of all its colours.

She lay on a couch, in a corner, covered with an eiderdown quilt which had been pink before it turned grey. Reggie saw in her no likeness to her lank, ungainly daughter. The old face was tired and sorrowful, but composed to calm endurance. Above the quilt, her dress showed an ample bosom. Everything about her was in a pretty order—the abundance of grey hair, the little, plump, white hands, the lace at her neck. But her dark, deep-set eyes gazed at the two men as if they were not there.

Underwood began with something apologetic about necessary enquiries. "I understand," she said gently. "Pray forgive me, I am not as young as I was. Ask me what you wish. I will tell you anything I can."

"Needn't ask you very much," Reggie murmured. "Did your son know his wife was coming here last night?"

"Dear me, no. Nobody knew. Nobody thought of the poor child coming till Minnie suggested telephoning to ask her to sit with me. It was just Minnie's idea."

"I see." Reggie nodded. "And how was the lady when she came?"

"Quite well. Just as usual."

"Oh, yes. Did it occur to you she'd been drinking?"

Mrs. Colson raised herself a little. "I never thought of such a thing. It is cruel to suggest it."

"You think so? She did drink, didn't she?"

"That is an amazing thing to say."

"Really? Never thought of it before? Well, well. Was her husband on good terms with her?"

"Perfectly. Alfred was devoted to her. I don't know what can have put this into your head."

"No? Well, well. Do you know where Alfred was last night?"

"He was in Town. He was dining at his club."

"Oh, he'd told you that. Yes. And when did his wife leave you?"

"I am not sure of the time. Minnie had only just gone. If she had gone. She always takes so long to get ready."

"Mrs. Alfred didn't sit with you long, then?"

"She wanted to go as soon as it grew dark. She never liked the dark, poor thing."

"Left at dusk," Reggie repeated. "Half past seven or eight. And Alfred dined at his club. Well, well." He gave Underwood a long, impressive stare. "That's all, Mrs. Colson. Thank you."

He led the way back to the little morning-room, and there turned on the puzzled Underwood. "My dear chap! Oh, my dear chap! Get on. Bring in Alfred, the son."

Alfred Colson was brought. He also had no likeness to the lean, long Minnie. He took after his mother: a well-made man, rather solid, with neat, small hands and feet, and a regular oval of a face almost as feminine as hers. But he was not so well preserved. His complexion was mottled; he had a loose double chin; his eyes and his hands were unsteady.

"I want to know where you were when your grandfather died," Reggie snapped.

Alfred's mouth came open. "I don't remember. How should I? It's twenty years ago."

"You were living here?"

"Of course I was. What's all this about?"

"He fell where your wife fell. How much money did he leave?"

"I don't know." Alfred stared sullen fear. "He left everything to my father."

"You must know. How much?"

"About seventy thousand, I think."

"And when your father died—gastric influenza, that was called—how much did he leave?"

"He left everything to mother."

"Did he? And much less than grandfather?"

"It was nearly fifty thousand," Alfred said loudly.

"Good deal less. Someone had spent some money. Not on this house, what?"

"There was the war in between. Everything was down."

"And when your mother dies, who does the money go to?"

"Under father's will, it's divided between Minnie and me." Alfred licked his lips. "What are you asking all this for?"

"Clearin' up the case. Where were you when your wife died?"

"I was dining at the club."

"Sure?" Reggie drawled.

"What do you mean? I don't know when she died exactly. I dined at the club."

"Time?"

"I don't know. About eight, I suppose. I was in the club all the evening."

"Any evidence?"

"What do you mean? Fellows must have seen me."

"Can you think of any fellows?"

Alfred's hands fidgeted. "I didn't notice. Why should I?"

"Your affair. When did you arrange to dine at the club last night?"

"I often do."

"Oh, yes. Told your wife you would?"

Alfred took time to think what he should answer, and decided to say, "Yes."

"Why?" Reggie drawled. "Why leave your wife to dine alone?"

"Nothing unusual," Alfred snarled.

"Wasn't it? Not on good terms with her. What was the trouble? Drink? Money?"

"There wasn't any trouble."

"Oh. Somebody had been spending the family money, though. How much have you and your wife drawn from the estate?"

"I can't tell you. What is it to do with you?"

"Quite a lot. And with you. But you can't tell me. Better think it over. Go on." Reggie waved him away, and, after a flinching look of enquiry and fear, he went in a hurry.

Reggie sat erect and alert.

"I say, you handled him rough, sir," said Underwood uneasily. "I—"

Reggie put up a finger and he stopped, and, in silence, they listened. Over Reggie's face came a slow benign smile. "There you are," he whispered. "Upstairs. Into mother's room. That's the reaction. To talk over my cruel suspicions." He slid to the door, and, without a sound, opened it and sat down again...

After a while they heard more movement overhead: a heavy-footed bustle. "Sister Minnie," Reggie murmured. A door opened and shut on a high-voiced question. "Sister Minnie gone to ask how things are goin'. The more they are together the happier they'll be."

"What's the idea, sir?" Underwood whispered.

"Next reaction. Shut up."

It was some time before the bedroom door sounded again. Then came a hurry of heavy feet on the stairs and away down the hall.

"Gone to the kitchen," Underwood indicated.

"Yes. That is indicated. Come on. Quiet."

They made their way to the kitchen door. That was open, but they saw only the cook and the daily maid sitting over their tea. "Where is Miss Colson?" Reggie said softly.

The cook jumped. "Miss Minnie's in the scullery, sir. Warming a glass of milk for the mistress."

"Oh, all right." Reggie drew back behind Underwood, and whispered in his ear: "Take her away for a minute. Ask how mother is. Something like that. Three or four minutes." He slipped out of sight round a corner of the hall.

Underwood went into the scullery. He saw Minnie Colson's untidy head bent over a saucepan on the gas-stove. At the sound of the door she started back, looking, it remains in his memory, like a frightened horse. When he said he wanted to speak to her, she made stammering difficulties. Oh, but she couldn't; the milk would boil over, and mother hadn't had anything all day. Underwood turned off the gas. "Come along. It's your mother I want to ask you about." He took her off.

Then Reggie strolled into the kitchen. "I can get out to the garden through the scullery, can't I?" He smiled at the cook. "Door opens under the terrace? Thanks."

Into the scullery he went, and closed the door behind him. He sniffed at the milk in the saucepan, looked round, opened the larder, and in it found a bottle of milk three parts empty, another sealed. The sealed bottle he took, and, returning to the scullery, poured a portion of it into a clean saucepan. The saucepan with the milk which Minnie had prepared he set down outside in the garden. Under his own saucepan he lit the gas, and stood by it till he heard Minnie's heavy steps returning. Then he put out the gas and slid away through the garden door, to stop, out of sight, beyond the window.

He watched Minnie take the saucepan with hurried bungling hands, taste the milk, pour it into a jug. She spilt some; she exclaimed hysterically, wiped up the mess, and thudded away.

Then he came in, and followed her quickly to meet Underwood in the hall. "Up you go," he muttered. "After her. See her give it to her mother. Then call her away. Ask her anything you dam' like. Don't let her make any more food for mother, that's all. Anything mother wants, the cook must make. Stay here till further notice. See?"

"What, you mean that milk—?" Underwood gasped.

"The milk she's taken is all right. I've got the milk she cooked. Get on, get on."

Underwood ran upstairs, and, as he went, Alfred came down, gave a sidelong look of fear and hate at Reggie, and left the house. Reggie followed, but only to take a rug from his car. When he returned to the car, the saucepan and the bottle of milk were hidden under the rug. He drove away to his laboratory...

It was some hours later; he was not in the laboratory, but in the room beyond—in an easy chair, on the small of his back—when the telephone rang.

The voice of Underwood came to him, emotional and aggrieved: "I've been ringing up your house, sir. There's the very devil of a business here. The old lady's been taken bad. Sick and convulsions, and I don't know what. She can't hardly speak now, but she says Minnie poisoned her. Her doctor says it looks like arsenic poisoning."

"Oh, yes. Yes. I should think he's right," Reggie drawled. "I'll come and see."

"Did you expect it?" Underwood's voice rose.

"One of the possibilities. Yes," Reggie murmured, "probable possibility," and he rang off.

Again he came into Mrs. Colson's room. As he entered, his head jerked back and his nostrils dilated. There was a faint smell of garlic. A doctor and a nurse were by the bed, and from it came a groaning sound. But he went first to the gas-stove, and looked down into it. Though it was not alight, some charred matter lay on the hearth, and the upper part of the cream fire-brick bore a brown stain. He gave that a little smile of satisfaction.

Then he moved slowly to the bedside. The old face was now of a bluish pallor and drawn with pain, and beads of sweat stood upon it. The eyes were sunken—looked fear, looked at no one. The body was contorted in slow faint spasms...

He beckoned the doctor out, and took him to the dingy little room downstairs where Underwood waited, nervous and impatient. He sank into a chair and sighed. "Well, well. Quite clear, what?" He surveyed the doctor with placid eyes. "Acute poisonin'. As you said. Irritant poison. No doubt arsenic. You noticed the garlic smell? Also brown sublimation on the gas-stove? Arsenic has been burnt there. Resolute bit of poisonin'. I should say you won't save her."

"I'm afraid not, Mr. Fortune." The doctor shook a melancholy head. "She's old; she has no power of resistance. It's a dreadful tragedy."

"Yes. Tragic elements," Reggie murmured.

"Her own daughter!" the doctor exclaimed with horror.

"Oh, no. No." Reggie smiled. "Not her daughter. Herself."

The doctor drew back. "But she has said it was her daughter, sir. The inspector, here, has it written down. He—"

"That's right, Mr. Fortune," Underwood broke in. "It's like this. First I knew of her being taken bad—there was a scream, and I ran up, and she was in a ghastly mess; and she said, 'Minnie, Minnie,' and cried, and then afterwards—she couldn't speak properly—she wrote down—look—"

He produced a paper, and Reggie saw written, in a shaken hand, "Milk Minnie gave me. Tasted strange. She poisoned me."

"Here is some of the milk left, sir." The doctor pointed to a jug and a dirty glass on the table. "You have only to make a test."

"And I shall find arsenic. Yes. I believe you. But this isn't the milk Minnie prepared. This is milk that I prepared from a sealed bottle." He turned on Underwood. "You watched Minnie take it into her?"

"I did, sir," Underwood answered eagerly. "And she didn't put anything into it, I'll swear. As soon as she set it down, I took her away, and I had her here, under examination, till there was a scream, and I ran up and found the old lady being sick and saying it was Minnie. That's how it was. Minnie can't have done it."

"No. Quite impossible. You see, doctor? The milk which Minnie did prepare I took away; and I've tested it, and there was no arsenic in it, nor in the sealed bottle of milk from which I sent up that jugful. Absolutely clear case. Mrs. Colson put arsenic into the milk herself from a store she had in the bedroom, and burnt the rest on the gas-stove; then she swallowed the dose, and, when the pangs came on, accused Minnie. No probable, possible shadow of doubt; no possible doubt whatever. Suicide by mother in order to convict daughter of murder. Case with elements of tragedy, as you say."

"My God! It's horrible," the doctor gasped.

"You think so? Yes. However. We've prevented the worst. We've made an end. You'd better go back to your patient."

"I can't do anything," the doctor muttered.

"Oh, no. No. But she might as well die as easy as may be." The doctor stared at him, and went slowly out.

"Mr. Fortune," said Underwood, and stopped. "I mean to say, did you expect this?" Reggie gazed at his keen, anxious face with closing eyes. "When you changed the milk—when you sent me up to make sure Minnie didn't dope what you got ready—I made sure you were going to catch Minnie out by testing the first lot."

"One of the possibilities," Reggie murmured. "Never probable possibility. But one must try everything. Broken toad indicated criminal was person of determination—Minnie isn't."

"You did think the old lady would poison herself?"

A small smile curled Reggie's lips. "What I thought isn't evidence. I was protectin' the innocent. Our job, Underwood. We haven't been very efficient. But some success at last. Also our job to punish the sinner. That we have done. See the sequence, don't you? Murders of grandfather and father committed to enrich the darlin' son. Murder of constable accidental in attempt to murder darlin' son's wife, subsequently achieved. Motive of that; deliverance of darlin' son from extravagant and vicious wife. If daughter could be convicted of the murder, whole of family fortune would be left for son. Hence daughter's string used for trip line, and daughter's shoes scratched on the broken toad. Devoted mother. Absolute devotion. When police were gettin' dangerous about the murders—when darlin' son came runnin' to her in a fright that they were makin' a case against him—final effort to save him by proving, with her own death, daughter was the family murderer. Beautiful self-sacrifice."

"Good God!" said Underwood, under his breath. "That's why you bullied Alfred into a funk!"

"My dear chap! Oh, my dear chap!" Reggie murmured. "Experiment made to observe reactions. Where have you put Minnie?"

"She's up in her room, poor woman. That Miss Pearse is with her. When we had the big upset, Miss Pearse came in, hearing the row, and took her in hand. I was glad of it, I own. Minnie was pretty well throwing fits."

"Poor soul. Yes," Reggie sighed. "Go and ask Miss Pearse to come and see me a minute, will you?"

Miss Pearse came. She was tightly neat still, and still her little meek face had the assurance of power over everything.

"You're very kind," said Reggie.

"Minnie is helpless," said Miss Pearse.

"It's all over. Does she know that?"

"I have told her the doctor says her mother won't recover. What do you want her to be told?"

"That there's no blame on her. For her mother. For anything."

Miss Pearse gave him a cold smile. "You have made sure of that? I congratulate you."

"Oh, no. No. Your work. You gave me the key, Miss Pearse. When you made it so clear Mrs. Colson was a devoted mother. Confirmed by broken toad."

"You are very acute, sir," said Miss Pearse primly.

"Thanks very much. I value that." Reggie bowed.

"Mrs. Colson committed suicide, of course?"

"Yes. Last act. Yes."

"I have told Minnie that she did. Can you imagine what Minnie said?"

"I think so. Yes," Reggie sighed. "Probably said it ought to have been her."

"You are quite right. She said, 'Why wasn't it me; oh, it should have been me?' These self-sacrificing people! I have no patience with them."

"No. Nuisance." Reggie smiled. "You'll look after her, won't you!"

"Of course I shall," said Miss Pearse.

IN THE TEETH OF THE EVIDENCE

Dorothy L. Sayers

Dorothy Leigh Sayers (1893–1957) was one of the most influential figures in the history of crime writing, even though she had a relatively short career as a detective novelist. Her first novel, *Whose Body?*, introduced Lord Peter Wimsey in 1923; her last, *Busman's Honeymoon* (which began life as a play co-written with Muriel St Claire Byrne, and has the ominous sub-title *A Love Story with Detective Interruptions*) appeared a mere fourteen years later. In the last two decades of her life she preferred to concentrate on theological writing and translating Dante, producing only a handful of detective short stories, none of which were especially significant. Nevertheless, she made a lasting impression on the genre as an author, historian, and reviewer. In addition, she played a leading role in the formation of the Detection Club, of which she became the third president, remaining in office from 1949 until her death.

Sayers was not a scientist—she studied languages at Somerville College, Oxford, and worked in advertising before becoming a full-time writer—but her interest in the scientific is evident in several of her most memorable detective stories, such as *Unnatural Death* (aka *The Dawson Pedigree*, 1927), which features a highly unusual murder method. The title story from *In the Teeth of the Evidence* (1939) concerns forensic dentistry, and is one of her best short stories about Lord Peter. The reference in the text to a "Rouse case" is to the sensational real-life "blazing car murder" committed in 1930 by A. A. Rouse; the victim has never been identified.

"Furnace" was Samuel James Furnace, a killer who committed suicide by swallowing hydrochloric acid while in police custody in 1933.

"WELL, OLD SON," SAID MR. LAMPLOUGH, "AND WHAT can we do for you today?"

"Oh, some of your whizz-bang business, I suppose," said Lord Peter Wimsey, seating himself resentfully in the green velvet torture-chair and making a face in the direction of the drill. "Jolly old left-hand upper grinder come to bits on me. I was only eating an ome-lette, too. Can't understand why they always pick these moments. If I'd been cracking nuts or chewing peppermint jumbles I could understand it."

"Yes?" said Mr. Lamplough, soothingly. He drew an electric bulb, complete with mirror, as though by magic out of a kind of Maskelyne-and-Devant contraption on Lord Peter's left; a trail of flex followed it, issuing apparently from the bowels of the earth. "Any pain?"

"No *pain*," said Wimsey irritably, "unless you count a sharp edge fit to saw your tongue off. Point is, why should it go pop like that? I wasn't doing anything to it."

"No?" said Mr. Lamplough, his manner hovering between the professional and the friendly, for he was an old Winchester man and a member of one of Wimsey's clubs, and had frequently met him on the cricket-field in the days of their youth. "Well, if you'll stop talking half a moment, we'll have a look at it. Ah!"

"Don't say 'Ah!' like that, as if you'd found pyorrhoea and necro-sis of the jaw and were gloating over it, you damned old ghoul. Just carve it out and stop it up and be hanged to you. And, by the way, what have you been up to? Why should I meet an inspector of police on your doorstep? You needn't pretend he came to have his bridge-work attended to, because I saw his sergeant waiting for him outside."

"Well, it was rather curious," said Mr. Lamplough, dexterously gagging his friend with one hand and dabbing cotton-wool into the offending cavity with the other. "I suppose I oughtn't to tell you, but if I don't, you'll get it all out of your friends at Scotland Yard. They wanted to see my predecessor's books. Possibly you noticed that bit in the papers about a dental man being found dead in a blazing garage on Wimbledon Common?"

"Yonk—ugh?" said Lord Peter Wimsey.

"Last night," said Mr. Lamplough. "Pooped off about nine pip emma, and it took them three hours to put it out. One of those wooden garages—and the big job was to keep the blaze away from the house. Fortunately it's at the end of the row, with nobody at home. Apparently this man Prendergast was all alone there—just going off for a holiday or something—and he contrived to set himself and his car and his garage alight last night and was burnt to death. In fact, when they found him, he was so badly charred that they couldn't be sure it was he. So, being sticklers for routine, they had a look at his teeth."

"Oh, yes?" said Wimsey, watching Mr. Lamplough fitting a new drill into its socket. "Didn't anybody have a go at putting the fire out?"

"Oh, yes—but as it was a wooden shed, full of petrol, it simply went up like a bonfire. Just a little bit over this way, please. That's splendid." Gr-r-r, whizz, gr-r-r. "As a matter of fact, they seem to think it might just possibly be suicide. The man's married, with three children, and immured and all that sort of thing." Whizz, gr-r-r, buzz, gr-r-r, whizz. "His family's down at Worthing, staying with his mother-in-law or something. Tell me if I hurt you." Gr-r-r. "And I don't suppose he was doing any too well. Still, of course, he may easily have had an accident when filling up. I gather he was starting off that night to join them."

"A—ow—oo—oo—uh—ihi—ih?" inquired Wimsey naturally enough.

"How do I come into it?" said Mr. Lamplough, who, from long experience was expert in the interpretation of mumblings. "Well, only because the chap whose practice I took over here did this fellow Prendergast's dental work for him." Whizz. "He died, but left his books behind him for my guidance, in case any of his old patients should feel inclined to trust me." Gr-r-r, whizz. "I'm sorry. Did you feel that? As a matter of fact, some of them actually do. I suppose it's an instinct to trundle round to the same old place when you're in pain, like the dying elephants. Will you rinse, please?"

"I see," said Wimsey, when he had finished washing out chips of himself and exploring his ravaged molar with his tongue. "How odd it is that these cavities always seem so large. I feel as if I could put my head into this one. Still, I suppose you know what you're about. And are Prendergast's teeth all right?"

"Haven't had time to hunt through the ledger, yet, but I've said I'll go down to have a look at them as soon as I've finished with you. It's my lunch-time anyway, and my two o'clock patient isn't coming, thank goodness. She usually brings five spoilt children, and they all want to sit round and watch, and play with the apparatus. One of them got loose last time and tried to electrocute itself on the X-ray plant next door. And she thinks that children should be done at half-price. A little wider if you can manage it." Gr-r-r. "Yes, that's very nice. Now we can dress that and put in a temporary. Rinse, please."

"Yes," said Wimsey, "and for goodness' sake make it firm and not too much of your foul oil of cloves. I don't want bits to come out in the middle of dinner. You can't imagine the nastiness of caviar flavoured with cloves."

"No?" said Mr. Lamplough. "You may find this a little cold." Squirt, swish. "Rinse, please. You may notice it when the dressing goes in. Oh, you did notice it? Good. That shows that the nerve's all right. Only a little longer now. There! Yes, you may get down now. Another rinse? Certainly. When would you like to come in again?"

"Don't be silly, old horse," said Wimsey. "I am coming out to Wimbledon with you straight away. You'll get there twice as fast if I drive you. I've never had a corpse-in-blazing-garage before, and I want to learn."

There is nothing really attractive about corpses in blazing garages. Even Wimsey's war experience did not quite reconcile him to the object that lay on the mortuary slab in the police station. Charred out of all resemblance to humanity, it turned even the police surgeon pale, while Mr. Lamplough was so overcome that he had to lay down the books he had brought with him and retire into the open to recover himself. Meanwhile Wimsey, having put himself on terms of mutual confidence and esteem with the police officials, thoughtfully turned over the little pile of blackened odds and ends that represented the contents of Mr. Prendergast's pockets. There was nothing remarkable about them. The leather note-case still held the remains of a thickish wad of notes—doubtless cash in hand for the holiday at Worthing. The handsome gold watch (obviously a presentation) had stopped at seven minutes past nine. Wimsey remarked on its good state of preservation. Sheltered between the left arm and the body—that seemed to be the explanation.

"Looks as though the first sudden blaze had regularly overcome him," said the police inspector. "He evidently made no attempt to get out. He'd simply fallen forward over the wheel, with his head on the dashboard. That's why the face is so disfigured. I'll show you the remains of the car presently if you're interested, my lord. If the other gentleman's feeling better we may as well take the body first."

Taking the body was a long and unpleasant job. Mr. Lamplough, nerving himself with an effort and producing a pair of forceps and a probe, went gingerly over the jaws—reduced almost to their bony structure by the furnace heat to which they had been exposed—while the police surgeon checked entries in the ledger. Mr. Prendergast had a dental history extending back over ten years in the ledger and had already had two or three fillings done before that time. These had been noted at the time when he first came to Mr. Lamplough's predecessor.

At the end of a long examination, the surgeon looked up from the notes he had been making.

"Well, now," he said, "let's check that again. Allowing for renewal of old work, I think we've got a pretty accurate picture of the present state of his mouth. There ought to be nine fillings in all. Small amalgam filling in right lower back wisdom tooth; big amalgam ditto in right lower back molar; amalgam fillings in right upper first and second bicuspids at point of contact; right upper incisor crowned—that all right?"

"I expect so," said Mr. Lamplough, "except that the right upper incisor seems to be missing altogether, but possibly the crown came loose and fell out." He probed delicately. "The jaw is very brittle—I can't make anything of the canal—but there's nothing against it."

"We may find the crown in the garage," suggested the Inspector.

"Fused porcelain filling in left upper canine," went on the surgeon; "amalgam fillings in left upper first bicuspid and lower second bicuspid and left lower thirteen-year-old molar. That seems to be all. No teeth missing and no artificials. How old was this man, Inspector?"

"About forty-five, Doc."

"My age. I only wish I had as good a set of teeth," said the surgeon. Mr. Lamplough agreed with him.

"Then I take it, this is Mr. Prendergast all right," said the Inspector.

"Not a doubt of it, I should say," replied Mr. Lamplough; "though I should like to find that missing crown."

"We'd better go round to the house, then," said the Inspector. "Well, yes, thank you, my lord, I shouldn't mind a lift in that. Some car. Well, the only point now is, whether it was accident or suicide. Round to the right, my lord, and then second on the left—I'll tell you as we go."

"A bit out of the way for a dental man," observed Mr. Lamplough, as they emerged upon some scattered houses near the Common.

The Inspector made a grimace.

"I thought the same, sir, but it appears Mrs. Prendergast persuaded him to come here. So good for the children. Not so good for the practice, though. If you ask me, I should say Mrs. P. was the biggest argument we have for suicide. Here we are."

The last sentence was scarcely necessary. There was a little crowd about the gate of a small detached villa at the end of a row of similar houses. From a pile of dismal debris in the garden a smell of burning still rose, disgustingly. The Inspector pushed through the gate with his companions, pursued by the comments of the bystanders.

"That's the Inspector... that's Dr. Maggs... that'll be another doctor, him with the little bag... who's the bloke in the eye-glass?...

Looks a proper nobleman, don't he, Florrie?... Why he'll be the insurance bloke... Coo! look at his grand car... that's where the money goes... That's a Rolls, that is... no, silly, it's a Daimler... Ow, well, it's all advertisement these days."

Wimsey giggled indecorously all the way up the garden path. The sight of the skeleton car amid the sodden and fire-blackened remains of the garage sobered him. Two police constables, crouched over the ruin with a sieve, stood up and saluted.

"How are you getting on, Jenkins?"

"Haven't got anything very much yet, sir, bar an ivory cigarette-holder. This gentleman"—indicating a stout, bald man in spectacles, who was squatting among the damaged coachwork, "is Mr. Tolley, from the motor-works, come with a note from the Superintendent, sir."

"Ah, yes. Can you give any opinion about this, Mr. Tolley? Dr. Maggs you know. Mr. Lamplough, Lord Peter Wimsey. By the way, Jenkins, Mr. Lamplough has been going into the corpse's dentistry, and he's looking for a lost tooth. You might see if you can find it. Now, Mr. Tolley?"

"Can't see much doubt about how it happened," said Mr. Tolley, picking his teeth thoughtfully. "Regular death-traps, these little saloons, when anything goes wrong unexpectedly. There's a front tank, you see, and it looks as though there might have been a bit of a leak behind the dash, somewhere. Possibly the seam of the tank had got strained a bit, or the union had come loose. It's loose now, as a matter of fact, but that's not unusual after a fire, Rouse case or no Rouse case. You can get quite a lot of slow dripping from a damaged tank or pipe, and there seems to have been a coconut mat round the controls, which would prevent you from noticing. There'd be a smell, of course, but these little garages do often get to smell of petrol, and he kept several cans of the stuff here. More than the legal amount—but *that's* not unusual either. Looks to me as though he'd filled up his tank—there are two empty tins near the bonnet, with the caps loose—got in, shut the door, started up the car, perhaps, and then lit a cigarette. Then, if there were any petrol fumes about from a leak, the whole show would go up in his face—whoosh!"

"How was the ignition?"

"Off. He may never have switched it on, but it's quite likely he switched it off again when the flames went up. Silly thing to do, but lots of people *do* do it. The proper thing, of course, is to switch off the petrol and leave the engine running so as to empty the carburettor, but you don't always think straight when you're being burnt alive. Or he may have meant to turn off the petrol and been overcome before he could manage it. The tank's over here to the left, you see."

"On the other hand," said Wimsey, "he may have committed suicide and faked the accident."

"Nasty way of committing suicide."

"Suppose he'd taken poison first."

"He'd have had to stay alive long enough to fire the car."

"That's true. Suppose he'd shot himself—would the flash from the—no, that's silly—you'd have found the weapon in the case. Or a hypodermic? Same objection. Prussic acid might have done it—I mean, he might just have had time to take a tablet and then fire the car. Prussic acid's pretty quick, but it isn't absolutely instantaneous."

"I'll have a look for it anyway," said Dr. Maggs.

They were interrupted by the constable.

"Excuse me, sir, but I think we've found the tooth. Mr. Lamplough says this is it."

Between his pudgy finger and thumb he held up a small, bony object, from which a small stalk of metal still protruded.

"That's a right upper incisor crown all right by the look of it," said Mr. Lamplough. "I suppose the cement gave way with the heat. Some cements are sensitive to heat, some, on the other hand, to damp. Well, that settles it, doesn't it?"

"Yes—well, we shall have to break it to the widow. Not that she can be in very much doubt, I imagine."

Mrs. Prendergast—a very much made-up lady with a face set in lines of habitual peevishness—received the news with a burst of loud sobs. She informed them, when she was sufficiently recovered, that Arthur had always been careless about petrol, that he smoked too much, that she had often warned him about the danger of small saloons, that she had told him he ought to get a bigger car, that the one he had was not really large enough for her and the whole family, that he *would* drive at night, though she had always said it was dangerous, and that if he'd listened to her, it would never have happened.

"Poor Arthur was not a good driver. Only last week, when he was taking us down to Worthing, he drove the car right up on a bank in trying to pass a lorry, and frightened us all dreadfully."

"Ah!" said the Inspector. "No doubt that's how the tank got strained." Very cautiously he inquired whether Mr. Prendergast could have had any reason for taking his own life. The widow was indignant. It was true that the practice had been declining of late, but Arthur would never have been so wicked as to do such a thing. Why, only three months ago, he had taken out a life-insurance for £500 and he'd never have invalidated it by committing suicide within the term stipulated by the policy. Inconsiderate of her as Arthur was, and whatever injuries he had done her as a wife, he wouldn't rob his innocent children.

The Inspector pricked up his ears at the word "injuries". What injuries?

Oh, well, of course, she'd known all the time that Arthur was carrying on with that Mrs. Fielding. You couldn't deceive her with all this stuff about teeth needing continual attention. And it was all very well to say that Mrs. Fielding's house was better run than her own. *That* wasn't surprising—a rich widow with no children and no responsibilities, of course she could afford to have everything nice. You couldn't expect a busy wife to do miracles on such a small housekeeping allowance. If Arthur had wanted things different, he should have been more generous, and it was easy enough for Mrs. Fielding to attract men, dressed up like a fashion plate and no better than she should be. She'd told Arthur that if it didn't stop she'd divorce him. And since then he'd taken to spending all his evenings in Town, and what was he doing there—

The Inspector stemmed the torrent by asking for Mrs. Fielding's address.

"I'm sure I don't know," said Mrs. Prendergast. "She did live at Number 57, but she went abroad after I made it clear I wasn't going to stand any more of it. It's very nice to be some people, with plenty of money to spend. I've never been abroad since our honeymoon, and that was only to Boulogne."

At the end of this conversation, the Inspector sought Dr. Maggs and begged him to be thorough in his search for prussic acid.

The remaining testimony was that of Gladys, the general servant. She had left Mr. Prendergast's house the day before at 6 o'clock. She was to have taken a week's holiday while the Prendergasts were at Worthing. She had thought that Mr. Prendergast had seemed worried and nervous the last few days, but that had not surprised her, because she knew he disliked staying with his wife's people. She (Gladys) had finished her work and put out a cold supper and then gone home with her employer's permission. He had a patient—a gentleman from Australia, or some such a place, who wanted his teeth attended to in a hurry before going off on his travels again. Mr. Prendergast had explained that he would be working late, and would shut up the house himself, and she need not wait. Further inquiry showed that Mr. Prendergast had "scarcely touched" his supper, being, presumably, in a hurry to get off. Apparently, then, the patient had been the last person to see Mr. Prendergast alive.

The dentist's appointment-book was next examined. The patient figured there as "Mr. Williams 5.30", and the address-book placed Mr. Williams at a small hotel in Bloomsbury. The manager of the hotel said that Mr. Williams had stayed there for a week. He had given no address except "Adelaide", and had mentioned that he was revisiting the old country for the first time after twenty years and had no friends in London. Unfortunately, he could not be interviewed. At about half-past ten the previous night, a messenger had called, bringing his card, to pay his bill and remove his luggage. No address had been left for forwarding letters. It was not a district messenger, but a man in a slouch hat and heavy dark overcoat. The night-porter had not seen his face very clearly, as only one light was on in the hall. He had told them to hurry up, as Mr. Williams wanted to catch the boat-train from Waterloo. Inquiry at the booking-office showed that a Mr. Williams had actually travelled on that train, being booked to Paris. The ticket had been taken that same night. So Mr. Williams had disappeared into the blue, and even if they could trace him, it seemed unlikely that he could throw much light on Mr. Prendergast's state of mind immediately previous to the disaster. It seemed a little odd, at first, that Mr. Williams, from Adelaide, staying in Bloomsbury, should have travelled to Wimbledon to get his teeth attended to, but the simple explanation was the likeliest: namely, that the friendless Williams had struck up an acquaintance with Prendergast in a café or some such place, and that a casual mention of his dental necessities had led to a project of mutual profit and assistance.

After which, nothing seemed to be left but for the coroner to bring in a verdict of Death by Misadventure and for the widow to send in her claim to the Insurance Company, when Dr. Maggs upset the whole scheme of things by announcing that he had discovered traces of a large injection of hyoscine in the body, and what about it? The Inspector, on hearing this, observed callously that he was not surprised. If ever a man had an excuse for suicide, he thought it was Mrs. Prendergast's husband. He thought that it would be desirable to make a careful search among the scorched laurels surrounding what had been Mr. Prendergast's garage. Lord Peter Wimsey agreed, but committed himself to the prophecy that the syringe would not be found.

Lord Peter Wimsey was entirely wrong. The syringe was found next day, in a position suggesting that it had been thrown out of the window of the garage after use. Traces of the poison were discovered to be present in it. "It's a slow-working drug," observed Dr. Maggs. "No doubt he jabbed himself, threw the syringe away, hoping it would never be looked for, and then, before he lost consciousness, climbed into the car and set light to it. A clumsy way of doing it."

"A damned ingenious way of doing it," said Wimsey. "I don't believe in that syringe, somehow." He rang up his dentist. "Lamplough, old horse," he said, "I wish you'd do something for me. I wish you'd go over those teeth again. No—not my teeth; Prendergast's."

"Oh, blow it!" said Mr. Lamplough, uneasily.

"No, but I wish you would," said his lordship.

The body was still unburied, Mr. Lamplough, grumbling very much, went down to Wimbledon with Wimsey, and again went through his distasteful task. This time he started on the left side.

"Lower thirteen-year-old molar and second bicuspid filled amalgam. The fire's got at those a bit, but they're all right. First upper bicuspid—bicuspids are stupid sort of teeth—always the first to go. That filling looks to have been rather carelessly put in—not what I should call good work; it seems to extend over the next tooth— possibly the fire did that. Left upper canine, cast porcelain filling on anterior face—"

"Half a jiff," said Wimsey, "Maggs' note says 'fused porcelain'. Is it the same thing?"

"No. Different process. Well, I suppose it's fused porcelain—difficult to see. I should have said it was cast, myself, but that's as may be."

"Let's verify it in the ledger. I wish Maggs had put the dates in—goodness knows how far I shall have to hunt back, and I don't understand this chap's writing or his dashed abbreviations."

"You won't have to go back very far if it's cast. The stuff only came in about 1928, from America. There was quite a rage for it then, but for some reason it didn't take on extraordinarily well over here. But some men use it."

"Oh, then it isn't cast," said Wimsey. "There's nothing here about canines, back to '28. Let's make sure; '27, '26, '25, '24, '23. Here you are. Canine, something or other."

"That's it," said Lamplough, coming to look over his shoulder. "Fused porcelain. I must be wrong, then. Easily see by taking it out. The grain's different, and so is the way it's put in."

"How, different?"

"Well," said Mr. Lamplough, "one's a cast, you see."

"And the other's fused. I did grasp that much. Well, go ahead and take it out."

"Can't very well; not here."

"Then take it home and do it there. Don't you see, Lamplough, how important it is? If it is cast porcelain, or whatever you call it, it *can't* have been done in '23. And if it was removed later, then another dentist must have done it. And he may have done other things—and in that case, those things ought to be there, and they're not. Don't you *see?*"

"I see you're getting rather agitato," said Mr. Lamplough; "all I can say is, I refuse to have this thing taken along to my surgery. Corpses aren't popular in Harley Street."

In the end, the body was removed, by permission, to the dental department of the local hospital. Here Mr. Lamplough, assisted by the staff dental expert, Dr. Maggs, and the police, delicately extracted the filling from the canine.

"If that," said he triumphantly, "is not cast porcelain I will extract all my own teeth without an anaesthetic and swallow them. What do you say, Benton?"

The hospital dentist agreed with him. Mr. Lamplough, who had suddenly developed an eager interest in the problem, nodded, and inserted a careful probe between the upper right bicuspids, with thir adjacent fillings.

"Come and look at this, Benton. Allowing for the action of the fire and all this muck, wouldn't you have said this was a very recent filling? There, at the point of contact. Might have been done yesterday. And—here—wait a minute. Where's the lower jaw gone to? Get that fitted up. Give me a bit of carbon. Look at the tremendous bite there ought to be here, with that big molar coming down on to it. That filling's miles too high for the job. Wimsey—when was this bottom right-hand back molar filled?"

"Two years ago," said Wimsey.

"That's impossible," said the two dentists together, and Mr. Benton added:

"If you clean away the mess, you'll see it's a new filling. Never been bitten on, I should say. Look here, Mr. Lamplough, there's something odd here."

"Odd? I should say there was. I never thought about it when I was checking it up yesterday, but look at this old cavity in the lateral here. Why didn't he have that filled when all this other work was done? Now it's cleaned out you can see it plainly. Have you got a long probe? It's quite deep and must have given him jip. I say, Inspector, I want to have some of these fillings out. Do you mind?"

"Go ahead," said the Inspector, "we've got plenty of witnesses."

With Mr. Benton supporting the grisly patient, and Mr. Lamplough manipulating the drill, the filling of one of the molars was speedily drilled out, and Mr. Lamplough said: "Oh, gosh!"— which, as Lord Peter remarked, just showed you what a dentist meant when he said "Ah!"

"Try the bicuspids," suggested Mr. Benton.

"Or this thirteen-year-old," chimed in his colleague.

"Hold hard, gentlemen," protested the Inspector, "don't spoil the specimen altogether."

Mr. Lamplough drilled away without heeding him. Another filling came out, and Mr. Lamplough said "Gosh!" again.

"It's all right," said Wimsey, grinning, "you can get out your warrant, Inspector."

"What's that, my lord?"

"Murder," said Wimsey.

"Why?" said the Inspector. "Do these gentlemen mean that Mr. Prendergast got a new dentist who poisoned his teeth for him?"

"No," said Mr. Lamplough; "at least, not what you mean by poisoning. But I've never seen such work in my life. Why, in two places the man hasn't even troubled to clear out the decay at all. He's just enlarged the cavity and stopped it up again anyhow. Why this chap didn't get thundering abscesses I don't know."

"Perhaps," said Wimsey, "the stoppings were put in too recently. Hullo! what now?"

"This one's all right. No decay here. Doesn't look as if there ever had been, either. But one can't tell about that."

"I dare say there never was. Get your warrant out, Inspector."

"For the murder of Mr. Prendergast? And against whom?"

"No. Against Arthur Prendergast for the murder of one Mr. Williams, and, incidentally, for arson and attempted fraud. And against Mrs. Fielding too, if you like, for conspiracy. Though you mayn't be able to prove that part of it."

It turned out, when they found Mr. Prendergast in Rouen, that he had thought out the scheme well in advance. The one thing he had had to wait for had been to find a patient of his own height and build, with a good set of teeth and few home ties. When the unhappy Williams had fallen into his clutches, he had few preparations to make. Mrs. Prendergast had to be packed off to Worthing—a journey she was ready enough to take at any time—and the maid given a holiday. Then the necessary dental accessories had to be prepared and the victim invited out to tea at Wimbledon. Then the murder— a stunning blow from behind, followed by an injection. Then, the slow and horrid process of faking the teeth to correspond with Mr. Prendergast's own. Next, the exchange of clothes and the body carried down and placed in the car. The hypodermic put where it might be overlooked on a casual inspection and yet might plausibly be found if the presence of the drug should be discovered; ready, in the one case, to support a verdict of Accident and, in the second, of Suicide. Then the car soaked in petrol, the union loosened, the cans left about. The garage door and window left open, to lend colour to the story and provide a draught, and, finally, light set to the car by means of a train of petrol laid through the garage door. Then, flight to the station through the winter darkness and so by underground to London. The risk of being recognised on the underground was small, in Williams' hat and clothes and with a scarf wound about the lower part of the face. The next step was to pick up Williams' luggage and take the boat-train to join the wealthy and enamoured Mrs. Fielding in France. After which, Williams and Mrs. Williams could have returned to England, or not, as they pleased.

"Quite a student of criminology," remarked Wimsey, at the conclusion of this little adventure. "He'd studied Rouse and Furnace all right, and profited by their mistakes. Pity he overlooked that matter of the cast porcelain. Makes a quicker job, does it, Lamplough? Well, more haste, less speed. I do wonder, though, at what point of the proceedings Williams actually died."

"Shut up," said Mr. Lamplough, "and, by the way, I've still got to finish that filling for you."

THE CASE OF THE CHEMIST
IN THE CUPBOARD

Ernest Dudley

Vivian Ernest Coltman-Allen (1908–2006), who worked under the name Ernest Dudley, was a modestly successful actor who turned to journalism in the 1930s. According to his obituary in *The Times*, he "worked for various newspapers, as a boxing correspondent, crime reporter, jazz critic and gossip columnist. At one point, he was nightclub correspondent for the *Daily Mail*, a position which allowed him to indulge his taste for the high life. In one scoop, he described how he helped Fred Astaire to create a new dance step." During the war he worked for the BBC, and was asked to write a crime series; the result was a series of radio programmes featuring Doctor Morelle, a character inspired by Dudley's memories of the actor and director Erich von Stroheim.

Morelle, a scientific and medical expert with a fondness for criminology (and fencing) became a hugely popular character, and appeared in fourteen novels, over one hundred short stories and a film. This story is taken from *Meet Doctor Morelle* (1943); the back of the dust jacket proclaimed: "*Meet Doctor Morelle* has been on the air twice weekly for nine months—a record-breaking run. As millions of readers will know, these episodes are based on the memoirs of Doctor Morelle, that strange and sardonic character who wields an almost hypnotic influence over his assistant, Miss Frayle." The book was a selection of the Crime Book Society, but in inscribing one first edition, Dudley noted wryly that he'd been commissioned to write the stories and been paid £300, "but no further royalties"!

"QUICKLY—THE ACID, MISS FRAYLE!"

Miss Frayle rapidly scanned the row of test tubes and bottles.

"The small phial—next to the iron sulphate—" snapped Doctor Morelle, his hand outstretched impatiently.

His peremptory command flustered her for a moment. She snatched the phial and caught it against a large container of distilled water. There was a crash and tinkling of broken glass. Without a word and with incredible quickness the Doctor took Miss Frayle's hand and placed it under the full force of the cold water tap. Then he examined it carefully.

"You are singularly fortunate. You might have sustained a very nasty burn."

Miss Frayle readjusted her glasses and regained her breath.

"I—I'm sorry, Doctor Morelle," she managed to stammer. "It slipped and—"

"I am not incapable of perceiving you do not appear to exercise full control over your digital extremities! Has the acid splashed your clothes at all?"

"No—just the corner of my overall."

He seized a bottle of alkaline solution and applied it liberally to the part of her overall indicated. Then he turned out the Bunsen burner beneath the retort which had been emitting a pungent odour.

"That brings our little experiment to an abrupt conclusion for the time being at any rate," he said, with a chilling glance at her.

"I'm so sorry, Doctor," she apologised again.

"I think your expressions of regret might well take a practical form, Miss Frayle. Perhaps you would care to procure another phial of acid for me."

"If you'll tell me the name—"

"I'll write it down. It's just possible that Mr. Jordan may be of some assistance to me. You know his shop?"

"The little chemist's shop in the turning off Welbeck Street? Will there be anyone there at this time?"

"Mr. Jordan resides on the establishment. You will ring at the side entrance. I have written the formula on this card of mine—you will present it to Mr. Jordan with my compliments."

She took the card upon which he had scribbled his requirements. He went on:

"I am confident he will have a sufficient supply to enable me to carry on with my work tonight. So that if you will hasten, Miss Frayle, I should have time in which to complete the experiment I am engaged upon before retiring for the night."

Miss Frayle hurried off, while Doctor Morelle lit an inevitable Le Sphinx cigarette and then divested himself of his white coat. In a moment he had returned to his study to make some notes.

Despite its undistinguished frontage, Miss Frayle had no difficulty in finding Mr. Jordan's chemist shop. She made her way to the side door which was in a narrow entrance between the shop and a garage. She rang three times, but there was no response. No sound of any movement within. She knocked loudly. It was then she realised that the door was not firmly fastened. Her first knock sent it slightly ajar. She banged the old iron knocker again, but there was still no reply. After a pause she stepped inside with some idea of perhaps finding Mr. Jordan in a room at the back. A strong smell of antiseptics greeted her as she hesitated for some moments, trying to make up her mind whether to call out or not.

She called quietly at first: "Mr. Jordan?" Then louder. But no reply.

At the far end of the tiny hallway, she noticed a flight of stairs. Thinking the chemist might be occupied in an upstairs room and perhaps slightly deaf, she decided she had better investigate further. It was a choice between that and going back without the precious acid. She decided she could not face the sardonic rebuffs from Doctor Morelle if she should return empty-handed.

Very gingerly, she began to climb the stairs. It was only a short flight, opening on to a small landing which was crowded with crates, packing cases and cardboard boxes of all descriptions. She tapped on the door immediately facing her, and as there was no reply, tried the handle, feeling more and more like a person intent upon some guilty purpose.

The door opened to reveal an unusual-looking room. It was a combination of warehouse, laboratory, office and living room. Nearest the door were still more packages and shelves containing innumerable bottles, whilst under the window was a large sink and bench, obviously used for dispensing. In the wall opposite were large cupboards, and near the fireplace was a table upon which were the remnants of a hasty meal. Two or three chairs made up the rest of the furniture.

It was growing dusk, so she snapped on the electric light switch by the door. This, she felt should convince anyone that she did not seek concealment, and that her presence in the place was not for some dishonest motive.

The only sound emanated from an old-fashioned, noisy wall clock, and once again Miss Frayle stood nonplussed as to what she had better do next. Then she caught sight of the telephone perched on a roll-top desk in a corner near the fire. If she rang up Doctor Morelle and explained the position, she argued to herself, perhaps he would suggest some other chemist. Or he might even have some idea where Mr. Jordan was likely to be found. At any rate, those saturnine features would not be visible at the other end of the wire. She was assailed by doubts once more. Suppose Mr. Jordan came in and found her using his telephone? Well, she would have to explain that's all, she told herself. It would be embarrassing, but a vision of the Doctor awaiting her return with increasing impatience spurred her to action. She went over to the instrument and dialled.

In a moment there came Doctor Morelle's familiar tones:

"Yes?"

"Oh Doctor Morelle, it's me," she stammered. "I mean it's 'I'—Miss Frayle—" She hastily corrected her grammatical error and prayed he hadn't noticed it. All he said was:

"I am not incapable of recognising that the sounds impinging on my ear emanate from your vocal chords," his voice crackled over the wire. "From where are you telephoning?"

"Mr. Jordan's. I'm upstairs in his laboratory. He isn't here."

"Then where is he?"

"I—I'm afraid I don't know."

"Who admitted you then?"

"I knocked and rang, but no one answered. I tried the side door and as it wasn't locked I went in. I called out, still no reply. Then I thought he might be working upstairs so I came up. But no one's here at all." She drew a deep breath, "I've telephoned to know if you would like me to wait till Mr. Jordan comes back or—"

Doctor Morelle heard her break off with a sharp intake of breath, then give a terrified scream.

"Miss Frayle!"

There came another scream, which died into a moan. Followed a clattering thud, as if the telephone receiver had fallen.

"Miss Frayle—what is it! Answer me—what happened?" He waited a moment or two, then murmured himself. "Confounded nuisance she is!... Here am I waiting to proceed with my experiment... Frightened by a mouse no doubt!..." He flashed the receiver bar impatiently..."Hello?... Miss Frayle?..." After one more attempt, he replaced the instrument.

"Ah, well," he snapped to himself, "I suppose I had better go round and revive her."

It was now dark outside, and he might have had some little difficulty in finding the chemist's side door, but for the fact that he had his narrow examination torch with him. The door was as Miss Frayle had found it, half-open. He walked in quickly, called: "Is anyone there?" Then made his way swiftly upstairs. By his torch he could see the door slightly open at the top of the stairs. He went in, found the switch and flooded the room with light, to reveal Miss Frayle lying crumpled by the desk. In her fall, she had somehow contrived to wrench the telephone receiver from its cord, and the useless instrument lay on the floor. He picked it up and placed it on the desk, then turned his attention to Miss Frayle. She was still unconscious. Her face was ashen. He picked her up and laid her flat on an old couch that ran along one side of the room. Then he opened the window. Within a few moments she began to show signs of recovery. She moaned once or twice, then opened her eyes and blinked at him. She pushed her spectacles which had fallen awry back into position. Fortunately they had not been broken.

"Oh, Doctor, I must have fainted... I'm so sorry..."

"Why apologise?" he retorted with heavy sarcasm. "You are little more than semi-conscious at any time!" She passed her hand over her forehead in bewilderment, then struggled into a sitting position. He steadied her. He continued:

"However, perhaps you can recall what caused you *completely* to lose consciousness?"

She looked up at him in utter bewilderment for a moment. Then suddenly her eyes dilated with horror behind her spectacles and she swung her feet to the floor. She clutched at his arm:

"Where—where is it?"

He regarded her narrowly.

"Where is what?"

"The body! It fell out of that cupboard over there." She shuddered, and for a second looked as if she might be about to faint again. "It was horrible! Horrible!"

"Come, come!" said Doctor Morelle sharply. "Pull yourself together! As you can see, there is no body anywhere."

Miss Frayle blinked short-sightedly.

"But I saw it! While I was 'phoning you, the cupboard door over there started to open—it's open now—"

"Cupboards have opened before now as a result of traffic vibration from the street."

"That's what made me scream," she went on, not listening to his suggested explanation. The picture of what she had seen was too vivid in her mind. "When the door had swung open, the man fell out—and I fainted."

"Can you recall what he looked like?"

"His face was ghastly… there was blood on the side of his head… his hair was grey… he had a moustache… oh, it was terrible!" She shuddered once more. "Do you think it might have been Mr. Jordan?" she asked.

"He could answer to that very incomplete description," he agreed, but there was doubt in his voice. He said smoothly:

"There is, however, an aspect of this case which interests me particularly, Miss Frayle. Briefly it is how you managed to distinguish this man's appearance in the dark."

Miss Frayle sat straight upright with a jerk.

"In the dark?"

Doctor Morelle nodded, a sardonic expression on his face. "Yes, my *dear* Miss Frayle. When I arrived here this room was in complete darkness. While it may have been only dusk when you arrived here, still it would not have been light enough for you to observe—"

"But I put the light on when I came in," she said. And added quickly: "Otherwise, how would I have seen to telephone?"

He regarded her closely. There was no doubt about the certainty with which she spoke. She went on:

"Somebody must have come into the room while I was unconscious—and moved the body. And *they* switched off the light when they went out."

"H'm, that would have been possible, I suppose." He conceded the point reluctantly. He was annoyed that her explanation would cause him to abandon his theory that Miss Frayle had been suffering from some stupid hallucination. "I wish you would adjust your spectacles, instead of blinking at me in that astigmatic fashion," he snapped suddenly.

They had slipped again in Miss Frayle's excited vehemence. She put them into position once more. Meanwhile the Doctor was carefully examining the cupboard she had indicated. He discovered a small, dark, wet stain that might have been blood.

He surveyed the rest of the room. Standing on a small cupboard near the sink he found a bowl containing two or three goldfish.

"Somewhat incongruous," he mused. "Mr. Jordan's laboratory would appear to be adequately equipped." His gaze rested upon a collection of test-tubes and various chemical apparatus. To his experienced eye they told him the chemist had obviously been engaged in research work of some nature.

He moved over to the table and gave a cursory glance at the remains of Mr. Jordan's tea, which had been laid on a check cloth covering only half the table's surface. He was about to pass on when he noticed a cigarette-end almost concealed by a folded evening newspaper. It had apparently burnt itself out on the edge of the table.

"Do you recall noticing this before?" he asked Miss Frayle, pointing to the cigarette end. She shook her head.

"Then perhaps you will assist me to look for an ash-tray."

Puzzled by his request, Miss Frayle nevertheless obeyed. They searched every likely place during the next few minutes. At length, having failed to find any ash-tray, he murmured:

"It would appear indicative that Mr. Jordan is—or was—a non-smoker. That might, in turn, suggest he recently entertained a visitor who did smoke."

"Yes—yes, that would be it," agreed Miss Frayle enthusiastically. "Perhaps we could trace the man that way—if we could find out the make of cigarette—" she concluded somewhat vaguely.

"I had already ascertained the name of the manufacturers of the brand in question," replied the Doctor with a frosty smile. "As, however, I imagine they sell the better part of a million a day of this particular brand this knowledge would not seem to be of much assistance to us!"

Miss Frayle subsided.

Doctor Morelle continued to survey the room in search of some sort of clue. Finally, he went to the window. With some difficulty he managed to open it to its full extent, and stood looking out on the yard of the garage below. It was moonlight. "I wonder," he mused, "if the body could have been removed by way of this window?"

Miss Frayle joined him and too looked out.

"It isn't very high from the ground," she said helpfully. He nodded and thoughtfully lit a cigarette. "It is just possible that man cleaning his car down there may have noticed something unusual."

"I'll call him," said Miss Frayle promptly, and proceeded to do so. The man looked up and replied in a Cockney accent. He wore overalls, but there was a taxi-driver's hat perched on the back of his head.

"Wot's the trouble?" he asked, looking up from his work.

"Er—do you—have you...?" Miss Frayle became incoherent, not knowing what question would be quite the one to ask. Doctor Morelle unceremoniously edged her aside.

"During this evening, have you, by any chance, observed a person or persons descending from this window?" he said.

The man eyed him quizzically, then pushed his cap even further back on his head.

"No, guv'nor, I ain't seen no person or persons. I ain't seen nobody. But then I been inside the garridge this last 'alf-hour, cleaning up the old taxi. I reckons to give 'er a sluice twice a week, and it's usually about this time, on account of business bein' a bit slack. So I takes this opportunity to—"

"Quite so," Doctor Morelle cut short the garrulous explanation.

"I can't say as I've ever seen anybody climb out o' that window," pursued the taxi-driver. "But wiv' that spout," he waved in the direction of where a rain-spout might be, "it shouldn't be much trouble—especially to one of these cat burglars. Why—is there anything wrong?"

"Nothing wrong," replied the Doctor and pulled down the window.

"There would not appear to be any egress in that direction," he murmured.

"Wasn't he smoking a cigarette?" asked Miss Frayle. "I saw the glow of it, I'm sure."

"That fact alone would not necessarily implicate him in this affair," replied the Doctor acidly. "At this moment, there are possibly five million people in London, including the murderer, smoking a cigarette. Even I am indulging in the pernicious habit!"

With a saturnine smile he flicked the ash of his Le Sphinx. Then he leaned against the edge of the table and surveyed the room once more. Miss Frayle regarded him anxiously.

"What are you going to do now, Doctor? Don't you think we ought to notify the police?"

"All in good time, my dear Miss Frayle, all in good time! First, I wish to consider the evidence so far manifest. There are several quite amateurish aspects of this case which should not render the mystery particularly difficult to elucidate."

"Well, I don't quite see that we're getting much further... Perhaps if the police could examine some fingerprints or—"

"Such elementary routine, while it may serve to fire your somewhat fevered imagination, would merely hinder the process of deduction at this stage."

He took out his magnifying glass and examined another blotch on the floor, just outside the cupboard from which Miss Frayle had seen the body fall. For the greater part uncovered, the floor was marked with stains of all sizes and descriptions, but this particular one seemed to be fresh, and also had the appearance of blood.

"No doubt a slight effusion from the wound when the body fell," he murmured thoughtfully. "If only you could have contrived to retain control of your senses at that moment, Miss Frayle."

"But I've never seen a body fall from a cupboard like that before, Doctor!" she protested.

"I hope you are now satisfied. But that is of no assistance to me in discovering the identity of—"

He was interrupted by a ring at the side-door bell.

Miss Frayle jumped. "Oh—what's that?" she cried.

His mouth twisted into a smile. "Merely the result of electrical impetus upon a mechanical device, actuated through pressure applied by a human agency upon another mechanical device!"

Miss Frayle goggled at him through her spectacles as one word magniloquently followed its predecessor.

"You mean it's the door bell?" she managed to murmur at last.

"Precisely, Miss Frayle!"

He stubbed out his cigarette.

"Who is it, I wonder?" she asked.

"That," he said suavely, "may be ascertained by proceeding to the door in question and opening it."

"I'll go." But he motioned to her to remain where she was.

"I would rather you remained here—and sat down," he said.

"Thank you, Doctor." She gave him a grateful look. "I *am* still feeling a bit shaky."

"Do not misunderstand me," he replied quickly as he made for the door. "I am merely anxious to avoid the irritation of your again losing that little consciousness with which you are normally endowed!"

Miss Frayle, however, no longer appeared to be paying attention.

"Listen!" she whispered, her eyes widening. "Whoever it is, they've got tired of waiting."

There was a sound of footsteps ascending the wooden stairs.

"Alfred—you there?" called a man's voice.

Doctor Morelle, who had paused at the door and stood waiting, made no reply.

Miss Frayle breathed: "It's a man!"

"Brilliant, Miss Frayle!" the Doctor said, without taking his eyes off the door.

In a moment the door opened. A short, thickset man wearing a bowler hat stood there. He removed it to reveal light, almost sandy hair. His eyebrows seemed to be non-existent; and he boasted a straggly sandy moustache. His blue suit was rather shabby, and inclined to be shiny at the elbows. His rather bleary eyes were somewhat shifty, and as he saw them he appeared to assume an air of confident ease which seemed to require of him not a little effort.

"Hello, what's all this?" he exclaimed heartily, as he came into the room.

"Good evening," replied the Doctor smoothly, waiting for a further explanation.

"Isn't Alfred—Mr. Jordan here?" demanded the visitor.

"I fear I cannot tell you." Doctor Morelle surveyed the newcomer with narrowed eyes calculated to make anyone feel uncomfortable.

"He—he's disappeared," Miss Frayle said.

"Disappeared?" repeated the man. "How d'you mean 'disappeared'? I expect he's popped out to see one of his pals, more likely than not. Or a customer, maybe. He's sure to be back soon. You see he was expecting me. I'm his brother-in-law, by the way. Green's my name."

"I am Doctor Morelle, and this is my assistant, Miss Frayle."

Green nodded.

"Have you been here long, Doctor?"

"Some considerable time. I—er—wanted a particular acid from him at rather short notice. But he seems to have vanished in somewhat odd circumstances. A cigarette?"

Green shook his head.

"No thanks—don't smoke. Funny old Alfred isn't here. It was rather a particular matter of business I wanted to see him about. I wonder if he got my message wrong? Thought he was to meet me round at my place?"

He raised the hand holding his bowler and scratched his sandy head.

"This is a blooming nuisance! Taken me half an hour to get here, and now he's out. I wish I knew if he'd gone to my place." He gave Doctor Morelle a genial grin, who coldly ignored it, and went on to suggest:

"I suppose there is no possibility of telephoning your residence in order to ascertain whether or no he is there?"

"Er—yes—could do that—if his 'phone here had been working."

"Doubtless there is a call-box within easy reach?"

"Just round the corner, there is as a matter of fact."

"We will go out together," said Doctor Morelle. "If you will excuse me a moment..."

He went to the window and flung it open. The taxi-man was busily polishing the radiator of his cab.

"You again, guv'nor?" he grinned, looking up.

"Would you bring your taxi round to the front immediately?"

"Okay—couple of shakes! Just give me time to get me coat on..."

The Doctor closed the window.

"But why do we want a taxi, Doctor?" Miss Frayle asked, a puzzled expression on her face.

"For the purpose of transit to the nearest police station," replied Doctor Morelle deliberately.

She glanced quickly at Green, who had swung round at the last two words.

"Police station?" he repeated. "What's on your mind, Doctor?"

Doctor Morelle showed no sign of perturbation. "I have an idea the mystery of the missing Mr. Jordan will very soon be elucidated," he replied evenly. "Elucidated by me, of course—after which it will be merely a matter of form to hand the culprit over to the appropriate authorities."

"Anyone would think there's been some sort of crime," the other expostulated. "Just because old Alfred pops up the road—"

"If you will come down and make your telephone call, perhaps you may be able to give us some further information regarding Mr. Jordan's movements?"

"Yes—all right—I'm ready," agreed the other, moving towards the door. "I hope nothing *has* happened to him." he went on. "But I'm sure you're taking it too seriously."

"Possibly," said Doctor Morelle curtly, turning to Miss Frayle.

"Perhaps you will wait here for the taxi-driver and direct him to the telephone box? We shall be awaiting him."

"Yes—of course, Doctor Morelle."

The Doctor followed Green down the narrow stair. Miss Frayle came after them. They went out through the side door and Doctor Morelle and the other went off. She waited at the front of the shop until the taxi appeared.

The Doctor and Green reached the call-box, and the man went inside to make his call.

While he was speaking on the telephone, the taxi drove up, Miss Frayle opened the door to find the Doctor waiting, quietly smoking a cigarette.

"Have you really discovered the murderer of Mr. Jordan?" she asked him in a whisper with a hurried glance at the man in the call-box.

"Indubitably, my dear Miss Frayle. He is at present quite busily occupied inside this telephone box." She gasped and he proceeded smoothly: "We may have a little difficulty in persuading him to visit the police station. However—"

Miss Frayle interrupted him. "Don't worry about that, Doctor Morelle! We shall have no trouble at all!"

He gave her a quick, quizzical look.

"I am afraid I fail to comprehend you, Miss Frayle. Perhaps you will kindly—?"

Again she interrupted him. This time a triumphant smile lit up her face.

"There isn't much to explain, Doctor," she said. "Simply that I've brought a policeman with me!"

And she indicated the stalwart figure of a police constable who was at that moment clambering out of the taxi.

It was over an hour later that Miss Frayle, waiting in the study of the house in Harley Street, heard the front door open, and Doctor Morelle came in. She rushed into the hall to greet him.

"Did he confess?" she gasped excitedly.

"Pray control your exuberance, Miss Frayle," he replied calmly, divesting himself of hat and coat with maddening deliberation.

"But the man Green—did he kill his brother-in-law?"

"Of course." Doctor Morelle led the way into the study with Miss Frayle hurrying after him. He seated himself in the chair at his desk.

"The mystery proved quite simple when reduced to its elementals," he said, taking a Le Sphinx from the skull which had been ingeniously made into a somewhat macabre-looking cigarette-box.

"Under pressure, Green confessed he had paid a visit to his brother-in-law shortly after eight-thirty this evening, quarrelled with him over financial matters and struck him down. This occurred just at the moment you arrived at the side door and rang the bell. Of course, you heard nothing—even if your mind had been alert!" he added sardonically. He went on: "Realising there was no time to be lost, he pushed Jordan's body into the cupboard and at the same time secreted himself there."

Miss Frayle shuddered. "How awful—if I'd known that horrible man was in there…"

The Doctor lit his cigarette. "It must have been a cramped space," he continued through a cloud of cigarette-smoke, "hence the door burst open, with the result that you fainted. During your period of unconsciousness, Green dragged the body to another room, from where it has now been recovered. My rapid arrival upset his calculations, and he left the premises, planning to return later to dispose of the body. Then he recalled he had left his cigarette. He *did* indulge in the tobacco-smoking habit after all—"

"Yes, I know," she smiled.

"Indeed?" His eyebrows were raised in inquiry. "May I ask how you formed that opinion."

"I noticed nicotine stain on his moustache."

"Yes, yes, quite obvious, of course!" Doctor Morelle said, in a tone of annoyance. "That roused my suspicions, too. He was fearful the remains of the cigarette would incriminate him and he returned, hoping to regain it. My suspicions were confirmed by his complete lack of surprise when he referred to the telephone being out of order… This inferred he must have been in the room earlier in the evening to have observed this fact." He paused dramatically: *"In the room between the time you used the telephone and my arrival!* How otherwise could he have known so conclusively it was damaged?"

Miss Frayle nodded vigorously. "Of course!" she said.

He said with a thin smile: "And now, my *dear* Miss Frayle… I am anxious to resume my experimental work in the laboratory at the point where unfortunately our attention was distracted."

She looked at him with a slightly dazed expression.

"But—but, Doctor," she stammered, "the acid?"

He paused with his cigarette half way to his lips. "Do you mean to inform me," he said, his voice sharp and bitter, "that you have omitted to obtain another phial to replace the one you so carelessly broke?"

She goggled at him. "Well—I—I—Yes, I didn't—" She broke off floundering.

"Really, your careless inattention to your work is most reprehensible—"

"I'm so sorry, Doctor," she apologised. But even as she spoke she realised it was no good. She could not prevent that flow of pompously precise words of censure that began to fall from his lips. Miss Frayle sighed resignedly and sat down to wait until Doctor Morelle finished the tirade directed against her.

THE PURPLE LINE

John Rhode

John Rhode was the principal pen-name adopted by the industrious detective writer Cecil John Street MC OBE (1884–1964). He also published three novels as Cecil Waye, and a long series of books as Miles Burton. Most of the Burton novels featured Desmond Merrion, and *The Secret of High Eldersham* (aka *The Mystery of High Eldersham*, 1930) and *Death in the Tunnel* (aka *Dark is the Tunnel*, 1936) have been reprinted as British Library Crime Classics. Rhode introduced Dr Lancelot Priestley in *The Paddington Mystery* (1925) and this crotchety but brilliant Great Detective continued to appear in Rhode's novels until the early 1960s.

In his younger days, Rhode served in the army, and in particular in military intelligence, with considerable distinction. He was also an electrical engineer, and his detective stories are the product of a highly practical mind. His interest in and knowledge of gadgetry came into play time and again; many of his best stories turn on tricks concerning methods of murder. The m.o. of Rhode's killers is often unlikely, but his straightforward and authoritative writing about technicalities facilitated the suspension of disbelief. "The Purple Line" is one of his few short stories; it first appeared in the *Evening Standard* in 1950, and is characteristic of his style of puzzle-making.

I NSPECTOR PURLEY PICKED UP THE TELEPHONE. BUT THE TOR-
rent of words which poured into his ears was so turbid that he
could make little of it. Something about a wife and a water-butt. The
fellow was obviously in such a state that questioning him would elicit
no coherent answer. "I'll come along at once," said Purley. "Holly
Bungalow, you say? On the Cadford road? Right!"

He took the police car, in which he drove out of the fair-sized
market town of Faythorpe. The villas on the outskirts extended
for a short distance, with a scarlet telephone kiosk near the further
end. Beyond this the road, bordered with trees on either side, ran
through agricultural country.

Purley kept a sharp look-out as he went, for he was by no
means sure of the exact location of Holly Bungalow. It wasn't any
too easy, for it was growing dark on a February afternoon, and it
was pouring with rain, as it had been all day. Then, about half a
mile beyond the kiosk, he saw, on the left, a white- painted gate
between the trees and, standing beside it, a man with a bicycle.
The Inspector slowed up as he saw "Holly Bungalow" painted on
the gate.

As he got out of the car the man at the gate began gabbling and
gesticulating. He was short and stocky, round-faced and goggle-eyed,
and was evidently labouring under some violent emotion. He wore
a mackintosh, sodden with wet, and was hatless, with the rain pouring from his hair over his face. "Rode at once to the kiosk," he was
rambling incoherently. "That's where I rang you up from. We're

not on the telephone, you know. I didn't know what else to do. It's a dreadful thing. Come, I'll show you."

He turned and almost ran up the path leading from the gate. Purley followed him towards the bungalow, a few yards away. The man turned off round the side of the building to the back and stopped abruptly. "There, look!"

At the back of the bungalow was a verandah, looking out over a lawn and garden surrounded by trees. At the further end of the verandah was a round galvanised water-butt, overflowing with the water pouring into it from a spout in the eaves. Projecting from the top of the butt, and resting against the edge, was a pair of inverted high-heeled shoes. "It's my wife!" the little man exclaimed.

The butt was about five feet high and two feet six inches in diameter, standing on a brick foundation. Beside it was a folding wooden garden chair. Purley climbed on to this and leaned over the edge of the butt. Within it, completely submerged but for the feet, was a woman, head down and fully clothed.

The first problem was how to get her out. It might be possible to push the butt over on its side. He managed to tilt the butt, the water surging over the edge.

"Here, come and bear a hand!" he exclaimed. Between them they tilted the butt still further, the water pouring out and streaming across the lawn. Then it fell on its side.

The little man made no attempt to help Purley as he drew the woman out by the legs. She was fairly tall and slim, apparently in the thirties, wearing a dark frock, silk stockings and high-heeled shoes, with no hat. Purley glanced into the butt. The water had drained out of it, and all it now contained was a layer of slime and a broken ridge-tile, which had at some time presumably fallen into it from the roof.

Purley carried the body into the shelter of the verandah. The little man was quivering like a jelly. "You'd better come with me," said Purley.

In a dazed fashion the other followed him back to the car. Purley drove to the kiosk, where he telephoned to the police station. Then the two drove back to the bungalow. "We'll go inside, out of the rain," said Purley. "There you can tell me what you know about this."

They entered by the front door. The bungalow was not large— lounge, dining-room, a couple of bedrooms, and the usual domestic offices. The furnishings, if not luxurious, were well-to-do. In the dining-room a French window leading on to the verandah was open. On the table were still some remains of a meal, apparently lunch, with one place only laid. Beside this, a tumbler, a siphon, and a bottle of whisky, half full.

As they sat down Purley took out his notebook and headed a page "Monday, Feb. 13". He said, "You told me the name was Briston, I think?"

The other nodded. "That's right. I am Henry Briston. My wife's name was Shirley. She had seemed rather depressed for the last few days. I wouldn't have left her alone if it had ever entered my head that she would do a thing like that."

"When did you last see her alive?"

"About eight o'clock this morning," Briston replied. "She was in bed then. I got up early, for I was going to Mawnchester to see my brother, and I took her a cup of tea. She seemed quite cheerful then. I got my own breakfast, and while the egg was frying I put a new chart in the barograph yonder."

He pointed to the instrument on a bracket fixed to the dining-room wall. Purley was familiar with barographs—there was one in the window of the optician's next door to the police station. The one on the wall was of the conventional type, with a revolving drum driven by clockwork, and a pen at the end of a long needle. The chart stuck round the drum bore out Briston's words. It ran from Monday to Sunday, ruled in two-hour divisions, the lines an eighth of an inch apart.

The pen had been set at eight o'clock that morning, and filled rather clumsily, for the deep purple oily ink had overflowed and run vertically down the chart. The time was now seven o'clock, and the pen pointed correctly between the six and eight o'clock lines. The graph it had drawn ran horizontally for an eighth of an inch, from eight to ten. After that time it sloped steeply downwards, indicating rapidly falling pressure.

"And after breakfast?" Purley asked. "You saw Mrs. Briston again?"

"I didn't see her," Briston replied. "I called through the door and told her I was going, and she answered me. Then I jumped on my bicycle and rode to the station to catch the 8.50 to Mawnchester."

"Was Mrs. Briston expecting anyone to call here during your absence?"

Briston shook his head. "Not that I know of. The postman must have called, for I met him on the road as I was riding to the station. I called out to ask him if he had anything for me, and he said only a parcel for my wife."

"Was that garden chair standing by the water-butt when you left home?"

"I don't think so. If it was, I didn't put it there. At this time of year it's kept folded up in the verandah. I sometimes use it to stand on and look into the butt to see how much water there is. But this morning the butt was empty. During the dry spell we had last week we used all the water for the plants in the greenhouse. It would have taken three or four hours to fill even with the heavy rain today."

"Did you put this bottle of whisky on the table here?"

"No, I found it there when I came home. Latterly my wife had taken to drinking rather more than I liked to see. I didn't clear away my breakfast things before I left this morning. My wife must have done that, and got her own lunch later on."

"You went to Mawnchester by the 8.50. What time did you come back?"

"By the train that gets to Faythorpe at 4.45. The ticket collector will remember that—we had some conversation. I had taken a cheap day ticket, but it wasn't available for return as early as the 4.45, and I had to pay the full fare. I lunched with my brother in Mawnchester, and saw several other people there."

There came a loud knock. Purley opened the door, to find the divisional surgeon. "This way, Doctor," he said, leading him round the bungalow to the verandah. "What can you tell me?" he asked.

"Not very much more than you can see for yourself," said the doctor. "She's been dead some hours. Death was due to drowning. There's a pretty severe contusion on the top of the head. It wouldn't have been fatal, for the skull isn't fractured. But you'll want to account for it, I expect."

"Have a look inside the butt," said Purley. "You see that broken ridge-tile?"

The doctor nodded. "Yes, I see it. You found her head downwards in the butt, you say? If, when she dived in, her head had struck the tile, the contusion would be accounted for."

Another loud knock brought Purley once more to the front door. This time it was a couple of ambulance men with a stretcher. The body was carried to the ambulance, which set off for the mortuary, the doctor following in his car. Purley returned to the dining-room, to find Briston looking utterly dejected and exhausted. Purley feared he might have a second suicide on his hands. "I don't think you ought to stop here all alone, Mr. Briston," he suggested.

"Oh, I shall be all right," Briston replied drearily. "I'll go along to the kiosk by-and-by and ring up my brother. If he can't come here he'll let me go to him, I daresay."

Purley went back to Faythorpe. Accident, murder, or suicide? The only way she could have fallen headlong into the butt by accident was if she had been clambering about on the roof; such behaviour might surely be ruled out. Murder? By whom? Her husband's alibi seemed perfectly good, though of course it would have to be checked. And there was this finally convincing point. Nobody, certainly not her puny little husband, could, with the help only of the garden chair, have lifted a struggling victim above his shoulders and plunged her head downwards into the butt.

Suicide, then. Everything pointed to that. The depression from which Shirley Briston had been suffering. And possibly the whisky to supply Dutch courage. It had started to rain about half-past nine that morning, and had never ceased all day. Three or four hours, Briston had said. The butt would have been full by the time she might be expected to have had her lunch. She had taken out the garden chair, climbed on to it, and dived into the butt.

Verification of Briston's alibi followed naturally. The ticket collector remembered him perfectly well. "I couldn't say what train he went by in the morning, for I wasn't on duty then," he told Purley. "But he came off the 4.45 and gave up the return half of a cheap day to Mawnchester. I told him that was no good, as cheap tickets are only available by trains leaving Mawnchester after six. So he paid me the difference, and I gave him a receipt for it."

Purley ran the postman to earth in the bar of the Red Admiral. "This morning's delivery?" he replied to Purley's question. "Yes,

I do recollect seeing Mr. Briston while I was on my way to Cadford. He was riding his bike towards the town here, and as he passed he called out and asked me if I had anything for him. I told him that all there was for Holly Bungalow was a parcel for Mrs. Briston."

"You delivered the parcel, I suppose?" Purley remarked. "Did you see anyone at the bungalow?"

"Why, yes," the postman replied. "The parcel was too big to go through the letter-box, so I knocked on the door. After a bit Mrs. Briston opened it and took in the parcel. She wasn't what you might call properly dressed, but had a sort of wrap round her."

"Can you tell me what time this was?"

"It must have been round about half-past eight when I spoke to Mr. Briston. And maybe five minutes later when I got to the bungalow."

All that remained was a final word with the doctor. There was just one possibility. Briston had arrived at Faythorpe station at 4.45. He should have reached home by 5.15. It had been after six when Purley had first seen the body in the butt. Only the faintest possibility, of course.

The doctor was at home when Purley called, and frowned irritably at his question. "How the dickens can I tell to a split second? I'm ready to testify on oath that death was due to drowning. But I'm not prepared to say exactly when it took place. When a body has been in water for any length of time, that's impossible. My opinion is that the woman died not later than midday or thereabouts."

So that settled it. Mrs. Briston had been seen alive after her husband left the house that morning. The medical evidence showed that she must have been dead before his return that evening. Clearly, then, a case of suicide.

Next morning, Purley went to Holly Bungalow fairly early. The door was opened by a man who bore some resemblance to Henry Briston, though he was taller and not so plump. "Do you want to see my brother?" he asked. "I am Edward Briston, from Mawnchester. Henry rang me up last night and told me what had happened, and I came over at once. He's had a very bad night, and I told him he'd better stay in bed for a bit."

"I won't disturb him," Purley replied. "I only looked in to see he was all right. You saw your brother in Mawnchester yesterday, didn't you, Mr. Briston?"

"Yes, he lunched with me, and we spent the afternoon together in my office, till he left to catch his train."

Purley nodded. "Have you any, personal knowledge of your sister-in-law's state of mind recently?"

Edward Briston glanced over his shoulder, led the way into the dining-room and shut the door. "It was to talk about Shirley that Henry came to see me yesterday," he said in a hushed voice. "He told me she was terribly depressed. Just as if she had something on her mind that she wouldn't tell him about.

"I'm going to tell you something, Inspector, that I didn't tell Henry, and never shall, now. One day last week I saw Shirley in Mawnchester. She was with a man I didn't know, and they seemed to be getting on remarkably well together. I know she saw me, but the couple hurried away together in the opposite direction. It's my belief the poor woman had got herself into a situation from which she could see only one way of escape."

That might be the case, Purley thought. Glancing round the room, he caught sight of the barograph. After that flat step, an eighth of an inch wide, the purple line traced by the pen had fallen steadily till about midnight. Then it had become horizontal, and was now beginning to rise. Fine weather might be expected. The prosperous appearance of the room prompted Purley's next question. "Your brother is in comfortable circumstances?"

"Well, yes," Edward Briston replied. "Henry hasn't much of his own, but Shirley had considerable means. She was a widow when he married her, and her first husband had left her quite well off."

Henry Briston's alibi was complete. There could be no doubt now that his wife had committed suicide, and Edward Briston's guess might explain why. Purley went back to the police station, and caught sight of the barograph in the window next door.

He looked at the instrument more closely. It was very similar to the one at Holly Bungalow; the only difference that Purley could see was the chart on the drum, which ran from Sunday to Saturday. A new chart had been fitted at ten o'clock the previous Sunday, for that was where the purple graph began. For the greater part of Sunday it ran almost horizontally. Then, late that evening, it began to decline. By the early hours of Monday morning, this decline had become a steep slope. As with the instrument at Holly Bungalow, this fall had continued till about midnight.

The queer thing about this graph was that it showed no horizontal step between eight and ten on Monday morning. Briston's barograph must be out of order. But it couldn't be, for in every other respect the two purple lines were exactly similar.

Purley went into the police station. A discrepancy only an eighth of an inch long in the graphs could be of no importance. And then the only possible explanation revealed itself to him.

His thoughts began to race. There was no confirmation of Henry Briston having left Faythorpe by the 8.50. He had certainly been seen by the postman riding in the direction of the station about 8.30. But he might have turned back when the postman had passed the bungalow on his way to Cadford. A later train would have given him plenty of time to meet his brother for lunch in Mawnchester.

Back to the bungalow, to find his wife dressed and having breakfast. Perhaps he had contrived to meet the postman. He could easily have ordered something to be sent her by post. That contusion the doctor had found. The kitchen poker! A blow, not enough to kill her, but to knock her out.

But it would manifestly have been beyond Briston's power to lift even an inert body over the edge of the butt. No, it wouldn't do. By jove, yes, it would! It hadn't begun to rain till 9.30, and before then the butt had been empty. Briston had tipped the butt over on its side. Easy enough, for it was of thin sheet metal, and comparatively light when empty.

First the broken tile, to explain the contusion that must be found. Then the unconscious woman, dragged through the French window of the dining-room and thrust head first into the butt. An effort, and the butt with its contents was upended in place. Perhaps the rainwater was already beginning to trickle into it from the spout. Then to set the scene, so as to suggest that the victim had been alive at a much later hour. To clear away the breakfast, and to lay the appearance of lunch, with that significant whisky bottle.

In his preoccupation with the crime, he had forgotten to change the barograph chart. It was by then ten o'clock. He put on a new chart, and set the pen on the eight o'clock line, to suggest the time of his action. Then he turned the drum till the pen rested on the ten o'clock line. He was bound to do that, otherwise it might be noticed later that the instrument was two hours slow. That was the only possible explanation of the purple line being horizontal for that vital eighth of an inch.

The motive might be deduced from Edward Briston's revelation. The only evidence for Shirley Briston's depressed state was her husband's. She hadn't been depressed, but determined. She had told him she was going to leave him. And if she did that her money would go with her.

It was beyond any doubt that the barograph had been set not at eight, but at ten. If it could be proved that Henry Briston had set it, his alibi was destroyed. He must have been in a state of great agitation. He had clumsily overfilled the pen, so that the ink had run down the chart. Might he not in his agitation have got some of it on his fingers? That oily purple fluid was not a true ink, but a dye, defying soap and water.

Purley drove again to Holly Bungalow. This time Henry Briston himself opened the door. "Hold out your hands, Mr. Briston," said the Inspector sternly.

"My hands?" Briston replied. He held them out tremblingly, palms downwards. Purley seized the right hand and turned it over. There on the inner side of forefinger and thumb were two faint purple stains. "You will come with me in my car," said Purley sternly. "And I must caution you—".

Edmund Crispin

Robert Bruce Montgomery (1921–78) was a composer of light music responsible for the soundtracks of films such as *Raising the Wind*, *Eyewitness* and *The Brides of Fu Manchu*, to say nothing of four of the *Doctor* comedy films and half a dozen *Carry On* movies. Despite his success in this field, he was—and remains—better known for witty and ingenious detective stories written under the pen-name Edmund Crispin. Educated at St John's College, Oxford, Crispin made his series detective, Gervase Fen, an Oxford academic, an English professor at St Christopher's College, which Crispin located next to St John's. Between 1944 and 1951, Fen appeared in eight highly diverting novels. Thereafter, Crispin only managed to publish one more novel, the rather underwhelming *The Glimpses of the Moon*, which after a long gestation period finally appeared in 1977. He did, however, produce a long sequence of short stories, most of which are included in the collections *Beware of the Trains* (1953) and *Fen Country* (1979).

Most of Crispin's short stories were written for the *Evening Standard*, and accordingly subject to severe constraints of space. As a result, the plots tend to pivot on a single trick; as David Whittle says in his 2007 biography, *Bruce Montgomery/Edmund Crispin: a Life in Music and Books*: "He usually concentrates on apparently small details, such as the position of a bolt on a door, the difference between the speed of sound and light, or the condition of a typewriter ribbon. Fen also likes to show that things are not always what they seem." This story, first published in the *Evening Standard* in 1954, turns on a point of ballistics, and is unusual in giving centre stage to DI Humbleby, who usually plays second fiddle to Fen.

"I'VE HEARD FROM THE BALLISTICS PEOPLE," SAID Superintendent MacCutcheon, "and they tell me there's no doubt whatever that the bullet was fired from Ellingham's gun. Is that what you yourself were expecting?"

"Oh, yes." At the other side of the desk, in the first-floor office at New Scotland Yard, Detective Inspector Humbleby nodded soberly. "Yes, I was expecting that all right," he said. "Taken together with the rest of the evidence, it makes a pretty good case."

"And your own report?"

Humbleby handed over a sheaf of typescript. "No verdict?" queried MacCutcheon, who had turned immediately to the final page.

"Certainly there's a verdict." Humbleby paused. "Implicit, I mean," he added. "You'll see."

"Nice of you," said MacCutcheon. "Nice of you DIs to try and keep my tottering intellect alive with little games. Well, I'll buy it. Smoke if you care to." And he settled down to read, while Humbleby, leaning back in his chair and lighting a cheroot, reconsidered the salient features of his visit to Harringford the previous day...

He had arrived there by train, with Detective Sergeant Pinder in tow, shortly before midday; and they had gone at once to the police station. Inspector Bentinck, who received them, proved to be a bony, discontented-looking man of fifty or thereabouts.

"Between ourselves," he said, as he led them to his office, "our County CID are a fairly feeble lot at the moment, so I'm glad the

CC had the sense to call you people in straightaway. And of course, having a ruddy lord involved... You knew that, did you?"

"It's about the only thing I do know," said Humbleby.

"I've got his gun here." They had reached the office, and Bentinck was unlocking a cupboard, from which presently he produced a 360 sporting rifle. Two slats of wood were tied to either side of the breech, and there was a loop of string for carrying the weapon.

"Not been tested for prints yet," said Humbleby intelligently; and Bentinck shook his head.

"Not been touched since I confiscated it yesterday morning. But in any case I shouldn't think you'll get any prints off it except his—Lord Ellingham's, I mean. He'd cleaned it, you see, by the time I caught up with him."

"Well, well, we can try," said Humbleby. "Pinder's brought all his paraphernalia with him. See what you can get, please," he added to the sergeant. "And meanwhile"—to Bentinck—"let's have the whole story from the beginning."

So Pinder went away to insufflate and photograph the rifle, and Bentinck talked. "Ellingham's one of what they call the backwoods peers," he said. "He's got a big estate about five miles from here, but I shouldn't think there's much left in the family coffers, because he lives in the lodge, not in the manor- house—that's shut up. He's about fifty, not married, lives alone.

"Well now, like everyone else, Ellingham's had his servant problems, and just recently—for the last year or so, that is—the only person he's been able to get to look after him has been this girl."

"Enid Bragg."

Bentinck assented. "Enid Bragg. And a fortnight ago even she packed it in—since when Ellingham's had to look after himself."

"What sort of girl was she?"

"Not bad looking in a trashy sort of way," said Bentinck. "I don't know that there's much else good to say about her... Anyway, point is, this Enid lives—lived—in a cottage with her parents not far from the Ellingham estate. And it was yesterday morning, while she was waiting for the 8:50 bus so as to come into town and do a bit of shopping, that someone picked her off with a rifle, presumably from behind the hedge opposite the bus-stop.

"Well, of course, when the bus came along, there she was with a hole in her head, and it wasn't long before me and the sergeant got out there and took over. We went through all the usual motions, but the only worth while thing we got out of it was the bullet." Bentinck opened a drawer in his desk and produced a small jeweller's box in which a squashed rifle bullet lay on a bed of cotton wool. "It'd gone clean through her and buried itself in an ash tree behind the bus-stop."

"No cartridge-case?"

"Not that we've been able to find. So I said to myself, well, better look up Ellingham first, because I knew he'd got a gun, and after all, the girl had been working for him until just recently, and what should I find but that—"

Here Bentinck broke off at the return of Pinder, who announced that he had dusted and photographed the two or three blurred prints on the rifle, and that it was now at everyone's disposal. Taking it from him, Humbleby squinted down the barrel.

"Clean as a new pin," he said cheerfully. But Pinder noticed that something had made him more than usually pensive.

"Well, that's it, you see," continued Bentinck, not very lucidly. "When I got to the lodge, there was Ellingham cleaning that thing, and it turned out he'd been out on his own, looking for something to shoot, since eight o'clock. I took the gun away from him, with all the usual gab about routine, and I'll say this for him, he didn't make any fuss about it. And until we see whether the murder bullet came from it, that's really all—oh, except for the autopsy. Five months gone, our Enid was."

"Oh, Lord," said Humbleby in genuine dismay. "Not that again. The number of times—"

"Yes, it's common enough, I suppose. Ah, well. If you get a nasty sort of girl like Enid Bragg into trouble, you must expect a bit of blackmail. And the only certain way of putting a stop to it—"

"Damn!" Thus Superintendent MacCutcheon, breaking in violently on Humbleby's thoughts in the first-floor office at Scotland Yard. He had finished reading the report, and now whacked it down angrily on the desk in front of him.

There was a long silence.

"Not pleasant," said MacCutcheon at last.

"Not pleasant at all, sir," Humbleby agreed. From the particular expression on his superior's face he was in no doubt that the evidence had been interpreted correctly. "And I don't think we're going to be able to pin the murder on him, either. There's no alibi—that much I found out before I left. And if we worked hard at it, I dare say we could establish the connection with the girl. But we'll never find the bullet, and without that—"

"We shall have to try," said MacCutcheon grimly. "If it's just a charge of fabricating evidence people will think he only did it to get a conviction. That's damaging enough, of course, but even so…"

He reached for a blue-bound book from the shelves behind him, and riffled through the pages until he found what he wanted.

"Gross' *Criminal Investigation*," he announced. "Third edition, page 157. 'A rifle barrel reasonably clean on one day will show plain traces of fouling next day. In such cases the barrel sweats after it has been cleaned.'

"But when you looked at it, the barrel of Ellingham's rifle was perfectly clean."

"Yes."

"It oughtn't to have been, if Bentinck's story was true."

"No."

"So Bentinck, the only person with access to that rifle, had recently cleaned it."

"Yes."

"And there'd be no point in his cleaning it unless he'd fired it."

"No."

"And there'd be no point in his firing it, and subsequently lying, unless he happened to want a bullet to substitute for the real murder bullet which he dug out of the tree."

Again there was silence. "I suppose there's no chance we're wrong?" MacCutcheon burst out fretfully. "I mean, there were even traces of blood and brains on that bullet he gave you… I suppose—"

"No, no chance at all." Humbleby was definite. "As to the traces— well, after all, a quick visit to the mortuary with a—a pair of twee-zers, say…"

"Yes." MacCutcheon relapsed into gloom again. "Yes… What gun do you think he used to kill the girl?"

"His own, I imagine. I got a look at the register, and he certainly has one, and it's a .360 all right. But his sergeant told me he'd hardly ever used it—which would account for his not realising about the fouling." Humbleby rose. "He had one morning's shooting, it seems, years ago, and after that never went out again… No stomach for blood sports, the sergeant said."

THE NEW CEMENT

Freeman Wills Crofts

Freeman Wills Crofts (1879–1957) pursued a career as a railway engineer in his native Ireland before his success as a detective novelist enabled him to move to England and write full-time. He was apprenticed to his uncle, who worked for the Belfast and Northern Counties Railway prior to being involved with the construction of an extension to the Donegal Railway. Subsequently, he became chief assistant engineer for part of the LMS railway network in north-east Ireland. Among other projects, he worked on the building of the Bleach Green railway viaduct, and chaired an inquiry into the Bann and Lough Neagh Drainage Scheme. The technical skills he developed in his day job influenced his approach to writing detective stories; the hallmark of his fiction was his meticulous method of construction.

Crofts, like John Rhode, has been damned with faint praise as a "Humdrum" writer by the novelist and genre historian Julian Symons. Admittedly, Crofts didn't indulge in literary flourishes, and his gifts of characterisation were limited, but there is compensation to be had in the soundness of his plotting. That readers enjoy well-made stories of the kind in which Crofts specialised is evidenced by the success of recent reprints of several of his novels. Excellent examples include the "inverted mystery" *Antidote to Venom* (1938) and *The Hog's Back Mystery* (aka *The Strange Case of Dr Earle*, 1933), both of which have appeared in the British Library's Crime Classics series. "The New Cement", taken from *Many a Slip* (1955) is typical of his short fiction, brief and to the point.

Providential was the adjective Superintendent French always used when he told of his call on his old friend Mark Rudd precisely at the most critical moment of the latter's life. Tragedy threatened, and tragedy French could not wholly avert, but his visit reduced the calamity to one over which people shook their heads and said it really was for the best.

French was enjoying a week's leave in early spring and had set out for a tramp round Leith Hill. It was a day of bright sunshine, and he swung along revelling in the clear air with its scents of earth and wood and the great vista over the Weald stretching away to the blue line of the South Downs on the horizon. Rudd had built himself a bungalow among the pines, a low, rambling house full of unexpected corners and gables. His hobby was sculpture, and as he was very well off, he had included at one end a large studio. He did good work and had quite a name among the lesser lights of his art. Though turned sixty, he had recently married a comparatively young woman, a doctor's daughter and an ex-nurse. It had been a marriage more of convenience than of love, he wanting a housekeeper and she a home. Though French did not greatly admire Mrs. Rudd, the arrangement had seemed to work well.

There was no answer to French's ring and he turned to the studio. It had two doors, one out into the grounds, the other leading into the house. There he found Rudd, bending over bottles, a basin, and a heap of sand.

"Hullo, Rudd! Turned chemist for a change?"

The old man swung round. "My dear fellow! I'm delighted to see you. What good wind blows you here?"

They chatted while Rudd produced drinks and smokes. "Sorry Jean's not so well," he said, speaking of his wife. "She's just back from a few days in London with her father, the doctor, and is lying down. But you'll see her later."

French replied suitably, though secretly he was pleased. It was with Rudd that he had come to chat, and the presence of Mrs. Rudd cramped both their styles. Presently he pointed to the table. "What's the great work?"

Rudd turned back to his bottles. "I've had some new cement stuff sent me," he explained, "and I was just going to try it. But you wouldn't be interested."

"Yes, I should," returned French, sensing regret in his tone. "Let's see the doings."

Rudd brightened up. "It's a stuff called Petriflux. Chap invented it and sent me a sample to try out. It's in these two bottles, and as long as they're separate it keeps indefinitely. But when you mix them it begins to harden into a form of silicon, taking about twenty-four hours to do it."

The bottles were of good quality, with glass stoppers, tied down and sealed with parchment covers. French picked one up. It bore a typewritten label: "Petriflux—A. This preparation contains acid and must not be allowed to touch the skin." The liquid was clear and brownish. In the other bottle, which was marked "B" and had a wider mouth, was a white powder.

"How do you use them?" French asked.

"You empty the powder into a basin and pour the acid on it. The powder dissolves and makes a viscous liquid. Then you add sand or powdered stone, stirring till all the grains are coated. You press the compound into the shape you want and it hardens into sandstone or marble or granite, according to the sort of stone you've used."

"Sounds good."

"Well, that's the claim. I've not tried it yet."

"The acid may attack your basin." French pointed to a chip in the enamel showing dark metal.

"I'll try that first."

Rudd poured three or four drops from his "A" bottle on the defective spot. It boiled and smoked.

"Bless us," French grunted, "you've got strong stuff there." He took the bottle and put it gingerly to his nose. "Vitriol, I imagine." He replaced the stopper, picked up the second bottle, and pushed the blade of his knife slowly through the contents. For some moments he sat motionless, then his manner changed and he spoke more decisively. "I'd like to try an experiment."

Rudd was mystified, but French would not explain. He emptied a few grains of the powder into a saucer and placed it on the ground in the centre of a grass plot. Then he tied a small medicine glass to a fishing-rod and put six drops from the acid bottle into the glass. Lying down, he pushed it towards the saucer and carefully emptied in the drops. There was an instant reaction. A sharp explosion eliminated the saucer.

"I thought that not unlikely," he declared grimly. "That powder's chlorate of potash and mixed with vitriol, which as you know is commercial concentrated sulphuric acid, it explodes. I suppose you realise you were about to make enough to blow yourself to kingdom come?"

Rudd was overwhelmed. He discussed the affair wonderingly, though it was some time before he reached the inevitable conclusion.

At last he muttered shakily: "Someone surely must have intended to murder me!"

"You don't mean it?" French returned. "Well, someone did, and someone who knew your circumstances. That ingenious tale of the silicon cement spells 'sculptor' all through. It was quite a scheme, for all incriminating evidence would have been destroyed."

"I just can't believe it."

"I find that sooner or later I'm forced to believe the evidence of my eyes." French's voice was dry. "Now, Rudd, pull yourself together. We've got to get the chap who did this. Let's see what we know. First, show me the letter that came with the bottles and the packings of the parcel."

These were available, and French noted that the letter was on the usual sheet torn from the usual cheap block, and was typed with the usual machine with identifiable defects. It purported to come from Ralph Spence, of 26 Hillside Crescent, Battersea, and contained a statement as to the action of the alleged invention, together with Spence's earnest hope that a man of Rudd's eminence would be so kind as to test it. The packing was elaborate. One bottle—obviously the acid—had come in a cylindrical tin, held steady by sawdust. The other had been protected by corrugated cardboard. Placed together, the two had been rolled in more corrugated cardboard, covered with stout paper and corded.

"I don't wonder he took you in," said French. "Where's your telephone?"

Rudd indicated the hall. In a few minutes French returned.

"I thought that not unlikely also," he declared. "There's no Hillside Cresent in Battersea." He picked up the paper wrapping. "Posted yesterday at Charing Cross. H'm. That's not too hopeful. However, if we get a suspect from your statement, we'll nail him through the typewriter and probably the purchase of the chemicals. Very well, let that go for the moment and tell me about your enemies."

"Enemies?" Rudd blinked. "I have no enemies."

"Haven't you? You've at least one, you know. Think again, old man."

Rudd shook his head helplessly.

"Well, let's see." French looked at him speculatively. "You're a rich man, I always fancied, Rudd. Worth how much, if you don't mind? It's not curiosity."

"Of course not. About twenty thousand, though I don't get much out of it these days."

"Who would have got it if you had mixed your bottles?"

"Some to my wife, my own money: the greater portion to my nephew, James Rudd, a family inheritance."

"H'm. Tell me about him. Is he well-to-do also?"

"As a matter of fact he's hard up. I know because he wanted me to help him out quite recently. But I refused. It's no use. I've done it again and again, and it's always the same. He just throws everything away at the races."

"That so? What's his job?"

"He's a chemist in one of the big patent food firms: I forget which."

"A chemist? Good Lord! Rudd, what more do we want?"

Rudd looked profoundly shocked. "Oh, come now, French, you're not going to accuse him of such a thing. He's a bit of a waster, I admit, but a murderer! No, I couldn't believe that."

"I don't accuse him. I don't know who's guilty. Can you think of anyone else?"

"Well, no," hesitatingly. "But then I shouldn't have thought of him."

"Quite." French began to pace the room, obviously lost in thought. Then he swung round. "I believe we could find out at the Yard who sent that parcel, but I've an idea we might get the information more easily. Perhaps your nephew would tell us if he's guilty?"

"I suppose that remark has a meaning, but I admit I don't get it."

"Never mind," French smiled. "I think we'll try it. But you'll have to do what I ask you'll have to do what I ask you."

"I'm not the expert in murder. What do you want?"

"Having no *locus standi* here, I must first have a chat with the local police. Then I'll come back and tell you."

When French had gone, Rudd sat on, puzzling over the affair. He was a kindly old man, always looking for the best in people and for ways in which he might help them. He was on good terms with friends and neighbours and could think of no one who might have a spite against him. That his nephew—or for that matter anyone else—could have desired his death he could not believe. And yet French's demonstration was conclusive. The whole thing was most distressing. Indeed, the only bright spot in it was that French himself was available to take charge.

The afternoon was well advanced when French returned. He was close about how he had spent his time, except to say that he had seen the superintendent and asked for a constable to guard the bungalow during the night.

"My dear fellow," Rudd protested, "you surely don't expect—"

"Now you must trust me," French interrupted. "You'll see what I'm up to in due course. Tell me, can you ring up your nephew?"

"Yes, of course: at his works."

"Then do so. Be chatty and friendly. Say a Mr. Spence has sent you—what he said he sent you, and ask your nephew whether as a chemist he ever heard of the stuff? Say you think the invention might be of great value in repairing weathered stone on buildings, and that you're much interested. Then go on that by a lucky chance your friend So-and-so—mention some big pot in your own line—is coming down to see you tomorrow, and you're going to let him do the actual experiment. That'll give the stuff a great test and a great boost if it works. Finish by apologising for troubling your nephew and explain again that you had wondered if the inventor was a well-known man."

"I suppose there's a meaning in that too, French, but again—" Rudd shrugged resignedly.

"Well, don't you see, old man? If your nephew's guilty that message will put him in a cleft stick. Some innocent stranger will be blown to bits and you, you who will undoubtedly be able to put two and two together, you will probably survive. That is to say, unless he acts promptly he'll be facing a conviction for a murder he didn't wish to commit and which wouldn't benefit him. What will he do? Just answer that for yourself."

While Rudd was waiting for his call there was a step in the passage and Mrs. Rudd appeared. French sprang up to greet her. She certainly seemed ill, with her pale, haggard face, absent manner and slightly twitching hands. But she spoke to him normally enough, apologising for being unable to entertain him, and asked him to put a letter which she gave him with those for the post. A brief word of conversation, a briefer smile, and she disappeared and he heard the door of her room close. He turned to speak to Rudd, but just then the call came through. Nephew Jim seemed somewhat taken aback by his uncle's inquiry, though he expressed interest in the idea. Both inventor and invention were, he said, entirely unknown to him.

The day dragged on without further incident, and then about dusk a constable arrived with a photographers' flash lamp and camera, which he handed to French.

"Good," was the response. "Even if he gets away we'll have a photo of him in the act. Now come along to the studio and I'll explain what I want. See those two bottles? Put a private mark on them, so that you can swear to them again. But handle them carefully, for the acid's strong. I'll do the same. Right." He replaced the doubly marked bottles and turned to the door. "I want this outer door to be locked, with the key left in the inside and the windows hasped. Good. Then let's go out: we can do it through the house."

The studio window gave on a small plot of grass, with a crazy pavement path crossing it to the door. At the opposite end of the house, and standing out from it at right angles, was the porch, with its door at the side. From this porch door the studio door and window were clearly visible. French walked up and down memorising the lay-out, after which he gave the constable detailed orders for the night. He was to watch at the back door, ready on a signal to run out round the house and take a visitor to the studio in the rear. "We're all right for a hour or two," French went on to Rudd, "then we must take up our positions."

"Time for a drink," said the old man hospitably, leading the way to the lounge.

They chatted for some time, then French made a move. Having posted the constable, he sat down himself in the porch, leaving the door slightly ajar.

Rudd insisted on sharing the vigil, but regarded the door with disapproval. "Must you have it open?" he protested. "It's going to be cold, you know."

"No help for it, I'm afraid. I want to see the approach to the study, and it's the only way."

They settled down to watch. French would allow neither light nor smoking nor speech above a whisper. The night dragged. Time indeed seemed to stand still. It certainly was cold and the breeze moaned eerily among the pines. Except for this and the occasional hoot of an owl, it was very still.

Twelve came and one, then two. French was chilled and cramped and growing increasingly uneasy. Had he made a mistake? Was this nephew either innocent or sharper than he had allowed for?

Slowly the night crept on. Three came and after another aeon, four. When five struck and faint signs of light began to show in the east, French's chagrin was painful. He apologised grumpily to his friend and sent the constable home. But till the normal life of the bungalow had been resumed he kept watch himself.

Before going for a bath and shave he had a look round the studio. Everything there was as it had been the night before: the outer door locked, the windows hasped, the bottles bearing his private mark, the basin and the sand. But the acid bottle seemed somehow lighter in colour. He picked it up. It *was* lighter.

Puzzled, he shook it. No, the colouring matter had not settled. Slowly he withdrew the stopper and cautiously sniffed the contents. Then his jaw dropped and he stood staring helplessly. This was not vitriol, it was vinegar!

In a way, he had expected something of the kind: it was the basis of his trap. Rudd's message would have convinced Nephew Jim that the explosive possibilities of the "cement" were unknown, and if he were guilty, substitution of some harmless chemical for the contents of one or both bottles was the only way in which he could save himself. True, his murder plan would have failed, but he could not be convicted of crime.

But Nephew Jim had not made the substitution. No one had entered the studio. No one could have opened door or window without leaving traces—or being seen.

As French found himself driven relentlessly to the only conclusion possible, he felt sick with aversion and loathing for what must follow. Rudd himself had been sitting with him all night: he could not have approached the studio. The woman who helped during the day had gone home in the evening. Only from one room could a secret visit have been paid.

Screwing up his courage, French went to the room and knocked. There was no reply, and he opened the door. Entering, he stood in the middle of the floor and let his eyes pass slowly over the contents. How within the bungalow could a powerful acid like vitriol be got rid of silently and without leaving traces? French did not believe it could be done. But if the acid were poured into another bottle…

For a couple of minutes he stood, looking and pondering. On one wall was a small white enamelled cabinet of the kind in which medicines are kept. He stepped over and opened it. Among the bottles was a tall glass-stoppered one containing a clear brownish liquid. Cautiously he lifted it down.

As he did so there was a scream from behind him. Jean Rudd was running across the room. She paused for a moment at the fireplace to pick up the poker, then advanced on him like a fury. But that pause gave French his chance. He was able to replace the bottle before she reached him. Then in the nick of time he seized her arms. To control her he had to use his full strength. She screamed and struggled and called down horrible curses on him, but at last he got her arms in a lock and she was helpless. Then all the fight seemed to go out of her and she collapsed limply. As French laid her on her bed, Rudd's appalled face appeared at the door.

"I'm afraid it's her mind," French said with profound sympathy in his tones. "Better ring up the doctor."

French followed him to the telephone, but he did not make a call. Rudd, thinking later over this action, could never make up his mind as to his friend's motive. French seemed in no hurry to make a move, then at last he returned to the bedroom. Immediately there came an urgent call. Rudd hurried after him.

"Bad news," French warned. "Prepare yourself for a shock. She's taken prussic acid."

Rudd gasped. "Can't we do anything?"

French shook his head. "I'm afraid it's a matter of a very few minutes. She's unconscious already."

The doctor turned up quickly, but before he arrived the unhappy lady had ceased to breathe.

Later French propounded his theory, for the benefit principally of Rudd. "It was no doubt the common case of a mentally unstable person turning against the one most loved. When she sent those chemicals one cannot suppose she was responsible. Then from her point of view things went wrong: I turned up and there was no explosion. She must have suspected me of interference and doubtless watched us both. She heard someone telephoning, came to learn what she could, and certainly hid and listened to the message. Not knowing that we had learnt what was in the bottles, she obviously understood what your nephew was intended to understand. To destroy the evidence was her only hope, and she removed the acid during the night, substituting vinegar. No doubt she intended to get rid of it on the first opportunity. But when she saw me with the bottle in my hand she realised I knew all."

Though this view was officially accepted by the police and coroner, it did not convince French himself. He had heard rumours about Jean and a neighbour and he had a certain suspicion that freedom and money were what the lady sought. He therefore made some unofficial inquiries. He traced her purchase of the vitriol from a London shop "to clean a sink with damaged glaze", and of chlorate of potash "as a weed-killer". A sufficient quantity of potassium cyanide was missing from her father's surgery. Having once acted as his dispenser, she knew where it was. She no doubt believed that even if he suspected, he would not give his own daughter away. The typewriter she had borrowed from a friend. The plan, French imagined, had been suggested by the nature of the nephew's profession. She probably calculated that he would be suspected, but that nothing could be proved against him. Finally French learnt that the neighbour had been at his home when the parcel was posted. From these facts he concluded that only Jean was implicated. No use therefore in stirring up mud which would hurt his friend without serving the ends of justice. French's conscience was clear. Through his efforts his friend was safe and the guilty party was dead: what more could be desired of him?

EDITED BY
MARTIN EDWARDS

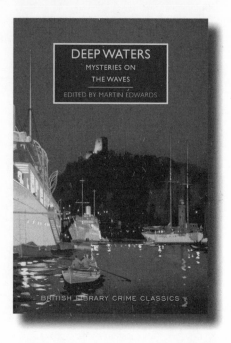

From picturesque canals and quiet lakes to the swirling currents of the ocean, a world of secrets lies beneath the surface of the water.

The stories in this collection will dredge up delight in crime fiction fans, as watery graves claim unsuspecting victims on the sands of an estuary and disembodied whispers penetrate the sleeping quarters of a ship's captain. How might a thief plot their escape from a floating crime scene? And what is to follow when murder victims, lost to the ocean floor, inevitably resurface?

This British Library anthology collects the best mysteries set on choppy seas, along snaking rivers and even in the supposed safety of a swimming pool, including stories by Arthur Conan Doyle, C. S. Forester, Phyllis Bentley and R. Austin Freeman.

EDITED BY
MARTIN EDWARDS

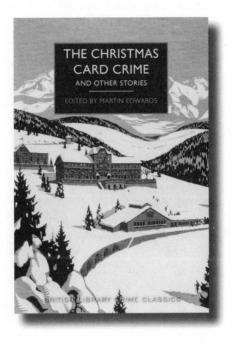

A Christmas party is punctuated by a gunshot under a policeman's watchful eye. A jewel heist is planned amidst the glitz and glamour of Oxford Street's Christmas shopping. Lost in a snowstorm, a man finds a motive for murder.

This collection of mysteries explores the darker side of the festive season – from unexplained disturbances in the fresh snow, to the darkness that lurks beneath the sparkling decorations.

With neglected stories by John Bude and E. C. R. Lorac, as well as tales by little-known writers of crime fiction, Martin Edwards blends the cosy atmosphere of the fireside story with a chill to match the temperature outside. This is a gripping seasonal collection sure to delight mystery fans.

EDITED BY
MARTIN EDWARDS

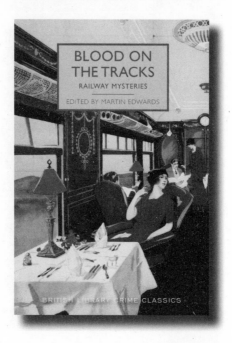

A signalman is found dead by a railway tunnel. A man identifies his wife as a victim of murder on the underground. Two passengers mysteriously disappear between stations, leaving behind a dead body.

Trains have been a favourite setting of many crime writers, providing the mobile equivalent of the "locked-room" scenario. Their enclosed carriages with a limited number of suspects lend themselves to seemingly impossible crimes. In an era of cancellations and delays, alibis reliant upon a timely train service no longer ring true, yet the railway detective has enjoyed a resurgence of popularity in the twenty-first century.

Both train buffs and crime fans will delight in this selection of fifteen railway-themed mysteries, featuring some of the most popular authors of their day alongside less familiar names. This is a collection to beguile even the most wearied commuter.

ALSO BY
MARTIN EDWARDS

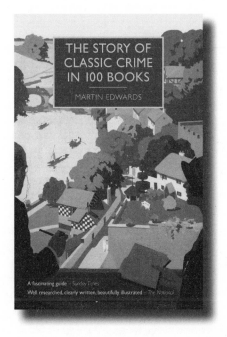

'A cabinet of criminal curiosities that novices and aficionados alike can happily search for titles to match their tastes.'   *Times Literary Supplement*

'No one could doubt the extent of Edwards's knowledge.' *Mail on Sunday*

.   .   .

This book tells the story of crime fiction published during the first half of the twentieth century. The diversity of this much-loved genre is breath-taking, and so much greater than many critics have suggested. To illustrate this, the leading expert on classic crime discusses one hundred books ranging from *The Hound of the Baskervilles* to *Strangers on a Train* which highlight the entertaining plots, the literary achievements, and the social significance of vintage crime fiction.

BRITISH LIBRARY CRIME CLASSICS

ALSO AVAILABLE

Many of our titles are also available in eBook and audio editions